Daniele-Marie Lawrenson was born in Devonshire to an English father and a French mother. She studied English and French at St. Luke's College in Exeter. She is married to Stephen Lawrenson, a retired teacher, and they live in a small village in Cambridgeshire where they raised their five children.

Dedication

My thanks to my husband Stephen for his support and encouragement, and also to our children; James, Juliette, Christopher, Edward and Elizabeth, who all have a crazy sense of humour and fun that kept me going.
Not forgetting my friend Hilary, who read each chapter as I progressed, with heartening comments which kept me on track.

Daniele-Marie Lawrenson

Narcissist

'Narcissism is a highly dangerous trait, which stems often from people who have been unloved in childhood, compensating in later life with grandiose self-belief, arrogance, a tendency to make unreasonable demands, unstable temper and violent mood swings, and, very significantly and dangerously, that familiar attribute of the psychopath: a lack of empathy.'

Austin Macauley Publishers™
London • Cambridge • New York • Sharjah

A CIP catalogue record for this title is available from the British Library.

ISBN 9781786936226 (Paperback)
ISBN 9781786936233 (Hardback)
ISBN 9781786936240 (E-Book)
www.austinmacauley.com

First Published (2017)
Austin Macauley Publishers Ltd.
25 Canada Square
Canary Wharf
London
E14 5LQ

Acknowledgements

I have always liked the idea of setting the location of a work of fiction in two countries. Being the child of an English father and a French mother made this a possibility for me. Although married to an English man and living with our children in Cambridgeshire, I was lucky that my husband shared my love of France, where we spent every available summer camping with our children.

I would also like to thank Matthew Smith and Vinh Tran from the production team at Austin Macauley Publishers who answered my queries promptly and helpfully.

Chapter One

That Promise of Rain

Saturday 12th February 2011
Cornwall

She sat back in her chair, enjoying the companionable peace, one eye on the book in her hand, the other on the television. A woman in a tight red dress was talking cheerfully about the likelihood of more heavy rain and the threat of floods. Céline glanced across at her husband, her lips parted to form a comment, only to see that he had fallen into a doze, his chin squashed onto his chest, his mouth half open.

"Hello you…!" she whispered.

Where was that vibrant young man she had married thirty-one years ago? The seventeen years between their ages, hardly noticeable on their wedding day, was horribly evident on the face before her. Who would have recognised this prone sixty-six-year-old fellow as the same impulsive Thomas of younger days? The stirring buzz of warm flesh triggered by linked fingers, sleepy colliding feet, just a glance sometimes, catching sight of that dimple or falling chunk of hair across the brow. Céline frowned. She could still see that face superimposed on this one, as fresh as ever. She had the memory, and now she had the amazing man behind the ageing façade. She knew which side of her bread was buttered and she grinned, knowing just how lucky she'd been to be loved by him.

The sudden jarring jangle of the doorbell made her jump. Thomas opened his eyes with a cough, gripping the arms of his chair in an effort to stand up.

"I'll go…" Céline announced, wondering who should come calling on a Saturday evening, prematurely darkened by that promise of rain. She switched on the porch light and sensibly looked through the peephole. Then she opened the door.

"Elizabeth!" she said in a shocked voice. A whirl of chilly wind swept between them, lifting the hem of Elizabeth's inadequate coat. A spattering of cold drops was flung into Céline's face as she reached for Elizabeth's sleeve, pulling her forwards with a violent movement. An alarmed expression passed across Elizabeth's face. Céline wondered if she'd been expecting a blow.

"Come in then," she said in a low voice. "This is very unexpected…"

Elizabeth put her bag down. "Sorry," she said, gazing expressionlessly at Céline with her large green eyes. "Sorry for not warning you I was coming… It was a spur of the moment decision. It's half-term this coming week so I've got space to think clearly… I feel we need to clear the air. This situation is intolerable."

"Is it?" Céline murmured coldly. "Well we can hardly turn you away, I suppose. Go in and say hello to Thomas."

Elizabeth made her way into the lounge and bent down to grasp the hand of the tall grey-haired man sitting in his usual chair. He removed his hand from hers and stared at the young dark-haired woman in front of him. Céline motioned her towards a chair opposite Thomas, into which Elizabeth sat, her eyes still gazing at him. He looked up to catch his wife's expression.

Céline avoided his searching glance. "Well…! Tea? Coffee?" she asked brightly, turning towards the kitchen and carefully averting her eyes from the overnight bag squatting menacingly in the hall.

Behind her, Thomas said curtly, "Well Elizabeth. What do you want?"

Without listening to the reply, Céline began to hum to herself as she switched on the kettle, turned it off again, and reached instead for the bottle opener and three glasses. "If she's staying the night, we'll need this…" she muttered, frowning. A bottle of red wine breathing, she opened the fridge and regretfully eyed the two small pork chops huddled apologetically under a blanket of waxed paper. She opened the freezer instead and removed three small trout. She lay them out on a white dish, 'like bodies in a morgue' she thought grimly.

Impatiently, before the wine had had chance to gasp, let alone breathe, she filled the three glasses and arranged two of them onto a tray, wedging a ceramic bowl of glistening green olives safely between them. She then carried it carefully to the room where her husband was listening intently to his daughter-in-law, who was fixing him with a serious expression, speaking low and fast.

"Here we are…make a space, Thomas," interrupted Céline, choosing to ignore Elizabeth's annoyed raised eyebrows. "I'm going to fix us something for later… Do you like trout, Elizabeth? I'll do it in garlic and white wine." She placed the tray firmly down on the coffee table. Thomas snatched his reading glasses out of the way.

Elizabeth looked up at Céline and smiled. "Thanks! That would be lovely. I don't expect you to go to any trouble though…"

"I don't expect to go to any, dear." Céline smiled back. "I imagine you'll be staying the night? Having come all this way…?"

"If it's no bother," Elizabeth said, picking up her wine and taking a large slug.

"Well then. I'll get on with a few things. I won't be long."

Céline tried to resume humming the tune that was circling her mind like a trapped wasp, but the sound stuck in her throat, filling her ears discordantly. She began to make a white sauce, deftly dicing an onion with vicious strokes of the knife. As circles of sliced potato browned slowly in hot butter, Céline wondered why she was going to such lengths to prepare this meal. Elizabeth certainly did not deserve it. She thumped a half bottle of cold white wine onto the work surface and shook out a handful of pasty-looking almonds from a packet, ready for toasting to a healthier hue later under a hot grill. She poked at the potatoes irritably with a fork, turning them over deftly and slamming a lid on to the pan. She wondered for the hundredth time what had brought Elizabeth all the way from Exeter to visit her in-laws here in Cornwall without warning.

Céline drained her glass of wine, poured herself another, and took it with her up the stairs. She placed it carefully on a small table and opened the slatted doors of the airing cupboard, her well-attuned eye seeking out the dark greens of the guest bedding. She found them near the bottom of the crisp lavender-scented pile of linen. She tried to remember when she had last made up the guest bed. Reaching into the cupboard, her brain was suddenly aware of the rise and fall of voices below.

Céline stepped back abruptly. Thomas's voice was raised in a sudden bellow of what she could only interpret as anger. Alarmed, she steadied herself, her hand on the wall beside her. She looked in the direction of the stairwell, puzzled.

Now she could hear Elizabeth's voice…shouting…her tone high-pitched. Céline could not make out the words. She turned swiftly, intent on disrupting this outrageous argument going on downstairs, in her house.

A sound like an animal in pain loomed out of the sudden silence. Céline froze uncomprehendingly and then lurched clumsily towards the top of the staircase, catching the table with her hip. It rocked sideways, sending the full glass of wine flying. Céline watched the arc of purple spray in a fan shape, the glass landing intact on its side, the thick pile of the cream carpet soaking up the spilled wine thirstily.

Beginning to sob, Céline ran down the stairs. It was like running through treacle, her senses seemed dulled, but still her ears rang with the groans that could only be coming from her husband.

He was slumped in his armchair, sweat beading in the haggard folds of his face, right hand clutching at his left arm, and that awful noise grinding out of gritted teeth, eyes clamped shut, lips blue.

"What? What is it? Elizabeth?" cried Céline in terror.

Elizabeth was on her knees next to Thomas. She was emitting a high keening sound, not at first audible through Thomas's growls of pain. Céline grabbed the phone which sat on a low window seat. She called 999, managing to describe what she was seeing, and giving the necessary information. She listened for a moment and then said quickly, "I'll try, yes, yes, okay. But come quickly…oh please!" Her mouth was obeying her sluggish brain, while her eyes refused to compute the scene before her.

Released from the phone, she ran to Thomas's side. "Elizabeth! Help me! We have to help him! Do something!"

Elizabeth turned agonised eyes to her, her wails continuing ceaselessly.

Céline put one hand flat on her husband's grey cable-knitted chest, then with the other hand pressed on top, she began pushing down rhythmically with all her might, terrified of hurting him more, and not really sure that she was doing this right. Shouldn't he be lying on his back? The thought of pulling his already pain-wracked body off the chair was unbearable. Her noisy sobs matched the frantic movements of her hands.

"Elizabeth!" she suddenly cried, "I forgot, you have to go outside and wait for the ambulance. Show them where to come!"

Elizabeth stumbled to her feet, hands covering her mouth as she ran to the front door.

Céline, realising with a start that Thomas's moans were quieting, looked with alarmed hope at his face. His eyes were open. "It's all right, chéri." she whispered. "I'm here. I love you."

Thomas looked at her, an expression so full of anguish on his face that she stopped breathing. He spoke one word. "Luke!" It grated in his mouth like a barb caught in a fish's gullet. And then Thomas Johnson just stopped.

When the paramedics entered the room, they found her, her head resting on her husband's chest, the hands that had tried so bravely to save him, stilled.

The room was silent at last.

One of the paramedics walked over to Céline and laid a comforting hand on her arm, before confirming what she already knew.

The other went to investigate the acrid stench of burning potatoes emanating from the open kitchen door.

Chapter Two
Time to Call It a Day

Saturday 12th February 2011
South-West France

Luke Johnson tipped the last barrow-load of cement into the base he'd prepared. He levelled the surface and wiped his face dry with the front of his t-shirt. A quick glance towards his wrist told him it was six thirty. The last rays of the setting sun glanced along his forearm, reddening the hairs on his skin as the sun dipped down below the horizon. The warmth of the last few days had lured out the hibernating pipistrelles, tiny bats which squeaked and swept across the darkening sky, stitching together the orange streaks like black cotton tacking.

Time to call it a day. Luke loved this mindless manual work after nine years of teaching craft, technology and design at a secondary school in Exeter. Now, here in South-West France, they called him an artisan. Another, recently retired artisan, who also happened to be an old friend and neighbour, had shown him the basic tricks of the trade. He had learnt how to renovate derelict properties, to rebuild the walls with large creamy-gold stones, and to lay long orange tiles onto the low roofs. To his French vocabulary, not bad, thanks to his mother, Céline, he could now add new words; 'aggloméré', 'couche de fond', 'béton' rolled off his Gallically pursed lips like old friends. Life was simple yet enormously satisfying. He definitely preferred renovating old buildings, but even having spent the last few weeks on this soulless structure, a box-like new build, he was feeling the fierce thrill of pleasure at this manual toil.

He would not even tempt fate by describing himself as at peace, but here in this beautiful part of France, he was becoming more and more aware of moments of content. These moments would arrive unannounced, like walking through a dark fog which disperses suddenly, revealing a momentary brightness that lifts the heart. The panic attacks and feelings of dark gloom were still having the upper hand in the constant battle living inside Luke's mind, but content was definitely lifting its cautious head more and more often.

He slowly cycled home along the winding road through dark fields of stubble. He was looking forward to the warmer months, when swathes of sunflowers would drench these fields with their golden burst of colour. He had been brought to this part of France summer after summer by his parents. His mother was French, and this beautiful stretch of coast along the mouth of the Gironde estuary had been the choice of her own family for summer holidays since she had been a tiny child. Where else to escape when his life as he knew it was threatening to dissolve?

Approaching the tiny hamlet, Luke noticed that the scattered low buildings were mostly in darkness. Only one or two lights showed, the winter custom of shuttering up the windows as dusk falls still being followed on this dark February evening. To his incredulous joy, he had discovered that he was able to rent the same cottage that his grandparents, and later his parents had rented all those summers ago. He followed the narrow lane, looking forward to a hot shower and a glass of wine. A dark shape suddenly barrelled out from the side of a stone wall, tail wagging joyfully, emitting little grunts of friendly greeting.

"Hello Ella! What a nice welcome!" Luke leant down to fondle the silken floppy ears of the long-furred mongrel. She belonged to his next-door neighbour, Gaston, the retired artisan who had helped Luke so much in the early days. He raised a hand in greeting to the figure standing in the shadow of a large fig tree.

"Bonsoir Gaston!" he called, receiving a friendly gesture in response. Gaston's gnarled hand, clutching his ancient well-loved pipe, described an arc of salute through the cold air. The bitter smell of pipe smoke wafted across as Gaston turned back to his kitchen. He was a man of few words, disguising a generous heart, despite a slightly jaundiced outlook on the world. Ella threw Luke a look of reluctant farewell before following her beloved master.

As Luke unlocked and pushed open the heavy oak door to his own property, he was greeted by the sound of the distant ringing of the telephone from the dark exterior.

Luke kicked off his boots in the hall and padded in his socks towards the kitchen, flicking on lights as he went. The butterscotch-coloured floor tiles gleamed, copper pans glinted. Suspended from the low ceiling, they were caught up by the cool draft from the opened front door, swaying gently. Luke strode across to a busy kitchen worktop, plucking the handset of the phone from a jumble of stuff, a bike pump, a half-eaten French stick, a flutter of scribbled Post-It notes. The shrill sound was arrested mid-ring as Luke placed the receiver against his ear.

The sweet voice, broken by sobs, caused Luke a physical pain in his chest as his heart dropped in fear.

"Mum! Slow down! What are you telling me?"

"It's your father Luke... He's gone..."

It took Luke a while to focus; his thoughts moved sluggishly, swimming against a tide of denial. He gazed unseeing at the untidy table while slowly grasping the gist of what he was hearing. His mother's words reached across the hundreds of miles of land and sea to lodge forever in his memory, so that for the rest of his days, he would recall exactly where he had been when he learnt about his father's death.

Death! It didn't seem possible. He was only sixty-six, no age. At least he had died at home in his own armchair, and his mother had been with him. He hadn't been alone. Thank God for that. A massive heart attack, and...

"No," answered his mother to his question, "there'd been no warning."

"I'll come home straight away, Mum... I'll arrange everything. Don't worry! What about Alexis?"

"She's on her way too.... Oh, Luke! What am I going to do? I can't bear this!"

"You mustn't be on your own, Mum! Can't Mrs Thing, next-door sit with you? What's her name?"

There was a pause, a hesitation...

"Mum? Are you there?"

"Yes... don't worry. I'm not alone, I'm with Elizabeth. Elizabeth is here with me... Let me know how soon you'll be here, darling!"

"Mum...did he suffer?" This last question came out on a slight moment of hesitation. It hung terrifyingly unanswered as the airwaves vibrated in his ear. Luke stared at the phone numbly as he heard the click of the replaced receiver.

He wondered why on earth his wife would be there with his mother. Maybe she meant another Elizabeth. Was there some friend of his mother's also called Elizabeth? He couldn't think straight. He sat down heavily, trying to make sense of things. With a groan, he put his hands up to his face, his cheeks wet beneath his fingers. He could tick them off, that brutal list that lurked in his brain, unfolding like ticker-tape at three o'clock in the morning when his defences were down. And as each failing was ticked off, it crumbled away a small piece of him, leaving him flaky, belittled.

Later, Luke sat quietly by his bedroom window. The dark line of the sea in the distance was interrupted by silver winking lights of a small port at the mouth of the estuary. His thoughts took him back in time; the death of his father suddenly transporting him back to his childhood. He remembered the scent of Old Spice and chalk dust as his father pulled him into a hug when he returned from work. He recalled the giddy joy of his father's strong arms lifting him onto his shoulders so that he could see the top of his mother's dark head, the dust on top of the door.

Memories of bedtimes. A blue cover, the only light falling in a golden stripe from the half open door, the soft voice, usually of their mother, telling the tale.

"Tell it again!" one or both boys would insist.

Their mother put her fingers to her lips, a reminder not to wake Alexis, in the next room, too small for stories like this. "Well…where to start…"

"Tell it from the beginning!" they whispered in unison, brown eyes watching her mouth, pink full lips changing from dry to that flat wet ribbon of intimate skin that appeared and disappeared as she formed the words.

Chapter Three

There Might Be Other Summers

Thirty Years Earlier
Friday 24th July 1981
Paris

Céline furiously thumped the bolt of cloth onto the cutting table. 'Merde!" she swore under her breath.

"Mon Dieu, I heard that!" scolded her mother, who had entered the shop in her soft-soled shoes, unheard by her daughter. "Don't be such a baby! These things happen…"

"Why did Jacques have to go and break his stupid arm? My whole summer is ruined!"

Mathilde tutted as she began straightening a pile of colourful reels of cotton which had spilled onto the counter. "Grow up, Céline! You are eighteen, not eight! You can hardly believe that your brother broke his arm for fun, or just to annoy you! And it wouldn't have been fair to your father to expect him to manage the shop on his own until September."

Céline shot her mother a reproachful glance. "I know Jacques always does his bit in the shop while we take our summer break…but that's the trouble! You know I love going to the cottage so much…you could have left me there on my own, couldn't you?"

"Oh Céline! We've been through this! Your father wouldn't hear of it. A hot-headed girl like you with that crowd of youngsters! Without me as a chaperone? What would people think? No, we pull together as a family; there will be other summers."

Céline sighed. What was the point of arguing? It would make no difference. Paris was hot, all her local friends were away on holiday, and she couldn't care less about the stupid shop that her parents ran in the slightly rundown area of the Rue St. Martin.

"There might be other summers," thought Céline, "but this one could never be repeated."

This one would have been a bittersweet preparation for the parting of the ways as new futures were faced, new choices made.

She gulped down a sob of frustration. Her mother had no idea just what she was missing. Céline closed her eyes and imagined the hot sun beating down, the crash and suck of the waves, creating a relentless background to her friends' voices.

Céline had known these friends since she was young. They were local to this part of south-west France, where Céline's parents had always rented a little cottage from a friend who kept it empty especially for them when they needed it. As she grew older, Céline would get out the old rusty bike from the cobwebby shed, and cycle the hot mile to the beach alone. Her bare feet in their summer espadrilles would pump the pedals tirelessly. There she would find them, playing like a bundle of puppies, not a care between them.

She remembered their horrified faces when she told them she had to return to Paris. They all hugged and kissed her, tanned arms around her, the girls wet eyed, the boys pushing each other, showing off to prove that they were the one she would miss the most. But in truth, she was in love with them all, together they were the epitome of all that was youth at its most reckless, at its most beautiful, those golden hours before the bubble was burst by the sharp thrust of reality.

Her mother's voice startled her out of her thoughts. "By the way, I forgot to mention it, but Papa and I have some business to attend to tomorrow morning. We'll only be a couple of hours…can you manage the shop until we get back? Then you can have the rest of the day off. Does that sound fair?"

Céline gave her mother a begrudging smile. "I suppose so… I've nothing else to do, have I?"

The Next Day

Hot rays of sunshine filtered their way through the slatted blinds, dust motes danced in the strips of light. Céline was bored. This shop was boring…a mixture of a drapery cum haberdashery, along with a jaded range of women's clothes, neither one thing nor another. Céline was always complaining that the clothes were dated and unexciting, but her words of advice fell unheeded on the ancient deaf ears of her parents.

Business was sporadic at this time of year, many shops preparing to close for the summer break. She loved the sunshine, so being imprisoned here in the claustrophobic shop was unbearable. She wore a yellow sundress which swirled around her tanned legs. She moved around the shop, a couple of chunky gold bangles clinking at her wrist as she fiddled with various bits of merchandise, trying to look busy.

The bell jangled as the door opened. Tiredly, Céline forced a smile onto her face which did not quite reach her eyes. "May I help you madame?" she asked of the white-haired old lady in front of her.

Despite the heat, she was dressed neatly in a blue skirt with a matching jacket. Céline's eyes took in the sensible lace-up shoes and thick tights. Mon Dieu! She must be in danger of heat stroke in all that! Céline sent up a prayer that this would not happen while the old dear was still on the premises. After fifteen minutes of fingering various garments, loitering rather alarmingly at the lingerie rail, the old lady reluctantly chose a reel of black cotton worth a few centimes, paid and left. Seething, Céline put everything back in its place, checking the time on her watch. Her parents should be back soon, thank God.

She was just thinking about making herself a swift cup of coffee in the back room when the bell rang out again. The small hammers of pain in her head notched up a level. Irritated, she looked up. Someone stood there, back to the stripy glare of the window. She could just make out a tall dark shape surrounded in a halo of dusty light.

"Monsieur? Q'uest-ce-que vous voulez?" she greeted him frostily.

The man stepped closer to the counter, a smile on his tanned, friendly face, untidy fair hair falling into his eyes. "Bonjour," he said in a strong English accent. "Sorry, I just need to ask you directions to the nearest tube station."

Céline eyed him carefully. "Are you meaning to tell me you are not going to purchase anything?" she asked coolly, in her careful impeccable English.

He cast his gaze doubtfully at the array of colourful knick-knacks around him. He looked as much at home in this shop as a juggler in a crowded lift. The thought made Céline smile.

The man let out a sigh of relief. "Phew, you are human after all!" He grinned widely at her, his dark-blue eyes crinkling at the corners.

Céline looked down demurely, wary of this tall friendly man. Was he flirting with her? She was used to boys of her own age, could tease and joke with them, but she felt uncomfortably shy now. "There is a Métro not far from here..." she informed him seriously. "Where do you need to go?"

"Anywhere!" He laughed. "It's my first time in Paris. What do you suggest?" He studied her intently while she seemed to consider his question. She had a sheet of raven-black hair falling to her shoulders like silk. She twirled the ends of it between her fingers thoughtfully. He stared at her, mesmerised.

"Le bateau-mouche!" she said brightly at last. "You will see Paris from the comfort of a lovely boat, with a friendly person telling you all about the sights around you. You will love this!"

"Where did you learn such good English?" he asked admiringly.

"At school of course!" she replied dismissively.

"You're still at school?"

Céline took in his worried expression before reassuring him. "Not any more! I am an adult, ready for the large life. The world is my…how do you say? My mussel?"

"Your oyster, I think you mean," he corrected solemnly, struggling to conceal his amusement. He leaned forward and offered her his hand. "Hello. I'm Thomas Johnson."

Céline hesitated a second before placing her hand tentatively into his large one. Her blood seemed to leap, kicking a buzz of heat through to the surface of her skin. Time froze as her hand remained in his. A trapped fly vibrated lethargically against a hot window pane. Somewhere a clock chimed the hour.

"And now you are supposed to tell me your name," he reminded her politely, taking note of the pale blush rising to her cheeks.

Her hand still lay in his, his blue eyes blazed into hers, with such heat that she was unable to look away. Her face felt scorched. His sudden grin and the pressure on her fingers shook her out of her trance.

"I am Céline," she said, flustered, swiftly reclaiming her unreliable fingers. "Céline Martel. My parents will be back soon. This is their shop. I am in charge until their return."

At that moment, the door to the rear of the shop opened. Monsieur and Madame Martel entered, talking animatedly to each other. They stopped and smiled at the sight of their daughter tending to her customer so correctly and warmly, an intense look of interest raising her eyebrows gracefully, instead of the usual long-suffering expression her face was accustomed to wearing.

"Well," Thomas said quietly, "thank you for your help, mademoiselle." He then leaned towards her and whispered, "I am now going to sit in the little café opposite, where I will order two coffees, and hope very much that I will soon be joined by a beautiful young girl with hair as black as night."

Céline watched him leave the shop, his blond hair shining gold in the sun. He turned slightly, and she caught the slow lazy wink of his eye, meant for her alone.

Céline's father walked around the counter, looking pleased. "That meeting went well!"

Céline glanced at him alarmed. Had he seen the wink, and approved? Surely not!

"Your mother and I have had a very pleasing meeting, n'est-ce pas, Yvonne?" Registering the totally blank expression on his daughter's face, he smiled at her fondly. "You don't want to listen to our boring business details, I'm sure, Céline," he said. "But tell us, have you been busy? Plenty of customers?"

Céline rolled her eyes. Why was her father always so patronising? She wasn't his little girl any more. "Not really, Papa..." she replied, sighing. "It's been too hot to expect many customers..."

"What about that gentleman? Did he not find anything he liked?" asked her mother.

Céline busied herself stacking and tidying a pile of papers in front of her. "Oh yes... I think he did," she replied dreamily. "Do you need me any more? I thought I'd take a walk, get a breath of fresh air." She couldn't wait to get away, from the stuffy atmosphere, from the interrogation, from the parents whom she loved dearly, but who got on her nerves! They were so old! She felt suffocated. There was a new life waiting for her out there. She blew her parents a kiss from the tips of her fingers as she opened the door, not realising that she was kissing her childhood goodbye forever.

Her parents watched her with affection as she hurried out into the hot sunshine, her eyes shining, her face flushed.

"She's a good girl, isn't she?" murmured Yvonne.

"The best, chérie! I really thought she'd still be sulking after being dragged back from the beach. It looks like she's growing up at last." The father spoke proudly and smiled at his wife.

"Oh Henri, it's going to be so hard when she leaves for college. I'm really going to miss her."

Marriage had come late to Yvonne and Henri, due to lack of finances; Jacques, was born when Yvonne was thirty-six years old, Céline three years later. They adored their children, thinking of them as a bonus to an already very happy reunion.

Henri pulled his wife into an impulsive embrace, which evolved into a passionate mouth-to-mouth kiss, startling the little old lady who had returned to the shop on a whim. She had daringly decided to splash out on that see-through nightdress in black silk that she had admired earlier. Her eager desire to own such a forbidden item had over-ridden the thought of facing the disinterested and sulky young woman who had served her before.

Having reassured herself that what she was seeing was not an attempt at resuscitation, she coughed discreetly until the middle-aged couple had returned to their senses of decorum. She wondered to herself whether, in the face of this rather racy behaviour, she would be justified in adding a pair of lacy cami-knickers to her order without arousing any feelings of disapproval.

Chapter Four
He Led Her All the Way

Later the Same Day

Mathilde Martel slowed her steps as she passed the little café on the corner. She was on her way to the local bakery, but nearing the café, her eyes were drawn curiously to the back of a familiar figure sitting there. That cascade of shiny black hair gave it away… Yes! It was her daughter Céline, sitting opposite the lanky fellow with the blond hair flopping onto his forehead. She recognised him as the gentleman in her shop less than an hour before. She turned up the collar of her jacket to obscure her face, but soon realised that the two people sitting there would not have noticed if a herd of wildebeest had stampeded past playing harmonicas. Their heads were nearly touching, their hands plainly joined on the table; no effort at discretion. Mathilde was unable to avert her eyes as she walked, she watched as their faces came together for a kiss. A long, lingering kiss.

Mathilde muttered an apology to the person in front of her, whose heels she had trodden on. She was seething with emotions she could not explain. Her daughter was old enough to choose her companions after all, but this companion was old enough to know better! How old was he, she wondered? Well, she didn't think he would see thirty again. And it was the unseemly haste of it all. She knew young people did things differently these days, but even so…to be kissing a man in public who she'd met only an hour ago seemed excessively inappropriate.

For a wild moment, she half turned round with the intention of marching up to Céline, grabbing her arm and ordering her to come home at once! But the realization came that some acquaintance, some nosey old neighbour, could well be watching, ready to gleefully spread her tasty morsels of gossip to eager ears. So Mathilde gritted her teeth and continued on her quest for her evening baguette. She would have to be patient and snare her wayward daughter later, at dinner. Except that her daughter did not come home to dinner that night.

Thomas Johnson gazed into Céline's eyes like the love-struck cliché he had become. He was a sensible thirty-five-year-old schoolteacher, what the hell was going on? His insides melted whenever he studied her slightly upturned nose with its spattering of golden freckles, the expressive wings of her dark eyebrows which took on a life of their own when punctuating her funny little stories. Even these mesmerised him; her breathy chattering about the little snippets of her life; her broken English in that slightly husky voice of hers that was sending weird messages down his spine to lodge alarmingly deep in his groin…

Céline fell silent, looking at him questioningly. "Thomas? Ça va?" She reached up to cup his cheek with her small hand, her thumb rubbing across his skin. "You look very serious! Tell me what are you thinking?"

Thomas smiled gently. "If I told you, I think your strict maman would beat me senseless with a broom, if your papa had not reached me first with his meat-cleaver…"

Céline laughed out loud, showing small white teeth and a very pink tongue. "Meat what?" she asked with an accomplished giggle. Before he could answer, she had leaned forward and placed her open mouth gently on to his smile.

And after that, there was really no going back. Thomas paid for the untouched coffee, took her by the hand, and led her across the hot cobbles to the heavy wooden door of the cheap pension. The stairwell was pitch black after the white sunshine, but Thomas led the way, shedding his qualms and common sense as they went. She held tightly to his hand, a lamb, not quite to the slaughter, her big brown eyes were too knowing for that, but a lamb just the same. And still he led her, their hands tight together, he led her all the way.

The bed was high and white; a big French bed, with square pillows which they discarded onto the floor. The dust motes danced in the narrow strip of silver light allowed through the almost closed curtains. They moved together in the semi-dark, like fish in a dappled green pool. They moved as if they were dancing, in and out of the shadows, in and out of that beam of sunshine which lit them up like performers on a stage.

Later, her head resting on his chest, he stroked her hair gently, and then her cheek. His fingers came away wet. He tilted her face up to look at her; her sooty eyelashes shone with tears. Without speaking, he wrapped her closer to him. They fell asleep like that; his heart full with the knowledge that this was what he had been waiting for, someone to protect, someone to keep safe. She curled into his arms, secure in the belief that her future lay mapped out before her, all her anxieties melting away as the last light of the day faded.

Two Weeks Later

Mathilde settled herself more comfortably in her chair. She turned her face towards the still warm rays of the late evening sun and closed her eyes in contentment. Their small balcony was her favourite place to sit on a sunny summer evening after a long day working. It overlooked a pretty tree-lined square stretching between their flat and a beautiful grey stone church.

Their large two-story flat was situated above the shop. Henri had inherited the whole business from his parents, being an only child. He could never have afforded to purchase this on his wage as a window dresser in one of the large fancy shops in the centre of Paris.

Henri, sitting beside her, shook his newspaper irritably, sending barbs of discontent into Mathilde's serene mood. "There they go again," observed Henri grumpily. He stared down into the street where Céline, her pink summer skirt swaying in the light breeze, and Thomas, tall, and so British-looking in pale slacks and a white vee-necked cricket jumper, could be seen wheeling their bikes along the pavement. "How long is he going to hang about like this? Surely his holiday must be up?"

Mathilde sighed, wondering how many times they were going to have this conversation. "Don't be so edgy, Henri. You know he's a schoolteacher...he doesn't have to be back until mid-September. There's no harm in him. I think it's just a holiday fling, and you must admit, it's taken her mind off having to come back from her holiday."

"I wouldn't mind if she was doing her share in the shop! She's lucky that you are such a soft touch, doing more than your share of hours just so she can go swanning off with that middle-aged charmer! You spoil her, Mathilde, you always have."

Mathilde bristled at this. She had always prided herself in being a loving, fair, but strict mother. Henri was the old softie! Céline had always been able to twist him round her little finger. Mathilde hated it when people said unfair things to her. It made her see red, in fact. She turned in her chair to look at him, her eyes flashing dangerously. "So when she stayed out all night, it was you, was it, who waited up for hours? Who caught her creeping in at five o'clock in the morning, and gave her such a scolding that she broke down in tears?" She glared at Henri. "Well?" she demanded.

Henri looked at her, startled at this sudden tirade. "Most unfair!" he murmured. "I would have gone out looking for her, you know that."

"Ha!" cried his wife. "And why didn't you? Because you were fast asleep in your armchair as soon as dinner was over! Oblivious to the world...a gang of men could have robbed the shop and carried me off with them for all you'd know about it!"

Henri was about to protest that the thought of anyone wanting to carry her off at her time of life was most unlikely, but one look at her expression and he closed his mouth.

As an afterthought, after an uncomfortable silence, Henri added, unwisely, "What good is staying up all night waiting, anyway? You might as well close the barn door after the horse has bolted. N'est-ce pas?"

One Week Later

The Sunday church bells announcing morning Mass pealed clearly across on the fresh morning breeze.

Mathilde did the buttons up on her chic summer jacket. It was a pretty shade of lavender, and looked well over her dark-blue dress; she added a scarf patterned with mauve and blue flowers, and admired the finished affect in the mirror of her dressing-table.

Henri came into the bedroom, humming. He looked dapper in his neat Sunday clothes. "Ready, chérie?" he asked, standing beside her and studying their reflections. "You look lovely as usual."

Mathilde turned to him, but before she could speak, there came the sweet voice of their daughter. "Maman? Papa? Are you up there?"

Mathilde smiled. "I told you she'd be up in time to go to Mass with us, Henri!" she whispered, delighted.

Céline's footsteps thudded on the thickly carpeted stairs, and then she arrived in the doorway, pink cheeked and glossy haired, reminding her parents of how she looked as a small child, freshly tumbled from her bed.

Henri stretched out his hands towards her, smiling his big fatherly smile. "Well, well! Good girl! We're just leaving…"

Céline's smile faltered. "Oh! Actually, I've come to tell you something… Can you come downstairs, now?"

Mathilde looked puzzled. "Is everything all right? What is it?"

"Yes, maman! Everything is all right! Just come now, please!"

Mathilde and Henri followed Céline downstairs, exchanging furtive baffled glances. Henri glanced at his watch with a frown.

Céline led the way into the lounge. Both of her parents stopped in their tracks as a tall figure unfolded itself from an easy chair. Céline ran to take the hand of her nervous lover, looking up at him expectantly.

Thomas coughed, pausing to choose his words carefully. "I would like…that is, WE would like, to announce to you, that um…"

"Get on with it young man!" Henri interrupted gruffly, not liking the sound of this at all. "We're going to be late for church…can't this wait?"

Céline stepped in front of Thomas and spoke clearly, "Thomas has asked me to marry him. I have accepted, and will travel home to England with him to meet his parents and arrange our wedding there."

There followed a painful silence as this news was digested. Mathilde spoke first, as glancing at her husband's flushed face, she feared a fit of apoplexy might overtake him at any moment. She herself tried to remain calm. "I'm sure we can discuss this sensibly," she murmured. "After all, you've only known each other three weeks!" She gave a little laugh, to show how absurd the whole thing was.

Céline translated what her mother had said. Thomas looked glum. This was not looking promising.

Henri's power of speech returned to him in this pause. He pointed a shaking finger at Thomas and barked, "How dare you come here! You waltz in, snatch our daughter away from us with your foreign wiles, seduce her without a by your leave, and then fill her head with nonsense about weddings! She has plans for the future. She is going to college. Get out of my house! Now!"

Thomas had no idea what Henri had said, but he had a pretty good idea that it wasn't likely to be followed up by a pat on the back and a glass of champagne.

Mathilde put a hand on her husband's arm. "Steady Henri… Seduce is a bit of a strong word, isn't it? Why don't I make a cup of coffee and we can talk without losing our tempers. The thing is there's no rush, is there? Maybe when you have completed your college course in three years' time, we will see how you feel about each other. Until then…"

Céline looked straight at her parents. She held her head up and said, "You don't understand, maman. By then, our baby will be walking and talking. So you see, we are not asking your permission, we are simply explaining our plans to you."

Chapter Five

They Imagined What Might Have Been

Mathilde and Henri Martel never really recovered from the shock of their daughter's defection to a foreign country. They were comforted by their son Jacques. He had married a girl who was two years younger than himself, who was level-headed, if a bit bossy, a good cook and mother to their two daughters, and last but not least, she was French...

But still, Céline was their golden girl. They never spoke badly of her, even to each other. But they grew older, and at night, lying side by side in their big French bed, white heads on their square white pillows, they would hold hands in the dark, and silently and separately nurse their broken hearts. She had forsaken them; that's what it boiled down to. They were too sensible to blame each other; why turn on the only person you had left? But sometimes if nerves were frayed, or bodies weary, they might eye each other thoughtfully, wondering if things might have turned out differently had one of them had perhaps been a stricter parent, or maybe whether one of them might have been guilty of turning a blind eye once too often.

As promised, Thomas whisked Céline home with him to his small cottage in a Cornwall village. She was introduced to his parents who lived close by in a comfortable old house where Thomas had been brought up. They did not know quite what to make of this beautiful young French girl. She was not the sort of person they were au fait with. Her foreignness made it difficult for them to ascertain her class, for example; they felt out of their depth. Her ancestors could be members of the French aristocracy for all they knew, or she could be a dancer from Les Folies Bergère. How were they to tell? And she was so young! It was hard not to equate her to one of his pupils from school! A seventeen-year gap in their ages was unwise, surely? Her interesting condition only added to their bewilderment; was this the only reason for Thomas to have taken leave of his senses? They found themselves fretting about the whole affair.

Céline had had her pregnancy confirmed by her own doctor in Paris by the end of August. Her expected date of delivery was to be the first of May 1982.

Thomas was back at work, teaching at the local secondary school, so Céline, with the help of her future in-laws, saw to all the details of the coming nuptials. The whirlwind wedding, set for Saturday 12th September, helped to distract the two sets of parents from their anxieties and uncertainties. Céline's parents arrived for the small affair, made welcome by Thomas's parents. All four had so many concerns and questions in common, that if there had been no language barrier, they would have got on like a house on fire. As it was, they nodded and smiled at each other a good deal, but remained as unaware of each other's true thoughts and feelings at the end of the few days, as at the beginning.

Mathilde and Henri returned home to Paris, not knowing when they would see their beloved daughter again. They discussed the wedding.

"Where was the church part of the marriage? Just twenty minutes in that cubicle, like a waiting room! They were not married in the eyes of God!" Mathilde felt faint at the thought and Henri had to help her to her chair.

Henri looked at her sadly, nodding in sympathy. "And that wedding breakfast! What was that? For a start, it was in another ugly room…"

"Those chairs! Mon Dieu! They were stacked up like in a schoolroom! And plastic tables. Don't the English use hotels for their celebrations?"

"I think lack of money might have been the problem," Henri announced with some insight. "That buffet was not fit for human consumption," he added, shuddering.

They both stared out of the window, recalling the memory of the curling sandwiches with unrecognizable pink fillings, the dry finger rolls topped with thin slabs of grey icing, the unlikely combination of squares of hard yellow cheese skewered to chunks of tinned fruit with wooden sticks usually used to clean one's teeth.

"We would have served Boeuf Bourguignon," whispered Mathilde dreamily. "With fresh crusty bread, platters of creamy cheeses, glistening green salads tossed with walnuts and pieces of avocado in my own homemade dressing…" Her voice drifted off as they imagined what might have been.

No mention was made of the hopes of a happy future for the giddy couple. Better to concentrate on what could have been done to make the day nicer. The fate of Céline and Thomas was now out of their hands and in the lap of the gods.

If the four worried parents of the happy couple could have used x-ray vision to see through the walls of the little Cornish cottage, they would have been pleasantly reassured. They would no doubt have averted their eyes from the amorous shenanigans going on, but would nod their old-fashioned approval at the small but telling signs of happiness. Thomas would ring Céline from school during his lunch breaks, making sure she wasn't overdoing things. Céline was loving her housewifely duties; producing suppers involving tasty sauces with plenty of garlic. He brought her flowers every week; bunches of the wildflowers he knew she favoured over funereal lilies. As the weather grew more Autumnal, she warmed his slippers in front of the log fire she had learnt to lay and light, with a promise not to carry anything too heavy.

Thomas insisted on running her a bath each evening to help her sleep well. She lay contentedly amongst the lavender-scented bubbles which circled her growing stomach. She would stroke it with a mixture of awe and fear, whispering little French songs under her breath, as much to soothe herself as the baby.

Thomas came in to massage her shoulders, as he often did. "Heavens! Your tummy is very…um…"

Céline tilted her head back to grin at him. "Go on! Say it! My tummy is very fat, isn't it?"

"Well! I wasn't going to say that exactly." He floundered. "It's just lovely and round, uh, rounder than it was, that is…"

"They call it being pregnant!" She laughed. "You know, I am going to see the doctor next week. If he asks me if we have any worries, I'll tell him that my husband is anxious about my tummy looking too round, should I?"

Céline squealed as Thomas grabbed the flannel and used it to flick a wave of water into her face.

The low sun was a red globe that bobbed just above the trees, turning the already russet and yellow leaves into fiery flames as the light hit them. Thomas drove home from work, enjoying his drive along the high hedged lanes and looking forward to the coming evening with its usual simple pleasures.

He threw his briefcase down onto the wooden hall floor. "Darling! I'm home!" he called, unwinding the old mauve scarf that was a memento of his college days. Being met with silence, he opened the lounge door quietly and peeped in, assuming that Céline had fallen asleep in there.

She was sitting, unmoving on the settee, her back to him. He walked around to face her, puzzled by her silence. She sat as still as a rock, the only movement was in her hands, twisting a soggy tissue back and forth. Her cheeks were wet, her eyes downcast. Thomas sat gently beside her, taking her hands in his.

"Céline?" he began, his heart heavy, as various possible scenarios flashed through his mind. "What did the doctor say? Are you all right?"

Céline raised her eyes, and Thomas could see she had been crying for some time.

"Okay, now, just tell me, please! You're scaring me... Is there something wrong with the baby?" he whispered, terrified of what she might say.

She swallowed, her voice thick with tears. "This will be a shock, Thomas. I am in a shock. I don't think I will be able to do this... I am so frightened!"

He waited, fighting the urge to shake her.

"The doctor, he thinks that my tummy *is* bigger than he was expecting. I should have known, you were right."

He stared at her while she continued to speak. "He is very certain, because I am bigger than my dates, that I am holding two babies, not one! Mon dieu! How will we manage?"

Thomas began to laugh and laugh; great gusts of mirth which brought tears to his eyes and hurt his ribs. He hugged Céline to him and began to rock her in his arms, still laughing helplessly until she was caught up by the infectious sound and there they sat, rocking and gasping together and then just calming down and grinning at each other like fools.

On April 8th 1982, Céline gave birth to two beautiful baby boys. They were born three weeks early, which she had been told was normal for twins. She cradled them in her arms, all pain and exhaustion wiped from her face, which shone with relief and joy. Thomas kissed the three of them in turn. There were tears in his eyes. Not a man to voice his feelings easily, he was now completely robbed of speech.

"Well, daddy, meet your sons; this one is Xavier, the older and wiser of the two," announced Céline solemnly. "And this little one, smaller but no less precious, is Luke." She looked up and smiled. "They are identical! At the moment it's easy to see who is who because of their size, but when Luke catches his brother up, it will be impossible!"

Thomas cleared his throat before managing to speak in a wobbly voice. "We'll have to dress them differently, then. One in stripes, and one in spots..."

"And have my babies be the laughing stop? They are not clowns!"

Thomas kept a straight face with difficulty. "It's 'laughing stock' not 'stop', sweetheart. And don't worry, I expect they'll develop their own little characteristics as they grow older."

As Thomas had predicted, the twins, despite looking identical in most respects, were very different in character. But Luke did not really catch up physically with his brother. He was slightly shorter, thinner, and more prone to childhood ailments. Xavier was a sturdier version altogether, and not only that, as he grew older he became known as the mischief maker, the daredevil, the one who did the opposite of what he was told. He tried relentlessly to lead Luke astray, but Luke was frightened of his own shadow, not to mention his parents' disapproval. He could not understand what made Xavier tick; why on earth risk being shouted at and punished for some silly prank?

But Luke was often confused. He felt that being well behaved and obedient was somehow not very interesting. When his parents' friends came round, the twins would be introduced as Xavier, 'the one who has all sorts of tricks up his sleeve, up to no good every five minutes! Who knew what devilment he was going to think up next? He was as clever and agile as a monkey! And this is Luke, who wouldn't say boo to a goose, he was a right little worrier, bless him! They were like chalk and cheese, couldn't be more different really, funny, wasn't it?'

To be honest, it was Luke's father who said these sorts of things. His mother was always ready to praise him, giving him an extra cuddle or offering to read him a story. Xavier was too busy racing around to bother with cuddles or stories. Sometimes when they had fallen out over something, Xavier would taunt Luke with being a sissy and a mummy's boy. Sometimes he made Luke cry, which only made things worse.

Alexis was born two years after the twins. She grew into a pretty little girl, her blonde hair contrasting with the boys' dark looks. They took after their mother. Alexis and Luke became very close. He adored his little sister, who was the only person he knew who looked up to him with admiration. He would have done anything for her.

It was during the summer after the boys' seventh birthday that something happened which would change the Johnson family forever.

Chapter Six
There Was Not a Breath of Air

Thursday 17th August 1989
Cornwall

Céline placed the last rinsed lettuce leaf into the salad spinner and glanced up. From her position at the sink, she could see down the length of the narrow cottage garden. Through the open window, Céline could hear the sweet high voice of her five-year-old daughter, Alexis. She was singing to her row of dolls as she poured cups of imaginary tea for them. Céline watched her for a moment, her little girl, so absorbed in her play, her tangle of blonde hair shining gold in the hot sunshine.

The sun beat down out a cloudless blue sky. Bees buzzed drowsily amongst the clover flowers growing profusely on the lawn. There was not a breath of air.

Céline checked that there was a bottle of tonic chilling in the fridge. There was, and a fat waxy lemon waiting to be sliced later. Thomas had been at school all day, supporting the students who were finding out their GCSE results. He would be emotionally drained on his return home, and would appreciate being welcomed with an ice-cold gin and tonic.

Through the sultry shimmering heat, Céline could hear her sons, shouting to each other as they played together further down the garden. They were hidden from sight by a willow tree, its trailing branches untrimmed to allow the children a green cave in which to play. Smiling to herself, she moved away into the cool depths of the cottage to lay the dining-room table for the children's tea.

The boys were bored, and the heat was making them fractious and irritable.

"What do you want to play then?" moaned Xavier.

Luke, lying on his back in the long grass, made a face. He knew what he didn't want to do; anything which involved physical tussling, hiding in unpleasant corners of the garden, or risking cobwebby hair exploring their dad's dark cluttered shed…all of which seemed to be inevitable if Xavier had anything to do with it. What Luke really wanted was to be left alone to lie on the cool surface of his bed with a colouring book and his new crayons. He closed his eyes, calmed by the swirls of gold and orange swimming through his eyelids.

His eyes flew open and he gasped as his brother landed with a thump on top of him. He lay still, trying not to cry as, winded, he tried to breathe normally.

Xavier tried a few half-hearted punches to Luke's arms, before pinning them to the ground. "Come on! Fight me!" he commanded. "You're so useless! Why won't you ever do anything fun?"

Luke looked straight up into his brother's face. He saw the skin close up, pink from exertion and heat, a scattering of damp freckles; a strand of black hair flopped forward, tickling Luke's forehead. It was like looking into a mirror. "This isn't fun..." whispered Luke. "Fighting isn't fun..."

Exasperated, Xavier rolled over and lay beside his brother. One boy kept his eyes closed in the hope of being left alone, the other was scanning his surroundings, planning the next plan of action.

The garden had a stone wall down one side, about five feet high, providing privacy and safety.

Luke had almost drifted into a doze, his limbs feeling light from the relief of the removal of his brother's weight. Alexis's voice drifted on the buzzing air, "Polly put the kettle on, kettle on...."

A sudden scraping noise brought Luke back from the brink of sleep. He opened one eye. Xavier was dragging one of the green plastic garden chairs away from the raised stone patio. He placed it carefully beside the wall, before returning his attention to the table, where his parents liked to sit with drinks and nibbles on warm evenings.

"Give us a hand, lazybones!" called Xavier, struggling to pull the table, which was proving an awkward shape to manoeuvre.

Luke shut his eyes firmly again, not wanting to be involved in Xavier's game. He did not see his brother succeed in yanking the table, bouncing the legs along the grass, until it was jiggled and pushed into place next to the chair.

With a satisfied smile, Xavier wiped his hot hands down the front of his stripy t-shirt, spat on them, and then climbed first onto the chair, and from there up onto the table. He stared down at Luke, the familiar feeling of irritation washing over him. What was the good of a brother who was scared of everything? He couldn't wait to get back to school, to his gang of friends who looked on him as a leader, yet weren't afraid to join him when he came up with some new reckless venture.

It wasn't hard for Xavier to pull himself up onto the top of the wall, sit astride it, and call down to Luke.

Luke sat up and stared at Xavier in dismay. "You shouldn't be up there!" he cried, his eyes round with fright.

"Says who?" replied Xavier scornfully.

"Mum'll go mad, you know she will."

Xavier pulled a face. "She's not looking though, is she? Unless you're going to tell tales on me as usual?" He glared at Luke.

Luke looked like he was going to cry. "I won't tell," he whispered, "Not if you promise to come down now…"

Xavier laughed. "Oh right, so I'll come down now, and it'll be our secret, yes? Just between you and me?"

"Yes!" gasped Luke thankfully, looking relieved.

"Or…" continued Xavier, "I could walk to the end of the wall, and then back again?"

Luke looked horrified at the thought. He clasped his knees and sank his face down against them. He hated these games. He groaned miserably. "You can't do that, it's too dangerous!"

Xavier's cheeks flushed pink. "Are you daring me, Luke? Are you saying I can't do it, or I won't do it, mmm?"

Luke watched as Xavier managed to push himself up to a standing position. The wall was a foot wide. He took a step forward.

"Don't…" said Luke.

"Watch me," said Xavier.

He took a few more faltering steps, then, gaining confidence, he took a few more, his arms outstretched. He had run out of wall at this point, it having reached a thick hedge growing at right angles to it, and marking out the end of the garden.

Luke sat stock still on the grass, terrified of saying anything, not wanting to break Xavier's concentration. He squinted upwards through his fingers, his heart hammering in his chest.

Xavier paused, realising that he would have to turn round to finish the challenge. He turned sideways, slowly moving his feet so that they were pointing back in the right direction. Luke closed his eyes.

With a big grin on his face, Xavier said, "Here I come! Didn't think I could do it, did you?" He took a step forward.

"That's it!" screamed Luke. "I'm going to get Mum!"

Xavier looked up in alarm, not noticing that a stone from the top surface of the wall had become dislodged. As he put his foot onto it, it slid to his right, taking the boy's foot sliding outwards. His hands clutched fresh air as he teetered on one leg, losing his balance.

He hardly made a sound as he fell, just a surprised sort of yelp. Luke's eyes widened at the sound. He saw his brother's falling body, the arms flailing, the puzzled expression on his white face. It wasn't a very long fall, and the grass was soft, but as he landed, his temple struck the edge of the patio with a sickening crack.

The bees continued to buzz, a dog barked in the distance, and Alexis continued to tell Polly to put the kettle on. Luke could hear nothing. He was enveloped in a shroud of silence. Minutes ticked by as Luke sat frozen on the grass. He saw his brother's blood staining the grass and soaking into the neck of his t-shirt, but he was unable to move. His body fell sideways, in a kind of trance, so that when, finally, Céline opened the back door to call the children in to tea, she thought Luke was asleep.

She stepped across to where he was lying in a foetal position, arms around his head. "Tea ready, sleepyhead!" she said, reaching down to touch his shoulder. It was then she realised that he was shaking from head to foot. It took Céline a while to realise that it was her other son who needed her attention, but by then it was too late. Xavier had bled to death.

Chapter Seven
"I Promise"

Christmas Eve 1989

Luke lay motionless in his bed. His mouth tasted minty, his sheets smelled of lavender, and if he lifted his head, he knew that he would see the bright red felt stocking tied to the wooden knob at the bottom of his bed. He knew that there was another identical stocking at the end of Alexis's bed, in the bedroom next to his. He could hear his mother reading Alexis a story. It was about a mummy elephant trying to have a few minutes' peace in the bath. He remembered loving that story, and the pictures sprang up clearly in his head, the yellow flowery shower cap sitting crazily on the elephant's head as she wallowed in the bubbles, delicately sipping from a cup of tea balanced on the edge of the bath…

He thought about the attic. It was always pitch dark in there, unless he climbed up the little fold-down ladder and turned on the single bulb which swung about on its wire, casting weird shadows. That was Mum or Dad's job. A few days ago, sitting on the landing, he'd watched his dad pass the Christmas baubles and stuff down to his mum. He'd seen the red stockings sticking out of the top of the cardboard box with 'Xmas Decorations' written in black marker pen on the side. His mother caught hold of the box as he swung it down to her. She'd frowned, taking one of the stockings out and quickly passing it back up to his dad, who leaned down through the square hole to snatch it out of her hand with a grimace.

"That's Xavier's," Luke informed them in a flat voice. "His is the one with the reindeer on it, Alexis has got a fairy, and mine…"

Céline interrupted him swiftly, using her jolly tone. "I know, poppet! We're just keeping it safe up here…"

"But Father Christmas will wonder why it's not at the end of his bed!" Luke's voice was shaky with panic.

His mother had managed to distract him with the promise of some treat or other, wrapping him in another layer of cotton wool, cushioning him against reality.

People had stopped asking Luke to explain what had happened that day. At first, he had been unable to speak at all. It was if he had disappeared into a bubble of pain, sitting for hours with his eyes closed. And later, when speech had returned, Luke said that he could not remember any of it.

Céline and Thomas were steeped in their own grief. Without realising it, their son's initial muteness allowed them to deal with their broken hearts at their own pace. It was difficult enough for them to contend with Alexis's baffled incomprehension and stream of puzzled unanswered questions.

Instinctively, Céline and Thomas closed ranks, supporting each other and finding huge comfort in each other's presence. They talked to each other for hours, remembering their son, his foolhardiness and stubborn character muted to their own version of a loveable daredevil.

"What a boy he was!" Thomas whispered in the darkness of their bedroom. He cradled Céline gently, shielding her against further hurt. "He lived every minute to the full, didn't he? Nothing fazed him…"

Céline clung to him, tears blurring her words. "He reminded me of you, chéri. So full of fun. And even at his young age, if he wanted something, he never gave up until he got it, did he?"

"I remember," agreed Thomas. "And I never gave up on you, did I? Like father, like son…"

And so they counselled each other, healing their wounds.

Meanwhile, Luke would lie dry-eyed in his room next-door. He too had been part of a twosome, and it felt like losing a limb. But he was alone now, cast up on a shore, unable to move forward. The loss of his twin haunted him in a way that he could not control nor fully understand. Sometimes he tried to remember the details of that day. He would warily probe his memory, like a tongue exploring the cavity left by an extracted tooth. Too painful and he would draw back in fright, slamming a door shut before the black yawning chasm of his memory swallowed him screaming and unable then to ever, ever forget.

At first, the hole left in Thomas's and Céline's life grew no bigger or smaller. Sometimes it became obscured by the sheer chaos of life, but it never disappeared. For Céline, being a mother, and having two small children who still needed her, softened the pain a little; she had less time to brood, unlike Thomas. A mother's job is all encompassing, it feeds her heart every hour of the day; from drying tears, creating comfort food for anxious appetites, wrapping the sweet-scented bodies in warmed towels, to the sharp words of sometimes needed reprimand, to the time given in reassurance and hugs when bedroom shadows lengthened and fears crowded the mind.

Thomas was not so lucky. The main bulk of his life was his work, time given ironically to other people's children. He returned each night to find that Luke and Alexis had been so cherished by Céline that there was nothing left for him to do. He didn't know that having been close to their mother with her softness, her clothes, her skin, her voice, that his children now needed and craved their father's masculinity, his strength, his silly jokes and exuberance, his rough cheek. Before the accident, it was Thomas's role to chase away the sleep, encouraged by Céline with her milky drinks and soporific stories. They looked forward to his rough and tumble games, hide and seek that ended with tickling and shrieks, the scary stories of wicked old women bundled into a bread oven, little children lured by their evil step-mother to starve in the forest. Now they were puzzled by their father's subdued tones and sombre expressions.

Luke's memory began to return in snippets and flashes. It caught him unaware when trying to think about something else. He was ten years old when he woke screaming in the middle of the night. He clapped his hands over his eyes, but it was too late. He had seen what his subconscious mind had hoped never to see again. A treacherous dream brought it back to him in full-blown Technicolor, like a film. Guilt hit him like a steam train, a feeling that no ten-year-old boy should ever have to feel.

Without being fully aware of it, at about this same time, Thomas began to watch Luke. He watched him through an open window, wheeling his bike into the drive, or sitting under a tree in the garden eating an apple, head in his school work. Luke's pale face, with its dark haunted eyes troubled Thomas deeply. He loved Luke so much. He felt huge guilt that he had not been there for Xavier, had not been able to save him. Now he looked at Luke and realised with shame that he had not really looked at him properly for a long time. He wondered when Luke had become so silent, so introverted and difficult to speak to. How had he not noticed the subtle change from a normal, all be it quiet little boy, to this nervous creature who would startle at the least thing, who seldom smiled let alone laughed. Thomas had known, and felt vaguely grateful, that unlike other parents who had lost a child, he wouldn't have to wonder what Xavier would have looked like as each year passed, he only had to look at Luke. But he had no such knowledge of how Xavier's character would have developed, he could only surmise, relying on his memories of that feisty seven-year-old fearless child, that he would still have these characteristics. And so he had watched Luke in order to be able to imagine that other child. Now he felt a wave of self-disgust that he had spent more time thinking about the son he had lost instead of the son within hugging reach. But to reach out to hug someone who avoids eye contact and physically steps away was impossibly difficult.

Luke, however, was very aware of being watched. He would glance up to catch the tail end of his father's heartbroken gaze, and be washed away by such a sick feeling that it made him feel physically ill.

It would not be until he grew older that he would recognise that feeling as guilt. He believed that his father wished that it had been him and not Xavier who died that day. This belief, combined with the truth of what really happened that terrible summer, haunted Luke, eating away his ability to develop a healthy relationship with his father. His very ability to mature emotionally seemed damaged, fractured by guilt.

Céline was comforted and relieved as the children grew older, to observe Luke and Alexis becoming closer. She also sometimes wondered whether she and Thomas were giving Luke the attention he needed. In the back of her mind was the memory of a hurtful observation made by Thomas, made when the boys were about five years old. He seldom criticised anything she did, which was why she had never forgotten it. He had accused her of babying Luke and turning him into a snivelling weakling. That memory made her hesitate to do what her instinct told her to; to wrap Luke up emotionally and physically. She knew that he needed to be reassured that Xavier's accident was just that…an accident. But instead, she put on a jolly persona, an act to show that life was safe and happy despite what had happened. Luke gazed at her, bewildered that his mother not only appeared not to mind very much that Xavier was dead, but that all the kisses and cuddles were heaped upon Alexis. He was not a jealous child, and he adored his little sister, but it was just another sign to him that he was less lovable now that Xavier was gone.

One bright spring evening, when Luke had just turned fourteen, both he and Alexis were sitting at the dining-room table. They had been busy with homework, and Luke closed his books with a sigh.

"All done?" Alexis asked, putting the finishing touches to a map of England she had traced for a geography project.

"Yep! Fancy a Coke?" Luke pushed his chair back and made his way to the kitchen.

Alexis picked up a dark-blue crayon and began shading in the coast line. She heard the hiss of released gas and the welcome sound of ice rattling against glass. Luke came back and plonked the brimming glasses on the table, slopping some onto the cloth. "Butterfingers!" She grinned, taking a long grateful gulp from her glass.

Luke sat down. On the sideboard, there was a professionally taken photo of the twins, aged four. They were dressed identically in white suits and between them on a white rug sat a chubby two-year old Alexis, clutching a teddy bear to her white smocked chest.

Alexis was staring at the photo over the rim of her glass. "Do you think about him every day?" she said.

Luke followed her eyes. He paused momentarily before replying. "Not every day," he admitted. "Do you?" he threw back at her guardedly.

Alexis turned to look at him, her startling dark-blue eyes so like her father's. "I don't remember him very well…" She faltered. "I can only recall his face because it's your face!" She smiled. "I was only five, and you boys were always playing together."

"Were you jealous? Didn't you feel left out?" he asked her curiously.

Alexis put her empty glass firmly down on the table. "No, I don't think so… All that tearing about and making silly noises! I don't actually think that Xavier liked me very much. Did he used to tease me? I remember feeling upset sometimes."

Luke gazed at her thoughtfully. "Yes, he did. You know that basket chair in your bedroom? He used to make you go underneath it, it's got that big wide base, and then he'd sit on it so you couldn't get out. You were such a stubborn little thing…you refused to cry!"

"I didn't like him much, Luke… That's awful, isn't it?"

Luke put his hand over hers. "It's honest," he said quietly. "You don't miss him then?"

Alexis stared at the table uncomfortably. She sighed. "I don't miss the boy he was, no. But he might have grown up and changed. We'll never know now, will we?"

Tears gathered in Alexis's eyes as she gripped Luke's hand. There was a lengthy silence. She looked at her brother. He was staring through the window at the garden. The shadows were lengthening as the sun sank lower; the patio paving stones shone golden in the thick warm light.

"He teased me too," he said suddenly. "I was scared of him. He was a bully."

Alexis gave an audible intake of breath.

"I hated him, but I never meant to kill him…"

By the time Luke told his sister exactly what he remembered had happened that day, the room was almost dark. There was an orange glow in the greenish sky, marking the place in the west where the sun had gone down.

"Did you leave him lying there on purpose?" Alexis whispered.

"I'm not sure. I can't remember! But why didn't I shout for help? I was old enough to understand how important it was… Why was I so useless? Just like Xavier always said I was!" He covered his face with his hands.

"Maybe…" Alexis said hesitantly, "it was because Xavier told you over and over that you were useless, that you believed it? You were just a little boy! You didn't kill him, Luke. He killed himself!" But she knew from the haunted expression in his eyes that he wasn't convinced. She wished she could comfort him, but she felt helpless.

Luke looked at her. "You're right. I didn't kill him by pushing him off that wall. I killed him by breaking my promise not to tell Mum. That's what made him fall…and then I did nothing, nothing at all." He reached across and took both her hands in his. "You are the only person who knows what I did that day, the only one. Promise that you will never tell anyone, please, Alexis? Promise me?"

She watched as the tears brimmed in his eyes and fell, warm and wet onto the backs of her hands. "I promise," she said, her voice husky. Looking down, she watched her tears mingling with his on their joined fingers, like drops of blood in a pact.

Chapter Eight

"Next Time, I'll Be Ready"

December 2006
Exeter

The room was long and low, the bar extending the whole length of one wall. People, mostly university students and young teachers, jostled shoulder to shoulder. With subdued lighting and very little clear floor space, the pub was a bottleneck, jamming together those piling in at the door, cold cheeked, unwinding scarves, with those crowding along the bar, hands held high to attract the one of several barmen's attention. At the far end, the continual flow to and from the toilets was hindered by lack of space between the stool-perchers at the bar and the groups of early arrivers who had grabbed comfort at the wooden benches lining the massive beer-stained tables. These stood beneath small-paned windows glowing orange from stubby candles within and streetlight from without.

Luke stamped the first fat snowflakes of the winter from his boots and ducked his way into the bar of The Suckling Pig. He fought his way through the smoky fug to the back, to join the friends he knew would be there, as they were every Friday. There was a shriek of wood on tile as chairs were shuffled along to make room for him.

At the age of twenty-four, Luke had lost the freckles, the rounded cheek had been honed down to a defined jawline, but the beautiful chocolate-brown eyes and jet-black hair were the same. A hank of it fell into his eyes as he gazed around the group of faces, animated, laughing, hands gesticulating, the rise and fall of voices as ideas were shared, opinions shredded. These were his friends, a safe band of people joined by their work, their ages, their interest in each other. They didn't judge. They were just there, and Luke accepted them unconditionally.

Someone passed a tall pint glass over to him, threading it between the shoulders of Jim and Mike, who were deep in a conversation involving some smirking and several dubious hand movements. Luke grabbed the freezing cold glass, his fingers already numbed with cold from the outside ice-spiked air, and mouthed his thanks to Annie, who taught P.E. and never shirked a round.

"Cheers!" said the girl next to him, clunking her glass against his and sending a wave of foam onto the back of his hand.

"Cheers, Sal!" he said back, "Like the hair…" He gazed at her fiery red locks, twiddled up into an impossible-looking knot on top of her head. She blushed and ducked her head down to suck a calming draught of lager. Surfacing, she bravely turned her eyes to catch Luke's, adding a tremulous smile to her shy overture.

Luke dropped his gaze to stare into his drink, uncomfortable with the suspicion that Sally was exhibiting increased signals of fancying him. He was aware of his facial muscles freezing into a lack of expression…they were outside his control, as was the invisible wall which always descended around him at times like this.

Normality to Luke now was avoiding any situation that brought people too close. He had struggled through secondary school; had shunned social contact, excelled at his studies, and avoided being bullied only because of his startling good looks. He shouldered his daily way through the clusters of students, tall, loose limbed, alert. The boys, the ones with their acne and inability to grasp the simplest concepts, made snide comments, called him autistic behind his back. But unease crept in to wipe the sneers from their faces as they witnessed the girls gazing after Luke with their knowing mascaraed eyes, tweaking the waistbands of their already too short skirts, their backs turning against them like a united wall.

He arrived unscathed one golden September morning at St. John's Teacher's Training College in Exeter. Here it was easier to melt into the crowd, the young men and women here mingled together, inhibitions shed by the adrenaline rush of college life.

Luke loved the freedom of living away from home for the first time in his life. He worked hard, enjoying the easy banter with the lecturers, the written work, essays, and lesson plans. Away from the claustrophobic love of his mother and troubled surveillance of his father, he was able to flourish. He was successful in continuing to dodge even the most outrageous manipulations of the female students, surrounding himself with a safe mix of friends who accepted him.

And now here they were, fully-fledged teachers. Some had chosen teaching posts in faraway locations, even abroad, but Luke and a handful of friends had opted to find jobs in local schools. Luke had considered moving even further away from the family home, but was reluctant to worsen the already strained atmosphere between himself and his parents, so had found a position in a secondary school in Exeter. And of course he needed to stay within reach of his sister, the most precious person in his life. He had found himself a quirky little cottage to rent in the harbour area of Exsham, a small fishing port nestling at the mouth of the River Exe. Meanwhile, Alexis was living in nurses' accommodation in a hospital in Exmouth, a sea-side town five miles away from Luke's cottage. They were a lifeline for each other.

Now, embarrassed by the lack of eye contact from Luke, Sally stood up suddenly, making her way towards the Ladies. Letting out a sigh of relief, Luke picked up his pint for a steadying draught. He raised his eyes, and there, past the place where Sally had sat, he saw a girl sitting alone at a small table. She was gazing out of the darkening window an untouched drink in front of her, seemingly totally absorbed. A squat orange candle sat nearby on polished wood. She suddenly turned to face him, and his whole perception of a normal Friday evening came crashing around his ears.

His ears rang with alarm bells as his skin prickled deliciously. He wondered that the fizzing crackle as each hair on his body rose was not audible to everyone in the room. But no, the fragmented cacophony of voices continued. There was no mass swivelling of heads in his direction. Luke had not been immune to pretty girls blocking his path on his blinkered stride through life. He had just programmed himself to sidestep.

The girl had turned away, staring into the middle distance. He was allowed to stare at her openly. Her dark hair was cut short; dead straight, it spiked unevenly to frame a small face with huge eyes. He couldn't see them now, but he knew they were green. He had been knocked nearly off the bench by them seconds earlier.

What was going on? She did not look remotely interested in him, was that it? Was he that vain?

The surge of sound around Luke was cranked up another few notches, as guffaws and shouted witty asides poured volubly from the well-lubricated throats of those around him. Wincing, he pushed back from the table, and unnoticed, made his way round to where the girl sat with her back to him. He observed the flickering candlelight coaxing a chestnut sheen from the depths of the dense darkness of her hair.

He made as if to walk past her, but as he drew level, he allowed his foot to slide out, like a dance step, to nudge the leg of her chair. Her hand moved out to touch her glass, as if to stop it toppling. He noticed her short, cut nails were painted green, and a grin lifted the corners of his mouth.

"And I've only had one sip of my beer," he murmured, almost to himself.

She looked up though, so that was a beginning of sorts.

She offered him an expression of such raised- eyebrow disbelief that he had to press a hand to his mouth to halt the laugh that was in danger of bubbling up. "Don't worry." She spoke in a low tone, as if imparting something serious. "Next time, I'll be ready. I won't be caught out a second time." She smiled up at him, her small smile revealing teeth that were a pleasure to see. She took a long sip of her drink.

"How long are you going to wait?" Luke asked her, conversationally.

"What, 'til you pass this way again?" she replied. Another comical movement of her eyebrows made him think of two small furry animals.

"No. 'Til you give up on whoever it is you're waiting for. Is he often late?" he said, realising with dismay what a corny chat up line that was.

In response, she pushed away the chair opposite her with a shove of her feet. "I'm getting a crick in my neck from looking at you," she complained.

Luke sat down obediently. He stared at her, taking advantage of his more equal position opposite. She was wearing an expensive-looking cream jumper. A green chunky pendant swung between her breasts on a silver chain. Green like her eyes. She sighed. He snapped his gaze away.

The girl shrugged. "I was meeting a girlfriend, but she sent me a text at the last minute. Thought I might as well have a drink, see what this pub's like."

"And?" he asked.

"Yeah…nice." She acceded. "I'll come again probably. But I'm off now." She drained her drink and stood up, reaching behind her for a black leather jacket with a dark fur collar.

Startled, Luke stood up as well. "Right…" he said, trying to sound unconcerned. "Nice to have met you…but I suppose now I'll never know…" He stood there, his hand extended towards her. She stared at it without moving.

"Never know what?" she asked, glancing out of the window.

He rubbed his hands across his face tiredly. "Anything really…what you're going to have for supper, what book you're reading at the moment, what your name is…?"

She turned and placed her hand in his. It felt like being handed a gift. "Elizabeth," she said, and shrugging her coat on, she disappeared towards the door and the black windows against which huge snowflakes twirled and stuck and melted.

He caught up with her on the pavement, walking beside her, hands in pockets, as if he knew her well.

"Far to go?" he queried, unconvinced that she would respond. All he could hear was the sounds of the city, revving up for the weekend. He was on the point of turning round to retrace his steps to the preferable warmth of the pub, when she caught hold of his arm.

"Ten miles!" she finally answered, "Are you offering to walk me home?" She stopped walking and looked up at him through her spiky black fringe. He thought her eyes glinted with humour, but he might have been mistaken.

"Where do you live, Elizabeth?" he said quietly. "Just answer me, or not. You're wearing me out to be honest."

"That's fair," she agreed. "Okay… I live in Exmouth. My car is parked down there in a side road, and you're welcome to a lift home, if you like? How fair is that?" She smiled properly then, and he felt his spirits rise.

He smiled back. "That sounds good…thanks. But how do you know I haven't got my own car?"

She looked at him thoughtfully. "You looked all set there to spend your Friday evening downing pints with your friends. Nothing wrong with that, but you don't seem the type to then drive home over the limit."

"I might live round the corner…?" What the hell was he doing? A gorgeous girl was offering him… what exactly? A lift in her car… Why was he prevaricating? It was hardly a proposition. But he couldn't resist one more hesitation, taking a risk that she might shrug and walk off.

"And how do you know I'm not dangerous?" he insisted, hating himself.

She studied him a moment before walking on. "With those eyes? And those shoes?" She laughed over her shoulder. He hurried after her, took hold of her hand and they began to run.

Chapter Nine

"Do You Always Do What You're Told?"

Saturday 9th December 2006
Exmouth

The corridor stretched in front of her eyes forever, the yawning length of it perforated by the black doorways. She ran as fast as she could, her laced-up shoes slapping the white surface like gunshots, but it seemed as if the floor were moving towards her so that she was running on the spot. The bell continued to drill its insistent clamour into her ears, but the bulbs above each door remained unlit, causing her to sob with panic.

"Alexis! Come on! Wake up…"

She was awake in an instant, looking blearily at her flatmate who was holding out her mobile phone to her. She took it from Cheryl's hand and pressed the green button to cease its ringing. She nodded to Cheryl's silently mouthed "Cup of tea?" and put the phone to her ear.

"Sorry! Just realised, you're on nights, aren't you? Did I wake you?"

"Yes, thank God! From a nightmare involving the terrors of night shifts! Don't worry, Luke…it's time I was up anyway. Are you okay?"

Luke laughed. "I'm fine. Just thought it might be nice to get a joint Christmas present this year for Mum and Dad? Any ideas?"

Alexis reached gratefully for the mug Cheryl had placed next to her. The hot liquid was nectar to her sleep-parched lips. "I'll have a think about it. Something practical for the house…?"

"Do you fancy a drink or something sometime soon? When will you be back to a normal routine? I don't know how you stand those insane hours!"

"Huh! Rather that than having to control thirty deranged testosterone-fuelled adolescents! Now that's insane! Anyway, yes, love to… I'll bus over to yours next Wednesday evening? I'll be back to the land of the living by then."

Luke blew a kiss down the line. "See you then, sis, love to Cheryl!"

Alexis smiled as she turned her phone off. "Sends his love!" She called through to the kitchen where Cheryl was busy throwing together a cheap student supper for them both.

Cheryl just avoided chopping off her little finger. "Oh, don't torment me Al!" She moaned. "If only! Why is your brother so bloody good looking? And why is he always so brotherly? You don't think he's gay, do you?"

Wednesday December 13th

Alexis jumped off the bus, her breath visible in the freezing winter air. She moved fast to keep warm, avoiding the temptation to linger at a favourite clothes shop showing models in dark-blue fishing smocks and thick stripy jumpers, hanks of knotted rope arranged in an arty sort of way. She made her way down the narrow high street of Exsham towards the harbour and soon reached the blistered black door of the old cottage which almost dangled its ancient toes over the harbour wall. The door opened at a push and she breathed in the fuggy welcome warmth, the sweet smell of burning wood. She slammed the door shut behind her to seal out the icy fingers which were deftly probing the air at her back.

Alexis followed the sound of something going on in the kitchen…crackles and rustling which promised the possibility of being offered food at some point. She looked round the half open door, delighted to find Luke unpacking an assortment of delectable-looking temptations onto the scrubbed wooden table.

Luke looked up and grinned at his sister, contemplating her rosy cheeks glowing from the cold. Her long ash-blonde hair tumbled from the confines of a bright red bobble hat. He rounded the table to give her a bear hug and a resounding kiss on each cheek. "God! You're like ice! Come and thaw out by the fire. Tea? Or we could go to The Lighthouse Inn when it opens."

Alexis thumped herself down on a shapeless beanbag which folded around her unnervingly. She unwound herself from layers of scarf, and stretched out a booted toe to prod a fat black cat that was sprawled on its back on the hearth rug. "Bit of decorum, you hussy!" she said to the cat, who opened one eye and then closed it again. "Oh let's stay in, Luke. I've no money as usual, and anyway it's so warm in here."

Ten minutes later Luke clanked a heavy tray onto a low table. He smiled when he saw that Alexis had fallen into an instant sleep like a child. The cat, despite its huge long-haired body, had half climbed onto her lap, front paws stretched towards her chin, the rest drooping, like a Salvador Dali painting; a waterfall of black fur.

Alexis sat up at the comforting sound of tea pouring, emptying the cat gently back on to the floor. She groaned with pleasure at the sight of a plate of golden-topped scones oozing clotted cream and jam. "I love you, Luke." She informed him solemnly.

Eventually, Alexis licked her fingers, and sat back happily.

"Doesn't take much to please you, does it?" Luke observed wryly.

Alexis looked at Luke carefully. "And what about you? You seem a lot jollier than usual...anything you want to tell me?"

Luke leant forward to pick up the tray. "Leave that," Alexis ordered quietly. "Look at me...no, properly! Honestly! You're hopeless, Luke. I can tell there's something, I know you too well. There's a glow about you, a satisfied sort of relief...." She gazed into his eyes until he coughed and looked away.

"Now, Alexis, don't get carried away," he warned, wagging a finger at her. "This is why I never tell you anything! You're such a girl!"

"I knew it! Who is she? How long have you known her? What's her name?"

Luke threw his hands up in despair, his lips twitching involuntarily at the sight of her grinning face. "I met someone, just once, last Friday night. That's all. No big deal..."

Alexis rolled her eyes. "Well, of course you did! You met someone...that's obvious. Now we need to find out whether you're going to see her again?" She waited patiently, hands on her knees, eyebrows raised.

Luke frowned, hesitating until the ticking of the clock on the wall became deafening. At last he spoke. "It's up to her, I suppose. She's quite unusual, a bit scary, to be honest..."

Alexis laughed, and then stifled it, seeing that Luke was serious. "How scary?" she asked tentatively.

"She likes to take charge..." He smiled uneasily. "She gave me a lift home from the pub, and then asked for my number. Then she drove off. I haven't heard from her since. Don't look at me like that, Al, I know I'm pathetic. It was all a bit weird...perhaps best if I don't see her again."

It wasn't until the following Saturday morning that Luke's phone rang in his cottage. He picked it up and sat on the bottom of his staircase, bare feet protruding from a pair of close-fitting blue jeans. He was expecting a call from Alexis about meeting up that evening, so at first he thought it was her voice.

"Luke...how are you doing? Fancy a walk on the beach? Wrap up warm, the sunshine is deceptive. I'll be waiting in the car, keeping the engine running."

Luke looked at the receiver in surprise and then slowly replaced it. He walked to the small bay window and saw the red sports car that Elizabeth had brought him home in; that Friday night seemed a long time ago, more than a week.

Elizabeth manoeuvred her car skilfully out of the village and was soon heading towards Exmouth. "Miss me?" she said, keeping her eyes on the road.

Luke hesitated before responding. He felt as if he were walking through a minefield. He wasn't good at games, and this one was making him feel uncomfortable.

She spoke again before he could think of a reply. "Why did you get into my car? Because I told you to? Do you always do what you're told?" There was a hint of laughter in Elizabeth's voice, but Luke wasn't amused.

"Okay, Elizabeth. You want to play games? Why did you come over today? Clearly not for my benefit, or yours. I suggest you turn round, take me home and…"

With a squeal of brakes, Elizabeth pulled the car into a layby, causing the car behind to sound his horn long and loud.

Shocked, Luke looked her in amazement. She sat slumped in the seat, her head resting on her hands still holding the steering wheel.

He put a hand on her shoulder, surprised to feel her trembling. "Are you okay, Elizabeth?" he asked softly.

She turned her head slowly to look at him. He drew in a deep breath as he took in her flushed cheek, her green eyes shone with tears. Her black fringe spiked down to meet her eyelashes, each blink threatening to cause a cascade. "I'm so sorry, Luke. I don't know what gets into me. If I just act normally, people treat me as if I'm invisible. So I decided to act outrageously and be noticed. I told myself not to do it with you, but it's hard to break a habit."

Luke reached towards her and wiped away the falling tear with his thumb. "You don't need to act anything other than yourself. You're lovely, who wouldn't think so? You're not invisible to me." The kiss that followed was so natural that they both laughed as they pulled away.

They sat there then, in the warm cab of the car. The windows steamed up as Elizabeth talked to him about the reasons for her behaviour. She told him that she never knew her parents; her mother had given her up for adoption at birth. She had been adopted from a children's home at the age of two, to a loving young couple. She remembered a comfy lap, hugs and kisses, pretty clothes.

But then her life changed forever when her adoptive parents died in a car crash when she was only six years old. With no other family, she had been returned to a children's home, only her feeling of abandonment twice over had made her create a shell around her. She became difficult, warding off kindness and love in an attempt not to be hurt again. She had immersed herself in her schoolwork, excelling in languages and doing well at her exams. When she became of age, she had inherited the proceeds from her adoptive parents' house, plus a large amount of money which had accrued a staggering amount of interest. She was alone in the world, but with money behind her, she had managed to attain a teaching degree at the women's teacher's training college in Exmouth, where she now taught at a primary school, not far from the flat she had bought for herself.

She stopped speaking and looked down at her lap. Luke squeezed her hand, moved beyond words. "I think it's time you start being yourself, Elizabeth. And I'm here for you if you want?"

"Oh yes," she breathed. "Please."

Luke pressed her hand once more. Maybe this could be a new start for him too…

The salty wind blew violently from across the sea, whipping up the waves into creamy foam, and playing havoc with Luke and Elizabeth's hair. The bright sunshine lit up the glassy peaks of the choppy water.

"Talk about blowing the cobwebs away!" Luke shouted.

"I love it!" replied Elizabeth, looking up as a ruffled seagull blew past them, calling loudly as if affronted by the wind's audacity. They both laughed.

They were walking arm in arm along the beach at Exmouth as planned. It was hard work, their words being whisked out of their mouths so that they trudged along with their heads bent close together.

They were so wrapped up in their own world that at first they didn't notice the girl walking towards them. She stopped and called out. "Hey Luke! Isn't it perfect here today?"

Luke stopped and looked up in surprise. "Hey! Alexis! How you doing?" he said, looking pleased. He pulled Elizabeth forwards. "Alexis…meet…"

"Elizabeth!" cried Alexis in astonishment. "You're a dark horse! How long have you two known each other?"

Elizabeth clung tighter to Luke's arm. She gave Alexis a slow smile. "Not long," she replied, looking up at Luke, who had a confused expression on his face.

"How do you two…?" he began, but Elizabeth interrupted him, looking at her watch.

"This is crazy, but I've just remembered I'm supposed to be meeting a friend from work this morning…it completely slipped my mind! Sorry, Luke, but I'm going to have to run…I'll take you home first."

Luke looked at Alexis apologetically. "See you tonight, Al, I'll be in the pub at seven…"

Alexis stared after them as they made a hurried exit from the beach. As Elizabeth drove back towards Exsham, she kept her eyes on the road ahead.

"Well...?" Luke broke the silence with a teasing tone. "Are you going to tell me how you know my sister?"

Elizabeth shot him a glance of surprise. "Sister? I didn't know she was your sister! I met her in the library. Seems we have similar taste in books; anything about relationships with an ending that makes us cry!"

"Known each other long? She hasn't mentioned you..."

"Fancy her being your sister though! You don't look alike...no, we only met about three weeks ago, and then when we bumped into each other again in the supermarket. She asked me back to her room for a cuppa. I really like her actually."

"I should hope so! What's not to like? She's my favourite sister, I love her to bits," Luke told her warmly.

"How many sisters do you have?" Elizabeth asked, curiously.

Luke grinned. "Only one!"

"And brothers?"

"No...no brothers," he said quickly. "Right, thanks for the lift, again. I'll be able to afford a little run around of my own soon, so I'll be able to return the favour. Do you fancy the cinema sometime next week? There's something called *Notes on a Scandal.* I think Judi Dench is in it, and it's supposed to be very good, but I don't know whether the ending will make you cry."

Luke jumped out of the car, blowing her a kiss. As he opened his front door, he glanced back. She'd started the engine, but was just sitting gazing in his direction. He waved and closed the door, wondering whether the meeting with her work colleague had slipped her mind again. It was a good few minutes before he heard her car pulling away.

Chapter Ten

"But I Gave Her a Second Look"

Saturday 16th December 2006
Later the Same Day
Exsham

Luke was sitting in a dark corner of the Lighthouse Inn, just a few steps away from his cottage. He always arrived early when meeting Alexis in a pub. He knew she hated to make an entrance alone. The place had recently had a makeover, sage-green walls replacing the dingy nicotine-stained ones, and the fishing nets that had hung across the corners of the room harbouring dusty unrecognizable marine items had vanished. Little paintings done by a local artist hung there, small fishing boats, depicted by no more than a colourful dab of paint for a sail, a black line for a hull, bobbed on dark-blue water.

Alexis blew in through the door, bringing a waft of salt air, and that particular sweetish scent of the glistening mud that oozed against the harbour wall at low tide. "That wind's manic!" she said, dumping a bulky raffia bag on to the floor. "It's been wild all day." She chucked her fleece-lined jacket onto an empty chair and tried to pull her hair back into submission while Luke went up to the bar for a glass of her favourite dry white wine.

She sighed with pleasure, enjoying the warmth from the logs burning fiercely in the massive open hearth, orange flames being sucked noisily up the chimney. Luke set her glass down, and sat down, rearranging his long legs as he did so. She eyed him through her fringe which was still tousled and ruffled. He caught her eye and waited.

"Was that her this morning then? The control freak?"

He frowned. "I don't think I called her that, did I?"

"Ah! So it is the same one! I thought you said it might be better if you didn't see her again?"

Luke rubbed a hand across his face. "I know. But I gave her a second look… She opened up a bit, and I liked what I saw…"

"I still don't get it. I only met her a couple of weeks ago, then you meet her, when? A week ago? That's a bit of a coincidence, isn't it?" Alexis took a sip of wine and a handful of crisps from the packet Luke had bought and torn open for them to share.

While she crunched her crisps, looking at him expectantly, he tried to explain the slightly weird details of meeting Elizabeth in Exeter. "I know I didn't paint a very reassuring picture of her before… When I first met her, she was different, I was intrigued," he insisted. "She didn't seem remotely interested in me. I had to chase after her, she left the pub so suddenly."

Alexis sat up straight and leaned forward. "So she was in the Suckling Pig, on her own, on Friday night?"

"Yes…" Luke said slowly. "So…what?"

"Well, hang on, I'm trying to remember… yes, it must have been Friday, the same one, because I popped into the supermarket for some bits for our dinner. I had an early shift. And Elizabeth was in there. I asked her back for a cup of tea…"

Luke stared at her. "I know all this…where's it going?"

Alexis waved her hand impatiently. "Wait, I've got to remember how it went…shush! Let me think…Yes! That's it, she was asking me about myself, did I have family nearby etcetera. I told her the parents live in Cornwall, then I told her about you and Xavier…"

Luke smacked his forehead with the palm of his hand. "You didn't need to mention him…" he groaned.

"Oh don't be daft, Luke, it's just part of our life. It's no big secret. Anyway, I showed her that photo of us both, Mum took it in Cornwall last year. Then she asked about you, she wanted to know all about you, just being polite, you know. Then I told her where you worked…and…"

"What, Alexis? And what?"

She looked at him for a moment. Then she said, "She said, that you look nice and maybe we could go out for a drink sometime, the three of us. And then she suggested me giving you a ring straight away to arrange something for that night. So I told her that your Friday nights were sacred, you always spent it in Exeter with your mates."

"And you told her the name of the pub we go to…?"

"Yes, she asked. I never thought…"

Luke looked at Alexis for a moment and then said, "You don't really think she manipulated meeting me…"

"It looks like it, Luke. She even asked if I knew what time you get to the pub." She flashed him a smile. "You should be flattered! How many people go to such lengths?"

Luke pushed his chair back from the table. "It's mad. I made the first move towards her. She really didn't want to know…she just upped and left. Hardly like someone with designs on me!" He laughed. "Drink up, I'll get you another."

There was now just over a week left before Christmas. As soon as their respective schools had closed, Elizabeth and Luke were able to spend a lot of time together. She dragged him off to Exeter, where the shops were blinding with colours, evocative music blasting away the winter blues; Slade and The Pogues repeated and overlapped from one store to another. Elizabeth helped Luke to choose a present for Alexis. She seemed to have a feeling for what Alexis would like, even though she hardly knew her at all. She picked out a pale pink fluffy dressing gown, perfect for curling up in on a girly night in.

"I suppose you'll be spending Christmas day with Alexis?" asked Elizabeth, insisting on carrying the bulky but light package out of the department store.

Luke took hold of her arm, steering her safely through the crushing crowd of manic Christmas-fuelled shoppers. "Of course!" He laughed. "It's a real family day for us… All the old traditions, we love it!"

After another few minutes of side-stepping and bruising of shoulders, Luke realised that Elizabeth had gone very quiet. He glanced at her, risking another collision with a large fierce-looking woman, holding her parcels in front of her like a battering-ram. "What's up? You feeling okay, love?" he asked, concerned about her pale face and pained expression. Instead of replying, Elizabeth hurried ahead of him, barging heedlessly into passers-by, not seeing or caring about the irritated faces frowning at her.

He managed to catch hold of her arm, pulling firmly to slow her down. "Hey, hey! What on earth's the matter? Elizabeth?"

She turned a furious face to him. "Talk about insensitive!" she hissed. "What do you think I'll be doing while you spend your fantastic day with your family?"

Luke looked at her, slightly puzzled. "I don't know…" he said honestly. "I don't know what you do on Christmas day. How could I?"

"Exactly! You didn't ask, did you? You know I have no family. I told you that, didn't I?"

Luke felt uneasy. Where had this attack come from? "Look, I'm sorry, love. But we haven't known each other very long, have we? You asked me what my plans were, and I told you, that's all." He shrugged. "If you'd asked me, I suppose I imagined that you'd spend Christmas with friends?"

Elizabeth's mouth was a thin hard line. He realised she was trying not to cry and he put a comforting arm around her.

"No, well I'm not." She pinned him with her eyes, unshed tears magnifying the shimmering green of them. "Don't make me ask, Luke," she begged in a low voice.

"Ask what?" he said, startled.

She sighed. "To spend the day with you and Alexis." The words came out through gritted teeth.

Luke felt a mixture of emotions. He felt a surge of concern for her, but it was early days, and besides, it wasn't that simple, he and Alexis were taking the train to Cornwall, to spend Christmas with their parents, as they always did. He could hardly turn up with a girl in tow who he had not yet mentioned to his parents. He felt cornered. "Actually, we're going to Cornwall," he told her eventually. "To our parents." He smiled at her gently.

Elizabeth response was immediate. Her smile blossomed and bloomed into a laugh of sheer happiness. "Are we? That would be amazing! I'd love to meet them… I can't believe it. Christmas with a proper family instead of walking about on my own through deserted streets, putting off sitting in an empty house!" She reached up to kiss Luke, the bulk of Alexis's gift squashed between them. "Thank you so much!"

Luke held her little face in his hands and pushed her away gently. Her beautiful little face, a pixie face, yet transformed by the spikes of black hair into something sultry and dangerous. "God, you're delicious!" he said, laughing. "Of course you can come home with us, they'll love you!" They stood there, their arms around each other, oblivious to the swirling mass of people, parting round them like waves around a rock.

Chapter Eleven
"I Feel at Home Here Already"

Tuesday 19th December 2006
Cornwall

"Of course not, no not at all! Don't be silly darling, it's no bother at all. Is she a very strict vegetarian? No, don't worry, I'll do something simple. No, no, just drive carefully, and text us when you are leaving. I know! But it makes me feel better…okay then, see you Monday evening…oh, your dad sends his love…!" Céline replaced the phone and looked at Thomas, who hadn't sent his love, actually.

Thomas frowned at her inquiringly. "Well? What was that about?"

Céline tucked a strand of hair behind her ear and began collecting up their empty teacups. "Oh well… They are arriving Monday evening, Christmas Eve, and will leave the day after Boxing Day. That's good. Alexis wasn't sure she'd be able to have that long off work…"

Thomas gave her his famous look as she tailed off. "What did he say, Céline? Who is this 'she' who is a vegetarian?"

Céline put the cups down again, breathed a sigh and plunged straight in. "A girl Luke's met. She's called Elizabeth, and he seems very taken with her. Alexis likes her too…"

"How long has he known her? He's not mentioned anyone recently, has he? It must be serious if he's inviting her home for Christmas?"

They both looked at each other, not needing to voice the fact that Luke had never mentioned any girlfriends so far, let alone invited any home.

Céline ploughed on, wondering why she felt it necessary to justify this girl's visit, she hadn't even met her, but she loved Luke so much she wanted this girl to be accepted, if she made him happy. "I don't know how long he's known her, but it doesn't matter. It seems the poor girl has no family. It's really no bother to invite her into our home."

"And have you running around cooking special faddy foods, and making up another bed. You're not thinking of putting them in the same bed, I hope?"

Céline smiled at her husband fondly. "You old hypocrite." She scolded him gently, "Speaks the man who had his way with an innocent virgin the first time he met her!"

Thomas coughed with embarrassment. It sometimes suited him to play the grumpy old man, but deep inside he could still vividly remember enough the excitement and joy of falling in love with Céline that day in Paris, twenty-five years before. Céline leant across and squeezed his knee provocatively, and was happily rewarded by a slow sexy wink from her husband.

Christmas Eve

"I think they're here!" cried Céline, peering through the dark window past which huge slow snowflakes were falling. She ran to open the door, standing with her arms crossed around her body, shivering as she watched the three young people climbing out of the taxi. They helped the driver to pull their cases out of the boot, and then the red tail lights were dwindling down the country lane and there they were, stamping their feet and all talking at once, snowflakes clinging to eyelashes as they wondered whether it would be a white Christmas.

"Come in, come in! Let's get that door closed!" They stood in the hall divesting themselves of gloves and scarves. Elizabeth stood quietly to one side. Céline stepped towards her and took her hands in her own. "I'm so glad you came! We want you to feel at home, dear."

Elizabeth smiled and held tightly to Céline's fingers. "Thank you, Mrs Johnson. I was afraid of making more work for you. This is such a gorgeous cottage." She looked round at the homely touches, bunches of dark-green holly, the bright berries shining through, the dark-red Aga visible through the open kitchen door, through which wafted the savoury smells of rich food. "I feel at home here already."

"Call me Céline."

Elizabeth reached towards the neat little dark-haired woman and placed a gentle kiss on her slightly surprised cheek. She was a little more reticent when introduced to Thomas, who stood up in his gentlemanly fashion to shake her hand. He promised to have drinks ready for when they had returned from freshening up. Céline showed them upstairs. Luke had been given Alexis's old bedroom, which had long since been decorated in muted green and grey, a dark-green cover on the single bed, not a Barbie doll or a pink anything in sight.

"But they are all in the attic…in case we have a granddaughter one day." Céline smiled. "I couldn't bear to give them away."

"I should hope not, Mum! They are mine after all," protested Alexis.

Céline opened the door to the adjacent room. "And this is for you and Elizabeth…I hope you don't mind sharing? There really wasn't another option." The room which had once held two bunk beds and shelves of Lego and shiny matchbox cars had been transformed into an elegant spare room. What had been the children's bathroom was now a smart en suite. Thick cream towels hung invitingly on heated rails, touches of lavender were in the blinds, and shower curtain and soaps were echoed tastefully in the pattern of the duvet on the double bed.

Alexis sat herself down on the bed, kicking off her shoes and curling her toes into the soft creamy fur of the sheepskin rug. "Delicious! I love the way you decorated this room last year. No, we don't mind sharing, do we, Elizabeth? There's heaps of room."

Only Luke noticed the crestfallen expression on Elizabeth's face as she made a little moue with her lips at him.

It was barely an hour later that the table, so beautifully laid with its white lace cloth, heavy silver cutlery, and dark-green damask napkins, each held captive by a chunky silver ring, had become a waste ground of crumbs, splashes of rich wine sauce, lipstick-stained glasses and a red wine ring on the cloth where Luke had been over zealous in topping up Alexis's glass. The meal had begun a little haltingly; Elizabeth had brought in a huge dish of Hungarian goulash, the thick glossy dark-red sauce, swimming with chunks of tender beef and swirling with cream, causing hungry groans of anticipation.

"Help yourselves," said Céline. "I'll just fetch the veg and Elizabeth's quiche." She returned, placing a dish of buttered ribbon noodles surrounded with bright green broccoli florets down, and in front of Elizabeth, an individual cheese and tomato quiche, golden and bubbling from the oven. "Careful, it's very hot!" she warned.

Elizabeth stared down at it, puzzlement and disappointment flickering across her face.

Luke noticed at once. "Are you okay, Elizabeth? What's the matter?" he asked in a low voice, leaning towards her.

Thomas frowned, and Céline stood up, half-smiling. "Oh dear, do you not eat any dairy? Luke said you were vegetarian, so I thought…"

"It's fine. Don't worry, I used to be a vegetarian, ages ago. It was only a fad. You can't have heard me properly, Luke. I don't mind. It looks lovely." She smiled reassuringly and picked up her cutlery, casting a yearning glance at the goulash.

"But you said…" began Luke.

Céline approached Elizabeth, "No, no, I'll take it back," she said, reaching for the dish with oven-gloved hands. "It'll freeze. Pass your plate to Alexis. There's plenty to go round!"

Apart from a slightly uncomfortable silence and a muted disapproving tutting from Thomas, the meal soon degenerated into a noisy raucous success. With promises to clear up, the youngsters ushered Thomas and Céline off to their beds, and then sat around enjoying the ambiance, soporific from the food and bonhomie.

Later, with the dishwasher churning away, (Céline would have to put the machine on again in the morning as they had loaded it incorrectly) they made their way up the stairs, shushing each other at every noise they made, making them noisier than ever. Alexis begged to use the en suite bathroom first. "Sorry, Elizabeth! I'm dying for a wee!"

Soundlessly, Elizabeth pushed a grinning Luke backwards into his bedroom, kicking the door shut with her black stiletto. He ran a hand through his tousled fringe, scooping her close and kissing her nose. "Happy Christmas!" he whispered. "Sleep well, sweetheart!" He turned her around and pushed her back towards the door.

"Oh Luke..." she moaned. "Can't I come to your room later? I can't believe they put us in different rooms!"

"What? What did you expect? They'd be horrified at the thought of us sleeping together so soon!" He regarded her rather crossly and added, "Anyway! I've been trying to get you into my bed all week! You didn't want to...what's changed?"

"This!" whispered Elizabeth. "This house where everything is perfect, a perfect family house...it would be so exciting, knowing how horrified they'd be!"

Luke stared at her, a glint in his eye belying his disapproving expression. He turned her round again and gave her bottom an affectionate smack. "Go on with you, quick...before Alexis comes looking for you."

Elizabeth's green eyes shone dangerously for a second, before her eyelids drooped sleepily, and he was able to propel her out into the corridor. The old cottage was settling for the night, creaks and rumbles as the beams shifted slightly, and the central heating turned itself off.

Alexis was already in her bed, just her eyes from the nose up, peeping out from the crisp sheets. Elizabeth squatted down to pull items out of her suitcase. She swiftly stripped off her clothes and pulled on blue checked pyjamas, before rustling around in the case once more.

"Hey! What are you doing? Get into bed! My mum's given us a hot-water bottle each...it's freezing!"

Elizabeth sat on the edge of the bed, holding two bulky objects in her hands. They crackled mysteriously. Curious, Alexis sat up.

"What are those?" She laughed quietly. "Christmas stockings?"

Elizabeth smiled at her, holding them up proudly. "Yes! This is the first Christmas I've ever spent with a family. These are for your parents, one each! Look, I've put a tag with their names and 'love Elizabeth'. What do you think?"

Alexis looked doubtful. "Well, we can't really creep into their room and hide them at the end of their bed…they'll hear us!"

Elizabeth looked so crestfallen that she amended hurriedly, "I know, we'll put them just outside their door. Mum gets up really early to make tea for her and Dad. She'll find them then. They'll be made up!"

Elizabeth nodded happily and Alexis watched her tiptoe to the door, clutching the two woolly sausage shapes to her checked chest. It was hard to watch. For some reason, Alexis felt a hard lump of sadness form in her throat.

Safely back in bed, Elizabeth fell into a deep and immediate sleep. She had not even turned her bedside light off. Alexis slipped out of bed, and crept round to turn it off for her. As she reached for the switch, she looked at Elizabeth. Her long black eyelashes fanned onto her flushed cheeks. She had a small teddy bear clutched in the fingers of one hand, and her mouth was firmly plugged by the thumb of her other hand, the index finger hooked across the bridge of her nose.

By the time she'd reached the middle stair, number seven, she'd counted them last night, she could hear that someone was already downstairs. The soft glugging of liquid filling a jug, the gurgle of a coffee machine, the soft humming which announced a contented female, happily working in her own space, creating comfort for her family. Elizabeth's slippers hit the final thirteenth step, and she entered the kitchen with a smile.

Céline looked up, smiling a welcome of her own. "Wow, you're up early! That was quite a late night for you, wasn't it? Thought you'd lie in!"

"On Christmas day? No way, not me anyway. This is so special for me, I don't want to miss a second." Her smile faltered momentarily as a rustle of newspaper alerted her to the fact that Céline was not the only one up. Thomas was sitting in an armchair tucked up near to the Aga, the way he had shaken the paper seemed to Elizabeth like irritation, but maybe she was being paranoid. Maybe it was just that she had hoped to find Céline on her own. "Did you like your stockings?" she asked shyly.

Céline laughed. "What an unexpected treat, at our age! We opened them in bed like three-year-olds, didn't we, darling?"

Thomas lowered his paper. His face broke into an unexpected grin. "Thank you, Elizabeth. Yes, a most refreshing gesture, and much appreciated."

Céline wiped her hands on her apron. "Right, well, I'll put the croissants in the Aga when I hear movement from those slugs upstairs. I'm off to sort some stuff out. Help yourself to coffee, Elizabeth."

Elizabeth moved around the kitchen, cradling her hot mug as she looked at a row of well-thumbed recipe books, and admired a lifetime of pretty knickknacks collected over the years. She reached out for framed photo which was hidden behind several more obviously recent ones. "How adorable!" she said.

Thomas looked up and she turned the photo towards him so he could see. "Oh, the children. The boys were four and Alexis was two. It was taken in a studio. I wasn't that taken with the sailor suits and staged format. A bit twee, don't you think? They never really looked like that. I preferred them when they were just mucking about with mud on their knees."

Elizabeth stared at the photo with a frown. "Two boys? Twins? Who are they?" she queried.

Thomas stared at her. "Well, Luke is the one on the right…and the other is Xavier. Didn't Luke tell you? He died in an unfortunate accident when he was seven years old."

Elizabeth put her hand to her mouth, her face registering shock. "I'm so sorry! I had no idea. Luke told me that he had no brothers, just a sister…"

Thomas faced her, a blank look which seemed to go on and on. "I wonder why on earth he would have said such a thing," he said coldly. The paper came up again to create a momentary end of further conversation.

Feeling dismissed, Elizabeth turned to go upstairs. She met Céline at the top. "Oh, I've just been admiring the photo of the children when they were little!" She put her hand on Céline's arm. "Weren't they gorgeous? You must be so proud…"

Céline stiffened slightly, not sure that she would ever be comfortable discussing her memories with someone she did not know very well. Before she could form a reply, Elizabeth continued.

"I've always thought twins must be such fun! Dressing them in the same things…you were lucky!" She applied pressure to Céline's arm, pulling her closer. "Tell me, is having twins hereditary? Wouldn't it be amazing if Luke and I had twins?"

Céline removed her arm from Elizabeth's grip, feeling slightly nauseated. How unfeeling of this girl to be speaking this way…and surely she and Luke had only just met? That's what she had understood from the conversation at dinner last night. She swallowed, finding it hard not to sound harsh. "No, Elizabeth. Having identical twins is not a hereditary condition. It's when one egg splits into two, and happens randomly. Having fraternal twins, however, is. It is caused by a condition called 'hyperovulation', when more than one egg is released at the same time, and is passed genetically on from mother to daughter." She gave Elizabeth a frosty stare. "I had no idea you and Luke were so serious about each other."

Elizabeth grinned, seemingly unfazed. "I don't think Luke had either, actually!" She laughed, throwing her arms around Céline. "Oh! You don't know how lucky I am to have found such lovely people! I love you all. I promise to make Luke as happy as I can."

Céline found herself being moved by the girl's exuberance. "Well, my love, just take things steady. You've had a hard life, and so has Luke. I'd like nothing more than for you to be happy, but…"

"Oh, thank you! That means such a lot to me!"

Céline felt a flood of emotion in the face of such youthful enthusiasm. She felt that she wanted to protect Elizabeth from further hurt, as if Elizabeth were her own child.

The rest of the holiday passed in a blur of eating, drinking and present opening. Luke's family were taken aback by the expensive items Elizabeth gave them. Thinking that she was just a passing friend of Luke's, they had bought her token presents. She insisted that she hadn't expected anything, but Alexis thought she saw shadows of envy and doubt cross the other girl's face, as if she did not feel included in the family circle.

'Why should she?' thought Alexis, she's a sweet person, but new to them all. No matter what lonely life she came from, they had to let things happen naturally.

It was with some relief from most of the assembled company when it was time to return to normal.

Céline and Thomas stood outside the cottage, waving and blowing kisses, (Céline, not Thomas) as the taxi carried the sweet young things away. Thomas stomped back into the house, leaving Céline alone to stare at the empty lane. There had been no white Christmas after all, just a damp and slightly foggy one. Céline shivered and followed her husband inside.

Chapter Twelve
"So Why the Rush?"

January 2007

Alexis was delighted to observe her reticent, introspective brother falling headlong for the enigmatic Elizabeth. She praised Elizabeth to her mother. "She's always ready with a word of praise, encouraging Luke to open up and become more outgoing." She riffled through a colourful row of t-shirts with one hand, holding her mobile up to her ear with the other. "She's woken him up, Mum...brought him back to us."

"But what's she really like, Alexis? Do you feel you really know her?"

Alexis sighed. "Oh Mum. As well as you can ever know anyone, I suppose. Has Dad been getting at you? He's an old cynic. How did you ever fall for somebody so unromantic?"

Céline chuckled to herself. "He was very romantic when we met, I assure you! I think he's cynical now, and can you blame him after what we've been through? I think he lost his trust in God, and after that, his trust in people," she finished sadly.

Alexis felt exasperated, but hesitated to hurt her mother's feelings. She chose her words carefully. "It's about time he put those feelings behind him, Mum. There's so much else in life to feel sure about. He shouldn't let the past spoil the present."

"You are still very young, Alexis. Wait until you have children of your own, you may think differently then... talking of that, how is life going for you?"

"Oh Mum! You're incorrigible!"

"Well, I don't know that word, chérie, but I would love to hear that you have met someone special?"

"That's it!" Alexis laughed. "You don't change, I know exactly what you're thinking. No, is the answer to that! It's not easy to meet someone on the unsociable hours I do... But actually, I do have a bit of news; Elizabeth's flat is quite near the hospital, and she has a spare room. She's suggested I take it! To be honest, even though I love Cheryl, it'd be great to have a bit more privacy. She's offering it to me for a mate's rate too, what do you think?"

Céline digested this in silence for a while. "I think that it would be a good move. And if it doesn't work out, you can always move out again! I think that the day Elizabeth came into our lives was a good one; a fresh wind blowing our cobwebs away, a new start."

Alexis threw her phone onto the bed in delight. She tugged down a bright red t-shirt and held it up against her, smoothing the soft material with a caress. A dangerously cheerful colour suitable to her mood.

Saturday January 6th

Cheryl peeked through the kitchen blinds and turned round with shining eyes and a blush rising in a wave. "He's here, Alexis! At least I think it's him. What colour did you say his new car is?"

"I didn't! He just told me it was a Ford Fiesta…"

Cheryl shrugged. "That means nothing to me. If it's black, then it's probably him."

The sudden jarring vibration of the bell made Cheryl shiver. Alexis spoke into the intercom and buzzed Luke up. Cheryl darted into her bedroom to give herself a quick squirt of CK1. Alexis gave her a pitying grin before opening the door.

Luke strode in looking cool in a dark-brown leather jacket, dark trousers and a cream scarf knotted loosely round his neck. He kissed his sister, and then repeated the favour to Cheryl, who was so overcome she had to sit down. Alexis reminded herself to seriously start introducing her friend to more people.

She fingered his arm, stroking the soft material. "Nice outfit! New?" she admired.

"Christmas present from Elizabeth." He smiled, putting on a mock model pose. "Well…are you ready? Is this all your stuff?" he groaned, eyeballing the pile of bags and boxes sitting on the floor, an unused foot spa leaning against a pair of black knee-high boots that had on occasion stopped traffic. "We'll probably have to make two trips. At least it's not far."

"How's the car?" Alexis asked as the three of them made their way down to the carpark, their arms full of her paraphernalia. "Looks smart."

"I love it, it's in good condition and was a real bargain. Don't know how I managed without it."

Alexis clicked herself safely into the front seat, and wiggled her fingers at Cheryl, who was not looking at her, but was standing forlornly gazing at Luke as he manoeuvred the car out of the parking area.

They arrived at Elizabeth's flat within a few minutes.

"Thank God there's a lift." Alexis panted, her face red from exertion.

Elizabeth was waiting for them. She seemed unfazed by the amount of belongings beginning to mount up in her hall. She grabbed Alexis into a sisterly hug and kissed her on both cheeks.

Inside was white airiness, a light-catching, pulsating area of captured vibrancy. Elizabeth took Alexis's hand drawing her into her new home.

"I'm afraid there's another load to come!" Luke laughed. "I'll get it. You stay here, Alexis. It won't take me long."

"As long as you can escape Cheryl's clutches!" Alexis warned. "She's got it bad!" she added, looking at Elizabeth with an amused glance.

"Perhaps we should feel sorry for her," said Elizabeth. "It's no joke being on your own, you know."

"Oh, she'll get over it," Alexis murmured. "She falls in and out of crushes all the time!"

"Thanks!" responded Luke on his way out of the door. "That takes my ego down a peg or two!" He disappeared out of sight, missing the troubled frown that appeared on Elizabeth's face.

Elizabeth and Luke were sitting in the kitchen, a just opened bottle of wine on the scrubbed wooden table. They could hear Alexis moving about in her new bedroom, singing an old Beatle number loudly and out of tune, while she opened drawers, rattled hangers, and clinked bottles onto an empty bathroom shelf.

"Alexis!" shouted Luke. "Glass of wine?"

Alexis skidded down the hall, her grinning face appearing round the door. She'd scraped her blonde hair into an untidy bundle on top of her head, rolled her sleeves up and appeared thoroughly pleased with herself. "Please…love one!" she said. "It's lovely, I've got so much storage space…much more than the nurse's accommodation. Thanks Elizabeth!" She sat down as Luke poured three glasses of wine, the last rays of the day's winter sun engorging the ruby liquid with a visual heat. Elizabeth smiled, picked up her glass, and raised it high in a salute.

"Cheers! To your new home," toasted Luke, lifting his glass to Alexis's. They all chinked together, the wine indeed warming their lips and throats with its richness.

Alexis sat nattering for a while, her exuberance overflowing into her chatter, sending her hands spreading and shaping as she talked. "Wow! Is that the time?" she interrupted herself. "I promised to pop back to see how Cheryl's doing… I won't be long!" She scooted her chair back noisily. "Oops, sorry, Elizabeth. Must remember to respect your flat…"

Luke laughed. "Go on with you. You're like a firework going off!"

Alexis grabbed her coat, a fluffy snug-looking collar vying inconsistently with a lack of sleeves. She blew them both a kiss, and ignoring the lift, seemed to descend the stairs two at a time, sounding like a stampede of small animals.

"I hope you know what you've got yourself into!" Luke said with a mock grimace.

Elizabeth looked at him, her transparent gaze fired through by sparks of amusement. "I have always trusted my own judgement," she assured him.

Luke stood up and stooped to put his arms around Elizabeth. "Such a tiny girl, aren't you?" he murmured, feeling her ribs through the soft pink sweater she wore. "You need looking after. I'm not going to let you out of my sight in a rush!" He pulled her to her feet and began to lead her by the hand towards her bedroom.

Elizabeth yanked her hand back, laughing. "Hey! Are you leading me astray?"

"Hardly astray…" admonished Luke. "Not after the week we've had! We spent more time in your bed than out of it I seem to recall! You're not going all coy on me now, are you?"

Elizabeth released her hand, creating a cool vacuum where her fingers had been. "Things are a bit different now though, aren't they? What with Alexis in the flat, I mean."

Luke stared at her, not sure if she was joking or not. "Well, she's not here at the moment, is she?" he observed.

Elizabeth's brow furrowed just a fraction. "No, but she could be back any minute. It could just get frustrating, not to mention inappropriate!" Her face cleared as she turned towards the kitchen. "Right! What do you fancy for supper?" she asked brightly. "I've got smoked salmon or steak? Or both! It's a celebration after all." She creaked open the heavy cutlery drawer and deftly dealt out three places, upending the last of the wine into their glasses. She glanced at Luke. "Would you open another bottle, sweetheart? It will need to breathe a bit so we can have it with our steak. How does Alexis like hers, rare or medium?"

With the start of the new school term, Luke's time was stretched to encompass the insurmountable minutiae of long hours teaching, plus marking tedious pages exuding inertia with each misspelt word. Elizabeth's days were more physically challenged, keeping abreast of thirty seven-year-old brains, ricocheting from the never-ending stream of unanswerable questions to just containing them safely within four walls. The ten miles between Exmouth and Exeter was not a very great distance in a car, but might as well have been a hundred after the stresses of the days sent them reeling into the arms of their respective armchairs. They soon fell into a routine of seeing each other on a Wednesday night if possible, and then all weekend. Luke was finding it weird that Alexis was seeing more of Elizabeth than he was. He was also finding it troubling that his and Elizabeth's love life was restricted by the inconsistent and unforeseeable vagueness of Alexis's hospital shifts.

"Is she on nights this weekend?" Luke would ask tentatively. All hope would be pinned on the answer; a whole weekend of nights with the flat to themselves! Elizabeth not only refused Luke's advances while Alexis was in the next room, but she refused to stay over at his cottage during the weekends that Alexis was on days.

"Why on earth not?" Luke questioned, when this rule had first been voiced.

"Because women can't just flit from one place to another like men! It's so easy for you, grab a pair of jeans and a couple of t-shirts and you're sorted. I have to colour co-ordinate my clothes, think of make-up, jewellery, hair-straighteners, perfume…."

"Stop! Why don't you leave stuff at the cottage? I don't mind clearing space for you…"

The withering look Elizabeth shot him would have proved the theory to a complete dullard that men and women were most definitely species apart.

"Just a thought…" he muttered despondently.

A couple of weeks later, stretching long bare legs deliciously under Elizabeth's crisp white duvet, Luke turned to face her, as she snuggled comfortably into his neck. The sleep-ruffled spikes of her hair, so dark against the white pillow made her look childlike and vulnerable. "You asleep?" he whispered.

She opened one eye. "I was…" she replied. "The little death they call it, don't they? You've completely exhausted me."

"Well, that's good. I aim to please. I just wish we were together more. I loathe Sunday nights."

Elizabeth sighed. "Well, there is a solution…" she said.

Luke sat up abruptly, the sheet falling. "There is?" he asked, feigning indifference.

She closed both eyes again and turned onto her back. Luke waited, thinking she had fallen asleep again.

"You could always ask me to marry you."

"Why such a rush?" grumbled Thomas to Céline when they heard the news. "She's not pregnant, is she?"

Céline was leaning over to dust a low table. She stood up, unable to disguise the exasperated expression on her face. "Would that be such a bad thing? They clearly love each other. And we managed all right, didn't we?"

Thomas scowled at her. He really was becoming grumpier as he got older, thought Céline. "Why do you always compare them with us?" he complained. "I don't want Luke to be forced into something he's not ready for."

Céline looked at him in dismay. "Like you were forced, you mean?" she asked unhappily.

"Now Céline, don't put words into my mouth, I never said that."

Céline looked relieved. "Well, she's not, as it happens," she said firmly.

"So why the rush?" repeated Thomas obstinately, raising his eyebrows at his wife, who flicked the duster at him in a gesture that was not as playful as it looked.

The date of the wedding was arranged. It was to be celebrated on Saturday April 7th, the day before Luke's twenty-fifth birthday. Preparations began swiftly, Elizabeth taking charge in her practical controlled way that left Luke dizzy with fearful admiration. It was to be a simple pretty affair. As Elizabeth had no family of her own, there was to be only a handful of guests. Alexis was delighted to be asked to be Elizabeth's bridesmaid.

At the harbour wall, Luke stopped to lean against the cold stone. The wind was full of salt and the sharp green smell of seaweed. Elizabeth joined him, her lean warmth fitting into his side. The tide was in, churning waves beating the sea wall and sending frothy spume into the wind in white shreds.

Elizabeth captured his arm tightly. "You know, we have to decide where we want to buy. Have you any thoughts?"

"Buy?" Luke studied the horizon; there was nothing to differentiate between sea and sky, just billowing blowing greyness.

"Yes. We need someone else in the flat…I thought Cheryl. What do you think?"

Luke's expression was guarded. "Well, I suppose the devil we know…" he stumbled the words out, not sure if he'd spoken out loud, they were whipped away by the wind so fast.

Elizabeth continued her thoughts, threading them together to form ideas which were obviously already reality. "There a few nice villages around, and unless one of us wants to move schools, I suppose we'll need to choose somewhere equidistant to each."

Luke made a noise between a gasp and a snort. Elizabeth eyed him carefully. "What?" she asked, disgruntled.

"Why on earth would we want to buy? What's wrong with my cottage? It's exactly situated between our work, in a gorgeous village. I thought you loved it? It never occurred to me that we'd live anywhere else!"

Elizabeth said nothing.

"Don't you like it, love?" he passed the question to her as if it were a fragile piece of glass.

She spoke at last, little hammer blows threatening damage. "There's no garden. There's only one bedroom. You're paying rent, a complete waste of money. It's standing next to water, dangerous stuff that...don't you care at all?"

He scratched his head crossly, feeling offended. "What are you on about Elizabeth? I'm not with you!"

"Our children!" she snapped. "That's what I'm on about! That's what married people do, didn't you know?"

Startled, Luke stepped back to scrutinise her. "God! You can't possibly be expecting, can you?"

The furious mask of Elizabeth's face unnerved him. But as he gazed at her, a weird transition pulled her features, almost against her will, into a calm neutral appearance. Her voice was low, controlled. "No sweetheart, I'm not! But I want to be, one day, don't you? And this cottage, sweet as it may be, will not be big enough, or safe enough."

Feeling chilled through, they walked back to the cottage. Luke threw a log onto the dying embers in the grate while Elizabeth filled the kettle, the drumming water giving her time to think. They sat opposite each other, warmth from their mugs loosening their tongues.

They both spoke simultaneously, but Luke's words came strong and confidently overrode hers. He explained how up to recently, he had not felt independent. That's why this cottage meant so much to him, as did his car. He felt slightly undermined by Elizabeth's wealth, to be honest, and was reluctant to give it all up at once.

Mango the cat came in between them, weaving and purring in anticipation of attention. Elizabeth fondled the silky black fur. She spoke to Luke while looking at the cat. "I'm sorry, Luke. I've been pretty selfish, I didn't mean to undermine you. I think of us as equal, and my extra money is ours now, not mine. Can we compromise? Why don't we try and buy this cottage, if the landlord agrees? That way we can enjoy it until we need to move to somewhere bigger..."

Before Luke could answer, Elizabeth was walking her fingers up under his jumper, and back down towards the heavy buckle of his belt. Mango stared at them through disapproving sea-green slits, huffing off to her food bowl with her fat black brush of a tail stuck in the air.

Chapter Thirteen
"No More Secrets"

Saturday 3rd March 2007

"You don't want these, do you? They're so big!"

Luke looked up from the list he was holding, his biro poised above a doodled mess of leaves and branches intertwined. The shapely jean-clad bottom balanced on a pair of bright white trainers pleased his eyes. "Mm? What are they? Can't see, love..."

Elizabeth withdrew her head from the low kitchen cupboard with an unladylike expletive. She rubbed the back of her head, holding up a large demi-john, greasy with kitchen dust. "What is it anyway?" she demanded.

Luke stared at it fondly. "To make homemade beer in, made loads when we were poor students, saved a fortune!"

Elizabeth added two of them to a pile of discarded objects, swelling bit by bit as Elizabeth rummaged through the drawers and cupboards in the cottage kitchen. Luke opened his mouth to object, but closed it again resignedly as Elizabeth assured him that from now on they could afford as much beer as he wanted from the supermarket. "All these weird things you've got, Luke! Loads of stuff, but nothing you can actually cook with!" She tossed a large stained funnel onto the heap.

"Hey! That's very useful...!"

"Looks like it's had engine oil in it!"

"Well...it has actually. But..."

Elizabeth sighed. "It belongs in the garage, not in the kitchen. I know, I know! You don't have a garage! Which is why I wanted..."

Luke stood up abruptly, throwing his pen onto the table. It rolled off and hit the tiles with an annoying click. "Give it a rest, can't you?" he said quietly. She noticed a tic jumping near his temple, and she realised he was seriously pissed off.

She approached him, wary of his hardened eyes, the set of his mouth. Without a word, she placed her arms loosely around his waist and let her head fall onto his chest. It was her way, these days, of showing complete surrender. It took her a few seconds to realise that this time it wasn't working; his hands remained stubbornly motionless by his sides. She looked up at him, widening her eyes and parting her lips just a fraction. Luke's expression remained stony.

He stepped back, causing her arms to fall away. He rubbed his hand tiredly across and around his mouth, a tiny abrasive sound of calloused flesh on bristle. "We agreed to compromise; we'll stay here until we need to move. There's no point in persisting in moaning about everything that annoys you about my things." He stared at her as she grabbed her coat, (a new one, he noted, red and warmly padded) and slammed out of the cottage.

He looked down at the list he had been trying to compile, of things he should do before the wedding. Apart from the doodle, the list was empty. Elizabeth had seen to everything, she had even bought the rings and booked a hotel for one night in a hotel. He felt a wave of depression pressing him down. A gust of wind threw itself against the kitchen window, setting the old casement rattling. Dark clouds were accumulating. He really ought to find her… He knew she'd be by the harbour wall, where an ancient path called the Goat Walk, wound its way round the sea wall, but he felt exhausted by the repetition, the sharp words. These were always followed by her worming her way back, always ending in a session of lovemaking that sometimes seemed more like a struggle to destroy each other than love.

Seriously disturbed by his thoughts, his immediate reaction was to talk to Alexis. He was reluctant to ring her mobile, knowing that although Cheryl had not moved in with Alexis yet, she might be in the flat spending time there. She often did at the weekends. He didn't want the conversation overheard. He couldn't text either. He knew that it wasn't always easy to convey what he wanted to in text-speak.

Luke brought his computer to the kitchen table with a thump that sent Mango scurrying out through the cat flap, an affronted look on her face. He began to type out a message to Alexis, intent on getting his thoughts down swiftly before his anger dissipated.

TO Alexis Johnson

FROM Luke Johnson SAT 3 MAR 10:58

Hi sis, I'm having a serious bout of wedding nerves. Sorry to be a pain, but I just needed to let off steam. Elizabeth is being great, don't get me wrong...sorting out the cottage, tidying and cleaning, (stuff I don't get round to) and throwing out loads! I should be grateful for all her hard work, but it's getting on my nerves. It's like she's removing my personality, do you know what I mean?

I suppose in the back of my mind, I've still got this doubt that I deserve any happiness. All these things that Xavier ought to be enjoying, a nice home, a career, someone to love. He never got a chance at life, did he? I saw to that. So why should I take it all? I love Elizabeth, there's no doubt about that, but she represents the icing on the cake, I suppose. I feel I'm being greedy to want it all when he's cold and dead, because of me. I watched his blood leave his body. That is imprinted on my memory forever, and I'll never forgive myself.

Sorry for ranting on, but I feel really low sometimes. Just ignore me.

Hope I haven't wrecked your Saturday!

Love Luke xx (your pain in the bum brother)

Luke nearly hit the junk button when he had read his letter through, but some impulse moved him to press send, and his words flicked and flew away to Alexis's computer before he had time to change his mind.

He sat at the table staring into space. Having spewed his thoughts out, he felt empty and purposeless. The wind unnerved him. He moved restlessly about the room, picking up random objects and putting them down again. He had been looking forward to the weekend, and now it was just a pointless amount of time to be endured. He hated arguing, he hated himself. He was not in a good place.

A rattle and sound of a thump startled him out of his apathy. He turned round, expecting to see Elizabeth at the kitchen door, but it was only Mango coming through the cat flap. She plumped herself on the rough mat and began to wash herself vigorously, one leg straight up like an aerial. Her fur was ruffled into black spikes by the wind. She halted in mid lick, head up and green gaze fixed on to his face.

"You minx! You remind me of Elizabeth with those eyes and…"

There was another sound as the door flew open, and Elizabeth blew in, her hair whipped into peaks, eyes suspiciously pink.

Luke found himself smiling at her, all anger gone. "Thank God…I thought you'd been blown into the harbour. You nutter, you must be freezing!"

"I am!" she answered, "Why are you laughing at me?" She pulled self-consciously at her wayward hair.

"Because you and Mango both look seriously alike when you've been out in a gale! And I love you both."

Elizabeth looked at him doubtfully. "You do? I thought the wedding was off," she said worriedly.

Luke cradled her, turning her face up to kiss each eye in turn. "I'm sorry…pre-wedding nerves, that's all. I'm a bad-tempered bore sometimes. How do you fancy a drink at the Lighthouse? We could have a bite to eat there? Go up and wash your face, your eyes still look sad!"

Elizabeth smiled at him warily before going to get ready.

Luke glanced at his computer and noticed a new e-mail. He sat down to open it up.

TO Luke Johnson

FROM Alexis Johnson SAT 3rd MAR 11:24

Right. Listen to me, and listen properly. You are mad, seriously. You deserve everything you have, how can you possibly think for one moment that what happened when you were seven years old should stop you living life now? To be brutal, do you think Xavier would have put his life on hold if it had been the other way round? You have to think of Elizabeth...is Xavier more important than her, really? I know you get depressed at times, but I think it's part of your make-up. Don't blame it on the past, it's a separate issue. It's bound to be scary sharing your life with someone, Elizabeth is only doing her nesting thing! You are a lovely gentle guy, she is lucky to have you. That's it; my agony aunt (or sister) bit done. Love as always, Alexis.

Luke read Alexis's words and felt strange. This was his little sister giving him words of comfort and hope. And he did feel comforted, as if he'd been carrying a massive weight and then off-loaded it. He'd always suffered from moods, morose one minute, cheerful the next.

When Elizabeth came into the room, in a cloud of her favourite scent, Luke was all smiles.

"About time! I'm starving!" He grabbed his jacket and they stepped into the narrow street. There had been a cloudburst since Elizabeth had come in. The air smelt clean, puddles reflecting blue sky and white puffs of cloud replacing the earlier darkness.

Plump cushions lined the wooden settle that curved beneath a sunny window. They shrugged off their coats in the sudden unexpected warmth and studied the menu.

Luke felt so calmed and comfortable that he stretched his legs out under the table and looked at Elizabeth.

"Can I ask you something?" he asked her, stroking her hand affectionately.

Elizabeth hesitated a fraction. "Anything!" she replied playfully.

"I know this sounds big-headed of me, but did you track me down the night we first met?"

She studied the menu, a sparkle of mischief in her eyes. "Now, why would you think that?" She looked at him over the card in her hand. "How on earth would I have managed it? I'd never met you!"

Luke gripped her hand. In a mock-stern voice he said, "A little bird told me that you had all the information you needed to know exactly where I go every Friday night, at what time, and even what I looked like!" He laughed at her surprised expression.

"I didn't know then how close you and Alexis are!" she responded, looking cornered. "I admit it…aren't you flattered?"

"Yes, I am…and that's why I fell for you. You're devious, conniving, manipulating, cunning, and…."

"And? Is that all?"

"It's all you deserve for the moment," he teased. "Have you chosen?"

"Not yet. There's something I want to ask you first."

Luke waited, not sure what was coming.

"Who is Xavier?"

Luke looked stricken. "I should have told you myself. Who told you?"

"Alexis told me when I first met her, then the photo in your parents' house…"

Luke looked down. There followed a silence.

Elizabeth broke it. She spoke to him warmly, full of sympathy. "I know there was an accident, Luke. Alexis said he was always taking risks. It must have been a horrible time for you. You should have told me."

Luke smiled at her. "I know, I'm not good at opening up. That's why I fell for you…you've had a pretty rubbish life, yet you listen, you make it easy to talk…"

"Well." She grinned. "No more secrets… We tell each other everything from now on. Now, I fancy the quiche, what are you having?"

Chapter Fourteen
"Something and Nothing"

Friday 18th July 2008
Sixteen Months Later

Luke drove slowly out of the school carpark, a huge feeling of release washing over him. The milling bunches of children walked together in groups, seemingly unaware of the heavy weapon of his car edging them along. Normally this got on his nerves, their total inability to take in anything which didn't involve their paltry little worlds. Normally he would have sounded his horn, waving them furiously out of his way. He had spent endless hours attending to their every educational need, how dare they impede his exit to the freedom of his own world? They were nothing to him at the end of the day, a mere means to a good salary. Gone was his passion for teaching.

But today he felt warm towards them all. He lowered his window, calling out to the children in a friendly voice, "Have a great summer, kids!"

They looked up startled, heads coming up like a herd of deer; suspicious and watchful before nudging each other. "And you, sir!" shouted the class comedian. And they all took up his cry, mimicking Luke's posh accent as they echoed each other. "Have a jolly good summer, sir!"

Luke didn't care. He pulled away towards the school gates, executing a rude victory salute out of the open window. Six weeks of freedom. He was transported to his own school days, remembering the joy of being returned to himself after tedious weeks of having to be what other people wanted him to be.

His euphoria doubled as he spotted Elizabeth's little red MG already parked outside the cottage. A whole summer of freedom together…not for the first time he realised how great it was to have the same profession as his wife. They both understood the pressures and satisfaction of the job, not to mention sharing the holidays. He had stopped for petrol on his way home, and now he picked up the package he had put on the seat next to him. The cellophane crackled as he lifted the white roses up to smell their heady fragrance.

Luke could hardly believe that he and Elizabeth had been married for fifteen and a half months. The wedding seemed an age ago, but with the chaos of a busy term, settling together into the cottage and keeping tabs on how Alexis and Cheryl were getting on in the Exmouth flat, time had disappeared behind them like exhaust fumes from a speeding car.

The wedding had come and gone in a blur, blue skied and bright, daffodils had flashed their sunny trumpets in the wind. Elizabeth looked edible in the simplest froth of a dress, the white fall of its line broken only by a clutched posy at her breast. It consisted of her favourite yellow freesias and primroses mingled with baby's breath. She clutched the arm of Sam, a friend from her college days who had agreed to give her away. Alexis wore an ankle-length yellow bridesmaid's dress with spaghetti straps and a smart little jacket in cream. There was only a small number of friends and family, both Thomas's and Céline's parents having passed away, her mother Mathilde the last to go at the age of eighty, four years before. They stood shoulder to shoulder in the tiny village church of Exsham, outwardly supportive, yet each with their own hidden thoughts.

Céline dabbed at her eyes with a linen handkerchief as her daughter walked past, remembering her as a little girl, singing to her dolls. She wished, with a guilty pang, that this was Alexis's wedding day. Thomas kept his gaze on Luke, his only son, standing there at the altar so hopefully, Jim, his colleague and friend fiddling nervously with his cuffs, worrying about his coming speech. Luke looked so handsome in his smart grey suit with yellow cravat, his black hair in a modern boyish quiff. And that's the worry, had thought Thomas. Luke was just that, a boy. He hadn't had time to flex his wings, let alone fly yet. He feared for his son, who had not only grown up painfully, but was still going through the process. He needed a mature partner in life, not this spiky, needy girl who nobody could quite get the hang of. He frowned and Céline prodded him in the ribs. He caught Luke's worried eye. The granite set of his jaw softened, and his face broke into a proud smile. A slow lazy wink sealed Luke's feeling of relief and confidence.

Later, as the wind blew cool across the estuary, the small group made their way to The Old Bridge Hotel which sprawled its many extended pink buildings to the very edge of the River Exe, just down the road from Luke's cottage. Phyllis, the friendly landlady, ushered them into a small private bar kept for friends. The bay window, with its inviting padded window seat, overlooked the water. Alexis made herself comfortable, making room for Cheryl, resplendent in a green dress, matching fascinator perched jauntily in her mousy hair. She looked through the window, the setting sun highlighting the warmth of the ancient wooden table and heavy comfortable chairs. "I've not been in this pub before, it's gorgeous!" she said to Alexis. "So quiet, look out there, see those swans peeping at us through the reeds…" She smiled at Alexis, her eyes then sliding away, her attention suddenly arrested.

Alexis smiled at her and then followed her gaze to see Luke and Elizabeth standing at the bar with her parents. Luke had removed his jacket, and slung it over his shoulder, dangling it from bent fingers. His other hand snaked round Elizabeth's waist, tiny in snug blue jeans, a cream sweater draped over a pale-blue shirt. She looked crisply smart, ready to leave shortly with her new husband. A barmaid brought a tray of champagne round. The girls each accepted one and Alexis touched her glass to Cheryl's. "Penny for them?" she murmured softly. "How are you feeling?"

Chery grimaced and took a big slug of champagne. "Better after a lot more of this," she stated, lifting her glass to her mouth again.

"You've really got it bad, haven't you? I didn't think you were serious about him?"

Cheryl cast Alexis a mortified look. "I suppose I played the fool about it, but I really have feelings for him even though I knew he'd never find me attractive. He was always so nice to me, it made me have fantasies…and crazy hopes…"

"He does like you, Cheryl, but only as a friend. He was jokey with you because he felt safe. You know Elizabeth is his first girlfriend." Alexis put her hand over her friend's.

"Lucky cow." Cheryl stared gloomily into her drink. "Well, she's got him in her clutches now. I just hope she makes him happy. She doesn't deserve him." She tipped up the rest of her champagne into one long swallow and held out her glass to the passing barmaid who took it and swapped it for a full one as Alexis looked on doubtfully.

"Elizabeth is a nice person, Cheryl. She adores Luke, and God knows he needs that now. You know what a tough time he's had of fitting in socially. You can't help who you fall for, as you should know!"

Cheryl rolled her eyes in agreement.

"Come on, cheer up! They'll be off to their secret honeymoon destination soon, and Mum and Dad said we could join them at the cottage for a bite to eat. They are staying there for a couple of nights while the lovebirds are away. You ought to get something down you to soak up some of that booze!"

Cheryl's response had been to down her whole glass in one and then burst into tears.

Now Luke locked his car and sauntered down to the harbour before going into the cottage. The sun was still high in the blue sky, beating heat into his neck and warming his arms where he had rolled up his shirt-sleeves. The tide was in, the turquoise water breaking into lazy little peaks of froth and evening out again into a glassy swell. A seagull chuckled as it swooped past him, beady eyes on the lookout for dropped chips. Luke took in a deep breath of salt air, sighing it out with satisfaction. What a place to live… he never tired of the ever-changing view. He turned whistling towards home.

He opened the front door, threw his work folder onto a small table already cluttered with keys and unopened mail, and sauntered into the kitchen. Elizabeth stood with her back to him, leaning against the table. She held the receiver of the house phone to her ear, and Luke realised she had not heard him come in.

Elizabeth sighed loudly and shifted her weight. She spoke into the phone, sounding slightly agitated. "I don't know why Alexis won't talk to you about it. If it's clear she's not happy…"

Luke coughed to let her know he was there without alarming her. Elizabeth turned round, smiling and curling her fingers into a welcome wave at him. "Don't worry, Cheryl. It's probably just her time of the month! Must go now… bye, love."

Luke raised his eyebrows. "What's up? Trouble with the girls?" he asked.

Elizabeth moved round towards him, grabbing the roses out of his hands and giving him a hug. "Oh something and nothing!" She laughed. "Thanks for these. I love them! I can't believe the term's ended! I so need this break. We have to decide where to go for a couple of weeks…" She reached up to a high shelf for a chunky glass vase, trimmed stalks and dropped the roses in with a sunlit stream from the tap. They settled into a natural arrangement, no effort needed. Luke watched her with interest.

Luke took the vase and walked through, placing it onto the low coffee table. Elizabeth followed him and they both sank onto the settee, sighing at the simple pleasure.

"I think we can afford somewhere hot with a beach, where we can lie all day reading books until the cocktail hour," suggested Luke, leaning back and closing his eyes.

"Spain!" cried Elizabeth happily. "Benidorm…that would be bliss."

"Mmmm… maybe somewhere a bit more off the beaten track? Some little village where we can try the local fare, where no one speaks English and we can go for long walks without fighting our way through tourists."

"Heaven!" Elizabeth agreed. We'll have a look at cheap flights tomorrow. Fancy a cuppa? I do, I'm parched."

She began to stand up, but Luke pulled her back. "Tell me what you were talking to Cheryl about first." He put his arms around her, smelling the lemony scent of her hair.

Elizabeth turned round to face him. "Oh yes, a bit odd really, she rang to speak to you really. I told her you wouldn't be long. Then she said she was worried about Alexis."

Luke looked concerned. "Why? What did she say?"

"Well…just that she's seemed a bit down recently. Cheryl said she thinks she's heard her crying in her room. She tried to ask her what was troubling her, but Alexis wouldn't say. Cheryl said you'd be better talking to her, in fact she asked if you'd go over and see her…"

Luke sat up, pushing his fingers through his hair. "Of course I will. I should go now. Did she say if Alexis is there?"

Elizabeth thought for a moment. "I think she said she'd gone out for some milk. She'll be back home by now I should think. Do you want me to come with you?"

Luke pulled her close to place a kiss on her nose. "You're sweet, but no, don't worry. I don't suppose I'll be long."

The traffic was slow, as to be expected on the last Friday of term. His thoughts had been concentrated on his worry over Alexis. Sunlight flashed and shimmered off hot metal, fingers drummed on steering wheels, windows buzzed open to cool sweating skin. He pulled at last in to the shared carpark of the flats, hoping that he would not have to stay too long.

Eagerness to be home again with Elizabeth carried him in swift strides to the entrance door, finding, thankfully, that the lift was unoccupied at ground level. At the top, Luke rang the bell, nearly falling into the hallway, the door being opened so promptly. He stumbled inside, unprepared for the sight of the face before him. It was awash with tears, blotchy and bruised looking from the mascara trails daubing the pale palette of her cheeks. She gave an agonised wail and flung her hands across her face.

"Oh!" she gasped. "I thought you were Alexis! Don't look at me!"

Luke put his arms gently round the heaving shoulders. "Shhh…it's okay. You look fine. Just take a few deep breaths."

Cheryl hid her face gratefully against Luke's shirt, unaware of the watery black smears she was leaving on it. Luke kept his arms round her, desperate to calm her down.

They both jumped as the front door swung open and Elizabeth stood there. "What's going on? Where's Alexis?" she shouted. She flew towards Cheryl, catching hold of her baggy cardigan and pulling her away from Luke with a screech. "You conniving bitch! You just can't keep your hands off him, can you? And as for you!" She glared up at Luke's concerned face.

"Hey! Slow down, Elizabeth! Cheryl's upset. I was just calming her down! Let go of her! You're crazy."

Elizabeth's eyes darted to his in fury. "Can't you see?" she spat. "She lied to get you over here. All that about Alexis needing you. Where is she anyway?"

Cheryl seemed to wake up from a trance. She stared at Elizabeth with a puzzled frown. "I told you on the phone. The hospital asked her to do a twilight shift tonight as someone's gone off sick."

Luke spoke firmly. "Let's get this straight. Did you ring Elizabeth saying Alexis was upset about something and asking for me to come over to see her?"

Elizabeth opened her mouth, but Luke held up his hand to silence her. "Well, Cheryl?"

"Elizabeth rang me," Cheryl said, rubbing a hand across her eyes and sniffing loudly. "She said she'd got the impression from Alexis that I've not been pulling my weight in the flat. She said I was lazy and slovenly and Alexis was fed up with me." She sobbed out a hiccup, but managed to continue. "She said Alexis couldn't talk to me about it because she was embarrassed, so she felt she had to tell me because it's not fair on Alexis. It's not true though! Alexis teases me about being too pernickety about things! She actually said I was OCD about cleaning!" Her voice raised to a wail.

Luke stepped back shaking his head in frustration. "This is mad," he stated, raking his hair with his fingers.

"Of course it's mad," agreed Elizabeth quietly. "I wouldn't ever upset anyone like that. Just ask Alexis," she said simply, raising her hands in the air. "She's never complained about Cheryl, she wouldn't. This one's a good actress, I'll give her that…" she added, casting a disgusted look at Cheryl, whose mouth was opening and closing like an automatic door.

Luke gazed at the two women. He felt completely at a loss as what to say. He certainly knew that Cheryl seemed to have a crush on him. Alexis had confided this to him after the wedding, and he felt uncomfortable at the memory of laughing about it rather unkindly with his sister at the time.

He also knew that Elizabeth had a slightly flaky side to her, but this contrivance seemed most unlikely.

They left the flat, Cheryl having fled to her bedroom and slammed the door. Elizabeth rolled her eyes and together they stepped into the lift.

"She'll get over you eventually," Elizabeth told him, holding on to his arm. "Mind you, if I hadn't come in when I did….would you have been tempted?"

Luke looked at her in mock horror. "You witch! When I've got you at home waiting for me? Never in a million years!"

They walked hand in hand to Elizabeth's car parked next to his. "By the way…" Luke said, frowning, "Why did you follow me?"

Elizabeth smiled at him. "It occurred to me that Alexis might need me if she's having girly problems. She is my sister-in-law, after all. Sometimes a brother just isn't good enough for the job…"

Cheryl twitched aside her bedroom curtain. She glared through tear-blurred eyes at Elizabeth standing there looking so smug and beautiful. If her eyes were capable of sending sharpened knives flying at speed across the carpark, Elizabeth would be perforated through and through, and like a paper doll, it would be possible to tear her into tiny fragments and blow her away.

Chapter Fifteen
Sounds of Possible Destruction

Friday 30th October 2009

The journey home was not pleasurable. The roads were writhing with slow-moving traffic, drivers becoming impatient, taking chances that weren't theirs to take.

"Stupid sod..." Luke muttered as the car in front braked, the lights unnaturally red in the twilight gloom.

Elizabeth retrieved her mobile phone from the floor. "God! Careful, Luke! You were right up his backside..."

Luke thought about how strange it was that normally Friday was a day to enjoy, a small last step of the week before the weekend arrived. But today was the last day of half-term, transforming the coming two days into smaller amounts of time than usual. Last Friday, the whole week ahead had swelled like a sunny pathway, and he had looked forward to it with unusual fervour. Now that it was behind him, he felt that it had not come up to expectations. He felt disappointed with himself for having been taken in, at his age.

"Poor old Mango will be pleased to see us," Elizabeth commented. "I hope Mary made a fuss of her and didn't just plonk the food down." She glanced at Luke. He was staring at the road in silence. "What's up with you?" she asked when he made no response.

"Sorry...I always feel fed up when a week away goes so fast. There's no time to savour it, is there?"

She laughed. "To be honest, I think nearly five days with your parents was enough! I love them to bits, but it'll be nice to be home, just the two of us, don't you think?"

Luke leaned across to squeeze Elizabeth's hand briefly before turning off the dual carriageway from Cornwall onto the Exmouth road. The sky had darkened considerably in the last few minutes.

"Oh! Look there!"

Luke saw a house with a low wall on which were set a row of pumpkin heads, their eerie slitty eyes and craggy smiles pulsating from the flickering flames within.

"I love Halloween!" she cried, and Luke noticed with affection that Elizabeth actually clapped her hands.

Luke mulled over the last few days spent in Cornwall, trying to pinpoint the reasons that had made it a shadowed experience. He knew well enough that his father had not warmed to Elizabeth. He felt resentful on her behalf, and hurt too. It was another rejection as far as he was concerned; his choice of wife had not passed the paternal test. Céline, on the other hand, seemed to be bending over backwards to make Elizabeth feel included and loved…yet ironically, Elizabeth seemed to resent Céline, drawing back the more Céline metaphorically reached out to her. He sighed, deciding that he would never reach a day when everyone who mattered to him appeared to live in harmony.

Luke had offered to throw something simple together for supper. He was pressing spaghetti down into a pan of boiling water when Elizabeth joined him. She sat down heavily at the table, riffling through the few items of post that had welcomed them home, along with a grumpy Mango, who had ignored their arrival with her furry back turned to them.

"Rubbish! Not one single interesting thing. Just boring stuff." She puffed out a sigh and turned to the newspaper. "Nothing decent on the telly either."

"Cheer up!" Luke grinned. "You were full of beans just now. I'm making spaghetti carbonara, so it won't take long if you fancy laying the table?"

Another huge sigh. Luke glanced over to her and saw hooded eyes and mouth set in a line. He knew that face. One could not be married to someone for eighteen months and not be able to read their face. It was as clear as a barometer. Elizabeth's arrow had swung from fair to stormy from going up the stairs and returning down them again.

"I wonder why your father doesn't like me."

Luke rolled his eyes. "It that what this is about? Of course he likes you. He can be prickly with everyone, that's not your special prerogative, you know!"

"It's not funny," she replied sulkily. "I'm not stupid you know."

"Never said you were!" Luke laughed, testing a strand of spaghetti he'd trapped with a fork.

"He chills me out somehow. I always feel like I'm gabbling, as if he's not interested in what I'm saying…"

"Well, my mum thinks you're the best thing since fridge freezers were invented…"

"It's sliced bread actually…and she wasn't happy when she gave me that third degree."

"What about? Shove over and let me get to the cutlery drawer."

Elizabeth glared at him. "You know what!" she hissed. "The same old thing! As if it's any of her business!"

Luke turned the gas off under the pasta pan, tipped the contents into a colander over the sink and back into the pan. He sat down opposite Elizabeth, clattering spoons and forks noisily onto the table. "Oh love…she's worried, that's all. Of course it's her business! She can't wait to be a grandma, and she's probably feeling her age…"

"She only thinks of me as a means to a grandchild! I'd always hoped that the parents of the man I married would replace the parents I never had. Do you know what she told me? That she conceived you and Xavier straight away. She said that people say it seldom takes less than a year! So don't tell me that she's not suggesting there's something wrong with us!"

"So you only married me as a means of replacing your parents?" Luke said in a teasing tone.

Elizabeth looked at him sullenly.

"I'm sure there's nothing wrong, love. We just have to be calm and not get stressed… You'll feel better after something to eat, and then do you fancy an early night?"

"No, I don't!" she yelled, startling Luke. He stared at her. "I'm not hungry, and guess what? I've just started my period!"

She slammed out of the room. Luke gazed unseeingly at the cooling mound of food. His depression of earlier was back, filling his head with black despair.

March 2010

The wind came straight from the sea. It blew into town, swirling down the narrow streets, causing havoc. It veered round walls, hit dead-end corners and turned back on itself, scattering dust and debris into untidy circles. Later, when daylight broke, people would find splintered wood from unlatched gates, toppled bins spewing rotten food, and severed branches strewing the roads.

The rushing and rattling woke Luke early. He lay there uneasily, listening to alarming sounds of possible destruction. He closed his eyes, distracted, realising with a jolt of partial pleasure that it was Saturday. His next thought was that he hoped his cherished weekend was not going to be stolen from him by having to attend to the results of the wind's mindless rampage.

As daylight began to filter into the room, Luke was aware of pulsing light, shadows chased by brief streams of dusty glare. He imagined the clouds scudding about up there.

Luke stared into the room, the slope of the ceiling, a chair's shape disguised by the clothes he'd thrown there last night, his need for sleep paramount. The dressing table stood demurely against the wall, decorated with Elizabeth's jewellery and scarves like a woman waiting to be asked to dance. The room brightened again, and he looked into the mirror. There he lay, sleep-ruffled hair creating an illusion of a younger version of himself. And there behind him sat Elizabeth, staring over his shoulder, her face a pale oval. He could not make out her expression.

Luke twisted around to look at her. She stared down at him as if surprised to see him there. "You okay? I thought you were asleep."

She lay down again and reached out to stroke his cheek. "I was…the wind woke me."

They lay face to face. He studied her eyes. They were almost turquoise in the dappled light, fine white squiggles looped through, like unstirred cream through a glass of chartreuse liqueur. The rims were dark green.

"I went to see the doctor last month," she told him conversationally. "Nothing to worry about…" she reassured him, seeing his worried expression. "I told him, you know, about me not being pregnant yet. He asked me all the usual questions, and ran a series of tests…"

Luke looked at her in dismay. "Why didn't you tell me? We should have gone together! When was this?"

She smiled at him. "I went on the spur of the moment, during half-term. Don't look so morose! I didn't want to bother you with it, I know men aren't keen on doctors and…"

"Don't lump me with the term 'men'! I'm me! Your husband! This is the most joint thing we'll ever do, isn't it?"

Elizabeth shrugged. "I'm sorry, Luke, as I said, I didn't even plan it. I was just passing my surgery and went in. It's not as if we go to the same doctor. Don't you want to know what he said?"

Luke nodded, shamefaced. "Didn't mean to shout love…worried…"

Elizabeth held his gaze for one long moment. Luke found himself holding his breath. Then she said, looking down, "There's nothing wrong, with me. I'm absolutely fine…" Her eyes met his, filled with troubled sympathy. "But he suggests that maybe you ought to get checked out, Luke. Then we'll know."

A mixture of emotions made Luke breathe in deeply. He felt like the weather earlier, shadows chasing the sun. Bravely, he squeezed Elizabeth's hand. She reached round to hold him tightly and he hugged her desperately in return.

"We'll be fine." she whispered. She gazed over her husband's shoulder, examining her face in the mirror, seemingly devoid of emotion. She wondered what she was thinking, wishing she knew what secrets lay behind her eyes, and doubting that she ever would.

August 2010

Elizabeth paused, the rainbow bubbles steaming and popping. They clung to the backs of her hands, irritating her on this hottest of days. She lifted out the last plate and rinsed it carelessly, dying to be out in the fresh air. She looked up and considered the small courtyard, a meanly apportioned area in between the cottage and the road. There was a tiny corner where Luke had coaxed a few flowers to bloom. He stood there now, deadheading a few roses.

She couldn't but agree that the cottage had grown on her. It was low maintenance, set in the prettiest part of the town with the music of the sea a constant background rhythm of sound. Elizabeth had loved living here when she'd thought it to be only temporary; a stopgap between their marriage and the arrival of a baby. But now she felt confined, cramped, stopped forever within these cottage walls.

She turned blindly away from the sink, and her eyes shone wet as she faced the thoughts that tormented her daily now. The possibility of a second bedroom yawned its denial like a black barren womb. This room existed only in her head, she thought. Its invisible colours, silent nursery music and absence of herself standing near a cot were more real to Elizabeth than hope itself.

It wasn't until the end of the summer, just before the start of the dreaded term, that Luke was shaken into action by Elizabeth's gloomy moods. He had come across her standing staring at nothing too many times now. He is so afraid of the outcome, but he loves his wife, so he faces his demons and takes action at last. He makes an appointment, not encouraged by the cheerful efficient voice of the receptionist, to see his doctor as soon as possible.

Chapter Sixteen
Indian Summer

September 2010

"How bloody humiliating," Luke muttered, standing behind a flowery curtain and glaring at a lewd photo of a naked stranger. She was peeping at him through a tangle of blonde hair. 'Surely what was needed was an alluring photo of his wife! Not this simpering air-head. No wonder men shunned doctors. Women weren't faced with this sort of thing.'

Instead of focusing on the matter in hand, Luke found his thoughts straying to the conundrum of the difference between men and women. How was it that men thought nothing of stripping off in front of their partner but went all coy and embarrassed in the presence of a medical person? Whereas women, seemed quite happy to endure (with martyr-like submission) the indignities which always seemed to accompany a visit to the doctor, be it for contraceptive reasons or a recurring patch of dry skin in an awkward location. But when approaching a love-making situation, on came the cellulite-concealing garment and off went the lights.

But he had done it; had tolerated the probing questions, performed like Pavlov's Dog, and finally been delivered the result.

He found Elizabeth ironing her 'sensible teaching clothes' in readiness for the start of the new term in a few days. She raised her eyes, discerned it to be him, and contemplated the ironing board once more. This was what it'd been like for the past few months; nothing much said, but silences becoming more and more deafening.

Luke was disturbed by how his life recently had thrown him into such tangible misery. How could another person cause this distress? Her avoidance of him emotionally and physically had rocked him into the darkest of places. He supposed that if he took the gigantic risk of deciding to live closely with one person to the exclusion of all others, which was what marriage amounted to, and that person decided to turn her back on him, this was where he found himself. He asked himself whether solitary confinement wouldn't be preferable, and wasn't sure he liked his answer.

This, he realised, was what he had been avoiding all those years, never wanting to take that massive risk with anyone. He had always told himself that he was unlovable, a weak coward who faced with another life or death situation, would fail again, causing the death of another loved one. And here it was, Elizabeth no longer loved him, and he was grieving at the loss of her. She seemed to be so absorbed in her own life these days, as if she had simply removed him from her mind. He would rather she confronted him eye to eye than this dismissive looking through him.

He was not even really sure whether she knew he had been to seek advice at last. He would find her staring into the middle distance, her thoughts excluding him. But now that he had done what she'd implored him to do, he imagined that, knowing him so well, she must have felt something of his struggle to carry it out. He felt shocked to see her face closed against him still.

He sat down, examined his fingernails to avoid seeing her turned away face and launched straight in. "I've been undergoing a few tests…as you asked me to," he uttered.

Silence.

"It's a matter of, well…it's not completely hopeless. Although…"

Elizabeth had moved towards him as he had begun to speak. She held out her hands hopefully. He carefully took hold of them gratefully. She pulled him up to stand in front of her. "And? Please, Luke…just say it."

"I have a low sperm count. They say it's quite common, some men have none at all, but mine are just less. It doesn't mean we can't have a child, just that it might take longer."

Elizabeth let go of Luke's hands. Her eyes had dulled. He felt her leave, emotionally, heard the shutting of some internal door inside her. "Just how much longer, Luke?" she asked. "How much more can we take?"

New buoyant faces brimming with optimism. They greeted Luke and transferred some of their hopeful expectations to him. Each fresh autumn term used to spark a chance of success in Luke's soul, but by the following summer, the children had morphed mysteriously into their elder peers. Polite earnest faces were replaced by bored disinterest. At the start of his career, he had blamed himself, but now he knew that this was how the human cycle revolved, a few heartening exceptions aside.

This time, he began the term with no illusions, did not even rally when peppered with excited questions from his shining-eyed charges. Carrying the extra burden of his recent depreciating self-knowledge, he was plunged into a darker gloom than he'd ever experienced. Deep in his brain, beliefs existed which were out of his control. He knew they were not logical. He was not a religious man, yet they paralysed him with fear. He was convinced without a doubt, that his likelihood of not being able to father a child was directly linked to his inability to have saved his brother's life. He almost embraced it as proof of his guilt. He felt that he was not deemed capable of being responsible for a young life.

Luke dreaded a continuation of Elizabeth's silent rebuffs, so he was surprised to see her mood lighten visibly with her return to work.

The September term was under way, and the last warm days were replaced by cold dawns fingering their way through the day until there was little memory of that heat steaming up from baking pavements. After another difficult day, Luke drove home along pale roads, the verges still straw like and parched despite the icy air. He entered the cottage, heard the rumble of the central heating just kicking in, and found Elizabeth sitting at the kitchen table surrounded by dog-eared exercise books filled with children's pencilled scrawls. She looked up at him with a welcoming smile.

"Hi sweetheart! Kettle's just boiled..."

Emboldened by her friendly greeting, Luke bent to kiss the top of her head on his way to take his favourite blue mug from its hook. "You seem happy. Had a good day?" he risked bravely.

"I did actually!" she agreed, sounding surprised. "This new class of seven-year-olds brings tears to my eyes at times! They're so funny and eager!" She picked up a book nearest to her. "I asked them to write a story about 'A Day in the Life Of ....' whatever they want. Well...this Sam in my class, he's a right chirpy chap, he chose a house spider. There the spider sits, minding his own business in his web in the corner of the lounge, when along comes this terrible noise and a tube chases him round the ceiling and sucks him down this black tunnel and lands him on a heap of dust and the dead bodies of other spiders who were all his friends before they recently went missing. So this triggers post-traumatic stress disorder in him and so on... It's hilarious. I love teaching these kids." Elizabeth smiled to herself, not noticing Luke's glum expression. She went on enthusiastically, "Did I ever mention that I got my French 'A' Level Luke? It's been a bit wasted as we don't teach French in most Primary schools, but I thought I'd try going to evening classes in advanced French...what do you think?"

Luke eyes her enviously, comparing her enthusiasm for teaching with his angry frustration. "I'm beginning to think I should have gone into primary school. The ones I'm faced with every day are killing me. They don't listen to me, don't look at me..." He is reminded suddenly of being at school himself, when his classmates treated him in exactly the same way. "I can't even put a hand on their shoulder in a fatherly way! They'd run to tell someone I'm a pervert, and that's the boys as well as the girls!"

Elizabeth recalled how just that morning, a five-year-old girl had fallen in the playground. She had dried the child's tears, made her laugh, and administered to the knee which in truth was hardly scratched. She looked sympathetically at Luke, thankful that her life was so much more rewarding than his. He returned the look with a sad smile, reassured that at least someone knew how unhappy he was.

The weather brightened and warmed momentarily for a few days, instantly bringing summer back. How fickle was the human condition that they forgot completely how they shivered just a few days before. Coats are returned to cupboards, grass turns greener and the heating is switched off.

Luke and Elizabeth had entered calmer waters, gliding side by side without the friction that had rubbed them raw of late. In an effort to continue this happier atmosphere, Luke carried two cups of tea through to the tiny courtyard where Elizabeth was sitting, her face turned up to the sun's fickle rays. Luke balanced the cups carefully on a low wall, kissed Elizabeth's cheek and settled next to her on a wooden seat that just fitted them both.

"I've just listened to the forecast. Looks as if this Indian summer is going to last another few days. Do you fancy inviting my parents over for the weekend? We haven't seen them properly in a while…before the short days set in, you know how my dad hates driving in the dark now."

"Oh yes, Luke. I'd like that. And maybe I could practise my French with your mum? It would be nice to have something in common with her."

"Apart from just me you mean?"

Luke was heartened to see a grin on Elizabeth's face.

Saturday 18th September

Céline was delighted to be invited to Devon again. Since Luke and Elizabeth's marriage, they had kept in touch pretty frequently, despite, or perhaps because, the relationship between Elizabeth and her parents-in-law was somewhat flimsy. Thomas had openly spoken of his distrust of Elizabeth, and Céline accepted that. But you would have thought that his desire to see Luke would have overruled his reluctance to spend time with his daughter-in-law. In spite of Thomas's disinclination, the short visits to and fro between both parties had been kept up quite successfully, albeit that the orchestration of these undertakings had been down to Céline.

She found Elizabeth easier to deal with. Females gravitated towards each other on so many levels that when they don't see eye to eye on some little item, it can be ignored for a while. But now, the small item that had previously been swept under the proverbial carpet had reared up too many times recently. Céline had been lulled by the warm friendship that had appeared to exist between her and Elizabeth, so during that visit of last October, she had confidently broached the subject of an addition to the family. She had honestly thought that this was the way to Elizabeth's heart…to offer her the support and interest that she obviously had never been able to receive from her own unknown mother. The sharp retort she had encountered from Elizabeth's mouth had stung her like a snake bite. Mind her own business? What did she mean? She had actually reared back physically, retreating to her bedroom where Thomas had found her shedding a few uncharacteristic tears. More fuel to feed his aversion to that unwelcome guest.

Since then, the two women have held back from each other, avoiding the elephant in the room by only discussing platitudes. They have lost a little of that warm chatty comfort zone which they had achieved. Céline was determined this visit to recapture Elizabeth's affection.

It had been arranged that they pick Alexis up from her flat on their way to Exsham. They had booked rooms for themselves and Alexis at The Old Bridge Hotel. That was the drawback of visiting Elizabeth and Luke; there was no room to sleep, or even eat comfortably at the small kitchen table. Céline was used to the comforts of her own home, and had become more critical as she grew older.

With Alexis safely in the back of the car, Céline's spirits lifted as they drove down Exsham high street. She was transported back to when the children were small, excited at the adventure of a car ride.

The narrow pavements thronged with people. The unexpected warm sunshine had brought them out to window shop and browse through the bright touristy shops, catching the eye with their blue and white boating themes, local fare of wooden tubs of golden clotted cream, and honey sold in its waxy fresh comb, the dripping amber calling out to be spread onto thickly buttered crusty bread.

"I can see the sea!" Alexis shouted in a high little girl's voice as the cottage came into view, a glimpse of blue waves as the high street disappeared before them to become part of the jetty. "Are we there yet?" She leant forward to squeeze her mother's shoulder with a grin.

Céline laughed and clapped her hands, moved to see the amused smile spreading on Thomas's face. "Oh don't! It seems like yesterday that you and Luke used to argue about who spotted the sea first!" Thomas reverted to form, grumbling as he struggled to park the car in the pocket-sized space between the cottage and the nearby Lighthouse Inn, but Céline knew that was just keeping up appearances. She jumped out of the car, pleased to see Luke and Elizabeth standing together at the gate, united smiles of welcome on their faces. Even Mango jumped onto the low wall, her eyes closed sensuously in the sunshine as she waited for her adoring minions to arrive.

Chapter Seventeen
She Delivered a Blow of Her Own

Saturday 18th September 2010

The two women hugged Elizabeth, thoughts flitting openly across their faces. Alexis grinned at her sister-in-law's warm embrace, considering she saw Elizabeth at least twice a week. Céline looked gratefully at Elizabeth's apparent warmth, while Elizabeth searched Céline's intense glance for signs of disapproval of her casual choice of cut-offs and slip-on shoes compared to Céline's crisp linen slacks and sensible lace-ups.

The three women moved into the cottage, with Thomas and Luke ducking in through the door behind them, Thomas loudly admiring the colourful border of snap-dragons that Luke had grown against the cottage wall.

Inside, the cottage seemed to have inhaled a deep breath of dismay at the intrusion. The five adults stood shoulder to shoulder in the diminutive lounge, as if the walls had been sucked in. No one attempted to sit down, as there was only a settee and Mango's bean-bag, already full of Mango.

Thomas immediately registered and pre-empted the expression of long-suffering irritation on Elizabeth's face. Before she could begin her diatribe on how inadequate Luke's cottage was, and how if he'd only agreed to move…etc. etc…he interrupted in a cheerful voice, "Why don't we go out and stretch our legs? Who fancies a drive out to Hay Tor? It's only half hour away?"

Various sighs of relief, queuing for the loo and borrowing of hats from Elizabeth, and the party was ready. They piled into Thomas's roomy Volvo Estate, the three 'children' sliding into the back seat, Luke gallantly sitting in the middle to allow the girls a better view of the pretty countryside, rolling past in the golden light.

"Oi! That's my slot, Luke! You're pinching my thighs!"

"Budge over a bit then! Have you put weight on, Al?"

At Alexis's outraged squeak, Thomas looked over his shoulder. "I'm not starting the engine until you've got your seat belts on! What are you both, four?"

Elizabeth laughed. This is what she loved about being part of a family; the mad banter that seemed to revert everybody back in time.

Thomas drove well. He loved his car and had driven Volvos most of his adult life. He knew it was one of the safest cars in case of accident. His children's safety was the most important thing to him, particularly since Xavier's death. Everyone relaxed, enjoying the smooth ride.

Thomas took the A38 through Kennford and on towards Bovey Tracey, passing open fields and copses of trees just touched with the yellows and russets of coming autumn. A flock of birds swept up, black against the blue firmament, the rich red of the Devon loam deepening the contrast between land and sky.

The quiet appreciation was interrupted when Elizabeth looked across at Alexis. "Love your jeans! Where did you get them?" she asked enviously. "They make you look positively waif like, I'd say you've lost weight, not put it on! Have you?"

Alexis blushed, a curtain of blonde hair falling across her face conveniently. "Oh…well, thanks. Got these in that new shop in Exmouth. I'm always looking for the bleached blue look in jeans and these really caught my eye."

Luke turned to his sister and cast a critical eye over her. "Mmmm, new jeans, nail polish." He leaned towards her to sniff. "Sun silk lemon-scented hair, and is that a new silver locket I spy round your still tanned from the summer neck?"

She punched Luke on the arm, looking pleased never the less. She made no reply, just sat there with a grin on her face.

"Well? Why are you looking so glowing? More than usual I mean," Luke persisted.

"Leave the poor girl alone!" Elizabeth laughed. "You've nothing to hide, have you, Alexis?" she added curiously.

Céline listened to the unfolding of the conversation with interest, watching the three faces reflected in the little mirror in her sun visor.

Alexis decided that she now knew what it felt like to be a fox, run to ground by several hounds. She was not going to shake these two off in a hurry. She was hopeless at lying, and she would have made a hopeless poker player. "Oh God, you're awful. There's nothing to tell really…"

"Just his name for a start."

"His age?"

"His job?"

"And of course…is he good-looking?" This from Céline, who received a rolling of eyes from Thomas.

Alexis groaned. "I give up. I am admittedly crumbling in the face of this cruel family inquisition, but honestly, he's just a friend…"

"Alexis!" four voices cried in unison. Céline gaped at Thomas, startled at his loud voice joining in. Whatever next?

Alexis gave up the fight and announced, "Okay…he's called Rob, he's thirty, he's a counsellor for young people, and yes, he's very good-looking. And here's a bonus for you, we've been going out for two months, and it's been bloody hard work hiding it for that long!"

There was a collective gasp at this revelation, with Elizabeth and Céline bombarding her with questions and opinions. There was a pause as everyone digested the possible change to the dynamics of the family that this Rob might bring.

"What a dark horse…" muttered Elizabeth, clearly put out not to have been confided in first. "I just hope he's as nice as you say. Why's a good-looking man of his age still unattached?" she asked suspiciously.

"That's wonderful, chérie!" Céline put in quickly. "You deserve some love in your life. I'm so happy for you!" She shot a frown in Elizabeth's direction.

Undaunted, Alexis laughed. "I can't win with you lot!" she said good-naturedly. "You're on my case when I'm single, and looking for trouble now I've met someone!"

"Well, I'm pleased for you Al," Luke spoke warmly. "Can't wait to meet the guy."

Alexis smiled. "It's early days, but I am very happy. My biological clock has been ticking more loudly than usual recently, so I thought it time to stop fighting off the usual losers who can't see beyond my blonde hair and nubile body. (Here a disapproving cough from Thomas) Rob's the first person I've met who seems genuinely interested in me."

This was quite an unusually long speech from Alexis and she fell silent.

At the mention of Alexis's biological clock, Luke had felt Elizabeth's left thigh tense up where it was wedged next to his, saw her hands ball into fists. He reached across to stroke her arm, but it was a while before she appeared to relax.

The Volvo cruised along the bright Devonshire roads. They soon reached Bovey Tracey, deciding to stop here in this pretty town on the edge of Dartmoor. They had perked up pretty swiftly when Thomas said he knew of a popular café which sounded perfect for a light lunch before the strenuous demands of climbing the Tor. They were early enough to be given a table of their choice at a sunny window, and were soon transported into the delights of a fresh crab salad, a small bowl of homemade creamy mayonnaise each to dip the succulent meat into, and warm crusty bread to mop up the vinaigrette that glistened on the crisp lettuce hearts. Conversation was put on hold until every last mouthful was finished.

Thomas threw his napkin on the table and signalled to the waiter for the bill. He waved away the protests, saying, "It's my treat. I suggested it. And now, are we sufficiently refreshed for a brisk walk?"

Alexis groaned. "I feel more like lying in the gorse and sleeping it off."

"Fat chance of that with Dad in charge!" Luke laughed. "I wouldn't be surprised if he makes us run up Hay Tor with backpacks on, military style!"

"Don't tempt me," warned Thomas, leading the way back to the car.

They were soon out on the open moor, purple heather stretching before them. More and more rocky outcrops came into view, dotting the grassy clearings, just as if a giant toddler had thrown his building bricks around in a tantrum.

"I've never been up here..." Elizabeth said, amazed at the vastness before her, the endless sky, nature at its most primeval.

"What?" Thomas asked in amazement. "How long have you lived in Devon? And you've never been on the moors?"

Elizabeth didn't answer, and Luke made a swift mental comparison of his and Alexis's childhood, the family outings every weekend exploring the countryside with their parents, and the bleak image of Elizabeth's life in a children's home, maybe a few local outings as a special treat, but nothing like this. He took hold of her hand and she looked at him gratefully.

Thomas did not seem to have noticed Elizabeth's discomfort. He launched into a potted geography lesson, explaining that the tors had been formed millions of years ago during the Ice Age. Frozen water had caused the granite rock to split, sending various-sized rocks tumbling downwards. Later, thawing had turned the ground to liquid mud, which had carried the rocks and boulders further afield. Over the years the surface of these huge masses was eroded by the weather, leaving the 'towers' or 'tors' the moors were covered with today.

"You can take the man out of teaching, but you can't take the teaching out of the man," Céline observed wryly.

Everyone laughed at her new take on an old saying.

"Oh Mum! You crack me up," Alexis teased. Luke noticed sadly that Elizabeth's expression remained cold, and she turned her head away to gaze out of the window.

The carpark was just a tarmacked space off the road, boulders placed around it to mark its boundary. There were only a handful of cars parked so late in the season.

The sun was still high and its rays strong enough to warm them through at the least exertion, despite a brisk wind whipping across the heather. They began with a walk to get their digestions moving, gulping exhilarating lungfuls of fresh air. Apart from a couple walking a dog in the distance, they seemed to be the only visitors. Then they crossed a small road and followed the well-worn path upwards towards the massive Tor looming above them.

As they reached the base of the Tor, they split up, Luke and Elizabeth branching off to start the climb on their own, while Thomas and Céline opted for the easier way. This meant steps cut helpfully into the granite, with strategic ropes placed to pull oneself up on. Alexis stayed with them, concerned as always when her parents attempted anything slightly strenuous.

"It's the nurse in her," Céline informed Thomas. "She's always fussing."

"I can hear you, Mum! I'm not deaf! I just don't want two aged parents needing to be stretchered off Hay Tor with broken ankles."

"Less of the aged," grumbled Thomas. "Sixty-four isn't aged these days."

They all met at the top, pink cheeked and wild haired and very pleased with themselves. They admired the view, Thomas pointing out Saddle Tor in the distance. But Alexis noticed her mother give a shiver as the wind gusted round her, nearly spinning her hat off her head. She clutched at it, laughing, but she seemed more than ready to descend to flatter ground. Alexis took her arm as they made their way carefully down again.

"I'm right behind you!" shouted Thomas into the wind. Luke and Elizabeth, undaunted, decided to go back the way they had come up.

Thomas re-joined his wife and daughter on a close cropped grassy clearing. "You look cold, darling," Thomas observed to Céline. "Why don't you go and sit in the car?" He tossed the car keys to Alexis and watched them ambling back, arm in arm. Thomas waited, expecting to see Luke and Elizabeth coming round from the side of the Tor at any minute. He also shivered. The September sun had definitely lost a little heat in the last half hour.

He decided to go back up the Tor, more to keep moving than anything. He was half-way up when he heard voices. He could plainly hear Elizabeth's complaining tone rising from the other side of a craggy rock.

"I'm not sulking, Luke! Honestly, you're so insensitive. I'm upset…if Alexis is worried about her biological clock, what hope is there for me?"

"Come on…! You're only twenty-seven…my low sperm count isn't the end of everything. You're so dramatic!"

"I'm depressed and angry! Can you blame me?"

"Angry with me?"

There was a silence. Thomas half expected to find himself face to face with Luke and Elizabeth at any second, but then he realised that they had stopped walking.

He heard Elizabeth reply then. "It's not all about you, Luke. I'm angry that we will probably never have children, yes, but I'm angry with you too. Do you care whether we have one or not? I'm angry that it took you so long to go and see a doctor, as if it never occurred to you that it might be your fault. Angry that the only thing I want is a baby, and I married someone who can't give me one!"

Thomas heard Elizabeth stifle a sob, it sounded very close to him, so he turned away abruptly, not wanting to be found eavesdropping. He made his way back to ground level as quickly as he could, but choosing his steps with care. He didn't want to trip and be found in an undignified heap at the bottom. He needed to process what he had just overheard.

Meanwhile, Luke was staring across the moor, as stony faced as the granite rock he was standing on. His thoughts were in a turmoil. He felt hurt that she didn't think he cared. Of course he was devastated that it appeared that he would never be able to give Elizabeth a child. But he had tried to hide his feelings from her, confused himself at his conflicting emotions. On one hand, he hoped desperately that his condition would just mean that it would take them longer to conceive than most people, but he also believed, illogically, that someone somewhere deemed him unfit to have a child. What was that song, 'He aint heavy, he's my brother…' He had to pay the ultimate price for allowing his twin brother to die, what better way than this? That Elizabeth was also suffering because of him only served to convince him that he was destined to hurt the people closest to him. How could he explain all this to her? She must never know what happened that day. She would lose all respect for him, maybe even hate him.

He was startled out of his deep reverie by Elizabeth's voice. She was speaking quietly, and at first he thought she was soothing him. Then he made sense of her words, coming and going in the wind so that he had to lean closer to her to hear.

"Perhaps it's for the best…it would be awful being terrified of leaving you alone with a baby. What would happen if you got one of your depressions and then lost your temper? It'd be like living on a knife-edge. I don't think I could live like that." She stared at him, the cold gusts of wind whipping her hair this way and that in spiky chunks.

Luke gazed at her, finding it hard to make sense of what she was saying. "Elizabeth…what are you saying? Why wouldn't you trust me?" He frowned, the sweat forming clammily on his face despite the chill.

"I know about you, Luke." she whispered. He leaned closer and she stepped back as if fearing a blow. He blinked, puzzled, and then she delivered a blow of her own. "I know that you murdered your brother."

Horrified, Luke stared at her blankly. "You can't...how…?" The pain that then contorted his face made him stagger. He clutched at the rock to steady himself. Then he sank to his knees and stammered, the words leaving him in gasps. "She told you…she promised me…she was the only one who knew… How could she? Oh Alexis…"

Chapter Eighteen
A Horrible Feeling of Déjà Vu

Saturday 18th September

The day's outing ended at last. The atmosphere was as altered as if a bucket of iced water had been chucked over the whole party. Never a man to dabble in small talk, Thomas drove the Volvo back to Exsham in silence. Céline was left wondering if she had said something to offend him. He could be so prickly at times. She sighed to herself several times before withdrawing to gaze out of the window. The frosty ambience surrounding the three in the back seat was no better. Alexis found herself unintentionally manoeuvred between Luke and Elizabeth, quickly realising that as neither of them uttered a word for the entire journey either, that one of them had upset the other. No prizes for guessing which one. A few times she tried to catch Luke's eye, eyebrows raised in questioning sympathy. When he eventually glanced at her, it was with such a venomous glare of injured fury that she looked away aghast, her heart beating fast in confusion.

Thomas pulled up outside the cottage with a sharp ratchety screech of the handbrake. He made his apologies for them not to expect Céline and himself to stay. "Céline is exhausted from that climb," he decided. "We'll have a quiet meal at the Bridge, and an early start home in the morning."

Céline, who did not feel at all exhausted, and who had been looking forward to a jolly bantering evening with 'her' youngsters, suddenly did look drained, pale and miserable from the shock of disappointment. Never before had she felt the age gap quite so strongly between herself and her husband as now. She felt six years old again, forbidden a longed for treat by her father. She began to form a sentence of protest, but Thomas spoke seconds before her, his deeper voice masking hers.

"You stay, Alexis…you don't want us old fogeys holding you back…"

Outraged that Alexis was being given the chance to enjoy what Thomas had so clearly denied her, she again began to speak again, only to find this time that it was Luke's voice cutting coldly across hers.

"Oh no. Give Alexis a nice meal, fatten her up. You haven't seen each other in ages. Thanks for the drive out, Dad…really enjoyed it." He spoke in a flat voice. A robot could have put more effort into it. Céline could have stamped her foot, she felt so frustrated with her tiring family!

In one last desperate attempt to save the day, Céline cried, "Oh Elizabeth! Your hats, don't forget them! Perhaps we could just come in for a moment?"

Elizabeth silently accepted the two straw hats that Céline and Alexis had borrowed. Alexis turned away, Thomas drummed his fingers on the steering wheel, and Céline's question hung unanswered on the air. Luke and Elizabeth climbed out of the car, each from their separate sides, and walked towards their gate with as much space as possible between them. Alexis stared after them unhappily, willing Luke to turn and wave, but he did not.

Later that evening, after a light supper, during which nothing much was said, let alone any amusing anecdotes shared by funny intelligent people who have much catching up to do, Thomas disappeared to his and Céline's room.

Céline and Alexis looked at each other glumly.

"Fancy a brandy, sweetheart?" offered Céline mutinously. "I'm going to!"

Alexis moved to the comfort of an early log fire, lit against an unexpected chill. The few days of Indian summer seemed to have dissipated.

Céline went off to find the bar. She returned, passed Alexis a glass, and sat down, clinking her own golden globe against Alexis's.

"I don't know what we're celebrating. What was all that about?"

"I don't know, chérie. But I do know that at this moment, you are the only person in this family who I feel comfortable with. Men! They reduce you to nothing in a second! A blink of the eyes!"

Alexis smiled. "Why was Dad being so boring and stiff? What have you been up to, maman?"

"Rien du tout!" She always resorted to her mother tongue after an injection of alcohol. "He was being sweet, worried I was cold on that rock, and then the shut face, his lips fermées comme la poche d'un avare!" She took a second restorative sip of brandy.

"What the heck does that mean? Oh, yes, I remember; 'closed like a miser's pocket'! Very apt."

"And toi, Alexis…why was Luke not so welcoming to you? You two never fall out!"

"I honestly don't know. I thought he must have argued with Elizabeth, but you should have seen the look he gave me in the car."

"I know what you mean, if an expression can murder you, then..."

"Something like that...yes...I'd be so dead by now!"

Both women stared thoughtfully into the fire, wondering how a happily anticipated family day could have deteriorated, just like that.

Three Days Later

Sunday had been a painful passing of time for Luke. Once again, the day that should have been spent in leisurely pleasure, had limped lethargically along. Luke and Elizabeth had managed, as any hostile couples sharing a confined space will recognize, somehow, to avoid each other successfully all day.

Luke had been fascinated how Elizabeth managed to transform herself into an ethereal wisp of smoke. She had gone to sleep early after the day out that Saturday night. She had brought down some bedding and burrowed down on the settee, skipping supper. Meanwhile, Luke had drunk too much white wine, sitting at the kitchen table. When he had finally stumbled past her in a cloud of self-pitying alcoholic fumes, he noticed that even in sleep, Elizabeth had become invisible, her face concealed under her a pale-blue quilt.

Luke rose late the following morning, his whole head wincing at the slightest sound, even the exuberant pealing of distant Sunday church bells. He came down to find Elizabeth gone, presumably for a walk. At this point, he hardly cared. But later, his headache diminished to a dull ache behind his eyes, he heard her quiet return to the cottage. Luke strained his ears to guess what she was up to, unable to concentrate on anything. He gave up reading the Sunday paper and just sat gazing at the door, desperately hoping she would come through it and at least talk to him. She was evident in the muffled flushing of the loo, a sneeze, the turning on of the radio, but she remained elusive. At the welcome rallying whistle of the kettle, his hopes were raised. He closed his eyes, listening to the clink of a mug set on tiles, the familiar sound of a spoon scraping coffee out of a blue canister, the fridge opening for milk. But that was that. She did not appear with a friendly smile, holding out an olive branch in the shape of his favourite mug. So when he heard her engaged in a sweet and soppy one-sided conversation with Mango, it fairly broke his heart with envy.

Monday brought its own distractions, as did Tuesday. Luke threw himself into his teaching day, managing with difficulty to ward off thoughts of Elizabeth's cruel attack, and, just as tormenting, Alexis's thoughtless betrayal.

That Tuesday evening, after a scraped together meal of bread and cheese, Luke slipped out of the cottage with his mobile phone. He had to make a decision one way or another. He had to find out why Alexis had broken her promise. The thought of confrontation made his fingers slippery with dread. He and Alexis had never argued seriously. She was the one constant in his life. His guts turned to water at the mere thought of losing her forever, yet the thought of continuing like this for another second was beyond endurance.

He had played out that imagined conversation too many times in his head. He could hear the whispers, the shocked intake of Elizabeth's breath as Alexis bowed her blonde deceitful head towards Elizabeth's dark one. How self-important one becomes when holder of a secret. A secret which will startle and engage another person's interest. How tempting! Could Alexis have really been so shallow to have fallen for such acclaim? Was she not too intelligent to foresee that her nugget of truth, handed over to Elizabeth like a poisoned sweet, would devastate his marriage? He began to doubt his fears, his haste at assuming straight away that Alexis must have told Elizabeth.

Until it started again; the pictures in his head playing out like a piece of jerky film, and then the cold creeping conviction that Alexis was the only person in the world who knew of the dreadful amount of time that had passed between Xavier hitting his head, and their mother screaming. Time. He saw it like a length of elastic, it stretched longer each time he remembered it. Sometimes he willed it to grow shorter, but sure enough, as he grew older and further away from that suspended moment in that sunny garden, those seconds grew longer and longer as his adult brain wrestled with the logic of it. And Alexis had been the only one he had told.

He made his way along the Goat Walk, a cold, blue autumn sky mocking his state of mind with its beauty. He found a bench and sat hunched over, a biting wind nipping at his fingers, slick with sweat despite the chill, so that the phone nearly slipped out of his grasp.

He gripped the phone and swiftly found Alexis's name in his contact list.

She answered on the third ring, her voice light and cheerful, an actor's voice, he thought.

"Luke! Hi…" A pause, stretching and growing thinner, like a bubble.

Luke spoke rapidly, hoping his voice did not wobble. "Alexis. We need to talk, not on the phone though… I have a free last lesson tomorrow. Can I see you? Can I come to the flat about two thirty?"

A hesitation. Then Alexis's words were spoken clearly and cheerfully. "Oh yes. My shift doesn't start 'til five o'clock. I'll be there!"

"I'll see you then."

"Luke? Can't you tell me what this is about? You're being so weird?"

As she held the phone to her ear, she heard a beep, and then silence.

Wednesday 22nd September 2010

A horrible feeling of déjà vu struck Luke as he parked outside Elizabeth's flat the following afternoon. He stared up at the blind sunlit windows, shaking off the irrational gloom as he approached the building. He stepped out of the lift as the door opened and Cheryl stood there. His heart plummeted as the memory of her last tearful scene flashed back to him. But he need not have worried, here stood a calm and smiling Cheryl, holding the door open for him.

"Alexis won't be long, honest!" She grinned at him. "We're both on evening shift tonight, so she's grabbing something easy for our tea. Talking of tea, do you fancy a cuppa?"

Luke sighed with relief. "Yes, please, love," he replied gratefully, following her into the kitchen. He perched on a stool while she filled the kettle.

Over the noise, Cheryl asked, "Everything all right between you and Al?"

Luke hesitated, not wanting to disclose anything. "Why do you ask? Has she said anything?"

Cheryl grimaced. "No, you know your sister…discretion itself where family's concerned. Just thought she's looked a bit distracted since the weekend. I worry about her, that's all."

Luke took the mug of tea from Cheryl and thanked her, looking away out of the window.

When the pause became uncomfortable, Cheryl said brightly, "Oh, don't mind me! Tell me to mind my own beeswax! How's Elizabeth?"

Luke flashed her a look of incredulity. "Don't pretend you really want to know!" he said with bitter amusement. An expression of extreme misery passed across his face before he had the wherewithal to hide it. He looked at Cheryl, who looked back, her face a picture of concern.

"Luke?" she said uncertainly.

Luke took in her kind freckled face, her sympathetic eyes, and he felt such a hopeless feeling wash over him. After the last few days, his alienation from Alexis, and the barren waste ground of his marriage, the smallest shred of human compassion brought him to the verge of tears. "I shouldn't say anything," he muttered. "It's just that marriage can be such a bloody lonely place, you know?"

Cheryl nodded, not knowing at all, how could she? She dared not speak, not wanting to break Luke's concentration.

"I love Elizabeth with all my heart," he said, not noticing Cheryl's involuntary wince. "But it's never enough. I'm never enough! I'm clearly not the man she thought I was…and there's nothing I can do about that!" He gave a weird half laugh, which worried Cheryl further.

She was about to speak, but at that moment they both heard the sound of a key in the flat door. Luke gave a start and frowned. "Sorry, Cheryl, forget all that…I'm not in a good place at the moment."

Cheryl looked up as Alexis sauntered into the kitchen, dumping a couple of bags on the work top.

"Supper!" she announced. "Sorry to keep you waiting, Luke." She raised her eyebrows questioningly at him.

He stood up and walked to the door. "Thanks for the tea, Cheryl. Alexis? Can we go for a coffee somewhere?"

Alexis shrugged her shoulders and threw a bewildered look at her friend. She followed her brother out of the flat.

Cheryl washed up the two mugs that she and Luke had used, wondering what on earth was going on with these two people she was so fond of. He'd just had a cup of tea, and now he wanted a cup of coffee? She sighed and began to unpack the bags that Alexis had brought home. All tidy, she picked up a glossy woman's magazine that Alexis had bought, one of their favourites. She settled down in an armchair with her feet up, and was soon lost in the latest antics of a famous starlet. It was a light relief from real life, and she was so engrossed that it took her a second to realise that the bell to the flat was being rung, urgently and repeatedly.

Startled out of her reverie, she scrambled to her feet, worried and not knowing who it might be. She was concerned that it might be Alexis. She yanked open the door, ready to offer more tea and sympathy, but it was Elizabeth standing there. And from the look on her face, it was not a social visit.

"Where is he?" Elizabeth spat the words, looking over Cheryl's shoulder.

"Oh, not again!" moaned Cheryl tiredly. "You're a nutter. He's not here…"

Elizabeth moved closer, and Cheryl observed dispassionately how anger can transform a normally attractive face into something quite ugly.

She moved closer still, pushing her face into Cheryl's personal space, her spittle landing in hot specks on Cheryl's cheek. "I can see his car in the carpark! I won't ask you again, moron. Where is he?"

Chapter Nineteen
Conflicting Emotions

Wednesday 22nd September

Outraged at this breach of civilised behaviour, Cheryl glared at Elizabeth without saying a word. Let her think the worst, make a fool of herself. There was nothing to hide here.

"Well? Do you both think I'm stupid? He's here, and I want to know what's been going on!"

Cheryl studied the woman standing there. She had everything going for her, good looks, a good job, money, and a lovely man. What was the matter with her? Why was she so hell bent on destroying her happiness? A fury born of pure envy and dislike boiled up in Cheryl's chest and exploded into life, the pent-up frustration of previous dealings with this spoilt woman lending vitriol to her words.

"Yes! He was here! Your good kind husband. Have you any idea how unhappy you've made him? Torment written all over his face! He never intended to tell me anything, he wouldn't have if I hadn't given him a sympathetic ear…that's all he craves, someone to listen to him. Which clearly you never do! And it's bloody you he wants! Why can't you see it? He said you made him feel he's not good enough for you, that nothing he does is good enough. When it's you who's not good enough for him! You don't deserve him, he's worth a hundred of you! You're poison…" And then, the added uncontrollable barb. "Be very careful. He's very vulnerable, thanks to you. What did you expect? You starve a man like that of love, he fell into my arms so readily. I've loved him so long, and that's all he wanted, someone to love him…"

Cheryl felt a huge jolt of fear as Elizabeth launched herself towards her with a shriek. She tried to slam the door shut, but Elizabeth was quicker. She blocked the door with her foot and sank her talon-like fingers into Cheryl's upper arms, dragging her out through the door, towards her. With an unnatural strength, Elizabeth pulled Cheryl towards a waist-high railing which ran along the centre of the hallway. To the left of this, the stairs descended to the foyer, the railing ending just left of the lift door at the end of the hall.

With a deft movement, Elizabeth twisted Cheryl round so that she was facing the railing. Cheryl felt her arms being twisted painfully up behind her back, as she was bent forwards over the rail. Real terror took hold of her as she felt one of Elizabeth's feet hook itself round her right ankle, pulling it back. "Don't do this, Elizabeth! For God's sake! Please! Oh God!" she screamed.

The sound of Elizabeth's savage snarl of rage increased her fear. Cold sweat slicked across her palms, her face, and trickled down her sides. She managed to croak out a few words despite the complete dryness of her mouth. "Don't...Luke loves you. He told me! Nothing happened between us. I made it up!"

"Too late! I don't believe you! You should have thought a bit harder before spewing out your sordid secret!"

Cheryl felt herself losing her balance, the hard edge of the railing digging into her stomach...

Elizabeth's mouth was close to Cheryl's ear. She could feel her hot angry breath, hear the brittle grating of Elizabeth's words hurting her ear drum. "You don't know him, you stupid cow. You don't know what he's capable of. He's bad, but he's mine! He's the only thing I've got, so just back off, bitch..."

They both heard the scrape of the key in the lock, the footsteps entering the foyer, and then the lift door shut with a clang and began to descend to where it had been summoned from below.

Elizabeth stepped back, releasing Cheryl so suddenly that she stumbled, grabbing the rail wildly to prevent losing her balance.

Elizabeth pushed her face aggressively again towards Cheryl's, and whispered loudly, "Listen! If you go near Luke again, or mention this to anyone, I will kill you...don't doubt it. And I want you out of my flat, and out of my life!" With that, she ran swiftly down the stairs, reaching the bottom just as the lift finished its ascent, arriving at the end of the hall.

Cheryl moved swiftly despite her shaking limbs, legs feeling like rubber, just managing to enter the flat and close the door before the lift door opened.

Alexis let herself in to the flat in a rush, needing Cheryl's sensible advice. "Cheryl?" she called. "I'm back, are you there?"

"In the bathroom..." came the muffled response. "Won't be a minute. Stick the kettle on, Al."

"Okay. You all right? You sound funny."

"I'm absolutely fine, honestly. Just fine," Cheryl answered, in such low tones that Alexis had to strain her ears towards the bathroom door.

Luke watched Alexis disappear into the entrance door of the flat and climbed into his car. He drove out of the carpark on auto drive, his thoughts weighing on his mind, his perceptions narrowed almost to a state of tunnel vision. So it was that he did not notice Elizabeth's red MG parked just a little way up a side road, clearly visible and facing him. Nor had he been able to see Elizabeth exit the flat just moments after Alexis had entered it.

He was too busy trying to find a solution as to how Elizabeth had guessed that he had somehow played a part in Xavier's death. When he had confronted Alexis with his accusation, sitting across a cheerful red-checked tablecloth in a nearby café, she had stared at him with such offended amazement, her cup suspended in mid-air, that he knew at once that it was not she who had informed Elizabeth. He found himself spending the following ten minutes calming her down and apologising for ever having doubted her. It was a huge relief on one hand, but on the other he was still floundering as to how Elizabeth knew. They parted on good terms, despite a spate of fresh tears as she kissed him, hugging him tightly.

Now, Elizabeth, shakily making her way to her car, was uttering hate-filled garbled sentences as she walked. Passers-by watched her warily. She climbed into the driving seat, gripped the steering wheel hard and leaned her sweating forehead on the leather rim.

Her worst nightmare had come to pass; Luke had been unfaithful to her…and with that dull, shapeless Cheryl! All her life this had been happening to her…all she'd ever wanted was to be loved, to have a normal loving family like other children, and then to marry and have her own babies. Why her, for God's sake? Why was every hope of happiness always snatched out of her grasp? Elizabeth began a low moaning monologue, words interspersed with whimpering sighs.

"Right from the start," she muttered bleakly. "Being given up by my own mother at birth! What a bloody start that was. And then, at two years old I got the foster parents from hell! Pretending to love me, and I believed them, didn't I? Stupid! Told me how sweet I was, and then going mad when I did just normal naughty things. They should never have been allowed to foster, let alone adopt another child! That was me put in my place…they loved Christopher right from the minute they brought him home! Stupid skinny kid, always crying…and they expected me to love him too! Said I was to look after him, when they should have been looking after me! I was only six for fuck's sake! I hated him! I never meant to hurt him…so how could they do that to me, send me back to the orphanage…

didn't they realise how it would affect me, being rejected again? I wish they had died in a car crash like I told Luke..."

A loud rapping on her window made Elizabeth open her eyes in fright, and her sobbing words petered away as she looked up to see the face of a man staring in. She reluctantly rolled down her window.

The traffic warden bent down to stare in at her, a concerned expression on his face. "You all right, miss? Need help?"

Elizabeth looked at him with wild eyes. "What?" she mumbled, looking confused. "What have I done?"

The man frowned. "Nothing, you're okay, are you? Fit to drive?"

Elizabeth closed up the window, shutting his silly worried face out. She started up the engine with a roar and drove away from the kerb. She waited for a gap in the traffic, and then turned right, nosing the MG in the direction Luke had taken. The traffic warden stared after her, scratching his head.

Elizabeth was oblivious of the dusty five-mile drive to Exsham. The still warm sun bobbed between the trees which lined the long straight road, throwing elongated shadows, bars of dark and light flickering across the windscreen.

Her head was crammed with darting thoughts and conflicting emotions; she hated Luke, yet loved him at the same time. She wanted to punish him, push him back to dreary Cheryl, it was all he deserved. And yet, he was her husband, her family, the only one she may ever have. Hot on the heels of this came the realisation that Luke was now imperfect in her eyes, he had shattered her dream by his declaration that he was unlikely to ever be able to give her a child...now the revelation of his murky past, some violence towards his brother that had ended in his death! God! How horrible! And now this...his breaking of his marriage vows! Tears of self-pity and bitterness rolled down her face.

Elizabeth shook her head as if to clear it. She turned down Exsham high street, driving slowly so as to gather her wits. She parked and, looking in the rear mirror, dabbed a wet wipe across her face, mopping mascara and tears away.

She must act carefully; what choice did she have, to be alone again? Or to hold on to this damaged marriage, which was all she had to call her own after all, and try to salvage something from it? It was her damned marriage after all, no one else's. She wasn't about to let him go that easily. She bit her lower lip hard, tasting blood.

She parked behind Luke's Ford Fiesta. Breathing deeply, she entered the cottage. She was feeling cool, collected and calmly in control. She could do this...

Luke sat on the edge of the double bed, flipping off his sensible lace-up school shoes. They fell with heavy thuds, one after the other. He felt a bit better already. He exchanged his trousers for jeans, pulled on a dark-green faded t-shirt and stood up. He glanced in the mirror and realised with a small shock how much weight he appeared to have lost over the last few days. His jeans were slipping down his hips. He pulled them up and sighed, looking towards the doorway at the sound of footsteps on the landing.

Elizabeth appeared, looking flushed, her hair in all directions, as if she'd been tearing her fingers through it. She smiled at him and his heart jumped. It was as if he were seeing her all over again, right from the start. She approached him slowly. He looked down, taking her in by degrees, from the chunky ankle boots to the smart chocolate-coloured cut-off trousers and topped with a soft, cream short sleeved jumper. She threw her tan jacket onto a nearby chair.

"Wow! You're back early. Everything all right?"

A wave of relief washed across Luke. "Fine, yeah. Forgot to mention I had a free last lesson…"

Elizabeth moved closer still. She looked up at him with a half-smile on her lips. "Well, we haven't really mentioned much since Saturday, have we?" she said softly.

Luke bent his head to place a kiss on her forehead. She raised her eyebrows comically.

"Oh, I see! I've turned into your sister now have I?" she teased. Before he could answer, she reached up on tiptoe, put her arms round his neck and pulled him down for a proper kiss. Luke felt his whole body tingling at the feel of her lips… A tight cord stretched, tugged gently from his lips down through his chest to attach itself firmly to his solar plexus. The sheer lovely lust of it wiped his brain clean. He walked her backwards, still mouth to mouth, back towards the bed.

Half an hour later they began to hear the sound of the sea through the open window. They slowly became aware of the bright day still outside, the birdsong, children shouting from the harbour.

"How long has it been?" Luke asked wonderingly into her hair. "It feels like a year."

"Silly! Two weeks?" Elizabeth curled up against his chest. "I can't even remember what we were cross about." She yawned.

"Neither can I," agreed Luke comfortably. "Something, I'd done I expect."

They looked at each other and laughed. Elizabeth rolled over and sat up.

"I'm going to shower first, okay?"

"Okay, but seriously…how did you find out? I need to know."

Elizabeth turned and stared at him. "Find out what, Luke?" she asked.

Luke frowned. "You know what…don't make me say it. I'm ashamed enough as it is. Who told you, really?"

"Take a guess, Luke!" Elizabeth spoke more sharply than she meant to. "There's only one person who knows what you've been up to, after all!"

Luke looked horrified. "I saw her today… She promised me that she would never say anything to anyone! I trust her, Elizabeth. Why would she tell you? Why tell you something that might damage our relationship? I don't believe you!"

Elizabeth stared at Luke as if he had taken leave of his senses. "I can't believe this. She couldn't wait to tell me! She wants to take you away from me! It's obvious. She wanted me to know the gory details, to know what you're really like. Why the hell would you trust her?"

Luke sank back into his pillows, looking completely bewildered. "Why would she want to take me away from you? I don't get it. She loves you like a sister!"

Elizabeth's laughter had a manic ring to it. Luke's concern grew. He wondered whether she was quite sane. "Well, if she loves me like a sister, she's got a funny way of showing it. If I had a sister I wouldn't expect her to seduce my husband…"

"You're surely not talking about Alexis…"

"Alexis? Of course I'm not!" she snapped. "Unless you slept with her too! I'm talking about Cheryl, you weirdo!"

They looked at each other in stunned silence. "Well? How could you, Luke?"

Luke opened his mouth.

"I wouldn't bother saying anything actually, because whatever you say, I won't believe a word."

Luke eyed her with narrowed eyes, and he could feel anger building up in his chest. "What is the matter with you? We've been over and over this. Read my lips…I have not slept with Cheryl. Why won't you believe me?"

Elizabeth rolled her eyes in exasperation. "I've just told you! She admitted that you went round there this afternoon, that you had sex…"

Luke gave a hollow laugh. "This is doing my head in! Firstly, Cheryl lives in her own fantasy land…and secondly I thought we were talking about Alexis!"

Elizabeth looked puzzled. "Alexis? Why? You asked me how I'd found out. What else did you mean?"

"Shit, Elizabeth! You know! You said you knew I'd caused Xavier's death…and you hinted that it was Alexis who told you! That's why I went to the flat, to find out why she told you." He stared at her coldly. "And I now know that she did not tell you. She hasn't got a disloyal bone in her body. I was a fool to believe you."

Elizabeth flashed her eyes. She rose up from the bed and stood up, looking back at Luke. "I never mentioned Alexis, actually. You assumed it was her, you doubted her all by yourself. You want to know how I found out about your sickening secret?"

Luke said nothing, he waited, appalled by his wife's ability to cause pain.

"I read about it, in your own guilty words. I've been checking your emails ever since Alexis told me that Cheryl has a 'thing' for you. I was sure that something was going on. But I found an email to Alexis instead, all about you watching your brother's life blood leaving his body, that it was all your fault."

Luke watched as Elizabeth disappeared into the bathroom, shutting the door firmly behind her with a conclusive click.

Chapter Twenty
She Lay Still and Listened to the Silence in Terror

Wednesday 22nd September 2010
Same Day
Exmouth

Alexis stared worriedly at the closed bathroom door. Its blank closed appearance was as ominous as a dead face. She moved swiftly to the kitchen area, a frown clouding her usual bright expression. She switched on the kettle and made as much noise as possible with the cups and saucers without actually breaking them. With the water boiling at full volume, she crept back to the bathroom door and listened intently. She heard a couple of gasping sobs, and then the unmistakeable sound of her friend being violently sick, followed by the flush of running water. Alarm and concern riveted Alexis to the spot. She stepped back as the door suddenly opened. Cheryl stood there, her face chalk white and shaking visibly. Without a word, Alexis pulled Cheryl into a hug before steering her towards the kitchen. With anguish, Cheryl could not help being reminded of being steered so recently towards that banister rail, by someone who had the complete opposite of her well-being in mind.

It was only when Alexis had sat Cheryl down and placed a comforting cup of tea in her hands, that she asked gently, "What is it, love? You look dreadful."

"Thanks!" Cheryl attempted a watery smile without much success. "Don't worry, Al." She managed finally. "It's just my time of the month. I don't often get it this badly. It's really painful."

Alexis studied Cheryl's face. From her pale skin and beads of sweat on her upper lip, she could empathise with how her friend was feeling. "You've been sick?" she asked.

"Yes, gross. It used to affect me this way when I was younger. I thought I'd outgrown it."

Alexis stood up, efficiency galvanising her into action. "Right, drink up that tea. I know you don't take sugar, but I've put two spoonsful in. You need it, and then get yourself to bed. It's okay," she added when she saw Cheryl's reluctant expression. "I'll ring the hospital and explain that you won't be able to work this evening. You on earlies tomorrow?"

"No. I've got the afternoon shift." She grimaced, pretending a pain she didn't feel, but not finding it difficult, as she was still pale and trembling from shock.

Five minutes later, Cheryl was sitting up obediently in her bed in her sensible grey pyjamas with pink buttons down the front. Alexis came in with a glass of water, two painkillers in an eggcup and a hot water bottle tucked under her arm.

"Take these," she ordered. "And this is for your stomach." She slipped the hot water bottle under the duvet. "And now try to sleep through the worst of it."

"Yes, nurse," Cheryl acquiesced, closing her eyes.

She opened them again briefly as Alexis positioned a bowl next to the bed. "Just in case…" she said kindly. She walked towards the door, but looked back as Cheryl called her name.

"Thank you, Alexis…you're a good friend. Um…I have something to tell you." She looked so miserable that Alexis came closer, intrigued. Cheryl looked troubled as she said, "I don't want to, but I've decided to move out of the flat. No, listen…" She held her hand up as Alexis opened her mouth in dismay. "I've thought about it for a while. I know Elizabeth's not charging us as much as she could, but even so, I've been finding it a bit of a struggle. I'm afraid I can't really afford it. I'm going to look into moving into a bed-sit I think."

"Does Elizabeth know?"

"Oh yes." Cheryl found the lump in her throat made it impossible to say anything else for the moment.

Alexis looked puzzled. "But surely, Cheryl, ninety pounds a week is pretty good? I don't think you'll find a better deal? Elizabeth's been very generous really."

Cheryl gulped, astounded that the 'mate's rate' she'd been offered was twenty pounds more than the amount Alexis was paying. She did not dare to divulge this information, fearing Alexis would think her foolish not to have checked the going rate, and worried that she might confront Elizabeth about it. She felt wretched and humiliated enough as it was. Cheryl put her hands over her stomach and groaned.

"Look, I'll leave you in peace. I'm gutted, though." Alexis looked at Cheryl sadly. Cheryl swallowed hard, her eyes bright with tears. Alexis moved towards her, but Cheryl closed her eyes to avoid further awkward questions, and Alexis quietly left the room.

Five minutes later, Alexis sent a message on her mobile. She waited for a reply, and then quickly threw on her jacket. She put her head round Cheryl's door, and reassured by the sound of her steady breathing, she let herself quietly out of the flat. Cheryl heard the faint clunk of the front door closing. She sat up in agitation as she realised that she was alone in the flat. The quicker she could arrange to leave this place, the safer she would be, she thought. She lay still, replaying the events of earlier in her mind and listened to the silence in terror.

It only took Alexis a few minutes to hurry through a narrow alleyway which was situated in a break between two rows of Victorian-terraced houses. She reached a wide tree-lined road, broad sweeping drives leading to large comfortable houses, recognizable as having been built in the nineteen fifties by their gables and rounded bay windows.

She crossed the road, and turned down a smaller side road. It was bordered by small identical bungalows, some with wheelchair ramps with handrails leading to the front doors. Alexis reached the end of this cul-de-sac, nipped around a wooden half gate, down another path, and at last she was in the park. She looked quickly towards a bench nestling beneath an oak tree with a view down a grassy slope, and was relieved to spot the lanky form already lounging there. He'd slung his jacket over his shoulder, and stretched his tanned arms along the back of the bench. The air was still warm, and Alexis's heart beat faster as she approached him, admiring his dark good looks, contrasting against his crisp white short-sleeved shirt. He glanced at his watch, running a hand through his thick brown hair. He looked up and a big grin spread over his face at the sight of her.

"Rob! Thanks for coming. How long have you got?"

Rob unfolded his long legs and stood up. He put his arms around Alexis and kissed her lightly on the lips. "About ten minutes." He smiled. "To be honest, I'm glad of some fresh air after my last session…and I'm seeing my next client in the hospital, so I think we can make that fifteen minutes."

Alexis and Rob had met at the hospital where he frequently worked, offering counselling to teenagers who had been hospitalised for such things as depression, anorexia, etc. They would meet here at their special bench for a quick chat whenever their work allowed.

Rob patted the warm seat next to him. "Come here…everything all right, love? How did your chat with Luke go?"

Alexis rolled her eyes at him. She plonked herself down and he took hold of her hand. "Oh that was okay, just a misunderstanding. No, I'm probably being silly…it's Cheryl I'm worried about. When I got back from seeing Luke, she was in a right state. I heard her being sick, and she was all pale and shaky."

Rob looked concerned. "Oh, poor girl!"

Alexis stared at their joined hands. Due to Rob's work, she knew that he was sensitive to young people's problems, and felt comfortable in confiding in him. "She said it was her period, normal enough, I feel that ropey sometimes, but Rob, I know for a fact that she had her last period two weeks ago!"

"How do you know?" Rob looked surprised.

Alexis laughed. "When two women share a bathroom, you know things like that, believe me. I was on mine as well, I remember reading once that when women live together they often begin to menstruate at the same time, so I definitely remember the date."

"Well! You learn something new every day!" Rob chortled. "But why would she lie about it? You don't think she's pregnant, do you?"

Alexis frowned, looking worried. Then she sighed. "No, she wouldn't know that quickly, that would be impossible. So I don't know why she would lie. She also dropped the bombshell that she's planning on moving out!"

"What! Why? I thought you were a great team there together?"

"So did I," she said glumly. "Apparently, she's finding the rent hard to find…which I find difficult to believe. She's earning the same as I am, and with the reduced amount Elizabeth's asking for, she shouldn't be finding it hard. We don't have time to spend much money with our anti-social shifts!"

Rob put his arm round Alexis. "Sounds like something's going on with her. But if she won't tell you, I don't see how you can help her."

They stood up as Rob took another look at his watch.

"Thanks for listening, love. It helps just to share things sometimes."

"Even though I was no help whatsoever!" He bent to kiss her again. "Bye sweetheart. I'll see you Friday night and maybe you'll have more idea of what's going on."

Thursday 23rd September 2010
Cornwall

Céline balanced her trug on a grassy hillock, eyeing a large sheep which had trundled alarmingly close to her in its mindless quest for the juiciest mouthful of greenery. It raised its head at her squeak of alarm and flapping hands, looked at her and skittered away to join its woolly friends.

With a sigh of relief, Céline turned to the task of picking as many blackberries as she could, or enough to add to the apples she had bought that morning, with the purpose of making a perfect 'crumble-top'. This was one of Thomas's favourite desserts, especially served with his beloved clotted cream. The children had always laughed at her, correcting her when she made a mispronunciation. She knew that the pudding was just called 'crumble' in English, but she preferred her version. She had been delighted with the golden-topped delicacy which Thomas's mother had served her in those early days of marriage, and was eager to learn and attempt all sorts of old-fashioned English recipes.

Also that morning, driving early to the local supermarket, she had bought two entrecote steaks, double cream and brandy. She was planning to cook Thomas 'Steak au Poivre', served with a simple green salad and her own homemade croquette potatoes. She did ask herself whether this pandering to Thomas's stomach was going to make any difference to his rather tortoise-like demeanour of late. Since the previous Saturday to be exact. He was not exactly unfriendly towards her, just distracted, and not aware of her presence. He'd often been like this over the years, and she knew something was troubling him, but she was fed up trying to catch the attention of her husband who clearly had his head so far retracted inside his own shell that he had stopped seeming to hear or see her at all.

She felt a tug as a blackberry bramble attached itself to her thick-knit oatmeal-coloured cardigan. "Zut, alors!" she swore mildly, pulling the thorn out of the wool carefully, and managing to embed it into her finger. "Merde!" she said, shocking herself. She looked at the black shining heap of berries in the shallow basket and decided she had suffered enough in the name of pandering to Thomas's whims. He'd better snap out of his shell soon or she might have to resort by dancing naked on the dining-room table.

"You are spoiling me tonight! If we hadn't celebrated our wedding anniversary a couple of weeks ago, I'd be wondering whether I'd missed something important."

Céline smiled smugly at him as she poured him more coffee and another glass of brandy. She had already added a couple of slugs of it to the cream sauce for the steak, not to mention the rich Bordeaux Red they had shared with the meal. "I don't need an excuse to spoil you…but I think that in return it might be kind of you to share the black dog that has been sitting on your shoulder recently. Fair deal?"

Thomas smiled at her, his mood sweet and mellow tonight, just as his wife had planned. "You are a devious person," he mused, cradling his brandy balloon. "And your command of the English language is coming along in leaps and bounds, so I suppose you need an apology from me…"

"Non, just talk to me please, and tell me what is in your head," she demanded.

Thomas sighed and pushed his chair back from the table. "Very well…but I'm afraid I don't come over very well myself. I have been guilty of eavesdropping." He looked at her with a comical contrite expression.

"Oh blink! I don't know that word Thomas. Eaves? I can't even guess what it means…is it very bad?"

"Well, it means listening to a conversation between other people that isn't intended for you. It was last Saturday when Luke and Elizabeth were at the top of Hay Tor. They were arguing and I was sort of stuck behind a rock… I never intended to listen."

"And?" urged Céline impatiently.

Thomas studied her face, not wanting to ruin the atmosphere. "It's not good, sweetheart. Apparently, Luke has a low sperm count, and although that isn't going to rule him out as a father completely, it might take them longer than usual."

Céline gasped and covered her face with her hands. She groaned, and Thomas knew that this news had really struck a nerve with her. "This is incroyable! The poor things…and I was so hoping for good news! A new little baby would have been so lovely!"

"I'm so sorry to tell you this, Céline. I was dismayed myself. But the worst of it was Elizabeth's attitude to Luke. She really laid into him as if he was doing it on purpose! He's obviously gutted about it, but she was offering him no support at all! I've never liked her, Céline, you know that, but now I am really worried about Luke. It seems he is trapped in a marriage with someone who is dangerously unpleasant."

Céline stood up suddenly and folded her arms. She glowered at Thomas so furiously that he stared at her in apprehension. "I know you have never liked her! You have made it very evident to us all, including to her. Poor girl! All she wants is a family, you know that, and you have refused to let her belong. You have pushed her away, Thomas!"

Thomas clenched his fists, his features hardened visibly as he made a huge effort not to lose his temper. "Céline, sit down and listen to me," he ordered. She flashed rebellious eyes at him, but sank back into her chair. "You, Céline, are a woman. Don't roll your eyes like that. I'm being serious. And as a woman, you see things through rose-tinted spectacles. Oh, not literally! It means you see the good side in everyone…"

"And you, mon chéri, are the other side of this money!"

"Coin," he corrected solemnly.

Céline tutted before continuing. "I know you too well. You frown that frown, looking for meanings behind words, distrusting people's reasonings… I can't find the words, but I think that if my glasses are pink, then yours are black! Look at your reaction to Alexis's news of this Rob…doubt and fear that no one is good enough for your princess."

Thomas sighed, resigned to the fact that reasoning with Céline was like wading through treacle. "All I know, is that Elizabeth is an unhappy, immature woman. We know nothing about her background, her parentage. She is like a needy child one minute and a trapped wasp the next. I think she has manipulated her way into Luke's affections, hoping to belong at last and to create the family she feels she never had. But as soon as there is a problem, instead of being a supporting mature wife, she lashes out, keen to hurt the person who has disappointed her. My loyalties lie with Luke, not with her. As should yours, Céline."

Céline gazed at him mournfully. "Well. All I know is that the urge to have a baby is like a physical pain inside. Men don't have it, so they will never understand. I feel sorry for her. She is hurting, and as a part of this family, she needs our love and support."

"And are you sure she loves Luke? Because I sure as hell don't!"

Thomas sat on at the table, staring gloomily into his brandy glass. Céline, suddenly feeling exhausted, got up and began to wearily clear the table.

Chapter Twenty-One

"Not Being Able to Kiss It Better"

Saturday 25th September 2010
Cornwall

"No, Céline! You can't ring him! I forbid you!"

"Forbid!" Céline shrieked. "What is this word, forbid?"

Patiently, Thomas replied, "It means…"

"Mon Dieu…I know what it means! It was la rhétorique, I don't know the English word…"

Thomas grunted his mounting irritation. "Yes, rhetorical, same word. I still forbid you."

Céline's eyes blazed with exasperation. "Thomas! I am not your child that you can forbid! I am your wife! Luke needs to know we are here to help him. Him and Elizabeth…she has no one else to turn to."

Thomas stepped firmly between his wife and the telephone. It was on a low window seat, the perfect place to snuggle up for a chat, but this was not the time. He gently took her hands in his and looked into her face. "Céline, calm down and think. I've just told you this worrying news, but I overheard it. They would be mortified to know that I was listening to their argument! How can we offer support if we are not supposed to know they have a problem?"

Céline thought for a while and then she said, "Oui, I understand that. I am not stupid…d'accord, then just let me ring to say hello. Just a normal little mother-to-son 'how are you' call."

She pressed his hands gently and he was drawn irresistibly to gaze into her dark eyes, still so mesmerising. Her hair, now threaded with silver, gave away the marching of the years, but her huge sooty-lashed eyes had not changed, and as always, Thomas found himself rendered speechless by their liquid beauty. He nodded at her, but could not help warning, "Don't get excited, though, Céline. Just keep it short and don't sound panicky. You would never have made it to the stage, you know."

Ignoring this insult, she plucked up the phone and dialled Luke's number, turning her back on Thomas so that she would not be maddened by his mobile eyebrows conveying disapproval or concern at her conversation.

"Hello?"

"Luke! It's me! How are things?"

There was a hesitation before Luke hedged an evasive, "Erm, I'm fine, Mum…what's up?"

"Why must there be something 'up'?" Céline said with a laugh.

"Oh…no reason. You're okay?"

"Luke! I'm fine! Dad's fine! Can't I just ring for a chat?"

Thomas walked round to face Céline and raised his eyebrows warningly. She pursed her lips at him crossly.

"Of course, sorry. It's just that you've caught us at a bad time, we're on our way out…" said Luke, lying through his teeth. Elizabeth had driven off somewhere on her own some time ago. Mango yawned widely, showing tiny top teeth gleaming sharply against the pink roof of her mouth. She glared at him accusingly. He put his tongue out at her.

"Okay, darling, I won't hold you. We just want you to know that you are both welcome to come for the weekend, any time…that last visit was a bit short…just one of those things…" her voice petered out as Thomas frowned, his face looming at her.

"Okay, Mum, thanks…"

"Luke! Are you sure you're…?"

"Got to go, Elizabeth's waiting. Bye Mum…"

Céline replaced the receiver, looking crestfallen. Thomas put his arms around her carefully, as if she might break. She rested her face gently against his chest while he patted her back. "It hurts," she mumbled into his jumper.

"What does sweetheart?"

"Not being able to kiss it better."

Luke stared at the silent phone and felt a yearning to rewind time and begin the conversation over again. He felt cold and shivered. He remembered that devastatingly lonely feeling of being seven years old and in desperate need of his mother's arms round him. He felt like that now, and the realisation of it made him shudder with a mixture of self-disgust and grief.

The realisation that as an adult he had to remain in control and true to himself, filled him with a feeling of dread. He had never felt so alone. Like a homeless man, he had no substance or fundamental starting point.

Elizabeth had now retracted any form of affection, which made living with her horrendous. It was like one of those dreams, where he could see her in the distance, but his legs refused to co-operate, so that he was unable to approach her. He felt tortured, yet at the same time apathetically accepting of her withdrawal.

It was impossible to turn to his parents. He had escaped them once already, his father's censure, his mother's stifling protection, and his pride would not let him regress.

And as for Alexis, she was his little sister, albeit with more stability it seemed than himself, but how could he explain to her about his unhappiness? She adored Elizabeth and would not be a willing ear to his doubts about her and the state of his marriage.

He just had to carry on, minute by minute, day by day, until things took a turn for the better. The rest of the weekend yawned ahead of him. It was fruitless to try hastening time, an impossible task and pointless anyway, as it would only hurry him on to another dreaded Monday morning. With a groan, he held his head in his hands, unable to think further than his next heartbeat, his next breath. Even the complexity of staying alive seemed an intolerably unreasonable task.

Monday 27th September 2010

There was an atmosphere of unease as the children sat in the school hall. A wind rose halfway through the usual mind-numbing assembly, stirring the air and shifting concentration. The children stared unheeding as Mr Jones, head of year eight, droned on to them about the coming week. A window banged somewhere and the branches of a nearby tree scraped across a window pane in disharmony, rendering the teacher's words momentarily inaudible. Distraction snatched the pupil's eyes to the window, to the door where a late comer sidled in hesitantly, letting the door bang behind him, and back to the window where a flurry of raindrops was pitched violently against the pane.

Mr Jones, who was about to commence his ninth September at this school, was well aware of the effect that wind has on animals and adolescent children, troubling and unsettling them. He wrapped up his spiel and signalled to Miss Jackson, who sprang to the piano to play the opening bars of the tune which accompanied the children as they single filed to their various first lesson of the day.

Luke was waiting impatiently for his class of twelve-year-olds to simmer down as they milled aimlessly around his classroom. They were unusually noisy this morning, the boys pushing and shoving, showing off to the handful of girls whispering to each other, smirking secrets, their eyes half concealed by long hair, seeking out the boys' approval. Irritated, Luke brought a board-rubber down hard on his desk, creating a wallop that silenced the insidious sounds of possible mutiny.

"Right!" Luke said coldly. "Calm down, and sit down... Before we retrieve your works of art out of your woodwork boxes, I want you to copy down some important points from the whiteboard into your books." Luke hated the sound of his voice. He wanted to appear friendly to these kids whom he'd taught for a year already and had become fond of...of some of them at least. But the careful bonhomie he had cultivated by the finish of the summer term had vanished into a mistrustful atmosphere of snide glances and cruel taunts uttered from lips obscured by spread hands. There was one particular boy, by the name of Desmond Smith. He had a short span of attention, resulting in silly behaviour and an infuriating ability to disrupt the class. Luke stared at him now, the red hair gelled into an unlikely quiff above his freckled grinning face. 'He looks like a zoo exhibit,' he thought uncharitably.

"Desmond!" Luke bawled across the restless crowd of children. "Make yourself useful and pass out these pencils to whoever needs one." 'Give the boy a job, make him feel useful...' thought Luke, trying to engender some sort of enthusiasm for the day ahead, when in reality he just wanted to go home and climb into his bed.

Desmond approached Luke's desk, prancing along the length of the work tables in an effeminate parody, hands on hips and throwing his head back. This inevitably produced snorts of laughter from left and right of him as he advanced, and a grimace of fury from Luke. He pushed a box of sharpened pencils towards Desmond, his eyes sending out daggers of warning, which landed unheeded on the waste ground of Desmond's powers of observation.

This became painfully apparent as Desmond skipped from table to table, offering the open box for scrutiny, like a wine-waiter showing an outstanding vintage of wine to diners at a top-notch restaurant. The girls snickered, and couple of boys grabbed at the pencils. Desmond, his short-lived claim to fame thwarted, tried to reinstate the girls' interest by using a fistful of dangerously sharpened writing implements as darts, aiming them at random children. This, added to the squealing and ducking of boys and girls alike, drove Luke into a deadly fury, and a red mist descended upon him robbing him of rational thought.

The unfortunate Desmond, oblivious of his peril, was returning up the aisle, another missile in hand, as he capered dangerously close to Luke who stood glaring, white-faced. "Shut up! Shut up all of you!" Luke roared, as the gabble and screech of indifferent voices rose in a tide to drown him out.

Luke felt his vision shift as a wave of rage swept through him, all sound suddenly receding into the distance.

Desmond's arm was surprisingly soft when Luke gripped it. He began to pull the child towards the door, but he was unready for the strength of the small fingers which enclosed like a vice onto the edge of Luke's heavy desk. Luke pulled with an adrenaline-enhanced strength, the fingers loosened, and the boy was flung, gasping through the air until the side of his head connected with the door frame.

One sensible girl had the presence of mind to seek help. Adults came running. They found a sea of white faces, all silenced now, just the odd whimper. An ambulance was called to attend to the boy slumped unmoving in the door-way, blood trickling from his temple, a livid purple bruise forming with alarming speed.

And then they noticed the middle-aged man, sitting curled up in a foetal position beneath his desk, arms around his head, shaking, his eyes tight shut.

Chapter Twenty-Two

"Now Then Sir, Let's Start at the Beginning, Shall We?"

Monday 27th September
The Same Morning

Elizabeth was called away from her classroom during her first lesson of the day. She knocked on the headmistress's door, her mind blank with fear. What was so important that she had been summoned to Ms Carter's inner sanctuary? Plenty of possibilities crowded at the peripheries of her mind, and outraged, she shuffled them away unexamined.

"Come!" came the order from within.

'Stuffy cow,' thought Elizabeth, hating the prim headmistress more than usual due to the probability that she might be harbouring bad news. She inched the door open, reluctant to invite the next few seconds to tick on. But there the woman sat, her lined face impassive as usual, making it impossible to guess her thoughts.

Ms Carter motioned the younger woman to the chair opposite her desk, but Elizabeth remained standing. "What is it, Ms Carter?" she asked abruptly, wondering frantically whether any of the children had said anything to their parents about her shouting the other day. She was only human, after all. Or, God forbid, that gobby child, Chelsea, had complained about Elizabeth squeezing her arm a bit hard to get her to sit down.

Ms Carter looked at Elizabeth over her spectacles. "It's your husband, Elizabeth. He's not quite himself."

Elizabeth almost laughed with relief. She felt like saying, 'who is he then?' but managed to bite her lip. "Oh, is he unwell?" she asked tentatively, unsure of what she was going to be told.

The headmistress scrutinised Elizabeth through narrowed eyes. "You might say that," she hedged. "Have you noticed any unusual behaviour recently?"

Elizabeth felt a flare of anger. How dare the patronising old bag quiz her like this? "We are talking about my husband, aren't we? You make him sound like a small child, or a pet dog. Just tell me what you've been told and I'll deal with it…" she snapped.

Ms Carter paused, her expression registering a possible unpleasant smell in her vicinity, before saying with obvious distaste, "It appears that he has been involved in some sort of incident, which has culminated in an unfortunate injury to a child in his class. Apparently, the paramedics are in attendance as we speak…"

Elizabeth gazed at Ms Carter, her mouth open. "And it's taken you ten minutes to tell me this? You're loving it, aren't you? This has nothing to do with you! Who had the nerve to divulge this information? Luke doesn't work here. All you had to do was to tell me to go to his school… It will take me the best part of half an hour to get there as it is…"

Elizabeth yanked the door open furiously, darted a venomous look at the startled headmistress, whose lips had all but disappeared into a thin line of shocked disapproval.

Without waiting for the words of permission reluctantly being formed in the older woman's mind, Elizabeth had flounced out, slamming the door behind her with no concern for the possible impact of her loss of control on her future.

Having at least made sure that someone had been appointed to take her class for the day, explaining that there was a family emergency, and that she may not be able to return to school until tomorrow, Elizabeth was soon heading on auto pilot towards Exeter in her MG. She began to regret her insolent words to the headmistress, not because she might have caused offense, but because she feared this last breach of etiquette might be used as a tool to lever her out of her job. She had skated on thin ice too many times recently, finding it harder and harder to remain unruffled when challenged on her sometimes chaotic performance in the classroom.

She tapped her fingers on the steering wheel, musing on these thoughts. With a sudden flinch of reality, she swerved slightly and braked to bring her speed down. Luke! What did they mean when they said he'd been involved in some sort of incident? She realised she hadn't properly taken it in…it must be the shock. And a child injured! Oh God! Was it Luke who was in danger of losing his job…or both of them? She drove the next two miles without noticing where she was, and she couldn't think in straight lines.

The wind had not abated, if anything it had become quite violent, swaying tree branches across the side windows, rustling half-turned leaves and skittering them across the road. Litter had blown and bunched against fences, like confetti in a graveyard. She slowed down as a school bus pulled laboriously away from the kerb, crawling in front of her and picking up speed sluggishly. She stared rudely at the small school-children's faces at the back window of the bus. They pulled their mouths into grotesque shapes with their fingers, laughing at her. The bus ground on, battling the branches of taller trees, which creaked and squeaked as they hit the roof.

Finally, she was driving into Exeter, negotiating the familiar streets. She turned into a wide, leafy road situated in the pretty suburbs before reaching the city centre. She followed the grey wall of old stone which marked the boundaries of the school on her right. It curved away, leading her to the open black gates through which she drove. She found herself wending her way between vast green swathes of grassy lawns for quite a way before nearing the school itself. The lawns morphed into a huge sports field, where several tiny figures in blue shorts and white tops were careering around. She realised that she had seldom visited Luke's work place. Their schools being ten miles apart, the opportunity had not arisen. The school building was a huge rambling collection of squares and oblongs of orange brick. The windows, door arches and many floor levels were delineated with cream bricks. Elizabeth was put in mind of a huge gingerbread house, the details piped on with whipped cream.

The carpark was virtually empty at this time of the day, apart from the cars belonging to staff which were in a separate section. She spied Luke's car there as she parked in the visitor's bay. She felt a further jolt in her stomach as she saw an ambulance and police car stopped nearby. It was as if her brain was refusing to concentrate on the reason she was here. She kept remembering it again, like a slap in the face. It was like a 'groundhog day' moment, looping back to the beginning and being told the shocking news once more.

Elizabeth walked across the tarmac towards a modern glass-fronted building which looked out of place. She blinked as the sunshine was reflected in the glass panes and thrown spitefully into her eyes. She neared the door marked 'entrance' and was let into the building by a secretary who had seen her approach. She made a few reassuring noises as she led Elizabeth down a corridor. Elizabeth made no reply. There was a strange hush apparent, she noticed ominously, but it could have been that the children were all attending lessons.

Suddenly, the secretary turned to Elizabeth saying, "In here, Mrs Johnson, will you be all right?"

Elizabeth stared at the other woman uncomprehendingly, but before she could form a reply, she had turned on her heel and walked away. Elizabeth pushed the door in front of her, pondering on whether to knock or not. She noticed the printed placard stating that this was the deputy head's room as she entered. The young woman behind the desk was concentrating on looking through various teacher's timetables, but she put them down and smiled as Elizabeth came in. She stood up, proffered her hand and shook Elizabeth's firmly. "Mrs Johnson? I've been expecting you…I am Susan Lewis…deputy head. Do sit down."

Elizabeth sat. "I'd like to see Luke, my husband, please," she stated stiffly.

Susan studied the elfin features of the girl sitting before her. She did not look old enough to have to cope with this troubling situation. A wave of sympathy washed over as she explained, "Luke seems to have been overcome this morning during his first lesson. We hadn't realised, but the children say that he has been acting erratically recently, not his usual cheerful self. Something seems to have triggered a loss of control, the boy in question has received a…um…an injury to his head."

"Can I see him? He'll be able to explain it to me, I'm sure. Where is Mr Collins? Shouldn't he be here?"

Susan was slightly taken aback by the seeming lack of comprehension displayed by Elizabeth Johnson. She felt dismissed and had to rally her nerve not to show irritation. She hesitated before speaking slowly and clearly, as if to a child, "I'm not sure you realise how serious this is. Luke is with Mr Collins, the headmaster at the moment. There are also two police officers present. I'm sure you can appreciate that at the moment, Luke could be removed to the police station for questioning…"

"What? That's ridiculous! Luke was probably driven to the ends of his patience by some exasperating child making his life impossible. I know what it's like! He's been a great teacher for what? Four years? And one misguided error, and he's going to be carted off to the nick?" Elizabeth was standing up, glowering with rage, hands on her hips.

Susan was eyeing her with alarm, but she kept her cool as she retaliated with the words, "Please calm down, Mrs Johnson. This isn't helping. The child's father is here too. He has every right to bring a charge against your husband."

"How is the boy?" Elizabeth asked, wonderingly. It was a question Susan felt should have been asked before this.

"The paramedics are with him in the medical room. They will check him over carefully before deciding whether to take him to hospital for the appropriate care. We will have to wait for that to happen before we know. "

"Did Luke hit him?" Elizabeth whispered.

Susan's expression was sombre. "We don't really know what happened. The other children who were present will have to be questioned…"

There was a tap on the door and Mr Collins's head appeared round it. He gave a curt nod to the deputy head. "Mrs Johnson? Hello. Would you like to see your husband now?"

Elizabeth followed Mr Collins's portly back down the corridor, the darts at the back of his tweed jacket flaring open where they strained against the roll of flesh which had accumulated steadily there over years of filling, if unimaginative meals, cooked by Mrs Collins. Conversation was ruled out by the fact that she was following in his wake, hurrying, it had to be said, as if he wanted to rush through the day and safely home to his creature comforts.

Elizabeth felt a wild urge to laugh. It was like being Alice in Wonderland, caught in a dreamlike nightmare where she spent hours at a time following people she hardly knew down corridors.

Another door was reached and pushed open. Mr Collins held it open for her. "I'll leave you alone for ten minutes," he announced sternly.

And there he was, sitting on a hard chair, his head bowed, his hands hanging loosely between his knees. As Elizabeth approached, both hands came up, and she thought he was going to hold them out to her, but he brought them to his face, rubbing his fingers across his cheeks and massaging his eyes.

She stepped close to him and stopped, willing him to look at her. "Luke, what the hell happened?" she hissed as he remained immobile, his eyes still closed. "Talk to me, Luke! We've got ten minutes to get your story straight, for God's sake!" She seemed to think she was acting in a police drama, or to have forgotten that there were at least thirty witnesses to Luke's actions. "This brat's father will press charges, you can bet on it…so talk to me!" she cried, shaking his shoulders so that his head rolled on his neck.

Luke's eyes stayed closed, but eventually he spoke in a monotone. "His hair was red, and then he slid backwards and the blood dripped into his hair and the blood was red and his hair was red, and then…" He stopped speaking. Elizabeth stared at him in silence, a horrified look creeping across her face. Nothing more was said until the headmaster returned to inform them that the police wanted a word.

Meanwhile, in the medical room, Norman Smith, Desmond's father, was standing nervously to one side of the small bed which was generally used by menstruating girls in pain, or boys who had finger injuries inflicted on them by themselves or other boys in the woodwork class. But here lay Desmond Smith, dried blood encrusting a portion of the bright white bandage which circled his head, with a rusty-brown stain. He lay on his back, grey faced, eyes closed. The school nurse stood near the door, her hands clasped in front of her.

The paramedics had done the usual vital checks, had reassured the child, even raising a watery reluctant smile from him. The older of the two men turned to Mr Smith. "He's a tough little chap, but he's lost a fair bit of blood, and as with any head injury, he will need to be monitored. We'll take him to hospital now where they can keep an eye on him. He'll probably have to stay in overnight."

Norman, managing to look relieved and terrified at the same time, asked timidly, "Can I go with him? I'll have to ring his mother. She's at home with little Daisy, otherwise she would have been here…" He jingled some loose change in his pocket, looking bewildered. In truth, he felt that he would have much preferred to be at home looking after his little daughter, who was no trouble, than here, facing a barrage of unsettling decisions concerning his difficult, foolish son.

He stepped towards Desmond, suddenly worried that he might be judged for not showing due concern. He looked down at the closed face, waiting a while before picking up the limp hand. He had not held his son's hand for a long time. He could not remember when. It was freckled on the back and felt moist to the touch. As he stepped back to let the paramedics get ready to lift Desmond onto a waiting stretcher, the boy made a gurgling sound. Norman mistakenly thought it was the beginning of a laugh, and smiled in readiness at his son. But the boy groaned and turned his head to one side, vomiting copiously with a loud splatter onto the sensibly tiled floor.

Norman looked away, embarrassed. He left the ambulance men to sort things out (he had never been good with this sort of thing) leaving the room to give his wife a quick call from his mobile.

As he returned to the room, he heard the last few words spoken to the school nurse by the younger paramedic. "…not a good sign, can't take any chances. We're ready to take him now…tell the dad to meet us…oh there you are Mr Smith…"

Elizabeth tore her tortured gaze away from her husband and looked up as the headmaster and two police officers entered the room. One was a rosy-cheeked young man who looked to Elizabeth as if he would look more comfortable behind a school desk. The other was even younger, an attractive female police officer with dark hair. She smiled at Elizabeth, who did not respond but stared through her vacantly. Luke did not appear to have noticed the two new arrivals. Elizabeth opened her mouth as if she would have liked a chance to intervene, but was ushered out by Mr Collins's fleshy hand beneath her elbow.

The policeman stepped forward, smiling in a friendly manner. "Good morning, Mr Johnson. I am Police Constable Taylor, and this is Police Constable Robinson. She will just step outside the door for a moment while I ask you a few questions if I may, sir? Take your time when answering. There's no rush."

He pulled a chair nearer to Luke and sat down. Opening a notebook, he pulled a pen out of his top pocket. "Now then, sir, let's start at the beginning, shall we?"

The female police officer left and made her way to the medical room. She was being brought up to date by the paramedics, when there was a sudden sound of the door being flung open. Police Constable Taylor strode swiftly into the room, looking flustered and more flushed than ever.

"I need one of you to take a look at Mr Johnson. He's not making sense, I think he's in need of urgent medical attention..."

It did not take long for the young paramedic to realise that Luke was having some sort of melt down. He was sitting on the floor now, rocking back and forth, his head in his hands and keeping up a monologue of incomprehensible mutterings. Elizabeth was asked for the name and location of Luke's doctor, and a call was made to inform him of the situation. Luke would be driven home by his wife, who would stay with him until the doctor could arrange a community psychiatric nurse to visit him as soon as possible.

Things were moving fast. Norman saw his son being carried into the back of the ambulance, and watched it pull away towards the road, the alternate lights flashing on and off. Then he heard the familiar, dreaded wailing sound of the siren starting up as it neared the exit gate. Norman gazed after it blankly, as if he were watching something on television. The nurse had to pull on his arm to remind him to make his way to the hospital as soon as he could. She escorted him to his car, making sure he knew how to get to the Royal Devon and Exeter Hospital.

His parting words to her were, "Do you think I ought to press charges against this teacher chap?"

Luke, despite being seemingly unable to communicate, was surprisingly docile. Elizabeth was asked to bring the car as close to the entrance as she could, and she and the two police officers helped him into the passenger seat. The paramedic had checked that he was fit to be moved, and had given Elizabeth a thermal blanket to wrap round him. She was relieved that he was so manageable, like a little boy. But still she made an emergency call to Alexis's mobile, explaining the situation briefly, and begging her to leave her work and be waiting at the cottage for them. She badly needed some emotional support. Alexis reassured her that she would get there as soon as possible.

"Don't cry, Elizabeth…you're not on your own. We'll deal with this together. He'll get through this, I know he will…" Alexis slipped her phone back in her pocket, realising that she had never heard her sister-in-law cry before. It was an oddly heart-warming experience.

Chapter Twenty-Three

"When is This Bloody Day Going to End?"

Monday 27th September 2010
The Same Morning

Cheryl walked unhappily along the narrow street, darkened by the unbroken shadow cast by the row of identical terraced houses. The wind lifted and flapped at her clothes, mean cold fingers probing the gaps and spaces where her flesh was exposed. Unable to pull her light coat round her due to the two heavy cases that dragged on each hand, her skin goose-bumped and she shivered. Litter swirled pointlessly hither and thither, chip paper, an empty lager can, cigarette butts; meaningless remnants of a desperate ploy to stretch and prevent a dismal Sunday evening from turning into an even more gloomy Monday morning. There were loads more things in her room at the flat which still needed to be shifted, but it was only a ten-minute walk, so she was confident that she would be able to move everything with a few trips.

Cheryl would have felt better on the other side of the street, where the sun shone in fitful spurts as scudding clouds raced across the sky. But the house she was on her way towards was numbered twenty-one, and the odd numbers were here on the dark side.

She had managed to throw herself into work at the hospital for the couple of days following her terrifying ordeal at Elizabeth's hands, even volunteering for an extra couple shifts when one of the other nurses went off sick. This had made it easier to avoid Alexis's worried concern and awkward questions.

It was on Friday evening that she had found the advertisement in the local paper, offering a room to let. She had phoned the number at once, before she could change her mind, and had arranged a meeting for the next afternoon. The appointment had been neither pleasurable or reassuring, but as Cheryl, in her haste to vacate Elizabeth's flat as soon as possible, would have agreed to move into a coal bunker if asked to, she seemed unfazed by the experience.

The front door on which Cheryl tentatively knocked was a faded mould colour. Only a fervent optimist would hazard a guess that it had once been painted a vibrant green. It was eventually creaked open an inch and an unsmiling face looked at her. It was a very wrinkled face, belonging to a very old man. He was wearing brown clothes; shapeless trousers, a lumpy jumper and shiny brown slippers partially encasing pale sockless feet.

Cheryl had spoken to a woman on the phone, so she asked him whether she could speak to a Mrs Peck. He continued to stare at her blankly. She was just about to repeat her request more loudly when the figure retreated backwards into the dark hall as if on wheels.

As he was pivoted away from Cheryl's sight she was able to see the mode of his removal. A large freckle-skinned woman stood in his place, hands on hips. "There, that's him sorted for five minutes. Can I help you?"

Cheryl was at a loss for words momentarily, absorbing the breathtaking sight of Mrs Peck's rotund shape packed into a pair of faded blue dungarees, a pink short-sleeved t-shirt, a pair of naked feet, continuing the freckled theme, planted on the ropey mat.

Having introduced herself, Cheryl was ushered inside. Having had her nerves shot to pieces through recent events, she was worried that she might be manhandled in the same way as the other occupant. But she was shown upstairs without interference, although the old man was waiting for them on the landing.

He looked at them as a cow will stare at a passing human. Mrs Peck was taking no chances though. Being a good foot taller than him, she took hold of his shoulders and with a brisk twist of her arms, pirouetted him smartly into a side room and shut the door. She brushed her hands together as if signalling another good job done.

"Is he a lodger?" Cheryl dared inquire, as they moved into a back room.

There was a harsh grating sound. Cheryl located the noise as coming from the landlady, and was startled to realise she was laughing. "Oh my days!" she snorted. "Him? That's Daddy! He just needs watching; give him an inch and he'll take a mile, that's him. Lodger! Oh you are a funny girl…we'll have a scream with you staying here, I can see."

Cheryl was better prepared for her second visit on the Monday morning and was able to accept the paucity of creature comforts with some alacrity. It was not as clean as she would have liked, but that was not a problem. There was a bed, that was the main thing. And although the thought of sharing a bathroom and kitchen was depressing after enjoying Elizabeth's lovely modern flat, the realisation that she was free from Elizabeth's clutches enabled her to breathe easily again. Alexis was concerned when she discovered that Cheryl was moving out so soon, and that she was moving her belongings on foot.

As Cheryl returned back to the flat with her two empty suitcases, ready to fill them again, she found Alexis there looking worried. "You can't do it all on your own, Cheryl," she protested. "What about the bulky stuff? You can't carry everything! Let me get Luke to take some of it in the car at least!"

"No! I'm fine, Alexis! Please, just let me do it…"

Alexis stared at her in consternation, realising that Cheryl was close to tears. She murmured words of reassurance and hugged her.

It was a few minutes after Cheryl had staggered out of the flat, and Alexis was just about to set off for her first shift of the day, that her mobile sprang into life and Alexis discovered that life had a nasty habit of throwing up predicaments that could change the future forever.

Elizabeth drove Luke home as carefully as she could. She tried to imagine that there was a glass of water on the dashboard, it was a steadying trick her driving instructor had suggested, and she'd try anything to prevent Luke from being tossed around. It was like having a box of eggs on the passenger seat. She could not be certain that he could brace himself against her braking or turning the car, had no way of knowing what was going on with him at all. The thought of his head smashing against something hard kept snaking horribly through her thoughts. Maniacally, she wondered whether his brain would look normal if spilled in a crash. Since hearing him speak so weirdly, she envisaged his brain to have turned to mush, like scrambled egg. She felt nauseated and appalled at being thrown into this situation.

Elizabeth kept her eyes riveted to the road ahead, terrified that Luke would suddenly rear up and strike her. She had no experience of this, no basis for knowing what to expect. She glanced at him furtively a couple of times. He sat with his head turned away from her, his arms under the blanket, which reflected the sun in flashes and crackled softly when his body moved.

Large tears continued to drip down Elizabeth's face. She had given up trying to swipe them away with the back of her hand. If someone had asked her why she was crying, she would have been hard put to explain it in words. She felt frightened and angry, robbed and cheated… She had worked so hard to reach this point in her life, she had fought against unfair odds and managed to engineer her path towards this marriage, which was her supposed ticket to happiness; her position as wife and then mother. It wasn't much to ask, yet here she was again, facing another huge setback.

It seemed hours later that she pulled over to park outside the cottage. Alexis was sitting waiting for her in her car. She leapt out and rushed over to yank open Elizabeth's door.

"You poor darling!" cried Alexis, putting an arm around Elizabeth's shaking shoulders and kissing her on the bit of cheek she could reach. Elizabeth's face was hidden, covered by her hands. "Just sit still a minute 'til you feel calmer. I'll need help to get Luke inside." She rubbed her sister-in-law's back for a second before skirting round the car to the passenger door. Alexis took a deep steadying breath before opening the door. Her brother looked up at her, no emotion in his face.

Alexis bent down so that she was level with his face. "Luke…we'll get you through this, I promise." She reached under the blanket to take hold of his hands. The foil rustled gently, but Luke did not respond to the pressure of her fingers.

The next few hours passed in a blur of confused activity. Neither Elizabeth or Alexis had spent a day quite like it. There were no boundaries or rules to it. It could most probably be likened to being in the presence of someone giving birth, not in any productive way, but in the chaos of not knowing what to do next, and in what order.

Getting Luke into the cottage was amazingly successful, if they could describe manipulating a grown man into a position where they felt he was safe and least threatening as successful. If it was any man, it would be bad enough, but when that man is your brother, your husband, it becomes surreal.

He was worryingly malleable. He was quiet and apparently without emotion, seeming to find it difficult to verbalise his thoughts.

There was a phone call from the police, and not much was said except that they should expect a visit that afternoon.

Alexis held it together until they had hauled him onto the settee, and Elizabeth was tucking a kitchen towel under his chin in an attempt to spoon some soup into him. Elizabeth looked up to see silent tears rolling down Alexis's face. It was the moment that they realised that nothing might ever be the same ever again.

A firm knocking at the front door made both women jump. Elizabeth had already received a call at around midday from the receptionist at Luke's surgery, asking how Luke was, and checking that they were coping. She informed them that a community psychiatric nurse would be calling within the next hour.

The pretty nurse who stepped into the cottage had an immediate effect of spreading an aura of calm and normality. She chatted easily, relaxing the atmosphere and looking capable enough to deal with anything that might be thrown at her. She introduced herself as Jaimie Porter.

She was lovely with Luke, sitting near him to explain the next course of action, in a down-to-earth, common-sense way, as if dealing with a broken leg, not a fractured state of mind. She was not patronising, but spoke quietly, pausing now and then in case Luke wanted to make any response. When she mentioned starting him on a course of medication, Luke turned his face towards her, a worried expression on his, up till then, apathetic face.

"No… I don't want anything that's…what's the word…? I don't want to be addicted to anything…" he spoke hesitantly.

Jaimie smiled reassuringly. "Don't worry, Mr Johnson, these would just be antidepressants, which are not addictive. Hopefully you won't need to be on them for long…at that point you will need to come off them slowly and safely to give your body time to adjust. We will help you to do that. However, they will take three to four weeks to kick in, so the quicker we start, the better."

"Thank you," murmured Luke politely. "And please call me Luke."

Alexis and Elizabeth showed Jaimie out, arrangements having been made for another visit from her in the near future. She explained that Luke needed what was termed as 'Crisis Therapy'. Luke would be asked to express his emotions around the crisis that had brought him to this point.

"Support from family is a crucial part of recovery," she said. "Home-care crisis treatment, coupled with an ongoing home-care package, is a viable alternative to hospital, except in severe cases where the patient is likely to self-harm, or present a danger to others." Here Elizabeth raised her eyebrows at Alexis, who looked away dismayed.

They thanked her, and as Alexis shut the door, she turned to take Elizabeth's arm. "She was great, wasn't she? I feel a lot better now. She really made it sound as if this is just a passing problem."

She looked at Elizabeth, who dropped her eyes and said, "She certainly had an instant effect on Luke. Did you see the way he perked up when she arrived? While we couldn't get a word out of him!"

Alexis blinked, before replying, "Yes…she was brilliant and obviously good at her job. Thank God he seemed to take to her!"

Elizabeth walked back into the lounge and stared down at Luke. He lay there, his eyes closed, seemingly unaware that Mango had draped herself across his chest, a paw each side of his face as if she was protecting him. A muscle twitched in Elizabeth's cheek as she ground her teeth together.

“Tea, you two?” called Alexis, heading towards the kitchen. She had decided that the only way forward was to act as naturally as possible. They would face whatever they needed to, together, as a family.

The afternoon moved along slowly. Elizabeth had popped out to the chemist with Luke’s prescription, leaving Alexis to hold the fort. She had managed to coax Luke to eat a little, and then he had slept. She wanted to call her parents, but when Elizabeth returned and she suggested it, Elizabeth begged her not to rush to do it yet.

“Wait until we have more idea of how things are going to pan out, Alexis. There’s no need to frighten them to death for nothing. At least let’s wait until the police have been.”

“Talk of the devil!” Alexis said in a choked voice, as a loud bang on the door made heart sink.

Elizabeth went to let them in. Constables Taylor and Robinson stood there. Elizabeth had the feeling of being in play, a farce, in which people kept reappearing and reciting their lines at her. The thing was, the whole thing was out of her control and she was beginning to feel like screaming. Maybe then they’d cart her off to the funny farm, and she would be left alone.

She rearranged her face into one of friendly welcome, stepping back so that the uniformed pair could enter.

“Could we have a quiet word in the kitchen, Mrs Johnson?” requested Constable Taylor after observing Luke soundly asleep on the settee. “We will have to discuss recent events with Luke as soon as possible. We will not be able to put it off much longer.”

At a nod from Elizabeth, Alexis followed them in and closed the door. Elizabeth pulled out chairs and the four of them sat around the table. Constable Robinson gazed around the attractive stylish kitchen with appreciative eyes. As if she was on a social visit, thought Elizabeth.

But a reluctant offer of tea was refused, and Constable Taylor began to speak. “This must all be very worrying for you. Firstly, I can tell you that Mr Smith and his wife, the parents of the unfortunate boy involved, have decided not to press charges.”

There was an audible sigh of relief from Elizabeth and Alexis. Constable Taylor looked at the two women, inviting questions. When none came, he continued. “But I’m afraid that may change.” His face took on a very serious expression.

“What?” gasped Elizabeth. “Why?”

Alexis locked her eyes, huge with anxiety, onto the policeman’s. “How is the child?” she whispered.

He cleared his throat and then said, "He remains in hospital…he has been pretty stable, but in the last couple of hours, he seems to have given them reason to believe that there is a medical complication. I am not able to go into details here. There are more assessments to be made, but at the moment it's just a matter of waiting, I'm afraid. We'll let ourselves out for now… We will be interviewing the children from Luke's class shortly." He glanced at his watch. "But we will be back after that to talk to Luke, to get his side of things." The two constables stood up and made their way out of the front door, just as the phone began to ring.

Elizabeth groaned. "What now?" she said shakily. She picked the phone up. "Yes, speaking…oh, of course, well, he's been seen by a psychiatric nurse and has been treated for shock, but I realise that…yes, of course. Half an hour? See you then."

Alexis looked at Elizabeth questioningly.

Elizabeth sat down heavily at the table again. "That was Mr Collins. He wants to speak to Luke. Oh Alexis! When is this bloody day going to end?"

Chapter Twenty-Four
Mike and Emma Exchanged Uneasy Glances

Same Bloody Day
Exsham

Alexis approached the settee where Luke was still asleep and placed a cup of tea and a cheese sandwich on the coffee table in front of him. The small clatter of china on wood roused him. He opened his eyes slowly, raising them up to his sister's face. He took in her worried frown, looking puzzled.

He swung his feet slowly to the floor and sat up, the blanket pooling round his ankles. "Where's Elizabeth?" he inquired.

Alexis sat herself down at his side, carefully so as not to disturb him. "Don't worry, she's just making a call to her headmistress, Ms Carter, telling her that she won't be in for the rest of the week." She pushed the plate closer to Luke, pulling the blanket up again and tucking it round him.

He pondered on what she had said for moment, staring into space. "She can't do that," he stated in a flat tone of voice.

"It's fine…it will give you both time to gather your thoughts, a chance to talk to each other and examine any problems…" She stopped, not wanting to panic Luke or put him under any pressure.

They were interrupted by Elizabeth coming in from the hall. "Oh good! Tea, just what we need," she declared cheerfully. "Did you make a pot, Al?"

Alexis stood up gratefully. "Sure, I'll pour us both a cup. And bring some more sandwiches if you fancy them? Luke needs to eat something before he takes more medication anyway. Sit next to him, Elizabeth. I'll have the beanbag, before Mango comes in and hogs it."

She escaped to the kitchen, aware that she was gabbling. She hoped the word 'medication' wouldn't trigger a nervous reaction from Luke. God, she felt out of her depth. She wished there was a guidebook to steer them down the right way of doing this. Every word was a potential minefield. What she really wanted to do, was to take him into a hug, ask him what terrible stresses he had endured which had led him to the unfolding of this day, and find out how she could help him. She buttered more bread, savagely, tearing holes in it with the knife, unable to see clearly for the force of her weeping.

Mr Collins arrived, officious and awkward, clearly ill at ease. He did not stay long. Alexis squeezed a hard chair into the room from the kitchen so that he could sit. The women remained outside of the room to give them some privacy.

Mr Collins faced Luke, smiling unconvincingly. The kitchen chair creaked ominously under the sudden pressure put upon it. There were a few beats of silence while both men looked at each other. "Well, Luke…this is a sorry business. Would you like to tell me what happened exactly?" He studied his hands closely as if expecting the answer to leap out from them.

Luke sighed and closed his eyes. Just when the headmaster thought he must have nodded off, Luke said patiently, "What happened, is that everything that has been making it difficult to get up in the mornings, has gathered itself up and thrown me into a situation that I never want to go through again."

He spread his fingers out before him. Mr Collins could see them trembling so violently that he was fearful of pushing Luke over the edge, but there was a question he had to ask. "Luke, for whatever reason, and I know how difficult these children can be, did you hit Desmond Smith, or cause him to hit his head?"

Luke's face paled, the muscles of his jaw were set in a rigid line, his breathing was shallow and a rapid beating pulse was visible at the base of his throat. He felt a slick of sweat greasing the palms of hands and wiped them roughly on the blanket. "It's a blur… They wouldn't listen, they never listen! They hate me. But I didn't hit him…I'm sure I didn't. I've never hit a child." Here he put his head in his hands, and began to sob, racking coughs of misery that caused Mr Collins to look out of the window in embarrassed alarm.

"Well, I think we'll leave it there…" The headmaster stood up, his hands hidden in the pockets of his raincoat. "Just to say that for the immediate future, I have no option than to inform you of your temporary suspension. This is a serious matter, and you must appreciate that the children's welfare is paramount. We can make no further decision until after the police have interviewed your class." He retrieved a hand from his pocket and leant forward to offer it to Luke, who stared at the plump appendage as if at something distasteful. He turned his face away, his cheeks shining wet with tears.

"I will hand my resignation in as soon as possible. I never want to teach again as long as I live," he muttered.

Mr Collins nodded and turned on his heel, desperate for some fresh air. “Steady though, Luke, no rash decisions!” he said with a ghastly grimace that was intended as a smile. Elizabeth was standing waiting at the door which was not quite closed. He was shown out of the cottage without another word being spoken.

The police had already set up an emergency interview room at the school, using a video so that the children did not have to write a written statement.

Some of the children interviewed by the police that afternoon were wary and frightened of saying something that might land them in trouble. They seemed to think the questions were there to trap them, so they avoided straightforward answers, saying they hadn’t been paying attention to what was going on, they were too busy looking at their books.

Emma Robinson wondered if these children hadn’t been watching too many crime dramas. “Honestly Mike…” she complained to Police Constable Taylor, “You’d think we were trying to trick them into incriminating themselves in the most hideous crimes of torture and murder.”

But there were enough of the quiet sensible ones. These were the children who, even though interviewed separately, agreed without exception that most of their classmates, themselves included, had led Mr Johnson a merry dance that day.

Sally Brown, a studious girl with a fat plait of glossy chestnut hair lying neatly down her back, spoke the words of many of the children, albeit more concisely and clearly, as she informed them sadly that; Mr Johnson is a lovely teacher. This was their second year with him, and he had always made his lessons really interesting and fun. It was only since the beginning of this term that he’d been different, more short-tempered and impatient. When kids like Desmond Smith start fooling around, it brought a bit of humour to the lesson. “A lot of the other boys egged him on,” she explained, “and it was hard not to join in. But Mr Johnson didn’t mean to hurt him, he just wanted to get him out of the room. If Desmond hadn’t held on to the teacher’s desk like that, the accident wouldn’t have happened. It was like pulling a rubber band, once Desmond let go, he flew through the air and hit the door all by himself.” Sally looked at Mike Taylor and Emma Robinson with her earnest brown eyes, confident that her statement had saved the day.

The wind had finally died down, and the sun was a red globe entangled in the branches of faraway trees on a hilly horizon, promising another fine day to come. Twilight was encroaching fast, street lamps picked out pale flowers in grass, whitewashed the sparkly pavements and drew attention to the police car neatly, legally, parked with its cheerful blue and yellow chequered sides.

Elizabeth shut the front door firmly on the two retreating uniformed backs with a huge sigh. All she wanted was to sleep. Tomorrow was another day. Luke looked absolutely drained after the final friendly, but intensive questioning by Constables Taylor and Robinson.

He had been more forthcoming with them than he had with Mr Collins, but that was more because he had never been able to stand the old-fashioned headmaster who seemed to struggle with any pretence at empathy or humour.

He was still finding stringing a coherent sentence together tiring, but managed to convey the essence of his frustration coupled with unidentified personal problems. They tried to encourage him to explain these to him, which he did with vague remarks alluding to lack of sleep due to panic attacks, feelings of dread, loss of appetite, and basically a feeling that the smallest task is too daunting. He gave an uncertain grin, apologising. "Sorry, you're not doctors, but it's the only way I can explain the lead up to such a mess."

Emma Robinson shook her head. "No, don't apologise. This explains a lot. Seems like you've come to the end of your tether. And you are certain that you did not intentionally hurt the boy?"

Luke shrugged. "As far as I can say, I was just going to escort him out of the room. Yes, he was resisting a bit, but suddenly he was flying towards the door. I can't remember after that..."

His face sagged, making him instantly look twice his age.

Mike Taylor picked up his hat. "You are seeking medical advice? There must be an underlying reason for the feelings you've described?" he asked kindly as he stood up.

Luke smirked mirthlessly. "Oh yes... I'll soon be medicated into submission. No more disgraceful behaviour from me, Constable. I'll just be wrapped in a blanket somewhere, popping happy pills and not minding about anything any more."

Mike and Emma exchanged uneasy glances.

Alexis had picked up her jacket, and was leaning over to give Luke a kiss when Elizabeth came in.

She looked up sympathetically. "What's the plan? Can I help you get a meal together before I go?"

Elizabeth shook her head. "No... I'm exhausted. I'll heat us up some soup. Is that okay, Luke?"

He grunted an assent.

“Ok! And I’ll ring the parents when I get home, reassure them. We don’t want them galloping over straight away! And I’ll make sure Mum doesn’t ring you tonight. I think you both need a bit of peace.”

They both thanked her, and she left them on their own, for the first time that day.

Luke sat quietly while Elizabeth fussed around, tidying up Sunday newspapers, removing the debris of all those cheerful cups of tea, and drawing the curtains closed. She had been itching to do this all day, feeling it was inappropriate while Luke lay so smitten on the settee in front of the almost constant audience of the sort of visitors she had neither liked nor welcomed into her home.

She took herself off to warm the soup, asking Luke if he wanted her to turn on the television.

When he made no reply, Elizabeth paused in the kitchen doorway. “Have you any idea what you’ve put me through today? Mmm? Have you? This has been one of the most horrendous days of my life. I was hoping for some sort of thanks, but you don’t care about anyone except yourself, do you?”

His silence infuriated her. Grievances boiled inside her, and black thoughts threw out words which backed up and spilled out of her mouth. “And what the hell were you thinking of, telling Mr Collins that you want to resign? Yes, I was listening. Have you no pride? It’s been awkward enough letting me shoulder the bulk of the financial burden of this marriage, but to give up on your job, without even discussing it with your wife? What sort of man are you?”

Luke got unsteadily to his feet. “A disillusioned and unhappy one, and also an incredibly tired one,” he said quietly.

Elizabeth watched him wearily climb the stairs, wishing she could turn the clock back and retract this last vitriolic outburst. Her whole life was spiralling out of control and she had a mounting suspicion that some of it might be her fault.

Chapter Twenty-Five

"Just Wondered if You'd Care for a Biscuit?"

Tuesday 28th September 2010

The insistent pealing reverberation clawed Alexis into a sitting position. Her eyes tried to penetrate the absolute darkness, failed and closed, giving way to her sense of smell. Was that smoke? Her immediate thought had been of fire; her dream had surely been about a massive wall of red, a distant roar.

The clatter and roaring rumble of the bin lorry, the alarm clock, blinking with a red eye, shrieking at her that it was six o'clock in the morning, penetrated her cotton wool brain cells. Now that there was no Cheryl to wake her gently with a sustaining cup of tea, she hated getting up for an early shift. Why was her head pounding though, her mouth so dry? Had she drank too much last night? These distressing anxiety attacks were becoming too frequent.

She clouted the clock into silence as reality kicked in with a wave of anxiety and depressing memories of the day before. She had gone straight to bed with a cup of hot chocolate, hoping to escape into a deep sleep. Instead of which, she had lain there, each new agitating thought about Luke revving up her heartbeats, prickling her skin with panicky sweat. Would he be taken to court? Lose his job? Recover from his obvious depression? She had thrown back the duvet to cool down, only to drift off and wake again to shivering clammy legs. She had eventually fallen into a shallow unrefreshing doze until the rude awakening.

'Oh God!' she realised, 'I didn't ring Mum and Dad…too tired.' She promised herself she would do it this afternoon, after her morning shift. It was too early to do it now. They'd freak out.

By two o'clock that afternoon, Alexis was practically asleep on her feet. She was looking forward to some chill time as she had the rest of the day off. It was tempting to get out of her uniform, shower, climb into her cuddly onesie, and eat a bowl of muesli before going back to bed for a couple of hours. But she knew she couldn't relax until she had made that phone call to her parents.

She cuddled up in a corner of the settee, plumped cushions around her and added one onto her lap for comfort. She dialled the number that she knew by heart. "Mum? It's me, can you chat for a moment?"

"Oh darling! At last…we've been trying to ring you all morning, and on your mobile…"

Alexis sat up straighter, a frown creasing her forehead. "Oh Mum…you know, don't you? How? I was supposed to ring you last night, but…I was so shattered, and now I've been at work all day, and you know I have to turn off my mobile in the hospital."

"Shush shush, it's okay…I rang Luke and Elizabeth last night, just to catch up? Elizabeth told us all about it."

Alexis was stumped for words. She had no idea how much Elizabeth had explained. Finally she asked, "Did you speak to Luke, Mum?"

It was Céline's turn to hesitate. "Well no…he was asleep, even though it was only nine o'clock! But Elizabeth says he started to feel funny in the morning? So why did no one think to tell us as soon as it happened?"

Alexis thought hard, deciding to continue quizzing Céline, rather than end up saying too much. "So Elizabeth's told you about it? It was all a bit chaotic to be honest…have you contacted them today?"

Céline sighed, her tension making it difficult to cope with the conversation; this was when her command of English let her down. "No, Elizabeth only said to me that Luke is having some problems, making him depressed. She has told me that he needs to be quiet and rest. I want to go and see them, but she says no. She is taking the week off, so maybe after. Your father says to leave them alone."

She sounded so sad. Alexis felt enormous sympathy for her mother. She hated hiding things from her, but supposed it was for the best. She told her mother that she loved her, promising to ring again soon.

Alexis found her mobile at the bottom of her bag. A quick glance showed five missed calls and several unopened text messages.

Her next call to Elizabeth was not easy. She was obviously irritated that Alexis had not kept her promise of ringing her parents. "The whole point was to play it down so they didn't worry! Honestly, Alexis, I've got enough to deal with without them arriving here."

"Well…I think I've calmed her down. She's accepted that there's no need to rush over. How is he today?"

"Sorry…didn't mean to moan at you, love. He's the same; not saying much, no appetite, stares out of the window…"

Alexis began to say that she would happily come and see him, but Elizabeth fended her off, saying he was best left to himself at the moment. "Anyway, Jaimie Porter, that CPN is due soon to spend a session with him."

"Okay, Elizabeth…just keep me in the loop. By the way, I meant to discuss this last week, but I didn't, and then yesterday wasn't an appropriate time." There was a pause so she rushed on. "Now that Cheryl has left, well, we were going to ask whether you had someone in mind to replace her?"

Elizabeth let slip a faint gasp. "Oh! She's left already? That was quick."

Alexis felt a jolt of surprise, surely Cheryl had told her she was going straight away? "Yes well, she moved out yesterday, wanted to be out by the end of the month, I suppose. I'll miss her like mad!" she tried to make light of it. Another silence. "Anyway, if you want to advertise, or perhaps you have already? But I thought, well, we thought…"

"Slow down, Al… I hadn't thought about it yet to be honest, told her there was no rush. What *did* you think?"

Alexis came straight to the point. "How would you feel about Rob moving in, taking Cheryl's place? We've been talking about getting a place together…"

Elizabeth laughed. "Oh Alexis! I'd be delighted to offer him Cheryl's tenancy! He's probably been staying over anyway… well now he can move in properly!"

Alexis breathed a sigh of relief. For some reason, she had feared that Elizabeth might be against the idea. Maybe because she and Rob were so happy, in the first flush of a new romance, while Elizabeth and Luke's relationship was seemingly showing cracks.

Elizabeth opened the door to Jaimie Porter with a big smile. Luke was sitting at the kitchen table, a half-drunk mug of coffee at his elbow, a paperback novel propped against a blue milk jug. He was staring at the table, eyes unfocused.

He looked up as Jaimie came through the door. She shrugged off her jacket and gave him a grin. Luke felt his lips stretching into a rusty response. "Hello…nice to see you again. Have a seat."

Jaimie tried to pull out the chair opposite him. "Somebody isn't keen to share this chair," she observed wryly.

"Just tip her off! She thinks she owns the place." advised Elizabeth, setting out two more mugs.

Instead, Jaimie chose the chair next to Luke and sat down. Luke laughed out loud as Mango immediately transferred herself to Jaimie's lap with a loud liquid purr.

Elizabeth looked up smartly from spooning coffee. She scrutinized Luke's face momentarily, before placing a mug in front of Jaimie. "I'll leave you to concentrate," she informed them, taking her own mug and the local newspaper through to the lounge.

Elizabeth settled down in the adjacent room. She shook out the paper and tried to concentrate on stories celebrating a seventieth wedding anniversary of a devoted couple, a fatal car crash, next to a snippet of news about a cat who had walked the five miles back to his original home after his owners had moved to another village.

But she didn't actually read a word, she sat straining to hear what was transpiring between Jaimie and Luke.

She heard Jaimie asking Luke if he felt able to express his emotions around yesterday's crisis. Jaimie's voice was clear, but she was unable to make out Luke's muffled responses. A car rumbled past, obliterating the next bit of Jaimie's sentence…she heard "clarification of the problem?" More mumbling from Luke followed by Jaimie suggesting they discuss some helpful coping mechanisms.

Elizabeth felt frustrated and shut out. What was Luke saying? Was he complaining about their marriage, blaming her for his stress? She stood up and moved closer to the door.

Jaimie said, "What is really important here, Luke, is for you to discourage inappropriate beliefs. Your mind can trick you into believing a distorted vision of events. What about keeping a diary of occurrences, something to focus your mind which you can relate to? Do you think there's something in the past which might be troubling you?"

Elizabeth felt sick. All this was the two of them ganging against her, two against one. This girl was insinuating that Luke was in a miserable relationship. She couldn't stand it. She yanked open the kitchen door just as Jaimie was explaining, "But of course, the paramount point is that you feel you have support from your family." She looked up at Elizabeth, and gave that warm encouraging smile again, "You, Elizabeth, are the most important aid to Luke's recovery. Oh yes! And you!" she stroked Mango's head.

Elizabeth stood stock still, distracted by the turn of the conversation. "Just wondered if you'd care for a biscuit?" she inquired falteringly.

At the end of the session, Jaimie reiterated to Elizabeth the importance of family support. "He's so lucky to have you and Alexis. And his parents aren't too far away, I gather? He's already showing positive signs. I know this is hard for you, but he has so much going for him."

Elizabeth nodded, lost for words. She swallowed hard. "Thanks. I realise his health is the most important thing, but we can't help worrying about his future too. Practical stuff..."

Jaimie put a hand on Elizabeth's arm. "Of course...anything in particular?"

"Is it okay to leave him on his own? I've got the rest of the week off, but after that I'm back to work...not to mention having to shop, oh, and of course I have to collect his car from his school. Alexis said her boyfriend has offered to come with me to drive it back."

"Elizabeth, don't be too anxious about everything. Luke needs you to be calm. His body has signalled that he needs help, but he doesn't need babysitting. Just be normal around him, and that means leading your life as usual."

When she had gone, Elizabeth followed her advice. She spent the rest of the afternoon lying on her bed reading a romance, took a nap, not venturing down again until it was time for the six o'clock news. She popped her head round the door once to look at Luke. He was sitting where she had left him, but by now it was almost dark. She waited a few seconds for him to speak. But there was nothing at that moment that he wanted to say.

Chapter Twenty-Six

"Something Good at Last"

Saturday 2nd October 2010
Exmouth

Rob's dark-blue Golf sat smugly in the parking bay outside the flat. An hour ago, it had been bursting with bags and suitcases.

Alexis pushed Rob out of the way and gazed down. She had a silly grin on her face as she began to dance around the bedroom.

"You're a nutcase! Come here…hey, what are the tears for? Alex! Slow down…" Rob grabbed his whirling girlfriend and sat her down on the bed. He tipped her face up towards him and kissed each weeping eye gently.

Alexis gave a long shuddering sigh followed by a loud hiccup. "Your car is sitting outside my flat, and I am so happy…" Her mouth wobbled as the tears flowed afresh.

Rob looked at her sternly. "Well, if we're going to have this drama each time you spy my toothbrush in the bathroom or my underpants in the wash basket, I may have to rethink this very serious move."

Alexis punched his chest, but before he could protest about domestic abuse, she was kissing his face and tangling the two of them up in the duvet she had so carefully put on the bed that morning, freshly washed and ironed.

Time had spun out its glorious minutes so that it was almost midday when Alexis sat herself down at her dressing table wrapped in a fluffy white towel. Steam from her mug of green tea brought the sharp scent of it to her nostrils. She grimaced as she took a sip. She hated the stuff, only drank it because all her nurse friends kept telling her about its amazing properties; promoting weight loss, preventing cancer, cholesterol and even Alzheimer's. But a recent five minutes' search on Google seemed to suggest that though all these properties couldn't be denied, neither could they be proved.

She wandered into the kitchen, smiled at the sound of Rob's slightly off-key version of 'Yesterday' swelling against the crashing of water onto the tiles, and reached for the coffee jar with one hand while pouring the tea down the sink with the other.

"What do you fancy doing today?" Rob asked later around a crunchy mouthful of toast.

Alexis, looking pretty in blue jeans and a dark-pink chunky sweater, mixed a blob of marmite with a smear of low-fat butter and spread it evenly to the edges of her own slice. She thought for a moment. "Look, tell me if you don't want to…but I thought I'd text Cheryl to see whether she's at home. If she is, I thought just a quick visit? It's weird, I've been so dying for you to meet her, and Luke and Elizabeth, and now it looks like Luke won't be up to it for a while, nor Elizabeth, and Cheryl's gone to ground in this bed-sit. I want to see it with my own eyes."

"I'm with you on that." Rob smiled. Alexis looked closely at his face, the crinkly laughter lines at the corners of those kind eyes, the generous mouth lifted halfway to a grin… He was like an open book. That was what had attracted her to him from the first second of meeting him. "Will you tell her about Luke?" he asked her.

Alexis hesitated, pondering the question. "I don't think so. I know I told you, but that's different. Cheryl seems pretty down herself at the moment. It won't help to swamp her with Luke's problems. I want to cheer her up, not make her more miserable!"

They were soon walking briskly towards Victoria Terrace, following the directions which Cheryl had set out in her text. She had asked them to send her a message on arrival so that she could let them in. She wanted to avoid an awkward confusion in the hall. The thought of trying to juggle Alexis and Rob past Mrs Peck and her father in that narrow space was too much to stomach.

Cheryl sat on her bed, waiting for her phone to beep. Then, the coast clear, she bounded down the stairs on slippered feet to open the door.

Alexis beamed at her, an introduction to Rob on her lips, but was silenced by Cheryl's finger on lips. They followed her stealthily up the stairs, quelling the urge to giggle.

Letting out a long held-in breath, Cheryl pushed open the door to her room. They followed her in, trying not mind the threadbare carpet and unrecognizable smell of something unspeakable cooking which had followed them up from below.

Alexis clutched Rob's arm at Cheryl's "Oh!" of alarm. The figure stood hunched just inside the door, his expressionless wrinkled face suspended beneath a few sparse tufts of beige hair. He gazed at them, cowering, as if they'd hunted him down.

Cheryl looked haunted and at a complete loss for words. Rob took over, unfazed by the situation. "Hello there! Seems you've taken a wrong turn. Let me show you out, there's a good fellow."

Cheryl nodded encouragingly. "He'll be no trouble," she whispered, as Rob gingerly took hold of the old man's flapping sleeve. He allowed himself to be guided out and pointed towards the stairs. A little push set him tottering on his way, like a clockwork toy.

"You can't stay here!" hissed Alexis. "How can you sleep at night?"

"Oh, it's cheap and the bedding's clean enough," said Cheryl morosely. "I should have locked my door, I do usually. Thanks for dealing with him, Rob."

Rob looked at her with concern. "He appears harmless enough. As long as you're not frightened of him?"

"Believe me, he's the last of my worries at the moment." She laughed unconvincingly.

Alexis rolled her eyes. "You would tell us, Cheryl, if something else is worrying you?"

Cheryl pressed her lips together, knowing if she tried to speak, her voice would wobble and give her away completely.

"Tell you what," began Rob, "I think Al here is worried that you're going to lose touch. Why don't we arrange for you to come to the flat whenever you need a bit of TLC?"

Alexis shot him a grateful glance. "Yes, you must, Cheryl, Rob's right. And we haven't told you our news… Rob's moved into the flat!" She studied Cheryl's face carefully to make sure the information hadn't upset her, but Cheryl looked at them both with delight.

"That's the best news ever! At least something good at last." She refrained from agreeing to visit, knowing that she would never step foot into that particular flat ever again. "Well, I've been a rotten host. Would you like a cup of tea to toast your moving in?"

Rob rubbed his hands together. "I think something a bit stronger, don't you? There's a bottle of champagne chilling in our fridge, shall we?" He strode to the door and opened it with a flourish, holding it for the two women to go through.

Cheryl stalled, not knowing how to refuse the invitation. "There's a nice pub down the road. It's not far." She tried weakly.

Rob tutted. "Why spend a fortune in the pub? Come on, get your shoes on, and make sure you lock this door behind you!"

They went through and she followed them meekly, her heart pounding at the thought of Elizabeth finding out that she had disobeyed the rules already.

Alexis linked arms with Cheryl, she felt a sensation of protective fondness overwhelm her. The three of them strode down one of the wide avenues that swept through the outskirts of the town. Leaves on the tall trees were turning, each type with their own particular hue. The resulting picture was a spectacular merging of oranges, dark-reds and limes with yellows not far behind.

As they neared the flat, Cheryl slowed her steps. She dragged back, looking round her anxiously, sure she would see Elizabeth's car parked nearby.

Alexis turned towards her, ever attuned to her friend's mood. "Whatever is it? You look terrified!"

Cheryl decided that the only way was to tell a half truth. "It's Elizabeth… I'm not her favourite person at the moment!" She made an exaggerated disconcerted expression, as if to make a joke of it. "She's not likely to turn up, is she?"

"Oh, I don't think so. Luke's a bit under the weather at the moment, flu or something. I think Elizabeth is busy administering to him," replied Alexis, dishing out her own white lie without turning a hair. "Why are you in her bad books?"

Cheryl took a deep breath. "Oh, nothing serious. She was a bit miffed at me deciding to move out so quickly, I suppose. People who are well off haven't got clue what it's like to be strapped for cash, have they?" She laughed it off, glad to end the conversation there as the three of them ascended in the lift.

They settled into the comfy armchairs in the lounge. Cheryl was quiet and obviously on edge for a while, but after her second glass of champagne, she sat further back in her chair and began to breathe normally. She was very impressed with Rob. He was the perfect partner for Alexis. They sat and relaxed, easy in each other's company. Cheryl could almost imagine that she was the third flatmate, how fantastic that would be.

Rob had opened a second bottle while Alexis had served up a big plate of cheese on toast to help soak it up. They were tucking in to this and laughing wildly at some ridiculous tale Rob was regaling them with, when Alexis's mobile phone chirruped loudly, signalling an incoming message.

Alexis read it and looked up at Cheryl apologetically. "It's Elizabeth! She's passing and wants to know if it's okay to pop up. She won't stay long, she says. She wants to ask what the best time is to fetch Luke's car from Exeter," she added, directing this last comment to Rob. "That's fine," he replied.

At the same moment, Cheryl leapt to her feet, almost sending her plate flying. Her face white as chalk. "Elizabeth?" she yelped. "Oh I'm sorry, I've got to go! Where is she?"

Rob looked at Cheryl in alarm. "It's okay…she won't bite you!" he said jokingly.

"She's on her way up, love," said Alexis, realising the depth of Cheryl's panic, who was looking wildly about, as if looking for a place to hide.

The front door opened and Elizabeth sauntered into the lounge. "Well hi… what are you all celebrating?" her voice was lacking its usual huskiness, it hit a high note, breaking on the last word. She walked over to Cheryl until they were a couple of inches apart. Cheryl tried to step back, but she was jammed tight against her chair. "Didn't expect to see you here, Cheryl… thought you'd moved on to pastures new? Move go all right? Mmm? Are you okay?" She frowned with concern. "You look awfully pale." She reached out a hand and placed it on Cheryl's arm.

Cheryl flinched as if she'd been burnt. "I was j…just off…" she stammered, shaking off Elizabeth's hand. She looked apologetically at Rob and Alexis, escaping in a rush for the door and was heard clattering down the staircase.

Elizabeth, perfectly composed, sat in the chair which Cheryl had just vacated.

"Well! She was in a hurry!" She smiled. "Strange girl…frightened of her own shadow! Well. You must be Rob, great to meet you at last."

Chapter Twenty-Seven

"Don't Let Them Grind You Down"

Friday 22nd October 2010
Three Weeks Later

Luke stared out of the window, appalled at how the continuing grey skies could suck up so much lustre. Mango sat blackly in her own absence of light, merging into the shadowed floor. Mugs and plates sat dully on the draining board, unwashed.

He supposed, without much interest, that feeling appalled was another emotion to add to the slowly growing list. Four weeks of medication was doing the trick; numbing those heart-pumping panic attacks and allowing him to recognise more normal feelings. These included disgust, cold, dislike, loneliness, to name but a few, but he was unable to engender much concern about any of them. And feel-good emotions appeared to have deserted the sinking ship.

Maybe they would think about returning if the weather would only buck up. Or maybe if he could find something to look forward to then the clouds would roll back. Whatever. His brain was tired so he closed his eyes.

Fifteen minutes later, he woke up. These cat naps were restorative, but as he had stopped wearing a watch, he was hardly aware of them.

What he was aware of, in a dispassionate sort of way, was that his marriage, as he knew it, was all but over. Elizabeth lived in the cottage, but that was all. She kept the fridge stocked, but only prepared food for herself. She went out to work, avoiding him on her return. He couldn't help but admire the lengths she went to in order to perfect this. She had requested that he sleep on the settee, which suited him fine.

He had vaguely been aware that Elizabeth had told him she had been invited to an old college friend for the coming week, being half term. She was going to leave early the next morning.

Sometimes, if their paths crossed, he would catch her watching him fearfully. Maybe she thought he might kill her in her sleep. Just the thought of that made him feel exhausted.

He had received several visits from Alexis, welcome enough, but it felt as if she was talking about someone else when she asked how he was. And then there was the inevitable visit from his parents. They were told that he was suffering from stress. Thomas seemed to think of it as a bad cold, to be recovered from as quickly. Céline was more astute, but Luke was no longer a little boy, to be pampered back to health. (Much as he would have liked to be.) The visit had been awkward for all concerned. They resorted, instead, to phone calls after that.

A week earlier, he had answered the phone. It was mid-morning on a Monday. He had expected it to be one of those cold calls, so was not ready for the voice at the other end of the line. It was that of Mr Collins, his headmaster. It was a voice he knew very well, but had not thought about for what seemed like a very long time.

The head said that he hoped that Luke was feeling brighter. He trusted that his convalescence was doing the trick. It also grieved him tremendously to have to request that Luke hand in his resignation. He waffled on for another couple of minutes. Luke heard the words 'unfortunate', 'out of my hands', 'in the interests of the children', but to be honest, he stopped listening after that.

When the silence had ticked on for several seconds, Luke became aware that the man had stopped speaking. He dragged his gaze back from the cereal packet he had been studying.

He said, "I took your advice. No rash decisions. I thought about it carefully and my letter of resignation to you is already in the post."

Now this conversation reminded Luke that he had one more important task to do before he could relax. He had no idea of the correct procedure, but made the call anyway. He rang through to the school secretary, and asked to speak to the nurse who presided over the medical room. He was put through after announcing himself as a concerned parent. He had the foresight to muffle his voice sufficiently by speaking through the sleeve of his jumper.

But he told the nurse his name. He had become quite friendly with her during his time at the school. He knew she would help him. "Janet, I just need to know, how is Desmond Smith? I don't know who else to ask, can you help?"

"Hi Luke! Yes, I can...I only know because these things are like Chinese Whispers. He's fully recovered, he had mild concussion for a while, and they kept him in because of a bleed. But it was under the scalp, on the outside of the skull. It took time, but now it's gone, and so have the headaches. Mrs Smith came in for a word actually, Desmond came back to school on Monday. She asked me to keep an eye on him. How are you though?" she asked in a concerned voice.

"Well…okay…better for knowing the boy's recovered."

"Will you be coming back, do you think?"

"No! Definitely not! But you take care, Janet. Don't let them grind you down."

Friday 29th October 2010

Driving home from her friend's house in Taunton, Elizabeth was amazed by a feeling that she could barely recognise. It was a flicker of anticipation for the coming weekend.

She had talked late into the nights with Deborah, over several glasses of wine, and had been persuaded that there was hope yet. She just had to give it time. She had tried to describe her feelings to Deborah, but it really was like explaining algebra to a two-year-old.

On her journey home, she thought about it and admitted to herself that the last few weeks had been a nightmarish suspension of time. She could not remember much of it, as each moment had been the same as the one before, the same as the one to come. She had stumbled through it as if on drugs, immune to what was going on around her, apart from flashes of abject horror when faced with her husband. So, having ascertained that he could fend for himself where his basic needs were concerned, she avoided him at all costs.

It did not really occur to her to consider his state of mind. It seemed to her that he had just stopped functioning on that dreadful morning. If someone had told her that he'd had a lobotomy, she would not have been in the least surprised. She seemed unable to wonder what had happened to him, or why. She was wired only to the inside of her own head, to her distressing realisation of being out of control.

The one thing which carried her through was her work. She was able to focus on her pupils, finding reassurance in being able to control them at least. She was also socialising better with her colleagues, playing the part of a concerned wife to those who inquired. It helped her to believe in this version of herself which she had concocted, so she opened up and chatted earnestly with adults who formerly she had ignored or avoided. She painted a tragic picture of a husband at home. She was vague about his ailment, but hinted at her loving involvement in his recovery. It jarred grotesquely with the truth.

However, during the last week before going to Taunton, there had been a subtle change; she likened it to a watery sun appearing momentarily after a particularly drear, dark passing of time. Like lightning flashes illuminating an obscured pleasure, if you blink, you'll miss it. Still tiptoeing around him like a nervous deer, he would startle her by greeting her with a cup of tea, or reading something amusing to her from the newspaper. She began to remain sitting when he entered the room. She considered preparing a meal for them both. She even found herself contemplating sex.

Jaimie was still arriving for Luke's therapy sessions. He knew that he would never talk about his past, but saw these visits merely as a step towards a relearned ability to communicate. Despite his cynical view of counselling, she seemed pleased with his progress.

Luke had begun driving again, just little spins into the country. This morning, he had driven to the chemist in Exsham High Street to collect a further month's tablets. Another visit to the bank to fill his wallet with some cash, and he felt that he had stepped back into the 'Land Of The Living'.

Luke set the iron on its end to cool. He had just folded up the board and slotted it into the tiny space under the stairs when Elizabeth blew into the kitchen, closing her umbrella and shaking her hair into shiny black points. Luke turned towards her, a ready smile as he took her coat and took it upstairs to hang in the shower cubicle to drip. On his return, he found her putting away some shopping, an opened bottle of red wine sitting on the table. Its scrubbed wood had been covered with a cheerful red and white checked cloth. Luke raised his eyes to Elizabeth's to show he had noticed.

She kept eye contact with him a beat longer than he expected, while lifting out a generous slab of fillet steak. She took down two wine glasses. "Join me?" she queried.

Luke nodded. "Jaimie says I can have the odd glass. Too much might make me drowsy, what with the medication." He considered asking how her week in Taunton had gone, but the moment passed.

Elizabeth poured the wine and they clinked glasses, ruby swirls climbing towards each rim.

He sat at the table, watching his wife chop and slice. She shook a pan, releasing the spit and sizzle of hot butter. She added tender fingers of French beans to rolling water in a pan, steam swirling in coils.

The steak was tender, pinkly undulating in folds. The chips were fat and glistening, the crunch opening up the floury texture onto the tongue. Luke sipped his wine, halving the amount of sips to mouthfuls of food to keep from nodding.

They ate at the table. Soft chunks of white bread soaked up the rich gravy. They ate the chips with their fingers, straight from an earthenware dish. Inevitably their fingers collided over a particularly succulent fragment of crisp potato. Their eyes met, hers beamed a green light of encouragement into his. He studied her with apprehension, still too bruised to break open the protective shell his damaged psyche had so recently equipped him with.

He was wary of her. She appeared to have cleared the last five weeks from her mind. His small step to recovery had given him the ability to think of someone else other than himself, and it had not occurred to him that that person might expect more.

Elizabeth deftly removed the debris from the table, piling the now grease-congealed dishes out of sight. She lit a couple of fat candles, cratered deeply from much use. The flames guttered and winked as she carried them to the table, wafted by the draught of her own movement.

"Good meal, thanks," Luke offered tentatively, seeming ready for flight now that the engrossing business of eating was over.

Elizabeth had switched off the main light. Shadows jumped and stretched, throwing her face into shadow as she slipped back into her seat. "It's what most wives do," she said softly. "I'm sorry, Luke. I'm not much good at this. I didn't know how to cope, but you seem so…I don't know…over the worst?"

"Am I?" he inquired wonderingly.

"Oh yes…" she murmured, reaching to touch his hand. "You're back, thank God! And we have to work with each other, not let you slip back. I suppose what I'm saying is that I'm here for you, Luke. We both lost our way back there. I've been quite terrified, if I'm honest, but we'll be fine, just fine." She proffered the wine bottle to Luke, who shook his head, so she up ended the last of it into her glass, filling it.

"I'm not sure, Elizabeth, I…" he began.

Elizabeth interrupted him, swallowing a large gulp of wine. "It won't be easy, I know it. That's what I'm saying. No secrets for a start, remember? That's what we agreed?" She regarded him with bright clear eyes, keen for a fresh start. "Well, I need to put right some stuff I told you ages ago… I hadn't known you long, so I suppose I…well anyway. The bit about my mother putting me up for adoption was true, and not ever knowing my father, but the couple who adopted me from the children's home when I was two? Well, they didn't die in a car crash for a start, so obviously I didn't inherit their money when I was twenty-one either." She braved a glance at Luke, he was staring at the candle in front of him as if mesmerised by the flame.

Elizabeth drank the rest of her wine, tipping her head back and continued. "Mum and Dad were quite loving to me at first, I suppose. But I wasn't very well behaved. I wasn't used to family life, was I? Well they got really strict with me when I annoyed them, which made me behave even more badly. So then they decided that I needed a sibling! That would make me nicer…just as if! So when I was six, they adopted a little boy, called Christopher. He was three years old and I hated him. He had floppy yellow hair, he was very small for his age, and always whining! They adored him from the word go, couldn't do enough for him. They clearly loved him more than they'd ever loved me, and shouted at me if I didn't fawn all over him all the time like they did. It was so unfair. They made me hate him. So when he fell down the stairs, they blamed me! Said I'd pushed him!" She glared at her empty wine glass and as Luke stared at her he could suddenly see the six-year-old girl she had been, the pouting lips, the sullen expression.

"Did you push him?" Luke asked. "No secrets…your rule."

Elizabeth's mouth opened and closed again. "Can't remember…"

"Too easy. Did you push him?"

Elizabeth stood up with a shriek of chair legs scraping the tiled floor. "Yes! Yes! Of course I bloody pushed him! Mum and Dad should have been nicer to me. I was their little girl. They'd told me they'd chosen me from all the others…I was their pretty little girl. And then they gave up on me because I was naughty! Replaced me with that stupid boy. He should have died, but he was just badly bruised. Anyway, they should have loved me whatever I did, but what happened? They took me back to the children's home. So I was rejected twice over, no wonder my head was fucked up…"

Luke felt a shiver run through him. "And the money? How did you get that?" he asked coldly.

Elizabeth spoke in monotone, eyes cast down. "When I was older, I managed to trace my birth mother. I wrote to her. She didn't want to know at first, and then she agreed to let me visit. She was obviously quite well off…she had a massive house in London. She'd been a model when she was young and was still very beautiful. She'd had a great career, very sought after. She had me when she was seventeen, right at the beginning of her success, and didn't know who my father was. She said she never wanted children so decided to put me up for adoption, said she would have aborted me if she'd realised she was pregnant early enough. She said she was lucky that she got her figure back because she was so young…great so far, isn't it?"

"Go on," said Luke, fighting the urge to put his arms around her.

"I didn't know she was taking drugs until after I'd left the home and moved in with her. I was seventeen, and I think she saw herself standing there. We looked very alike. She was drinking too. It was pretty awful. She didn't really want me there, but she was too weak to make me leave. Yay! I'd found my mother at last, but guess what? She didn't want to be found. I reminded her of the reason why she gave up. She hated me then and told me she still did now. I watched her disintegrate before my eyes. She was a mess. She died of an overdose when I was eighteen. I was allowed to stay in the house as I'd come of age. I also inherited a large amount of money, and she'd hidden cash all over the place. I hired an accountant who helped to sell the property for a fortune. All I really had in the whole world was money. It doesn't make you happy, I know that. I bought the flat in Exmouth, got my teaching degree, and you know the rest."

Luke raised troubled eyes to hers. "You've had an unfair start, I'll give you that…but to try to kill someone? My God, Elizabeth…"

"Says the boy who murdered his brother!" She laughed shrilly. "How did you do it, Luke? Throw something hard at him? Push him off a wall? We're just the same, you and I! I hated my brother, and you hated yours! Great to find we have something in common after all."

Luke's flesh felt on fire, and forgotten feelings rushed through him, injustice, anger, disgust. "No! I didn't hate him! I was scared of him, maybe, but I would never hurt him on purpose!" he shouted, nauseated. "I would never do that. I'm not like you. He fell doing a stupid stunt walking along a high wall. I just didn't call for help, I should have called for help, but I didn't. I was only seven years old!"

"And I was only six! No matter how you dress it up, you can't get away from the truth! We both wanted our brothers dead. It's quite amusing if you think about it. We deserve each other!"

Luke kicked himself back from the table. "What else did you do, Elizabeth?" he demanded urgently. "What else are you capable of? Did you want to kill your mother too? She abandoned you when you were a baby…but you gave her second chance, and she blew it. I can't imagine what it must have felt to be told by your mother that she hated you. It must have been easy to do, no? How hard is it to hold a pillow over the face of someone out of their head on drugs and booze?"

Elizabeth's face drained of all colour. She rose unsteadily in an effort to lunge towards him. He side stepped and she fell against the table.

Luke left the room, slamming the door behind him.

Elizabeth, whimpering and sobbing, lurched across to the counter and snatched a bottle of scotch from a selection of drinks. She tossed a large measure into her wine glass and downed it in one. Her head sagged to rest on her arms. She wept as the drink coursed through her blood. She filled her glass twice more until she passed out. The candles burned on and burned out, plunging the room into darkness.

When she came round, late the following morning, Luke had gone.

Chapter Twenty-Eight
It Was Time to Open the Door

Saturday 30th October 2010
On the Road to Somewhere

He'd left the cottage in darkness, not sure of what the time was, but determined not to be around when she woke up. It had not taken him long to gather a few important items into a travel bag, and swallow a mug of black coffee while stroking a sad farewell to Mango. She had taken the opportunity to fall into an instant coma upside down on his lap, offering him her throat to caress, twitching with pleasure. She was clearly not keen for him to leave, and it was with great reluctance that she allowed herself to be tipped gently into her bean bag.

He drove mindlessly for a while, just enough to put a few miles between him and that sensation of being reeled towards a black abyss, one which would swallow him down and keep him there.

Sleep was tugging at his senses. The small amount of wine he had drunk was surging through his blood, chasing the effects of the last dose of medication. He had to stop somewhere before his drooping eyelids slammed shut and slammed him into a tree.

A layby full of black potholes and a couple of slumbering articulated lorries beckoned him in, and a four-star hotel could not have looked more inviting. A thick picnic blanket and a pillow pinched from Elizabeth's bed rendered him cosy enough to be snoring within moments. He would have slept longer, but creeping tendrils of cold began to swirl between gaps in the blanket. They touched his stiff muscles and he woke, stretching aching legs with a groan. A swift check of his watch told him he'd slept for six hours. That would do. He would drive on until he found a greasy spoon transport café for breakfast.

The sky began to show yellow streaks in the east about an hour and a half later. A smoky, dull golden globe climbed slowly above the horizon, brightening the thickly wooded areas lining the road. Wispy clouds gathered in shredded lines around the sun, bleeding pink and violet streaks into the metallic haze. The colours of the trees dazzled Luke as the sun's rays took hold. Copper, burnt orange, deep yellow, whirling past like a kaleidoscope as he drove deeper into the countryside.

7.00 a.m.

As Luke turned off the main 'A' road and began to pass through small villages, he began to look out for signs advertising food. He was soon rewarded and turned gratefully onto the forecourt of a small white building with red trim. A sign on the wall spelled out 'The Stop Start Café'. It had two trestle picnic tables set up optimistically on the damp concrete. Luke ambled stiff-legged towards the door, suddenly realising that it was Saturday. Hopefully it would be open. He was in luck. His watch told him that it was ten past seven, but the café had just opened, an hour later than the usual weekly hours. The proprietor smiled a welcome, wiping his hands on a greasy apron.

Luke sank gratefully into a red plastic chair; his stomach gurgled and he realised that he was starving hungry. The memory of Elizabeth's steak and chips seemed days ago. He ordered the 'Full English' and sat back with a sigh, his hand curled possessively around a steaming cup of frothy coffee.

7.00 a.m.

There was an apricot glow growing above the roofs, lending a momentary shine to the orange tiles and creamy chimney pots. A swirl of birds swept blackly up against the sky, their beaks open at the possibility of an early squirming snack.

Cheryl, head down against the chilly still dark air, had mixed feelings about the gift of the clanking second-hand bike. Somebody, a friend of an acquaintance at the hospital, had taken pity on her leg-aching rushed journey to and fro from shift to her lodgings and back again. She ought to be grateful, really. It shortened her travel time. It was just the unpleasant intimacy of the wind as her knees rose up and down. It was the top-heavy feeling of her bag in the front basket, threatening to tip her onto the road at every turn of the handle bars. The slightest incline made her lungs sound like a pair of bag pipes. This meant she had to dismount at the bottom of the slight slope leading to the hospital entrance in case some good Samaritan thought she was having an asthma attack and carried her into A & E.

Another day, another shift; people calling for her non-stop, not because they were pleased to see her, but because they needed something, another rubbish convenience supper heated in the shared kitchen, always feeling in someone's way, another Saturday evening alone. Oh joy.

7.00 a.m.

Rob felt the pull and tug of the duvet, laying his legs bare. "Oi! Give over! It's flipping freezing!"

Alexis aimed a pillow at his head. "Morning Grumpy!" she retorted. "Need a wee…don't suppose you'd like a coffee?"

Rob groaned and put the pillow over his face. "Are you always so sprightly on a Saturday? What time is it? It feels like yesterday."

"Well, we're awake now so I'll take that as a yes." Alexis came back balancing a tray. She put the cups on each of their bedside tables and climbed back into bed, leaving her dressing gown on. It was the pink fluffy one which Elizabeth had picked out for her Christmas present almost four years ago. "I ought to ring Elizabeth today, see how she's getting on with Luke," she pondered aloud.

Rob sat up and made himself comfy before reaching for his coffee. "Seems like he's more himself now, don't you think?"

"I agree, but this is the dangerous time…it's a slow process, and they still need our support."

Rob blew her a kiss. "I do love you. Always thinking about someone else." He smiled at her.

Alexis reached out a foot to stroke his leg with and sipped her coffee. "Oh yuk! Does your coffee taste okay? This tastes like dishwater."

"Mine's okay…must be your taste buds."

Alexis quickly replaced her cup by her bed and swung her legs out. She disappeared out of the door in an urgent rush. She returned after several minutes looking pale and shaky.

"Are you okay, love? You look rotten…something you ate?" asked Rob with a worried frown.

Alexis sat down on the edge of the bed. She looked at him for a moment, a very sombre expression on his face. "Oh Rob. I don't know how to tell you this…this isn't what we planned at all."

She looked as if she was about to burst into tears.

Rob gazed at her, his eyes round with alarm. "Come on, sweetheart, tell me…are you ill? Whatever it is, we'll get through it…"

Alexis said it swiftly, with her eyes closed so that she wouldn't be able to see his expression of dismay and panic. "My period is three and a half weeks late," she whispered. "And I keep needing to wee, and…"

She felt warm arms around her. A resounding kiss ricocheted on her cheek and she opened her eyes to see Rob's face up close, stubbly chin and a huge grin spreading over his face. "Well, Miss Johnson…I hope this interesting condition is down to my irreverent behaviour and no one else's?"

Alexis pushed him in the chest, and then sank her face against its comforting warmth. "You're not upset?"

"No, love…not upset…terrified, shocked, amazed and extraordinarily happy, but upset? No, not upset."

7.00 a.m.

She tried prising her eyelids apart, not easy. They seemed glued together. And her chin was wet from the drool which had escaped her gaping mouth.

She managed to open her eyes with a sucking sound and stared perplexed at the blurred sideways view of a shadowy room, early light only just permeating the slatted blinds. Her stomach ached from the sitting position she had adopted all night, and her legs were freezing.

As her gaze focused, she marvelled at the swimmy amber mass blocking her left eye. The empty wine glass sat smearily to her right, and all at once she remembered the night before. She straightened up with a grunt, closing her eyes again to allow the shifting of her vision to settle down.

There was the whisky bottle, half empty. This time the sight of it brought a wave of nausea brimming to the back of her throat and she shivered.

Slightly steadied and fortified by strong black coffee, Elizabeth crept up to the bathroom, where she stripped off her stale crumpled clothes. The hot needles of water from the shower massaged her icy skin back to life. Mouth minty and wrapped in a huge fluffy towel, she hesitated before going into the bedroom. She had desperately been trying to remember last night's conversation with Luke. It was like falling asleep towards the end of a film, she could remember so much, and then nothing…as if someone had turned all the lights off.

The memory of the meal was there…it had been a good one. Luke had said he'd enjoyed it. Then…oh yes…she'd wanted a fresh start, no more secrets. She had decided to go back over her past, tell him the truth this time. She remembered that warm feeling of being honest with him for the first time. It was all coming together beautifully.

But then somehow it had turned ugly, Luke had shouted at her. He hadn't understood at all. What was it he'd accused her of? Her mum, that was it… Her heart seemed to stop as the memory hit her. She'd pushed the truth under so many layers of lies over the years that she hardly could believe she had done it. How had Luke been so sure? He had seen right through her.

Elizabeth pushed open the bedroom door and walked in. It took her a few seconds to realise that the bed was neatly made. No one had slept in it.

A couple of strides took her to the window. It was light enough to see that there was a space where Luke normally parked his car.

Indignation was her strongest emotion as she began to look through cupboards and drawers. He had certainly taken a load of belongings, hard to tell what. She thought of that game where you put ten objects on a tray to be memorised, before removing some. It was hard to recall what was no longer there.

Once she realised that he had left without a new batch of medication for the coming month, her anger quickly turned to anxiety as she began to wonder where he'd gone. In his state of mind, he might be capable of anything. The tears began to fall the more she imagined fearful images of bridges, deep water, ravines…

She opened the folder that held all their important documents. Her tears dried instantly as she processed the information that told her that Luke had taken his passport with him. Hers sat there alone in its maroon cover.

Nobody with a suicidal frame of mind took their passport with them, did they?

7.00 a.m.

Céline sighed as the bed sagged with a squeak of springs. The eiderdown with its candlewick bedspread slipped down as Thomas pushed his side of the covers back and heaved himself out with a huge yawn. She shivered and burrowed deeper into the bed.

This was one of the drawbacks of age, Céline thought. Seven o'clock wasn't early, but when Thomas had been up three times already to empty his bladder, it was a bit much. But it wasn't his fault, bless him. It was just that every time she just managed to get back to sleep, he woke her up again.

She threw back the bed clothes, drew her slippers on and padded downstairs. A cup of tea was what she needed.

Céline had switched the kettle on. It began its familiar ascending hiss. So she jumped when Thomas glided into her peripheral vision in silent tartan slippers.

She gasped, covering her heart with her hand.

"It's only me…who did you think I was? The mad man of Borneo?"

Céline's face folded into a scowl. "I don't know this man. But I thought you were a robber! Do you want to kill me sneaking up like that?"

Thomas put his arms around his wife, kissing the nape of her neck and inhaling the warm sleepy scent of her. "Mmm…I still think of you as a young girl…"

Céline stood still, holding the tea caddy in mid-air. She delighted in these romantic gestures. They didn't occur very often, so she savoured them all the more. “That’s because you are looking at the back of my head and can’t see my wrinkles.” She laughed.

“Does this cosy tea party in the kitchen mean that we are getting up?” Thomas asked mournfully.

“Go back to bed and I’ll bring you up your cuppa. Special treat.” She turned round and caught sight of the twinkle in Thomas’s eye. “But I’ll get into the shower, I’ve lots to do today,” she added hastily. ‘A kiss on the neck is quite enough at this time of the morning thank you,’ She thought. (In French)

Céline pottered about for another few minutes while waiting for the tea to brew. She prided herself on her ability to make a good English cup of tea. She wiped over a couple of already clean work tops, aligned the handles of matching saucepans on a shelf, and ran a tea towel over some renegade droplets of water which dared to mar the draining board. She smiled to herself, wondering why it was that a woman always used up a few spare minutes in useful activity, while men, and here she really meant Thomas, (she had observed him waiting for the kettle to boil) just leant against the nearest object and stared vacantly into the middle distance.

She poured tea from a white fat teapot decorated with a strawberry pattern into two matching cups sitting on matching saucers. She arranged these carefully on a tray. She carried it through the lounge and towards the stairs.

Nearing the front door, a crunch of steps on the gravel drive made her glance up. It was much too early for the postman. Who on earth was this? She set the tray down on a small table, suddenly feeling vulnerable in her dressing gown. She pulled the sash tighter round her.

The doorbell rang loudly. And then a second time. It was time to open the door.

Chapter Twenty-Nine

"Good Grief! You're Tying Me Up in Knots!"

Saturday 30th October 2010
Same Day

Elizabeth got dressed swiftly, grabbing a pair of jeans and an old jumper. She made her way downstairs, recoiling at the stale smell in the kitchen and avoiding the sight of the dirty dishes piled up near the sink. She tried to think rationally, but a red mist of fury kept descending on her and preventing logical thought processes. She snatched up her mobile and pressed the 'call' button. She threw it away from her in frustration when it went straight to Luke's voicemail.

She went in search of her jacket and car keys before she realised that it was still only half past eight on a Saturday morning…much too early to pay a visit on them.

Mango burst through the cat flap and began to weave back and forth against Elizabeth's legs. As Elizabeth bent to stroke her, Mango ran hopefully towards her food bowl, making urgent little meows. Elizabeth forked some nasty-looking meat of some description into Mango's filthy encrusted dish. The plastic mat underneath was covered in food splatters and muddy paw prints which obscured the cartoon picture of a smiling pussy cat.

Elizabeth made a mental note to do some cleaning up soon.

"Hey! How do you know for sure that you're pregnant without doing one of those kit things?"

"I just know…I am a nurse, you know."

"I know you are. Still, I think we ought to do it properly…you never know, you might have made a mistake?"

"Is this what I think it is?"

"What?"

"Are you hoping it will turn out negative?"

"Did I say that? I never said that…"

"But would you like it to be negative?"

"Would you?"

"What sort of question is that? You know I wouldn't!"

"Well…it's okay for you to ask me that question, even though you know what I would like it to be…so what are we arguing about?"

"Good grief! You're tying me up in knots!"

"There we are! That's all the proof we need! Your brain has already turned to baby mush!"

Rob dodged a screwed-up tissue as it flew past his nose. "Come on, hormonal one…get yourself in that shower and I'll make the bed for you, just this once."

Alexis let out a squeak of indignation.

"Hurry up! I can't wait to do this!" Rob grinned at her, grabbing up her dressing gown and placing it gently round her shoulders.

"Where are we going?"

"To the nearest chemist, of course. Don't complain that I never take you anywhere."

In the end, they bought three pregnancy tests, just to make absolutely sure. Rob hopped up and down in the doorway to the bathroom, holding a huge glass of water for Alexis to sip from.

They had followed the instructions carefully. "Is this big enough?" asked Rob, who had gone in search of a container for Alexis to wee into.

She blinked as he passed her an eggcup. "Er…not really. I'm not a man."

"I noticed…" Rob sighed. He finally found a nice wide container which could be wedged in the toilet bowl. "Do you want me to run a tap? Oh you've done it already…Now for the exciting part. It says 'Put the strip in at the end with an arrow.' Careful! Don't drop it…do you want me to…?"

"No! Well, sorry, you can help with the next one. Right, no further than the max line…okay one, two, three seconds." She handed the strip to Rob and he laid it on the edge of the bath. He let out a whoop as a new band appeared below the control band. It grew darker as he stared at it. A sure sign of a positive pregnancy.

He gazed with admiration at Alexis. "Wow…you're amazing…"

She burst into laughter. "What sitting on the loo?" she gasped.

"Especially sitting on the loo. Adorable. I will tell our son of this moment." He threw the first pregnancy strip onto the bed and handed her the second.

"It might be a girl."

"It might be twins…one of each?" The second test was positive. This one was thrown with even gayer abandon, landing in his empty teacup.

As the third one showed positive, Alexis leapt off the loo and she and Rob held hands and danced around. Rob put his arms around her and waltzed her through the bedroom and into the lounge. He held the strip aloft like a bunch of mistletoe and kissed her soundly, before whirling it up into the air. It landed amongst the sofa cushions.

Alexis went to the kitchen to prepare a celebration pan of scrambled eggs. "Answer that, would you Rob?" she called as the phone began to ring.

"Damn it! Where the hell have you been? I've been ringing you on and off for ages!" came the agitated voice of Elizabeth. Rob held the phone away from his ear and grimaced at Alexis.

She mouthed, "Who is it?" Rob shrugged, shaking his head.

"Who is this?" he asked in a calm voice.

"Elizabeth!" she shouted. "Oh, for God's sake! Let me speak to Alexis!"

"She's busy!" he snapped, feeling irritated. "Calm down, will you! We've been out. What's the emergency?"

"Don't either of you have a mobile phone?"

Rob sighed. "Look…get to the point…"

Alexis stopped stirring the eggs and mouthed, "What?" at Rob with eyebrows raised. He shrugged helplessly.

"He's only bloody gone!" Elizabeth hissed. "After all I've done! No thanks, no explanation…"

Rob leaned his elbows on the worktop near Alexis, frowning with consternation. "Whoa…slow down, Elizabeth! You're talking about Luke?"

"Who else?" she shouted crossly.

"Hey…simmer down. The bloke's not well, you know that. Just tell me calmly what happened. When did he go?"

"I don't know," said Elizabeth in a sullen voice. "I was asleep…he never came to bed last night."

"What? Did you argue? How was his mood? Did he seem troubled about anything? Have you tried ringing him?"

"Oh, don't start with the questions! I'm not one of your disturbed teenagers. He won't answer his phone. How do I know what was going on in his head? You said it yourself, he's not well."

Rob shot Alexis an exasperated look. She mimed taking the phone from him, but he turned away. "All the more reason to be worried…hang on a minute…did he take his car?"

"Yes…and some of his stuff…and his wallet…"

"Why didn't you say that before? No, no, don't go off on one. Come over to us and we'll try and think what to do. Are you ok to drive? Okay then, be careful and we'll see you soon." He slammed the phone down. "Did you get the gist of that, love?"

Alexis nodded.

Rob frowned with displeasure. "Well! What an unpleasant woman! I've just seen a side of your sister-in-law that I wasn't aware of. You made her sound sweet and vulnerable. That was some conversation! She's not thinking about Luke's welfare at all! She just seems put out that he's left her in the lurch! What a selfish bitch!"

Alexis stared at Rob in surprise. "Oh Rob, she's frightened and out of her depth! She's had an awful lot to deal with in her life… She needs friends right now, not a character assassination!"

They glared at each other for a moment. Rob was tempted to remind her that Luke was the one in need of friends and that poor Elizabeth's unhappy childhood was no excuse for her shallow behaviour…but he thought better of it.

Rob's face softened as he took in Alexis's worried face. "Okay, love, there's no need for us to fall out. We're stronger than that, aren't we? Let's just concentrate on Luke right now. He needs us, Al."

"Okay," she said, her eyes tearing up. "What do we do now then? Should we call the police?"

Rob took the wooden spoon out of her hand and put it down. He looked down at her, smoothing her hair back with his fingers. He thought for a moment before replying. "I don't think so. Luke's a rational man. He's been depressed, yes, but he's not shown any signs of irrational behaviour, as far as we know. I think it would be more important to get in touch with his CPN. He's still having sessions with her, so she needs to know that he's gone off somewhere. She's more likely to know about his state of mind, more than any of us."

Elizabeth entered the flat just over half an hour later. She wore no makeup, and her jeans were crumpled as if she had fished them out of the dirty clothes basket. Alexis moved to her side to envelope her in an embrace, but Elizabeth shook her off impatiently.

"God, you look rough," he greeted her rudely, taking in her tired looking, pink-rimmed eyes.

"Well… she's had a shock…" commented Alexis.

"You could call it that. I think she's more upset that Luke has left without permission…."

Alexis shot him a warning glance, and he shut his mouth reluctantly.

Elizabeth scowled at him. "I didn't come here to be hassled by you," she snapped. "You've no idea what it's been like, treading on eggshells round him…"

"Hey guys, this isn't helping," said Alexis quietly. "When is that Jaimie Porter due to see Luke again, Elizabeth?"

Elizabeth looked at her vaguely as if finding it hard to concentrate. "Um, Monday afternoon? Yeah, I think Luke said about two o'clock."

"We'll have to let her know what's happened. Have you got a contact number for her?"

Elizabeth nodded. She appeared to have lost all her hostility, slumping into a dejected mood.

Alexis still felt sorry for her sister-in-law. She couldn't help it. It was in her nature to try and put herself in other people's shoes. That was why she had always tried to give her the benefit of the doubt. "Go and sit down, Elizabeth, I'll make some coffee. Rob?" She smiled at him encouragingly and he grudgingly responded, ushering Elizabeth to the settee.

Elizabeth found Jaimie Porter's contact number in her mobile and pressed the call button. She was surprised when Jaimie answered at once. Elizabeth told her briefly what had occurred and was reassured by Jaimie's opinion that Luke probably just needed to get away to think. It could be a sign of recovery. She said if he hadn't been in touch by Monday morning, then to let her know. Elizabeth said she was worried that Luke would be running out of his medication shortly. Alexis and Rob looked up in concern at this added news. Jaimie assured her that she would be able to find out whether Luke had ordered the next month's tablets. She said she hoped that he would return by the end of the weekend, to just sit tight and try not to worry.

Elizabeth put her mobile down, looking crestfallen. Alexis put a cup of coffee next to her. Neither she nor Rob knew what to say.

Elizabeth gazed at the couple. The tears were very close to the surface. She felt so alone and frightened. And so jealous of Alexis with her good-looking kind partner and perfect life. She always seemed to be on the periphery of other people's lives. It was so unfair. She gave a sob, casting her eyes down. Her hands were clutching the soft seat of the settee in her distress, and her fingers caught hold of something half tucked under her thigh. She brought it out and looked at it numbly.

"Oh my God! Alexis! You're pregnant…oh God!"

Alexis gaped as she realised what Elizabeth had said. She stared at the strip in Elizabeth's hand.

She jumped up and walked over to her. “Oh Elizabeth! We weren’t going to tell anybody yet! We only found out this morning!” She laughed awkwardly.

Elizabeth just kept staring at the object in her hand as if she could not tear her eyes away from it. And the silence stretched on and on.

Chapter Thirty

"She Brought Her Own Destructive Damage to Your Door"

Saturday 30th October 2010
Same Day

Céline went up on her tiptoes to look through the peephole set into the front door. Finding it hard to balance steadily on her toes, she couldn't focus long enough to make out the person's features.

She withdrew, planning to be sensible and call Thomas down, when there was a firm knock on the door. She drew nearer hesitantly and placed her ear to the smooth surface.

"Mum…let me in, Mum. It's flaming cold out here."

"Who is it?" Céline asked loudly.

"It's Father Christmas. Who do you think it is?"

Long pause. "You do sound kind of woolly."

"If it puts your mind at rest, why don't you look through the letter box?"

Another dubious pause. Then Céline bent down and knelt on the door mat. She gingerly opened the flap and put her eyes to the gap.

"Céline! What in heavens name are you doing? Have you dropped something? I can hear voices."

"Don't tell anyone. They'll manhandle you off to a home." Céline chuckled, looking round at Thomas glowering in his pyjamas on the stairs.

"Well done! That's a good word, Céline. I just don't appreciate its use in this context."

"Have you two been drinking? Much as I admire your caution, I'd really like one of you to open the door?" came Luke's plaintive voice.

Céline sprang up from her knees and grasped the door handle. "It's okay, Thomas, it's Luke. I recognised his scarf."

Luke felt very strange ensconced on the settee. There was a red blanket over his knees, which brought back instant memories of days off school with tummy bugs. A plate holding two scones oozing homemade clotted cream was balanced next to him. He frowned at Céline, who was sitting opposite him with a concerned motherly expression.

"I'm not 'that' sort of ill, you know, Mum. I just needed a bit of calm. I would have rung, but I didn't want any fuss, really."

Thomas grunted from behind his paper. "See? I told you…he needs his own space, he's not five."

Céline flapped her hands crossly. "And nor am I! You treat me like a child, that's all right I suppose… but I'm forty-seven! And I don't understand why giving someone a nice warm scone is making a fuss. If we left all that sort of thing to you, Thomas, we'd all be eating dry bread on paper plates…"

Thomas tutted and rolled his eyes. "Shhh Céline…before we send the poor boy mad with our marital differences. Well, Luke, I think we need to discuss the situation. You said you left really early this morning…that suggests to me a difference of opinion? Is Elizabeth fine with your coming here?"

Luke swallowed and looked at his father. He decided to answer candidly. "The thing is, Elizabeth isn't coping very well with my…how would you describe it? My temporary malfunction." He gave his parents a watery smile. "Alexis has been lovely, but she cries a lot when she thinks I can't hear. The only real comfort has been Mango…but I could hardly kidnap her."

"Catnap," corrected Céline.

"Yes, but do they know you're here?"

Luke shook his head. "You're right, Alexis should be told. She's worrying enough about me as it is, without this. I've been selfish, but I couldn't really think straight."

"And Elizabeth? How did she take your escape into the night? Not well, I'm guessing?"

"She was asleep when I left. I don't really think she will miss me at all. She's finding it all a lot to contend with."

Céline looked at Luke in amazement. "What? You didn't tell her you are leaving? Mon Dieu…that poor girl! She will be thinking of you under a bus or down a hole somewhere! You must ring her immediately!"

Luke narrowed his eyes at her. "No, Mum, you don't understand. I mean absolutely nothing to her, so why should I bother to tell her where I am? Let her stew."

Céline opened her mouth, looking bewildered. Thomas explained, "He means 'let her be left in the dark'." Céline looked none the wiser.

With Céline safely out of the way, humming happily as she made her way upstairs to make up the bed for Luke in Alexis's old room, Thomas sat near his son and eyed him seriously.

"You have made your mother's day. She's so happy to have you home again, that she's unable to see past turning the radiator on in your room and I can see the shopping list already forming in her head in preparation for the making of your favourite meals."

Luke looked away as a shadow passed across his face. "That's okay, isn't it, Dad? She loves all that domestic stuff. She loves to be needed."

"Look at me, Luke. Let's be honest with each other. It's not food and a warm bed that you need, it is inner peace, a loving relationship; in other words, happiness. Am I right? I don't think even your mother is capable of waving that sort of magic wand over you, do you?"

"I'd happily settle for a bit of mothering actually. My marriage is over. I've accepted that now, and neither of you can mend that. I've been in a pretty bad place getting my head round things, but I've had some help. I'm taking the pills, and now I just need to stay here for a while and lick my wounds, if that's okay?"

Thomas sighed. "I'm not going to turn you out, am I? But you're wrong if you think I agree with your running away from the situation. What happened to 'for better, for worse'?

Luke gave a cynical grimace. "The same fate as what happened to 'in sickness and in health', I guess."

Thomas tutted irritably. "And have you considered the extremely foolish move of leaving your estranged wife in the marital home? She'll change the locks and claim that 'possession is nine tenths of the law'. You could end up homeless!"

Luke looked at his father miserably. "Dad, I'm tired, so tired. I really don't care…about anything. All I want is to remove myself from a black place, to stop the situations and people who are making me feel so worthless and insignificant. Elizabeth is killing me."

Thomas stood up slowly. Having never suffered from depression in his life, clinical or otherwise, he fought hard with the urge to tell Luke to pull himself together, to act like a man, fight for his marriage, or throw the baggage out.

He could imagine Céline's reaction to this however, so he said instead, "Well, I won't pretend I liked her. She brought her own destructive damage to your door, never mind about her captivating looks. I fell for your mother in exactly the same way, but luckily for me she had no hidden agendas. But there but for the grace of God go I, I suppose. You can stay here for as long as you like, of course. And now I'm going to go and call Alexis." He hesitated as he caught Luke's worried glance. "Don't worry, I'll ask her not to let Elizabeth know where you are. It'll be hard as she thinks the world of her, God knows why. Same as your mother. They both seem completely taken in by the 'poor little orphan Annie' story."

Thomas made the call in the privacy of his office. He was startled at the male voice which replied. He had forgotten that Alexis's boyfriend had moved in to her flat. Céline had announced the news gleefully to him a few weeks ago, but as his initial response was to drive over and remove the man physically, Céline had talked him into some semblance of acceptance and then removed him from the loop of her gossip. No wonder he had forgotten; he was more and more aware that the women in his life were choosing not to discuss certain things with him.

Thomas scowled at the receiver and spoke petulantly, "Hello…is that Bob?"

"Hello there. It's Rob, actually…did you want Alexis? She's out at the moment… who shall I say called?"

"This is her father. Yes, no, I mean I did want to speak to her, but hang on a minute…this is about Luke…"

Rob swallowed hard. He had to handle this delicately. If the old man was suddenly informed that his son had disappeared, the news might kill him. "Luke?" he queried in an off-hand manner.

"Have you spoken to him recently?" Thomas demanded.

"Um…not as such. We've not met yet actually." He floundered, wondering how to explain that he had been living with Alexis for almost a month, but had never met his girlfriend's brother. He knew that the depth of Luke's breakdown had been somewhat concealed from Thomas and Céline by Alexis. And certainly for the last month, Luke had been in no fit state for social introductions. It had been a tacit agreement that Rob should meet Luke when he had returned to full health.

He jumped as Thomas raised his voice in response. "So! You've wangled your way into my daughter's heart, not to mention her flat, without first meeting myself or her brother? What have you got to hide? Squirming like a coward through the back door! Have you no decency?"

At that moment, Céline entered the office from the hall where she had been listening to the conversation. She marched across to her husband and snatched the phone from him. "Hello? Robert? So lovely to speak to you…this is Céline. Excuse my husband, he has a very short memory these days of how he conducted his own approach to myself when we met! I will tell you all about it sometime if he continues to shout at you…" She tucked the phone into her neck and out of Thomas's exasperated reach. She continued, "It seems that Thomas has no intention to tell you himself, so I will...Luke is here, he has come home to recover himself. He is not his usual self, Robert, and so it is a good thing you have not met yet. When you do, it will be a pleasure to you. He is a good boy. Like you, I think. Alexis has told me all about you."

Rob opened his mouth and shut it again, not quite sure what to say to this delightful French voice that sounded like that of a much younger woman. "I'll tell Alexis that Luke is safe. She's been worried to death about how to tell you he had disappeared," he responded eventually. "She's not in at the moment. She and Elizabeth are out and about in Exmouth...girly shopping, you know."

"Well, you can tell them both! One bird killed by two stones, isn't it?"

Now it was Thomas's turn to take the phone from Céline. "Hello...Bob? I apologise for my rudeness, as usual my wife has poured oil on troubled waters." He raised his eyebrows at Céline's perplexed face. "Her grasp of English is extremely good, but it seems she is finding it hard to take in that Luke has no wish for his wife to know of his whereabouts at the moment. So I would appreciate it if you and Alexis keep it quiet. Thank you."

"Of course, no problem."

"Nice speaking to you, young man. Look after Alexis. She's the only daughter I have, so treat her well, you hear?"

Rob switched the phone off with a sigh. He felt wrung out after that conversation. It was like walking through a minefield. He quaked at the thought of announcing that Alexis was pregnant. He wouldn't be surprised if Thomas didn't suggest pistols at dawn...

Thomas and Céline sat in their usual chairs in the lounge. The settee, with Luke stretched out along it under his red blanket, lay between them like an unfolding mystery. His chin was sunk onto his chest, light snores rumbling from his open mouth.

Céline was thinking, 'poor boy with his troubles; the chance that he would never know the joy of fatherhood, the depression that was robbing him of his cheerful demeanour, his troubled marriage.'

Thomas was thinking, 'at last this might be the best thing to have happened to his son, a chance to escape his poisoned marriage, the fate that seemed to be ensuring that no child would be spawned from such a dangerous union, and a depression that if treated successfully might restore that happy side of Luke which Thomas had not really seen for a long time. If they could just help and support him through these next difficult months.'

Husband and wife shared an affectionate smile over the sleeping form of their troubled boy, united once more by the bonds of parenthood.

"Thomas?"

"Mmm?"
"What is this oil I have been pouring on these waters?"
Thomas closed his eyes. He'd done enough talking for one morning.

Chapter Thirty-One

"She's Threatened to Turn Up There and Make a Scene"

Three Weeks Later

These three weeks had passed swiftly for some and slowly for others.

For Alexis, the days were flying by. Her worries about Luke were put aside slightly by her euphoria of her pregnancy, and life with her gorgeous Rob. She could just about put up with the nausea, it was a small price to pay, and the nurse at the surgery assured her it would diminish soon. She rang her parents every few days, accepting grudgingly that Luke did not want to speak. Céline assured her that to recover from this temporary mental derangement, as her mother described it, ('I looked it up in la dictionaire, ma petite') Luke had to be calmed and left alone to pull round at his own pace.

Elizabeth, on the other hand, found time stretching out in an agonising nightmare. Behind her stacked up empty days which had dripped reluctantly into each other, like an ancient stalagmite, to form sluggish weeks. She was unable to grasp that Luke had gone; he had filled her thoughts constantly for so long, that when he was suddenly no longer there, it was as if she had been stopped mid-sentence.

It hardly occurred to her that she had been preoccupied with thoughts of him for all the wrong reasons. She had been trying to think back to what could have made him leave. She had accepted the news of his infertility, had tried to discuss the death of his brother in order to help him, even confided in him her own nugget of discomfort that she hated her own brother. She had been trying to share this information with him to make him feel better. She even forgave him his infidelity with Cheryl by inviting him straight into their marital bed. And then his horrendous behaviour at school! She hadn't seen that coming! And what did she do? Wrapped him up in cotton wool, taken time off work to mollycoddle him at home, only to be thanked by cold behaviour and his resignation from his job. She could hardly bear to recall that last humiliating evening. Bending over backwards to be a good understanding wife...that meal! Well, she had surpassed herself, all in an attempt for a fresh start, and he had slammed a final door in her face.

All her good intentions towards Luke had back-fired. She could not see that she had only been concentrating on her own forgiving and accepting behaviour, as she saw it, in the light of Luke's failures. She'd stepped on his fragile ego in an effort to boost herself even higher in her own esteem.

Now that he was gone, she had lost her footing. She was dangerously out of control. She immersed herself into her work, tried texting and calling Luke on his mobile twenty times a day, scoured and de-grimed every inch of the cottage, so that everything shone and sparkled, even Mango, and these things helped her believe that she was still on top, that Luke would return at any moment.

Saturday 20th November 2010

Alexis was finding herself in an awkward position; she desperately yearned for a female friend to share her hormonal highs and lows with, and Elizabeth was the obvious one to turn to, but this was not a very tactful move in the light of her husband's recent disappearance.

Alexis sat curled up on Elizabeth's settee, hugging a comforting cushion to her stomach. She gazed round the room, appreciating the polished surfaces, the fragrant scent wafting from a bowl of fresh limes and tangerines, the bunch of dark red and gold chrysanthemums in a chunky pottery vase.

"Have you told your mum and dad yet?" Elizabeth called from the kitchen over the sound of a drawer opening and closing.

"No, not yet, we wanted to wait 'til the twelve-week scan anyway…"

"Which is….?" asked Elizabeth, popping her head round the door.

"Around the first of December. But as they haven't even met Rob yet, we thought we'd go down and see them, make the proper introductions, and then announce it, if the meeting goes favourably!

"Don't worry, it'll be fine. He's a lovely bloke. Coffee or tea, Al?"

"Do you have green tea by any chance?"

"Yes…it might taste a bit musty. Someone gave it to me months ago and I only tried it once. Yuk! It's like pond water. Biscuit?"

"Better not! I'm going to become fat enough without going down that road!"

Elizabeth moved into the room carrying two mugs. "Honestly, Alexis!" She sighed as she passed the mug of grey scummy liquid over with distaste. "You don't have to make a martyr of yourself for the whole nine months you know!"

Alexis glanced at her friend doubtfully.

"I'm joking! If you get fat and lose your sense of humour too…well, there's no hope for you!"

Alexis smiled. "I'm just so happy. This is such a fantastic time for me, I feel I have to do everything just right. I would recommend this feeling to anyone, honestly Elizabeth!"

Elizabeth frowned. "That's not funny. Are we talking about a miraculous conception here? I think it's easier if both parties are in the same country at least, don't you?" she said bitterly.

Alexis blushed furiously, covering her face with her hands. "Oh God! I'm so stupid! Sorry, Elizabeth! But, what makes you think that Luke is out of the country?"

Elizabeth stared hard at Alexis. "And what makes you think that he isn't?" she asked.

Alexis, not accustomed to prevarication, floundered in an effort to formulate a convincing answer. "I don't know where he is!" she answered. "He's not a child. I'm sure he'll be in touch soon…"

"Don't treat me like an imbecile, Alexis. I don't believe you. You must know where he is. You'd be out of your mind with worry otherwise. Everyone keeps telling me that he's probably holed up somewhere, getting his head together. And where would he do that, Alexis? He was hardly feeding himself properly before he left…he's always been needy. First his mum, and then me. I don't get it that he's out there somewhere on his own!"

Alexis, her hormones driving her emotions to the surface, felt her bottom lip wobble, tears gathered and fell. She stared down at her hands.

"I'm fed up with you all ganging up on me!" Elizabeth suddenly snarled. "He's my husband! You all know something! Your bloody parents put the phone down on me when I try to call them. Tell me, Alexis! He's there, isn't he? In Cornwall? I thought I could trust you, of all people! If you don't tell me, I'll just have to go there and confront them. They can't stop me from seeing him. I hate all your family, Alexis…and most of all I hate you!"

Alexis had never felt the lash of Elizabeth's tongue, and it startled and mortified her. She had witnessed her sulks and moods at third hand, but this attack caved her in. She stumbled to her feet, slopping the still-full mug onto the coffee table, and left the cottage without looking back.

Rob was sitting at the dining room table studying a pile of case notes when Alexis returned to the flat. He looked up. "I thought you were going to give me a call when you needed picking up? Everything okay, sweetheart?"

Alexis approached him slowly, unwinding her red scarf. Rob caught hold of it and pulled her tenderly onto his lap. "You're freezing! Did you get the bus?"

Alexis nodded. "She was horrible to me, Rob! She thinks we're lying about Luke..."

"Well we are! You have to grow up a bit, Al... Elizabeth is not another kid in the playground. She's an angry spoilt young woman who goes crazy when she doesn't get her own way. Your trouble is that you never see people as they really are. I've tried to make you see that Elizabeth is capable of real destructive behaviour when crossed..."

Alexis pulled away. "I thought you'd stick up for me! It was never my idea to keep the truth from her!"

"I'm just saying that you refuse to face reality. Don't get upset. I love that you see the best in people, but I hate it when you can't see what's staring you in the face, and then get hurt. Luke hasn't helped. You tell me that he's never bad mouthed Elizabeth in your presence, even when it's obvious that she makes him unhappy."

"That's because he's loyal! We were brought up with certain standards! I really think she has the right to be told that Luke's in Cornwall! How would you feel if I'd disappeared and everyone knew where I was but hid it from you?"

"That's a ridiculous hypothetical argument. The difference being that Elizabeth is not good for Luke, and everyone can see it. How can you put her rights before your brother's happiness? Cheryl is your one of your best mates, yet she clearly has an issue with Elizabeth. You'd think she would have turned to you about it. The trouble is that people like you too much and don't want to upset you."

Alexis sighed heavily and sat down opposite him. "Why are you having a go at me?" she accused him sadly.

"Because the bloody woman is getting away with murder. I think a great deal of you, your parents, and what I've heard of Luke too. I can't just stand by and watch her cause such stress. I want to wake you up, Al, not protect you. That's not helpful. I love you. We never argue, and yet here we are, at hammer and tongs because of her!"

Alexis reached out and Rob gripped her hand warmly. She smiled at him. "I love you, too, even when you tell me off like a silly school girl. But I'm worried, Rob. Elizabeth is convinced that Luke is with our parents. She's threatened to turn up there and make a scene."

Rob looked thoughtful. "We have to warn them then. This could set Luke back. Did she say when she'll go?"

“No. She was so angry, I suppose there’s nothing to stop her driving there at once! What shall we do?”

“We’ll ring them now. Do you want me to do it, yeah? Okay, what’s the number?”

Chapter Thirty-Two

He Seemed Taller Than She Remembered

Saturday 20th November 2010
Cornwall

To be honest, Luke was quite relieved when his parents came in to tell him about Elizabeth's intentions. Days had passed in a haze of inactivity, never having to worry about even the most trivial domestic detail. His mother even put out a suggested choice of clothes to wear the next day. It had been a welcome therapy at first. When he had arrived here in the safe harbour of his old home, he had not given much thought to the future. He took each day as it came, spending his time gazing out of the windows at the bleak but beautiful views, rolling November skies stretching away, black, stunted trees, their branches bent into improbable angles, all leaning away from years of the violent winter gales that sweep across Cornwall. Soon he was taking longer and longer walks, returning to the cottage with wind-whipped cheeks and muddy boots, his pockets full of bits; a bird's wing, a fir cone, the skeleton of a leaf.

Sometimes he could hear the murmur of his parents' conversation through a closed door. He listened to them as he used to do as a child, small, but safe too, as he had felt then. At times, though, he made out Thomas's voice raised in irritation, and it occurred to him more and more as the healing raised him closer to the surface of normality that it was nearing the time when he would have to leave.

He had been here exactly three weeks. Céline's sweet administrations to his requirements were beginning to smother him. He felt as if he had been asleep in a cramped position for hours, and he needed to walk about and stretch his limbs. This need was growing, like a hunger.

His parents entered the room together like a comedy act, only their expressions were sombre.

Luke looked up at them questioningly. "What's up?" he asked.

Céline sat on the arm of his chair and ruffled his hair. He could not help twitching away slightly.

"Rob and Alexis just rang. They said that Elizabeth has told them that she knows you're here."

Luke turned to look up at her incredulously. "Who told her that? Oh God, will she never leave me alone?"

Thomas sat down opposite them. "Steady, Luke. She guessed...although it can't have been hard to work it out. Where else would you have gone? Apparently, she plans on driving down to talk to you."

Luke gave a mirthless laugh. "And when do we expect this pleasure? She's unbelievable."

Céline threw her hands out expressively. "That's it! They don't know! Any time..."

Thomas spoke soothingly, "Let's not panic. Are you sure it wouldn't be a good idea to talk to her Luke? You have things you need to discuss, surely?"

"No, not yet, Dad...I'm not ready for this. But I'm not panicking, you know, I was going to move on soon anyway." He held up his hand as his mother looked at him in dismay. "You've both been very supportive, but I'll be out of here by the end of the week."

Céline covered her mouth in distress. "Where will you go, mon chéri?"

"Somewhere where she won't find me," Luke said in a monotone.

"What if she arrives tomorrow? Or tonight? Mon Dieu!"

Thomas tutted loudly. "She's a silly selfish woman, not a mass serial killer! Let's get this into perspective. Luke doesn't have to talk to her if he doesn't want to. Now, if Luke is set on leaving in a few days, then we have to discuss his options. And pick up more medication. How are you off for money?"

Luke rolled his eyes. He was grateful, but the parental ties were pulling too strongly. It was definitely time to move on, while he felt strong enough to do it, before he gave up and went under again.

Despite Luke's nonchalance, he was relieved when the evening passed without that unwelcome knock at the door. The following day was harder to take. They knew it would take Elizabeth two hours to drive down from Exsham, whether she would bother to make the four-hour round trip on a Sunday was questionable, but by eleven o'clock that morning, fed up with jumping at every sound, Luke suggested that the three of them go out for the rest of the day. Thomas mentioned the name of a quaint pub in Newquay for a bite to eat, followed by a blustery walk along the coast. They all relaxed as the car left their small village of St. Evan behind.

"This is such a good idea!" Céline observed cheerfully. She sang a few words of a Georges Brassens song. "He was my mother's favourite," she said dreamily. "We should have done this before, it would have cheered Luke up."

Thomas turned to her affectionately. "You are such an optimist, my darling…most women would be thinking of their son recovering from a difficult marriage, his planned escape to a place unknown, and fleeing from the house to avoid meeting the poisonous daughter-in-law. You sound as if we are on a day out on our summer holidays!"

"Oh, you are an old grouse! Do you have to spoil everything? It's good to wear the pink glasses at times like this, n'est-ce pas?"

"I think you mean 'grouch', Mum. And yes, I agree with you, let's turn this into a great day out together. I refuse to let her get to me." Luke laughed properly for the first time in weeks.

After a simple but filling pub lunch of a Ploughman's; crusty rolls, creamy butter, tangy, crumbling Farmhouse cheddar and dark, spicy pickle, they climbed replete back into the car. "Where do you fancy walking?" asked Thomas of his passengers, who both looked more ready for a doze than anything.

"You are chauffeur…" murmured Céline sleepily. "Aha, this is a French word you have pinched."

Thomas glanced at his wife, who sat with her eyes closed and a smile on her lips. He swallowed the unexpected lump that had formed in his throat, and headed the car towards Mawgan Porth, a haven offering a delightful beach, rock pools alluring young and old alike, and a choice of walks north or south.

The six-mile journey from Newquay was long enough to elicit a few ladylike snores from Céline. She was not quite so genteel on being shaken awake, but the trio were soon making good headway on the one and a half-mile walk along the cliffs from Mawgan Porth towards Bedruthan steps.

Luke linked arms with Céline, laughing at her choice of footwear, brown suede boots lined with honey-coloured fur.

"Don't even go there!" warned Thomas. "I have long ago learned not to reply honestly when asked for my opinion on your mum's wardrobe decisions."

Céline looked down at her feet, mystified, as if expecting them to have grown ears or something equally amusing.

Unbeknownst to the three intrepid ramblers, their lengthy plans to vacate the house for the day had turned out to be a complete waste of time.

Elizabeth had indeed fully intended to set off early that Sunday, hoping to arrive midmorning. Her idea was to sweet talk Luke into returning home with her. Screaming and shouting was not an option, she realised, and she needed to prove to his parents that Luke would benefit from being restored to her capable and healing hands.

She was all organised, Mango fed, a chicken in the slow-cooker as an easy meal to share with Luke later, the lights on timer, curtains semi-closed…she was wrapped in her warmest red winter coat, sitting next to her bulging handbag, her fingers on the keys in the ignition, when there was a knock on her window.

He stood there, an old grey cardigan flapping over a faded t-shirt, miming her winding down her window, even though Elizabeth had only ever experienced electrically controlled windows.

"Lucky I noticed," he said, pointing downwards. "Flat tyre, unusual these days, but I always check mine before I go anywhere. Habit. You'll not get far on that," he observed cheerfully.

Elizabeth felt a childish surge of exasperation. If she'd left the house five minutes earlier, he might not have noticed. She bit her lip crossly, realising how stupid she was being, yet frustrated as hell. She just wanted to be on her way. Her impetuous decision had not included this setback.

Eventually she managed to calm her anger and actually to show some authentic gratitude to Bill Davis, who lived opposite on his own, and, now she came to think about it, had always shown a warm and friendly greeting for her and Luke.

She watched while he produced the spare temporary wheel (did he really call it a doughnut?) from her boot, a jack, and a metal thingy that fitted over the wheel nuts. It took him a while, aided by a mug of tea with several ginger biscuits, to do the job. When he'd finished, Elizabeth was suitably thankful, until he advised her not to drive on the doughnut very far.

"It'll get you as far as 'Tom's tyre and exhaust' in Countess Weir, know it?" he asked. "He'll fit you in, I'm sure. I'll ring him for you if you like. Be an idea to get two new front tyres, so they're balanced…"

Elizabeth groaned. "Yeah…I know where you mean, but how long will it take him?"

Bill awarded her with a wry smile. "You young things are so impatient! How long is a piece of string? Going far, were you? At least now you'll be roadworthy for work tomorrow."

So Elizabeth had abandoned her journey and it was not until the following Saturday that she was able to set out once again for Cornwall.

Thomas had insisted on lending Luke enough money to see him through several months to come. An overnight ferry crossing from Plymouth to St. Malo was booked for the coming Friday night, and Luke had managed to contact the owners of the cottage in the Gironde Estuary which had been such a hub of family holidays over the years. The cottage stood empty for most of the winter months, but the gravelly voice of old Madame Le Blanc, the owner who lived a few doors away, assured him that it could be cleaned and aired in moments, ready for him on his arrival on the Saturday. It was a good five-hour drive from the ferry, but he reckoned if he could get some sleep on the crossing, he would be refreshed and should arrive at the cottage by early afternoon.

His parents felt comforted at the thought of Luke staying in the cottage. It felt right, said Céline, as if he were going home. He put their minds at rest about how he would cope, optimistic that with his fluent French and practical skills, he would be able to find local work pretty quickly.

He had enough medication for the next month, and he was in contact by e-mail with Jaimie Porter, who was happy that he was doing the right thing. She only advised him that he see a doctor in France before weaning himself off the anti-depressants, when that time should come. She said that she thought that time wasn't far ahead.

Saturday 27th November 2010

Elizabeth breathed a sigh of relief as she drove through the narrow high hedged roads that led to the small village of St. Evan. Some superstition had been niggling at her. She could not believe that she would be allowed to reach her destination without another mishap. But the sun had shone throughout the journey, albeit low in the sky, making visibility hard at times, and apart from the traffic building up as the morning wore on, nothing occurred to delay her.

It was nearly eleven o'clock in the morning when she arrived. She pulled up outside her parent-in-laws' cottage, and flexed her hands. She had not realised how tense she had been for the two-hour journey. She must have been gripping the steering wheel really tightly.

She had run through what she planned to say to Luke a hundred times, but as she approached the front door, her mind went blank. She was shaking slightly, not with nerves, but with suppressed fury. This was not how she'd planned it. She wanted to be calm and upbeat, to show them all how sweet and sad she was. She clenched her fists to control herself, breathed deeply to slow her thudding heart, and reached up to press the doorbell, not even noticing that Thomas's Volvo was the only vehicle parked on the gravel drive.

Thomas opened the door halfway, a grim expression on his face. He seemed taller than she remembered. "He's not here," he barked abruptly, beginning to swing the door shut.

Taken aback, Elizabeth swung her handbag into the diminishing gap between the door and the frame. "Please! I have to talk to him! Just for a few minutes… I've come all this way!"

"For nothing!" Thomas exclaimed vehemently.

"Thomas…" came the soft voice of Céline from the shadowy hall. "Not too hard, hein? She's right, she's driven a long way. What harm to give her a cup of tea before she returns?"

Thomas grunted in disgust, but stepped away from the door. He turned his back and went in search of his crossword, too irritated to argue the toss.

Céline drew Elizabeth inside. "Just tea…to warm you up? And then you will go home."

The two women walked past Thomas and into the kitchen. Neither woman spoke until the kettle had boiled and Céline had finished clinking and clattering mugs and spoons. They sat opposite each other, the awkward silence settling between them.

Elizabeth spoke first. "Where is Luke? I'm not here to fight with anybody. I just need to know his plans."

Céline regarded her sympathetically. "He really isn't here. I feel sorry…but I have to protect Luke…"

"What from? Me?" The words had been uttered before Elizabeth had a chance to stop them. She attempted a rueful smile to soften the outrage printed on her face.

Céline said slowly, "Non, not you…. from, well, life I suppose. He has been very unhappy, Elizabeth. We are not blaming anyone, and normally I would tell Luke to face the problems in his marriage, but he is not well enough yet to deal with this. He needs more time to mend himself before he can move on. Can you understand?"

Elizabeth nodded, not daring to voice her thoughts. She wanted to shout that it wasn't fair, that they were using his breakdown as an excuse. Nobody wanted to know how she was feeling, for all they knew, she was having a mental meltdown too. Her real issue was that Luke had a loving family to back him up while, as always, she had no one to reassure her that she was being badly treated.

Another silence ensued, Elizabeth not trusting herself to control her temper, and Céline not knowing what else to say. They both sipped their tea and avoided each other's eyes. Elizabeth searched for a safe topic, coming up with an idea that, while it might upset Alexis, would diffuse the atmosphere a little.

She smiled at Céline brightly. "Let's change the subject…tell me, how do you feel about becoming grandparents?"

Céline made a poor attempt to disguise the look of horror that swept over her features. What terrible timing! To bring a baby into this troubled marriage! Quelle catastrophe! She struggled to find the appropriate words to form a reply. "Oh Elizabeth…this is very surprising news! We had no idea! And how are you feeling about it? You must have a mixture of feelings?"

Thoughts were tumbling through Elizabeth's mind as she realised that Céline had jumped to the conclusion that Elizabeth was talking about herself and Luke. She made the instant half-formed decision to go along with it. "I'm fine. I keep thinking that this is fate…a reason for Luke and I to face our problems together." The words fell from her lips without clear thought. "Being apart won't solve anything. Isn't this an omen, Céline?"

Céline was at a loss for words. Elizabeth continued, "So you see, I have to talk to Luke. When he hears about the baby, he'll want to support me, surely? He can't leave me now, can he?"

Céline's eyes were drawn to the doorway behind Elizabeth, where Thomas was standing. He had clearly overheard this last sentence, his face like thunder. He gripped the edge of the door, his knuckles white. "Do you really," he growled through gritted teeth, "really want to force Luke to return to you by using emotional blackmail? I will not stand by and watch my son ruin his life. Get out of this house, now!"

Chapter Thirty-Three
"Does a Dog Go Back to Its Own Vomit?"

Saturday 27th November 2010

Elizabeth's fury was making her drive dangerously. The car swallowed up the narrow lanes at breakneck speed, approached blind bends recklessly, twigs and leaves scraping the sides of the car with angry screeches. She slowed down as her heartbeat slackened its frenzied pace, and she realised that a head-on collision with an oncoming vehicle would solve nothing.

She drove into the pretty town of St Columb Major, taking in the wide high street and tall grey ancient buildings with high-pitch slated roofs. On a sudden whim, Elizabeth indicated left and turned sharply into the spacious carpark of a large hotel, causing the driver behind her to sound his horn waspishly. She turned her head swiftly, caught a glimpse of the man's frowning face and stuck out her tongue.

Crossly she rummaged through her handbag on the seat next to her, angry fingers pecking through the contents until she found her mobile phone. She jabbed with unnecessary violence at the keypad, finding the number for her parents-in-law, and hearing Thomas's voice at once, as if he'd been sitting with the receiver in his hand.

"Thomas Johnson speaking?"

"You may not be over the moon about becoming a grandfather to our baby, mine and Luke's, your only son..."

"I have no wish to speak to you."

"Oh, but I bring you good news! Your beloved daughter is expecting a baby too, out of wedlock and to a man you've never met, but hey, I don't suppose you'll mind about that. So you can turn your back on me with the knowledge that, even though Luke and I have been such a terrible disappointment to you, Alexis and Rob will step in to make you proud..."

Thomas cut the connection and stared into space, numbed by a confusion of emotions.

Elizabeth turned off her phone and gazed out of the windscreen with a satisfied smirk on her face.

Sunday 28th November 2010

"We can't just appear out of the blue! Why do you have these strange sayings, anyway? We are not birds!"

Thomas clicked his teeth impatiently. "Be that as it may…" He ignored his wife's dubious expression at this last onslaught onto her linguistic credibility and continued, "We have several things to discuss with Alexis!"

"And Rob…" Céline reminded him.

"I wouldn't know him if I fell over him…" Thomas grumbled. "But yes, him as well, seeing as he is the father of my grandchild. But anyway, we have to see them. It won't wait 'til next weekend, and a phone call won't do. We'll set off straight away to see them." Having made the decision, Thomas stood up and wandered out of the room, muttering about finding the car keys and commanding Céline to make sure the back door was locked.

Céline followed him to the foot of the stairs and called up, "We have to warn them. They might be going out for the day! Why don't you text Alexis while I get ready?"

Accepting Thomas's grunt as a sign of agreement, she disappeared to do all the several little jobs that a woman must always do before leaving the house, and which men seemed to think happened by magic. She turned on the dishwasher, which needed rinse aid, wiped the sink down, took out a cooked casserole from the freezer, placing it on a plate on the draining board to thaw for supper, emptied the washing machine and hung the clothes out on the airer, locked the back door, and then ran upstairs for her handbag. She found Thomas sitting on the bed, hunched over his mobile phone with an expression of deep concentration on his face.

"Bloody thing! Why do they make these button thingies so tiny?"

"Mon Dieu! Have you not done it yet? I have done ten jobs and you…"

"Shush! You're not helping…how do I do a question mark? Oh no! All the letters are coming out wrong! I want to say 'Are you at home?' and it's writing 'Are you good?' It's rubbish!"

Céline rolled her eyes, took the phone, disabled the predictive text mode, shooed Thomas out of the bedroom and quickly tapped in a message. Céline moved to the mirror to apply a fresh coat of pink lipstick and added a quick squirt of her favourite perfume.

"What are you doing now?" bellowed Thomas from the foot of the stairs. Céline declined to answer. She secured the front door and slipped in beside her husband who had already started the engine, impatient to be off.

"Right! Rob has suggested we meet halfway to make it easier. He says Lornstown is good…" Céline said cheerfully.

"Where?" Thomas asked. "Oh, Launceston!" He smiled as Céline spelled it out. "What would I do without you?" he growled reluctantly. Céline squeezed his thigh in a friendly manner, pleased to be in his good books once more.

Alexis and Rob were already settled in a quaint little café in the old Market Place of Launceston. They clutched cups of tea in their chilled hands and looked at each other worriedly.

"Why the summons to meet suddenly?" asked Rob, looking decidedly uncomfortable.

Alexis tucked a stray chunk of blonde hair under her red bobble hat. "I've told you, I've no idea. Mum wasn't forthcoming in her text. It takes her so long to write it, and she was trying to explain that Dad was waiting for her... He's not the most patient of men! Just that there were a couple things to discuss..."

"Well...we'll have to tell them our news now. Damn! I wanted to do it properly. Your dad won't freak out, will he? I wish I'd met him before this..."

"He'll probably take you outside to the War Memorial out there and shoot you," she replied with a deadpan expression, but taking pity on him as she noticed his face pale visibly. He let out a sigh of relief as Alexis gave him a grin. The café door pinged and they both looked up. Alexis nodded at Rob's questioning glance and they both got to their feet.

There was a flurry of coats and scarves being thrown off, hugs and handshakes. Rob avoided imminent cross-examining by disappearing to order more tea. A fresh pot, accompanied by a plate of scones was placed in the centre of the green and white flowered cloth. Thomas eyed Rob across the comforting accompaniments of social exchange. Alexis decided to break the ice, only fair, she thought, as she was the only person present to be known personally to all those present.

"Well, you must have read our minds! We were going to arrange to meet you next weekend. How's things?" She smiled cheerfully at her parents, while busily buttering a scone.

Céline studied Thomas's expressionless face and decided to brave his annoyance by speaking first. "We are all right, chérie, but what a busy weekend we have suffered! On Friday, Luke is gone...leaving us and escaping away from his troubles again!"

"Steady Céline!" boomed Thomas. "He has decided to start afresh for the moment, that's all. All quite sensibly thought out. Your mother makes it sound as if he's absconded to a region of darkest Africa!"

Alexis was not reassured by these words. “But where’s he gone? And why? I thought after a month staying with you, he’d be ready to go back home to Elizabeth!”

Thomas nearly choked on a morsel of scone in his haste to respond to this absurd observation. “Why can’t you get it into your thick heads that he will never go back to Elizabeth? Does a dog go back to its own vomit?”

Three alarmed faces gazed at him, taken aback by this vitriolic outburst. Céline gripped the edge of the table, begging Thomas with wide eyes to be calm. He coughed into his napkin and continued more quietly. “Luke knows what is best for him. He has gone to stay in our little holiday cottage in the Charente Maritime. It’s a brilliant idea…just what he needs. And if you want to call it an escape, then I suppose it is. And not a moment too soon! Elizabeth was on his tail…arrived a day too late, thank God! She came expecting to pluck him back to her, just like that. And when she discovered that he had already left the country, she came up with this cock and bull story…” (He paused to still Céline’s bemused query at yet another baffling sentence.) “…about being pregnant with his child! It was clearly just a ruse to get him to change his mind!”

Rob and Alexis looked at each other, unnerved by the direction the conversation was going. There was an uneasy silence. Then Céline burst out, “Thomas! Why have you not told me that she was lying? I believed her about the baby. I wasn’t happy about it, did you think I was? I’m not that stupid, I know that an unplanned child would not heal a breaking marriage. But I am sad that you never discuss anything with me!” Tears were threatening to fall.

Alexis looked horrified. “Come on you two, this is awful! Poor Rob here, it’s his first meeting with you both and he’s been shoved in right at the deep end. Have some feeling for him! It’s bad enough meeting your girlfriend’s parents for the first time, but to listen to all these skeletons clanking about in the proverbial cupboard is asking too much!”

They all stared at each other in silence, until Rob’s stifled cough turned into a guffaw, Thomas’s lips trembled into a smirk, which erupted into a belly laugh, Alexis also gave way, shaking with mirth, while Céline looked uncomprehending, still trying to work out how skeletons and cupboards had introduced themselves into the conversation.

Wiping the tears from their eyes, the atmosphere had lightened to an almost jovial level. Alexis was so relieved that she grinned at Rob and he nodded at her encouragingly. She took a deep breath and then said, “Now then, we have some news of our own. We wanted to wait another week, but well…here goes… I am pregnant!”

Céline and Thomas beamed at her. Thomas turned to shake Rob's hand and Céline's tears surfaced once more.

Alexis swallowed hard, delighted at the positive response. "I thought you'd be disappointed, you especially, Dad. You like things done properly, and let's face it, you hadn't even met Rob."

Thomas replied slowly, "I made up my mind in ten minutes that Rob has an open honest face and cares about you a great deal. That's enough for me. You have done things properly in my book…compared to someone I could mention, and I don't mean poor Luke."

Rob spoke then, quietly and seriously, "If it helps, Mr Johnson, I have been in agreement about Elizabeth from the first time I heard about her. So I will keep Alexis safe from her if I can, and although I've not yet met Luke, I feel I know him through Alexis, and will offer him any support if needed. I would also like to announce that Alexis and I became engaged yesterday."

Alexis showed her hand proudly, the pretty little ring sparkling in the overhead light.

"What? But you haven't asked my permission!" Thomas cried.

Céline gasped in dismay, and Alexis's eyes widened in surprise.

Grinning, Rob said, "Well, I know my future father-in-law better than the two women closest to him! He's joking!"

The two men clasped hands and Thomas growled, "And you'd better call me Thomas from now on."

Céline sat companionably next to Thomas as he drove home to Cornwall, the dark wintry skies showing the early signs of dusk, ribbons of birds flying home to roost in untidy lines like unravelling wool.

"Thank you, chéri."

"What for?"

"For not telling Alexis that we already knew about her baby."

"What, and give the Elizabeth the chance to spoil yet another special moment?"

Céline looked out of the window. No matter how dark and swirling it appeared outside, she was travelling safely home with the man she loved. He was grumpy and old fashioned, but he was also wise and observant. She wrapped her arms around herself feeling happy and secure.

Chapter Thirty-Four

She Was the Outcast, Belonging Nowhere

December 2010

The December days passed, as all days do, regardless of whether the humans existing in these times were in a contented frame of mind or not. Emotions flickered up and down, with only extremes making themselves regarded as one thing or another. Happiness was an absence of sadness and vice versa.

Thomas and Céline considered themselves more content than in recent months. Their daughter was with a good man, looking forward to the birth of their child in June, and a wedding planned for the following summer. Their worries about Luke had diminished. Now that he was safely out of the country and Elizabeth's clutches, they felt he was on his way to a new and happier life. He told them that he would not risk coming home for Christmas, but said that after that he would love them to visit him. He had found several jobs as an 'artisan' and enjoyed living the simple life.

Alexis was very cheerful; she was feeling well, all nausea and fatigue gone, although Rob insisted she lessen her hours at the hospital and cut down on the night shifts. She had had the twelve-week scan on the second day of December, and had been reassured that all the baby's organs were intact and healthy. This procedure included the 'nuchal transparency scan' by which the thickness of the fluid at the back of the baby's neck was measured by ultrasound. From the result of this, Alexis and Rob were told that their baby did not have Down Syndrome. They were given a scan photo in which the baby looked as if it were punching the air with a closed fist. Céline was in awe of all these reassurances. In her day, you crossed your fingers and prayed that your baby would be healthy.

Alexis kept in touch with Cheryl by text, still not happy with her living conditions, but having to accept that Cheryl was more and more unattainable, blaming her long hours and tiredness for not having time to meet up.

The only storm cloud on Alexis's blue horizon was the presence of Elizabeth. She visited frequently, calling unexpectedly, safe in the knowledge that Rob's hours were pretty much set in stone. Alexis was too polite to turn Elizabeth away, especially as she was a tenant in Elizabeth's flat, not to mention being her sister-in-law. To tell the truth, she had always been fond and more than a little in awe of her, and now she felt sympathy too. She, Alexis, felt she had everything she wanted compared to Elizabeth. She felt that Elizabeth, far from moaning about her life, was concocting a fake feeling of optimism, as if to convince herself and everyone else that her problems were just a blip in the otherwise smooth path of marriage.

It began to grate on Alexis's nerves. Usually hating plain speaking or confrontation, she spoke to Elizabeth on impulse. "You do know that Thomas doesn't believe you are expecting a baby, don't you?"

Elizabeth gave a mirthless laugh. "As I haven't seen him for over two weeks, I've no idea what he thinks! I know you don't want to think badly of him, Alexis, but it seems to me that he's terrified of Luke finding out that I'm pregnant and coming back to me. He hates me, Alexis. If I disappeared tomorrow, he'd be over the moon."

"That's not true! He just wants what's best for everybody..."

Elizabeth shook her head despondently. "You're nuts! You only see the good in people...but you believe me, don't you, Alexis?"

Alexis remained silent. Finally, she lifted her eyes and said, "I want to, of course I do. But I remember Luke hinting to me that you haven't been close in that way for a long time. He joked about spending more nights on the sofa than he'd like..."

Elizabeth took hold of Alexis's hands and looked into her eyes, the same blue as Thomas's but so much more trusting. "That's just it! We did go through a really rough patch. I never trusted that Cheryl, always making it so obvious that she fancied Luke like mad. You know I keep a diary? Well it was the twenty-second of September. Cheryl really got under my skin, hinting that she and Luke...well, it was awful. But it made me realise that I had to cling onto my marriage, I love Luke so much!"

"So...what happened?"

"I was waiting for him when he got home, wasn't I?" she said with a meaningful wink.

Alexis grinned. "You seduced your own husband? You minx!" She laughed, and then sobered as she realised that this was no happy ending. "And then he had this meltdown. Oh Elizabeth! What are you going to do? I don't think he plans to come back."

Elizabeth sat still for a moment before answering. "That's because he doesn't know he's going to be a dad...he'll be over the moon when he knows! It'll change everything…it's not fair to keep it from him. Think about it, Alexis! Please tell me where he is! Please?"

Alexis looked at Elizabeth with tears in her eyes. She felt as if she were being torn in two, but blood had to be thicker than water. She had made a promise to Luke. It was as simple as that. She shook her head miserably.

Elizabeth stood up and walked stiffly to the window. She stood there for some time, her forehead pressed against the cold glass, trying to calm her rage and rearrange her expression of pure hatred before being able to turn round and reassure Alexis that she understood. Of course she did.

Christmas was strange that year. Alexis went home with Rob to her parents in Cornwall, but without Luke there it was a rather bitter sweet occasion. There was a long telephone call from him on Christmas Day; he had cooked a traditional turkey lunch for himself and Gaston, Luke's wise old friend and neighbour. He had been very impressed with the pigs in blankets, "les cochons dans les couvertures? C'est bizarre, n'est-ce pas?" and even more so with the Christmas pudding which Luke had bought in a local 'Super U' store which specialised in a small English section. Luke warmed the brandy, poured it over the pudding and lit the holly on top with a brandish that set the whole thing shimmering with an undulating blue flame. Ella barked loudly and Gaston whooped with uncharacteristic delight.

Alexis had a tearful conversation with Luke, blaming it on her changing hormones. In reality it was because she had been forbidden by her father to even mention Elizabeth's 'phantom baby'. She was fed up with all these secrets, feeling that Thomas was manipulating them all like puppets. Luke, in his usual generous spirit had been delighted on hearing of Alexis's happy news and engagement to Rob.

"I'm so pleased for you, sis, I can't believe I'm going to be an uncle! I just wish I could meet Rob. Mum and Dad think the world of him…perhaps both of you would like to come out here and stay a while? In the early spring, before he or she arrives!"

"We'd love to! Happy Christmas, brother-in-law!" shouted Rob over Alexis's shoulder. Alexis smiled, longing for the day when their family would be back to normal.

Elizabeth spent her Christmas curled up on the settee with Mango, watching *The Wizard of Oz* and *Ben Hur* and eating chocolates. She pushed the boat out a couple of times, inviting a handful of female colleagues to dinner. It was more an exercise to keep occupied and keep up her cooking skills than a desire for company. She told them that Luke was away visiting a sick elderly relative while she stayed home to take care of Mango.

The two holiday weeks dragged by. Every waking moment was tortured by the knowledge that the 'family' were together, while she once again had been abandoned. She knew that Alexis and Rob were in Cornwall, but she mistakenly imagined Luke there too. She could see them all there, raising a glass to the new baby, the engagement, Luke's new life. She could hear them laughing, congratulating Luke on his escape from that weird woman. Thomas would be laughing as he hugged his son, Alexis sharing smirks and snide remarks with Céline about her, Rob clapping Luke on the back, man to man. Elizabeth had these thoughts continually in her head, as on a loop, going round and round, driving herself mad. Sitting there alone, she became almost delirious with the ferocity of her helpless outrage, slipping in and out of a dream-like state where she watched herself outside the Cornish cottage. It was freezing, her clothes were thin, letting the biting wind through to her bones. The night was pitch dark, the brightly lit window such a haven in contrast, throwing an orange rectangle onto the frosty grass. She crept closer, pushing her pale face against the icy glass, looking in. She was the outcast, belonging nowhere. She cried out, but her voice made no sound. She beat on the glass with frost-stiffened hands, but no one could hear her. Alexis stood there with Rob behind her, encircling her rounded stomach with his loving hands. Elizabeth felt a stirring within her own womb and cried out again for Luke to draw her into his arms. He seemed to see her at last. He walked towards the window, she stretched out her hands, and watched as he drew closed the curtains, blocking her out.

Elizabeth woke up in a cold sweat. The room was dark and she was alone. She made the decision there and then that sitting at home doing nothing was driving her mad. She had to find out where Luke was somehow.

Wednesday 5th January 2011
Exsham

Elizabeth had seen the New Year in alone at home, sinking a bottle of champagne on her own. She raised the last glass to Jools Holland, promising herself that 2011 was going to be a happy year. She would reconstruct her damaged marriage, forgiving Luke for all his difficult behaviour and murky past. "A fresh start, Jools!" she shouted towards the television. "That's what we need…here's to the future…bring it on!"

Now, the day before the new school term, Elizabeth put her new year's resolution to the test. She dialled Thomas and Céline's phone number once again, sitting on the edge of her chair. She gripped the receiver tightly, confident that this time she would not be fobbed off. The ringing tone went on and on. And just as it rang for the fifth time, a flustered breathless voice said, “Hello…can I help?”

Elizabeth hesitated, taken aback by the question, and not recognizing the voice. “Is Céline there?” she asked hopefully.

“No, I’m so sorry…they’ve gone away for a couple of weeks. Can I help?”

“And you are…?” Elizabeth queried cautiously.

“Oh yes, of course…I’m Dorothy Mason, next-door neighbour. I’m keeping an eye on things while they’re away. I was just watering Céline’s pot plants when you rang actually, had to run through from the kitchen!”

Elizabeth thought quickly, deciding to find out as much as she could from this unexpected source. “Well, that’s good of you, Dorothy. I’m a friend of Céline’s, haven’t seen her for ages and thought I’d have a catch-up gossip! Where have she and Thomas gone?”

“Oh dear, she did tell me but I’m not very good with foreign names. The furthest me and Ron have ever been is the Isle of White! It’s in France somewhere, that I do know. Gone to stay with that lovely son of theirs…Lewis? No, Luke…that’s it! He’s living out there now, got a job and everything! He was here for a while, did you know? Not been himself so she said…but listen to me going on! Can I give her a message from you for when they get back?”

“No, Dorothy, don’t worry. I’ll ring again…wanted it to be a surprise actually. Did they say exactly when they’d be home again?”

“Oh yes!” Dorothy said, pleased to be able to help, “they said they’ll be back late afternoon on Monday the seventeenth of January…I don’t think you told me your name…?”

But there was a click and an empty echo. Disappointed, Dorothy replaced the receiver onto its holder.

Later, dishing up Ron’s favourite supper of bubble and squeak, she regaled him with a repetition of the phone call, being the highlight of her rather otherwise dreary day. “She sounded ever so nice,” she recalled dreamily. “Must be nice to have an old friend look you up…”

Ron steered a well-balanced forkful of cabbage and unidentifiable meat towards his mouth, halting it precariously to say, “Let me get this right, Dot! You told this person that Thomas and Céline are away? Abroad no less? And did you clarify as to the date of their return?”

Dorothy blushed in confusion, hating to be cross-examined by her husband. He was always right, he told her often enough, but she ploughed on, “Yes Ron…I did, but she was an old friend, she said so! And she knew their names, and Lewis’s name, so she must be all right.”

“Talking of names, what was her name I’d like to know?”

Dorothy looked crestfallen. “She never said. Wanted it to be a surprise…” she mumbled.

Ron returned to the industrious business of eating once more. Dorothy was left to contemplate her silly behaviour which was impressed on her by the pointed refusal by Ron of a second helping. She made a private New Year’s resolution to avoid the urge to share every experience with her husband in future.

Chapter Thirty-Five

She Pulled the Envelope Free

Friday 14th January 2011

Elizabeth's first week back at school for the new term had been hectic, but was a welcome change from sitting and brooding. The previous weekend she had been overwhelmed with lesson plans and paperwork, and it wasn't until now that she had time to think about her personal life. So, Luke was in France. It wasn't much to go on but it was a start. That he had found the need to remove himself even farther geographically from her than ever, was hard to swallow, but she put it down to the drawbacks of living with his parents, critical Thomas and suffocating Céline. He was escaping from them, still needing time alone.

Her journey had to be made under cover of darkness, and it had to be done tonight. If she left it until tomorrow, she might lose her nerve and never do it. She was running out of time.

She'd arrived home from work sometime after four o'clock; that was the good thing about being a teacher, she could avoid the worst of the Friday night rush hour if she left on time. She was not in the least bit hungry, but shoved a bag of crisps and a couple of chocolate biscuits into a bag to take with her. She might need to boost her energy levels later on for the homeward drive. Elizabeth made her way upstairs, kicked off her shoes and crawled under her duvet, setting the alarm mode on her mobile phone for half-past nine. Lying on her back in the cold bed at this strange time of the day, she convinced herself that she would not be able to sleep…yet the next moment it seemed, the phone was jangling her awake.

The journey took much longer than she'd expected. It was nearly one o'clock in the morning when she pulled over to park. She positioned her car under a hedge at the end of a small cul-de-sac and climbed out to feel the chill air grab at her hands and face. Feeling weary and thirsty, she wrapped her black coat more closely round her as she navigated her way through a couple of linking roads towards her destination. She had forgotten to bring a drink with her, but knew she would soon be able to enjoy a long glass full of cold water. The thought spurred her on and she quickened her footsteps as she hurried through the quiet darkness of the winter evening.

At least being this bit later meant less chance of bumping into any late Friday-night drinkers, not that she expected to be recognised by anyone like that. Nevertheless, she pulled her dark-green scarf up over her face, glad she had found somewhere quiet and adequately concealed to park the car.

As she turned into the narrower country lane, she was relieved to see a couple of street lights still throwing their orange haze into the blackness. There was only a handful of old dwellings here, but they were clumped in twos and threes as if huddling together for warmth. As she neared the cottage, the nearest street light made it easier for her to pick her way up the drive, without throwing her ruthlessly under a spotlight. She was also vastly encouraged at the absence of a vehicle parked there. She had been worried that for some reason they might have returned home earlier than planned.

The house next door was in darkness, thank God. She had no desire to being submitted to awkward questioning from Dorothy of the run-away tongue. Her heart was racing quite enough with nerves and excitement at what she was doing. The front of the cottage was black with shadow, so Elizabeth risked turning on the tiny flashlight mode on her phone. With this, she easily spotted the small black plastic case screwed to the wall to the right of the front door. Elizabeth had noticed this on her first visit to the cottage; that Christmas in 2006. Céline had explained to her that it was a key safe; a four-digit code had to be tapped into the raised number buttons inside the case, which then made it possible to release a cover, giving access to the various house keys within. They had had it installed when Céline was expecting the twins. Céline had explained it to Elizabeth at the end of that same visit, after Elizabeth had quizzed Thomas about the photo of Luke and Xavier. Thomas had been anxious at Céline being alone at the cottage at this time, as onset of early labour was probable. This way, the code was given to the medical staff at the local surgery, enabling them to gain entry to the cottage in an emergency. Céline could ring for help from home if necessary. Céline had remembered with nostalgia that after the birth of the boys, Thomas has decided to keep the safe, musing that it would be useful when they were teenagers, coming in late at night with no excuse about mislaid keys. In a tender moment, Thomas had changed the code to a new one; '8482'; the date of the boys' birthday. It made it easy for Elizabeth to remember.

Now she juggled opening the black plastic lid with one hand, while holding the phone 'flashlight' in the other. She tapped in the code, praying that it had not been altered. The inside cover fell towards her easily, revealing three keys inside. Each one had a tiny label stuck to it; 'back door', 'conservatory', and 'front door'. Elizabeth breathed a huge sigh of relief. She selected the front door key, popping the others back and closing the little case up. The next second, she had unlocked the door and let herself into the cottage, feet slipping on a few envelopes that had gathered on the mat in her parent-in-laws' absence. She clicked her phone off and listened…the only sound was the slight sighing of wind through surrounding trees. She shut the front door quietly and firmly.

Leaving the mail where it was, she reminded herself not to move anything out of place, Thomas and Céline were both very neat by nature. She opened the door immediately to her left, entering the lounge. The curtains had been left half closed. Elizabeth pulled them together completely so that she could use the proper torch that she had put ready in the deep pocket of her coat. She played its beam around the room, confident that no one would be able to detect any light from outside.

The bureau was in the corner of the room. Shadows jumped and jerked as she made her way over to it. She tried to place the torch somewhere where its beam could light up the whole thing, but the span of the beam was too small. She had to manage by holding it trained on each drawer and cubby hole as she searched through everything methodically with one hand. It was a tedious nerve-wracking job.

She had imagined that there would be an address book holding the secret of Luke's address. Nowadays people kept postal addresses in their computers, but not Céline, she guessed. It took her longer than she'd planned to look through every nook and cranny of the bureau, stopping halfway through for that long promised drink of cold water. She drank it out of a mug, thinking it would be easier to dry and replace than a glass.

The bureau exhausted, she flashed the torch across the coffee table and surfaces where papers and books naturally seemed to congregate no matter how neat people were. Swearing under her breath, she began to panic, expecting to hear hammering on the front door at any moment. She was devious, but she had never done anything like this before, and the adrenaline kick was giving way to alarm.

She made a cursory search of the kitchen, which did not take long as it was so minimalist. This left upstairs. She ran quickly up to the main bedroom, again pulling the curtains closed before clicking the torch back on and locating the bedside table on Céline's side, easily identifiable by the stack of obviously female-targeted novels, and a box of flowery tissues. There was a cubby hole above and a drawer underneath. She tried the cubby hole first, pulling out old birthday cards, postcards, and a tube of antiseptic cream. Her fingers closed round the shiny leather cover of a small book, tucked right at the back. 'Address Book' was scrolled in gold lettering across the front. Bingo! She riffled through the pages awkwardly with one hand, cursing not being able to turn on the light. She looked under 'L' first…no address for Luke. She looked at the 'J's then, but nothing. In her frustration, she felt like hurling the book across the room, but managed to control herself, just.

Replacing everything, she wondered where Luke's French address could be. She was not to know that the address of the French cottage was engraved in Céline's brain. It had been like a second home for such a large part of her life, that the only place she had ever written it down was in the front of her diary, in case, heaven forbid, Thomas needed it and she was not around.

Before making her way downstairs, and more out of nosiness, Elizabeth pulled open the drawer. It held just a large box, probably it had once held chocolates. It was tied loosely with a pink ribbon. She pulled it free and lifted the lid; inside were tidy piles of unused writing paper and envelopes, unused Christmas and birthday cards, and a couple of pens. She was just about to replace the lid when she saw part of an envelope poking out from underneath. A man would possibly have ignored it, but Elizabeth was of that breed of woman who can never resist peeking into someone else's private life, especially when it was under her nose. She pulled the envelope free. It was a square cream-coloured envelope, addressed in black ink. The handwriting was bold, striking, but the postmark was too smudged to make out a date, or location. Intrigued, Elizabeth opened the envelope which had originally been slit open neatly with something sharp. With finger and thumb she pulled out the single page of cream paper, covered with the same bold black writing. She read it quickly and then once again, more slowly, processing the information it imparted with great interest. Time stood still as she knelt there on the rug beside Céline's bed, torch held transfixed, her eyes cast down, deep in thought.

A swift glance at her watch told her that it was past two o'clock already. The hour had flown. Again, some superstitious foreboding set her heart racing at the thought of Thomas deciding to return a couple of days early, taking an early evening crossing and arriving any second. She strained her ears to listen, was that the sound of a car engine in the distance? Nerves and paranoia made it hard to be sure. She had to get out of there, and fast.

Making sure the drawer was pushed shut properly, she pushed the letter back into its envelope and stuffed it deep into her pocket. She switched off the torch, twitched the curtains open slightly, as she had found them, and then she was downstairs, checking everything there was as she had found it.

Outside, she closed the front door behind her, and it locked automatically. She grappled with the key safe once more, opened it and pulled the front door key out of her pocket. She was just about to slip it to join the other two into the little space, when there was a sudden shout from nearby, a male voice, harshly angry. The key fell out of her grasp as she jerked in fright. She heard it clatter onto the concrete step and she folded down into a squat, shoving her mobile flashlight into her pocket to douse its perfidious beam. There was some altercation being played out in the lane, the jarring male voice jabbing accusations, a softer but moany female voice replying in turn. Elizabeth could not make out the words, but felt pretty sure that these were two late home comers, with the right amount of alcohol inside them to bring out the worst of their flaky relationship. She patted open hands over the gritty ground in front of her and was amazed to feel the cold outline of key-shaped metal almost immediately, and clutched it tightly.

The voices dwindled away as the inebriated pair weaved their way down the lane to their 'home sweet home'. Elizabeth had no intention of hesitating a moment longer. The key safely snapped back into its location, she ran silently through the once more silent roads, threw herself gratefully into the safety of her car, and pointed it homewards, reaching her destination finally as the sky began to lighten, streaks of orange and blood red spreading through the dark grey like a child's painting left out in the rain.

Saturday 29th January 2011
Exmouth

"I'm rather looking forward to tonight," commented Thomas, pleased that the journey had been problem free, the early Saturday evening roads not yet congested with drivers on their way out to their own choice of relaxation. The weather was mild for the time of year, but there was a possibility of rain, taking into account the building up of a few black clouds.

"Isn't it nice that we can stay the night?" murmured Céline. "I'm sorry that Luke won't be there, but it'll be lovely to stay with Alexis and Rob, instead of having to drive to that hotel."

It was just six o'clock when they rang the bell. Rob opened the door with a friendly smile. "Come in, come in…" he welcomed, helping Céline out of her coat, and taking the small overnight case from Thomas. "Go through…Alexis is in the lounge. I'll put this in your room."

The next two hours flew by as the four exchanged the questionably fascinating snippets of their lives. No doubt Alexis's details about her growing pregnancy were of great interest to her parents, and Thomas was indeed genuinely eager to hear about Rob's involvement with his troubled youngsters in his capacity as counsellor, being able to empathise from his experience as a secondary teacher.

Céline and Alexis had shared a pot of tea, and now they had moved into the kitchen to continue chatting over the assembling of dinner. The men settled more comfortably into their armchairs, each nursing a pint of beer while moving on to political topics.

"Oh! Your little bump is bigger than I thought now you are standing up! Can I stroke it?"

Alexis beamed with pleasure. "Of course! Oh Mum, I'm so excited...it seems real now that I can see and feel it!"

Céline placed a hand on the small of Alexis's back and the other on the bump, stroking and circling it with loving fingers. The two women embraced silently. "So, the twenty-week scan went okay last Wednesday, sweetheart! Thanks for texting me, and that's the last one now before the birth?"

"Yep! Everything is fine!" Alexis smiled.

Céline looked at her closely. "And do you know if it's a boy or a girl? I didn't dare ask before, it is so not important next to the healthy baby..."

"No Mum. Rob and I decided that now we know all is well, it'll be lovely to wait for the surprise when he or she comes."

Céline kissed her daughter soundly. "Very wise...it will be like a Christmas parcel. Can I do anything to help, chérie?" she asked after an emotional few minutes.

"Nothing, Mum," Alexis insisted. "Go and relax for five minutes while I put the finishing touches to the table and strain the vegetables. Here, take a glass of wine with you..." She ushered her mother back into the lounge and turned to the cooker just as there was a faint knock at the front door.

Alexis wiped her hands across the front of her red stripy apron, caressing the swelling there as she did so. She moved quickly to the door, opening it with a grin for the young woman standing there clutching a bunch of pink carnations. "Good timing! We're just about to eat...wow, these are lovely, thanks!" She pulled her sister-in-law into the hall and took her charcoal-coloured jacket.

She looked good in her dark blue jeans and white chunky jumper, her hair in slightly damp spikes. "It's just starting that fine drizzle that soaks you!" She laughed, shaking her hair like a puppy. "Are you sure Rob doesn't mind me coming here?"

Without answering, Alexis took her hand and led her into the lounge. "Look who's here!" she announced loudly. "We haven't seen Elizabeth for ages. I thought it'd be nice to get together...a new start to the New Year!"

There was a deathly silence as the others stopped speaking, their glasses arrested in mid-air. Elizabeth looked stricken. "You didn't tell Rob I was coming, did you, Alexis? And you didn't tell me that *they* would be here either…how could you? This is so horrible!" She turned away, threw the flowers down on the hall table, and struggled feebly with her jacket, trying to find the arm holes.

Alexis burst into tears. "Don't go, please!" she sobbed. "Mum? Dad? She's having Luke's baby! I know she is…we can't turn our backs on her! Let's just have a nice meal together! I thought if I arranged it all…"

"What?" Thomas spoke sternly. "That we'd all get on? Like a happy family? Oh Alexis, you are so naïve."

Rob stood up and moved next to Alexis. He put his arms around her. "Yes, Thomas, she is naïve, and that's what I love about her…don't be too hard on her. But it wouldn't work, sweetheart." He addressed himself to Alexis, "We owe it to Luke. How would he feel if he could see us now?"

Alexis sniffed miserably. Rob turned to Elizabeth, who stood there, ready to leave. Rob asked her in a quiet voice, "Elizabeth? Alexis has told me that your pregnancy dates are the same as hers…quite a coincidence, wouldn't you say? So how did your twelve-week scan go? Have you a scan photo to show us? It might help…"

"How dare you quiz me like this? I don't have to justify myself to anybody!" shrieked Elizabeth. As she turned towards the door, Rob reached out and put his hands over Elizabeth's stomach. She lurched away from him, but not before he felt the soft spongy feel of some sort of cushion underneath the loose jumper she was wearing.

Rob looked into her eyes then, seeing the shocked truth in her eyes and felt an overwhelming feeling of distaste for her. He turned round to face the others. "She's not pregnant," he stated, ashen faced. He looked back at Elizabeth and added, "I think you were so envious of Alexis that you decided to fabricate your own pregnancy. You mirrored her, so that you could follow the stages to make it look believable."

Elizabeth wrenched open the door and stumbled out onto the landing. The others stared at each other in discomfort.

"Someone go after her…who knows what she might do…" whispered Alexis.

Céline looked towards Thomas. "Thomas?" she spoke his name clearly, her hand on his arm.

Thomas stood and took himself to the door in a few long strides. He descended the stairs two at a time and burst through the entrance door. Elizabeth was nearly at her car. She triggered the locks open with a high-pitched note from her key fob, but Thomas had caught up with her before she could open the door. She stood there, glaring at him and breathing heavily. "Well? What have you to say to me, Thomas?"

"Nothing good, that's for sure," said Thomas emotionlessly. "The women still seem to be keen to give you the benefit of the doubt, but I don't. But then, I know more about you than they do…"

Elizabeth frowned. "So, what do you know? Has Luke been running to Mummy and Daddy with complaints? Typical!"

Thomas looked at her with disgust. "That shows how little you know your husband. He has remained loyal to you, and in return you have made it clear that you don't love him at all. You haven't supported him in any way…no wonder he's left you."

Elizabeth's eyes flashed dangerously. "He never needed my support! Not when he's being mollycoddled by you lot. He's never grown up!"

"Oh, and you're the mature one, are you? How did you help him when he had his crisis at school? And what did you do when he told you he had a low sperm count? You told him he was as good as useless!"

She glared with such hatred that he flinched. "And how do you know that? You couldn't have known that! Luke must have told you! My loyal husband!"

Thomas's vision shifted. He felt his control shifting too. He said quietly, "No, he didn't tell me. I overheard you arguing. You were blaming everything on him. Nothing is your fault, is it, Elizabeth? I knew from that moment that you would never make Luke a good wife."

Elizabeth gave a peal of laughter that sent shivers down Thomas's spine. "Luke doesn't deserve a wife! He's a coward, a depressive prone to manic behaviour. He has no backbone and he can't even hold down a job or father a child. Is that clear enough for you?"

Thomas studied her almost in wonder. "How in God's name did Luke ever fall in love with an aberration like you? This is the final proof of your devious character; a fake pregnancy to lure poor Luke back to a loveless shell of a marriage. You are an evil woman, and I hope none of us ever have to see or speak to you again." He turned on his heel and returned to the flat, wanting to return to the warmth of his family. Being physically close to Elizabeth had made him feel as if a poisonous web had settled over him. He shuddered, needing to shake himself clean of her, a feeling of nausea rising in the back of his throat.

Chapter Thirty-Six

She Began Her Attack Swiftly and Mercilessly

Saturday 12th February 2011
Cornwall

Elizabeth's thoughts were in turmoil. She knew she had to get through this, despite fearful misgivings. In her last conversation with Céline over the phone, her mother-in-law had been so sure, so certain that this was the right thing to do. It made sense; it would bring closure to the whole sorry mess.

Apparently, Thomas wanted to discuss practical issues on Luke's behalf. He had approached Luke on the assumption that he was now recovered from his recent indisposition. Luke, if he were honest, had no interest in dealing with Elizabeth over any shared possessions, with the exception of Mango of course. Thomas had ground Luke down with words like 'dignity,' 'pride,' and 'self-respect' until Luke had agreed on the condition that the practicalities would be discussed through emails, not face to face. It had been suggested that Elizabeth put the Exsham cottage up for sale, split the money with Luke, and then she could move back into her Exmouth flat and Alexis and Rob would rent somewhere else. These loose ends needed tidying up now that it was clear to everybody that the marriage was over. Clear to everybody that is except Elizabeth herself.

As she drove along the familiar roads towards the cottage, Elizabeth had a plan of her own. Did they think she was a puppet to be danced to their tune? An arrangement for her to visit Thomas and Céline had not actually been discussed. Céline had just outlined Thomas's concerns to Elizabeth to prepare her for what needed to be done.

Céline's final sentence to Elizabeth had been, "As soon as we've discussed things over with Luke, we'll be in touch, Elizabeth." Elizabeth however, had decided to put her own interpretation to the situation.

As she neared the cottage, Elizabeth considered how cosy it looked from outside. She felt bereft and bitter at the sight. The wind gusted round her as she walked up the path, and the sky was prematurely dark. She shivered as she reached out to ring the doorbell. The porch light came on above her head. There was a pause, and then Céline opened the door.

"Elizabeth!" she said in a shocked voice. A whirl of chilly wind swept between them, lifting the hem of Elizabeth's inadequate coat. A spattering of cold drops were flung into Céline's face as she reached for Elizabeth's sleeve, pulling her forwards with a violent movement. An alarmed expression passed across Elizabeth's face. She had half thought that Céline was going to strike her.

"Come in then," Céline said in a low voice. "This is very unexpected..."

Elizabeth put her bag down. "Sorry," she said, gazing expressionlessly at Céline with her large green eyes. "Sorry for not warning you I was coming. It was a spur of the moment decision. It's half-term this coming week so I've got space to think clearly. I feel we need to clear the air. This situation is intolerable. It's your idea, remember?" she added.

"Is it?" Céline murmured coldly. "Well, we can hardly turn you away, I suppose. Go in and say hello to Thomas." The order was uttered with a distinct lack of warmth or sincerity.

Elizabeth made her way into the lounge and bent down to take the hand of her father-in-law. He removed his hand from her grasp with a jerk and stared at the young dark-haired woman in front of him. Céline motioned her towards a chair opposite Thomas, into which Elizabeth sank, her eyes still gazing at him. He looked up to catch his wife's expression.

Céline avoided his searching glance. "Well...! Tea? Coffee?" she asked brightly, turning towards the kitchen.

Behind her, Thomas said curtly, "Well, Elizabeth. What do you want?"

Elizabeth raised her eyebrows. "Céline phoned me a week ago. She said you wanted to discuss a few things about my future..."

Thomas frowned. "I don't believe I said anything about discussing anything with you."

Elizabeth fixed him with cold determination. "Maybe not...but there's something I want to discuss with you! Last time we spoke, you took great pleasure in tearing me to bits. Now it's my turn..." she was speaking low and fast, but broke off as Céline returned to the room, bearing a tray with two glasses and a bowl of olives.

"Here we are...make a space, Thomas," she interrupted, choosing to ignore Elizabeth's irritated expression. "I'm going to fix us something for later...do you like trout, Elizabeth? I'll do it in garlic and white wine." She placed the tray firmly down on the coffee table. Thomas snatched his reading glasses out of the way, sending Céline an agonised look, not unlike a rabbit caught in headlights.

Elizabeth gave Céline an unconvincing smile. "Thanks! That would be lovely. I don't expect you to go to any trouble, though…"

"I don't expect to go to any, dear." Céline smiled back. "I imagine you'll be staying the night? Having come all this way….?" Thomas looked horrified, but Céline remained calm and collected.

"If it's no bother," Elizabeth answered, picking up her wine and taking a large slug.

"Well then. I'll get on with a few things. I won't be long."

Elizabeth listened to the sounds of chopping and the opening and closing of the heavy fridge door. She began her attack swiftly and mercilessly. Thomas's words spoken in the carpark that evening two weeks before were still raw in her memory. "You called me immature, evil, you said I never loved Luke…that I was a bad wife…you called me an aberration!" she spoke in a loud whisper, spittle flying from her sneering lips. "You don't know me at all! I loved your son…with all my heart…but it became clear over time that he was not the quiet kind man that I believed him to be." She paused as the noise of a heavy thump followed by what sounded like the slamming of metal on metal emanating from behind the closed kitchen door.

Thomas began to form an outraged response, but Elizabeth rudely cut him short. "Before you start pulling me apart again, answer me this…how well do you really know Luke?"

"Better than you, clearly!" Thomas spat derisively. "He's a saint compared to you!"

Elizabeth lowered her voice and began to speak clearly, but the sound of a door to the hall opening made her gasp and hesitate. The muffled light tread of Céline making her way upstairs halted Elizabeth full flow. She waited until it was apparent that Céline was not coming down again straight away. She continued, "What sort of son allows his brother to die in front of his eyes, mmm?"

Thomas's eyes widened in confusion. "What do you mean? Are you talking about Xavier's accident?"

Elizabeth nodded and continued to speak urgently, her voice rising in pitch. "Luke's told me what happened. It may have been an accident, but Xavier fell off that wall because Luke had promised not to tell Céline, and then changed his mind. That made Xavier panic and fall… Luke watched him land, he watched him crack his head open on the patio and he watched his brother's blood leave his body, not just for a few seconds, but long enough for Xavier to bleed to death And don't tell me he was only a child! He was a bright boy, he could have screamed for help, but he chose not to!"

Thomas gave a loud groan, head in his hands. "Why are you telling me this?"

"Because I want to hurt you!" she shouted. "You've treated me like dirt, pushed me away like everyone else in my life, now it's your turn to feel the pain! It's time you faced up to the truth. Luke was a spineless coward then and he hasn't changed! Oh, and while we're at it, I've got something to show you." Elizabeth produced the cream envelope from her pocket with a deadly flourish. Thomas eyed it warily, as if it might contain a bomb.

Elizabeth pulled out the sheet of paper. Making a point of emphasising the recipient's name, the date and location of the sender at the top of the letter, she read it out to him, ending with the composer's signature. As she read it, her voice rose in a triumphant shout, her eyes blazing.

Elizabeth paled in shock as Thomas seemed to disintegrate before her eyes. His face sagged and changed colour as a howl of pure desolation split the air. Elizabeth rocketed forwards, landing on her knees beside Thomas. She began her own high-pitched wailing. It was a sound of sheer unadulterated terror.

She hardly registered the appearance of Céline who was shouting, "What? What is it? Elizabeth?"

Elizabeth could hear nothing except Thomas's roars of pain and the sound of her own dread in her ears.

Then she was aware of Elizabeth's urgent appeal. "Elizabeth! Help me! We have to help him! Do something!" But she could make no sense of the words. Time passed and the Elizabeth knew that she was being asked to do something. She tried to concentrate on Céline's face. "Elizabeth! I forgot, you have to go outside and wait for the ambulance…show them where to come!"

Elizabeth stumbled to her feet, hands covering her mouth as she ran to the front door. She waited long enough to see the lights of the ambulance as it approached along the narrow lane. She waved her arms at it frantically until it stopped. Two paramedics pushed into the house carrying bags and equipment. She stepped back as they passed her. "In there…" she told them.

Elizabeth followed the men into the house, grabbed up her overnight bag which had been pushed aside by the rushing men, and returned back out of the front door.

Sobbing and shaking, Elizabeth ran, her bag bumping against her legs. She made it to her car, climbed in and drove away fast, tyres squealing.

Céline did not realise that Elizabeth had disappeared until someone asked her whether there was anyone nearby who could sit with her until her daughter arrived. She shouldn't, they said, be alone in the house at a time like this.

Chapter Thirty-Seven
Broken Heart Syndrome

Saturday 12th February 2011
After

Céline was not functioning well at all. The back of her throat was brimming continually with something so vast, that she knew that if she let it spill out, she would be destroyed forever. Alexis and Rob put her inactivity down to shock and misery. They moved quietly around her, respecting her diminished persona.

They had arrived as soon as possible after she had brokenly told them what had happened over the phone. The ambulance men had been so kind, making her drink tea, the older one holding her hand while they waited for the doctor to arrive to confirm Thomas's death.

Céline had gazed around her as these people moved around the room, talking in low voices, busy with pens, sheets of paper and medical objects. Her eyes would land now and then on Thomas's face. He would help her, surely? He couldn't leave her to cope with this this alone, it wasn't in his nature. He always looked after her. But as she studied his face, so grey, the lips blue, half open, she knew that not only had Thomas Johnson just stopped, but that she had too.

Someone had helped her find Luke's number in her mobile phone and had stayed near her while she spoke to him. She did everything that they told her to do. There seemed to be no alternative to this, and anyway it was strangely comforting. It was after this call that she realised that Elizabeth was no longer in the cottage. She was able to remember, with difficulty, the names of her next-door neighbours.

The activity round her seemed to slow down. She could sense that they were about to leave her. She clutched her throat in panic. She knew that another stage was about to begin, but she didn't want it to happen. It was so inconceivable that anything could move this moment on. Neither could she imagine what might happen to her next. She closed her eyes, and when she opened them again, Dorothy and Ron were standing in the doorway to the hall, disbelief and discomfort etched on their faces. She wondered why they were there…she did not see them very often, having little in common with the rather unimaginative English couple.

But here they were, reassuring Céline that they would stay with her until Rob and Alexis arrived. Ron escaped to the kitchen in search of more tea, while his wife bravely sat next to Céline, a damp tissue clutched in one hand, Céline's cold fingers in the other.

It was not down to chance that the Funeral Director arrived after Alexis and Rob. It was protocol to allow them a chance to see Thomas and say their goodbyes. Dorothy and Ron slipped away, congratulating themselves that their presence had been invaluable. Alexis had thanked them profusely for their help, her tears starting Dorothy off, despite her having had no more than a couple of stilted conversations with Thomas over the hedge in all the time they had lived next door. It was Céline who had asked Dorothy to keep her eye on the cottage whenever she and Thomas were away.

Alexis had taken hold of her mother's hands on first entering the room, tears pouring freely down her cheeks. She pulled her mother wordlessly towards her and into one of the most gentle but intense hugs that they had ever shared. They stood there together, neither wanting to end the moment, as close as only a mother and child can be. As Alexis finally released her suddenly tiny mother, Rob stepped in to support her in his strong arms. Céline was shaking with delayed shock and emotion as she whispered words of appreciation through trembling lips. Rob then had to physically support Alexis when she knelt at her father's side. She kissed his cold cheek. It reminded her of him returning from a brisk winter walk when she was small, picking her up to rub her soft cheek with his chilled one. Rob held her firmly, knowing she was on the verge of falling.

The removal of Thomas into the vehicle, ready to carry him to the Funeral Parlour, was done discreetly while Alexis bravely ushered her mother into the kitchen. Rob was informed that there would have to be an autopsy, nothing to worry about, it was just normal procedure when there was a sudden death at home, especially as Thomas had not seen a doctor recently. The body would be released for disposal as soon as possible.

Rob had to leave the next afternoon to be back at work on the Monday, but Alexis stayed with her mother, having been given permission not to report to back to work until she was able to. Luke had managed to get a flight from the nearest airport in La Rochelle on the Monday morning. Gaston had given him a lift there, his sympathy shown in the Gallic hug and comforting words as he hugged Luke goodbye.

Monday 14th February 2011

Céline stared out of the kitchen window at the scudding white clouds. The wind was fresh, whisking through the bare branches of a couple of small fruit trees that Thomas had planted at the place where Xavier had fallen twenty-two years before. Both deaths had pulled together into one huge anguish in her mind. Sunshine came and went in sheets of shining light chased by the clouds racing across the sky.

Alexis looked up from where she stood at the stove, stirring a pan of watercress soup she had made. "Mum?" she murmured softly. "Luke should be here any minute. Do you think you could try a little soup? You've eaten nothing since…"

Céline turned her head and tried out a watery smile which ended up in a wobble of misery. "Thank you, sweetie…maybe just a mouthful?"

They both heard the front door being opened and shut quietly again. The two women looked up hopefully, and there stood Luke, bringing in a clean windswept scent, his cheeks flushed with cold. He looked foreign somehow, his face more filled out, a light tan beneath a new dark stubble. The outdoor work suited him, his upper arms solid beneath the soft wool of a pale sweater, visible as he shrugged off a dark-blue jacket, modern with zips in unexpected places. He had had no trouble hiring a VW Polo from the Avis Hire Company at Newquay Airport. The entire journey to St. Evan via St. Mawgan and a couple of small towns had only taken him twenty minutes.

"Used the key safe," he informed them. And then he was striding across the room. Céline ran to meet him, flinging her arms around his neck. She reached up on tiptoe to press her hot cheek against his lips. He turned, a sob catching at the words in his throat. He opened an arm for Alexis to step into, hugging his diminished family close to his chest.

With Luke home, that Monday evening, Alexis was relieved to notice that Céline was at last able to speak a little. They believed her when she remembered that not long before hand, she had been counting her blessings. She gave a small smile. "I was remembering how much I loved him…instead of feeling irritated by all those stupid things that can build up. He was asleep…and then, well…I wasn't expecting…"

There was a pause as Luke and Alexis tried not to imagine what their mother had not been expecting.

Luke thought for a moment before asking hesitantly, "Mum, when you rang me, you mentioned that Elizabeth was here. Did you mean that? You weren't getting muddled were you, with someone else?"

Céline stared at him in consternation, as if he were asking her a question in Swahili. "Yes, she was here, that's right. I had almost forgotten! How strange…"

Alexis turned to look at Céline anxiously. "But why, Mum? Why was she here? After that last row, I thought she'd keep to herself! You didn't mention it when Rob and I arrived? Mind you, you weren't in any fit state to mention anything, especially after taking those pills the doctor gave you…"

"She just turned up, I think it was not long after six o'clock, the news was on. She seemed to think I wanted to see her."

"What for? I thought Dad didn't want to see her again?" queried Luke, puzzled.

"He didn't," she agreed decidedly. "But I think she wanted to talk about property and decisions that you and she were going to make, so I thought, let's get it over and move on."

"So what happened, Mum?"

Céline looked down, at a loss to find the words. She looked up unhappily. "I don't know what happened. I went upstairs to make up a bed. Next I could hear voices, very loud, and another sound, like pain. So I ran downstairs and your dad was having some sort…he was not right! He looked…affreux…dreadful! And moaning! It was awful, awful!"

Luke put his hand over his mother's. "Okay, Mum, don't think about it now. You did your best. You called the ambulance, you couldn't have done any more."

Alexis swept her tears away with the tips of her fingers and sniffed loudly. "Luke's right, Mum. You were with him, that will have been a comfort to him. What about Elizabeth, though? She wasn't here when Rob and I arrived…"

"No, chérie, I didn't see her after those kind men in green clothes arrived. I can never remember their proper names…she must have left then."

"Has she been in touch since?"

"No," said Céline. "I expect she is too upset…it was so very upsetting…"

Luke glanced at Alexis over his mother's bowed head. The unanswered question was mirrored in each other's eyes.

Friday seemed the best day to choose for the funeral, taking a day off before the weekend seemed less disruptive to working lives somehow. With the help of Céline's memories and the family address book. This was finally located in Céline's beside cabinet. She had forgotten that when Luke had decided to flee to France, he had asked her for Madame Le Blanc's telephone number to arrange booking the cottage at short notice. He had made the call from the upstairs extension and then shoved the book into bottom of the cabinet.

Rob and Alexis compiled a short list of Thomas's colleagues and friends. Most of them were able to accept the invitation to the funeral, to be held at St. Evan church. Rob and Alexis had been to visit the church after the service on that Sunday after Thomas's death. Alexis was emotionally blown away by the thirteenth-century building, standing quite alone and visible for miles around. She had been there as a child, but not frequently, and she had forgotten its raw beauty and strength, standing strong for all those centuries while fierce Cornish storms had beaten against the rugged walls.

"This place reminds me of Dad himself in a way," murmured Alexis, one gloved hand snuggling deeper into Rob's as she held her wind-whipped hair out of her eyes with the other one. "I don't think he was particularly religious, but Mum loved this church, even though she's Roman Catholic. My dad…he stood strong for me all my life, fending off anything that might hurt me. Like these walls, he made it against all the miseries life can throw at you…until now."

She stifled a sob and Rob held her tightly. "Do you remember when I first met your dad in that café in Launceston? Must have been around the end of November?"

"Of course I do! He was great with you, wasn't he? I was so nervous…"

"He was brilliant. He accepted me straight away, didn't he? And he said he could see how much I love you."

Alexis smiled at him, squeezing his fingers.

"And I told him that I would keep you safe, remember? Now I think of it, it was as if he was giving me his blessing to take over his role in looking after you. And that's what I'm going to do."

Alexis looked up at him. "I can't think of anyone nicer to step into his shoes. I love you, Rob."

With the unpleasant necessity of the autopsy out of the way, things could be prepared for the coming Friday. The results stated that Thomas had died from a heart attack caused by 'coronary atherosclerosis' which in a layman's terms meant sudden blood clots in the heart's arteries. He had not, to Céline's knowledge, suffered any warning pains during the months running up to his death. The doctor explained that there was nothing she could have done. These things happened.

In a quiet moment, Luke had googled 'heart attacks' on his laptop and had been quite startled after learning about complicated descriptions such as 'stress cardiomyopathy', to discover that there was an actual condition which mirrored all the symptoms of a heart attack; chest pains, breathlessness, etc. It was called 'broken heart syndrome', caused by a sudden shock. There were no other physical signs, such as clots or blocked arteries or scar tissue, and generally the victim of this recovered in a few days. However, Luke was alerted to the final sentence of the report. 'Broken heart syndrome can however lead to severe, short term heart muscle failure, and in rare cases it can be fatal.'

Luke swallowed uncomfortably. He preferred not to dwell on such morbid thoughts at the moment, and certainly did not feel like sharing them with Alexis or his mother. They were distraught enough, and he had plenty on his plate, what with steering them all through the funeral itself. He would be glad when Friday was over.

Friday 18th February 2011
The Funeral

The day dawned fresh, clear skies full of yellow light, but the air so chill that the three Johnsons were not surprised to find a sparkling frost touching the pavements and lying thicker on grass verges.

Rob had driven down again the previous evening, and the four of them drove together in the little blue hired Polo, arriving at the church minutes before the groups of Thomas's friends and acquaintances arrived. There were a few stilted conversations due partly to the sadness of the occasion, and partly to the fact that Céline had either not met some of the 'dearly beloved', or could not remember those she had.

The service was short, a mercy to most of the congregation who were not slow to observe that the church's heating was either defunct or had not been turned on early enough.

Luke and Alexis stood either side of their mother, Rob next to Alexis, each of them making frequent surreptitious glances back at the door, worried that Elizabeth might suddenly make an appearance. She did not.

The internment was brutally painful. Céline just about kept the hysterics at bay, but the tears ran down her cheeks as if they would never cease. Then suddenly it was all over.

Despite Céline's polite urgings to several of the sombre-faced strangers to return with them to the cottage, but to a man they dredged up worries about the possible onset of snow, long journeys that they desired to complete before nightfall, and even a dog or hamster that needed attention. Dorothy from next door's eyes lit up at the thought of being offered a choice of delicacies and beverages that she had not had to prepare herself for a change, but Ron dragged her firmly away by the arm, mumbling something about, "What about my bangers and mash? You know we always have that on a Friday. Don't want to spoil our appetites…"

So it was with a united feeling of relief that Alexis, Rob, Luke and Céline drove home unaccompanied to plates of tuna sandwiches and small fancy biscuits which Alexis had bought in a tin, whose lid pronounced it to contain 'petits fours'. Céline had eyed these very English biscuits with justified suspicion. She cling-filmed the sandwiches and had soon produced a nourishing lunch of homemade quiche, potatoes in their jackets oozing with butter and a pale-green mound of flageolets, dotted with freshly ground black pepper. Alexis and Luke exchanged encouraging looks; Céline seemed to be rallying somehow, if only temporarily. She must take each moment as it came. They even managed to tease her by referring to the often-used observation that in French, potatoes in their jackets became 'pommes de terre en robes de chambre'. That was, potatoes in their dressing-gowns. "How typical, French farce," Luke commented.

Céline actually chuckled. "You might laugh…but the Germans eat potatoes in their uniforms!"

Luke smiled and Rob grinned, feeling so comfortable within the confines of this bruised family.

They talked companionably, sitting cosily at the kitchen table. The bottle of wine that they shared encouraged nostalgic memories of Thomas at his funniest and most pompous. "He was such a lovable mix." They all agreed as they clinked glasses, which prompted the opening of a second bottle of wine.

Céline sighed and looked at the three young people sitting there. She folded her arms and announced suddenly. "Well…I have been thinking. And I have decided that I will return to France with Luke…if that is all right with you, mon chéri?"

Luke's mouth opened in surprise, followed by a huge look of relief. "What a brilliant idea, Mum! How long for? It's just what you need!"

Céline looked pleased. "I have not looked further than a couple of weeks," she admitted. "But the thought of being here in the cottage on my own is too much. If Alexis and Rob were closer, but, tant pis. This seems a good thing to do for a while. I'm not running away…am I?" she asked worriedly.

There was a chorus of reassurances. "And to be honest, Mum, I could do with some company right now, not to mention coming home to a home-cooked meal every evening. I work quite long hours though, which'll be even longer as the days pull out. You won't get lonely, will you?"

"Not as lonely as here. I thought that I could close this cottage up, work out my finances, and then fly out to you in a week or two? We have enough money to be quite comfortable, so I thought it would be good to buy a small car out there? I will be able to drive to the shops while you are at work."

Three pairs of eyes studied Céline with admiration. It seemed that she was not going to go completely to pieces from grief. It was still going to take a while to accept what had happened, but she was obviously a fighter.

"I'll drink to that!" stated Luke firmly, touching his glass to each of the others in turn.

Chapter Thirty-Eight

"Well, Well... At Last. I Did Wonder If You'd Be in Touch"

Sunday 20th February 2011

Luke replaced the phone and sat down opposite his mother. He rested his hands on his knees, looking pleased with himself. "Well, that's settled," he informed her. "Gaston is quite happy to take over the two or three jobs I was in the middle of."

"Is he fit enough? I thought you said he's retired?"

Luke laughed. "He's officially retired, Mum, but in fact he's never really given it up. He's as fit and agile as a man half his age. He avoids the really heavy stuff, but he's fine with doing what he can for me over the next couple of weeks. Everyone knows everybody else round the villages as you know, and they are very understanding. Madame Le Blanc sends her sympathy by the way."

Céline nodded her thanks. The perpetual lump in her throat rendered speech impossible at times.

She was grateful to Luke for the change of plan. It would be good to have him there for moral support while she sorted everything out before leaving with him for France. It had been decided that they would drive down to the French cottage in the family Volvo. It made sense not to have to buy another car in France. The black waves of grief were coming and going, but these plans helped her to focus on something else.

The door to the kitchen opened as Rob appeared, bearing a tray holding four mugs of steaming coffee. Alexis followed in his wake, a plate of ginger biscuits held aloft.

"Oh...you are looking very fine in my best apron!" Céline observed.

Rob set the tray down and did a twirl, narrowly avoiding a collision with the biscuit plate. "Right. Elevenses, even though it's only ten o'clock. Help yourselves...that one's got sugar in it."

"Why eleven? Surely it depends what time you had breakfast?"

Alexis rolled her eyes. "Don't start, Mum! Have a ginger nut," she urged, proffering the plate.

She then had to interrupt her mother who was off again, "Nut! Why is a biscuit called…?"

"Luke! Rob and I have been chatting and we need to say something. Don't you think you ought to talk to Elizabeth? Don't make that face. If you don't do it now, it'll just become impossible. Someone has to ask her what the hell she and Dad were talking about that evening…and she can't just go on living in Exsham, can she? I think Rob and I need to discuss the flat with her, too. Rob doesn't really feel comfortable with us being her tenants any more."

Luke looked thoughtful. "I know, I've been worrying about all of this. I wish I could buy Elizabeth out. It would solve a lot of problems."

Céline dunked a ginger nut into her cup, looking bemused to find herself just holding a small crescent of dry biscuit. "I will help you do this," she mumbled, fishing about in her coffee with a spoon.

"What Mum? What did you just say?" asked Luke.

Céline stared at him with a candid expression. "Your father has been very careful with our money," she said softly. "He has made sure I will not need to worry about anything." She swallowed with difficulty, hiding behind her mug. "If he were here now, this is what he would want. I can make you able to buy her share. That way we can move on without her. Imagine! Life without Elizabeth! I hate her now! I need to know what they were shouting, or what she was shouting… Thomas wasn't…he was in too much pain!" Her face contorted in an effort to control her tears.

It was impossible not be infected by her distress. Luke was finding it hard to keep his emotions steady. "Don't worry, Mum. I'm going to get to the bottom of it somehow. I can't bear the thought of her upsetting him, especially as he's not here to tell us what happened. There's nothing I'd like better than to have my cottage back. I couldn't handle the idea of having to sell it. Thanks, Mum!"

"On one condition," Céline cautioned seriously. "And this is, that we offer it to Alexis and Rob to rent from you, Luke? That means they can move out of Elizabeth's flat and leave her to…wait, I know this word…to stew!"

Luke stood up and began to pace the room. He dragged his fingers through his hair, looking troubled. "Hang on a minute. What do you guys think? You know how tiny the cottage is, especially with the baby on the way. You don't want this foisted off on you if you're not keen…"

Rob opened his mouth to speak, but Céline beat him to it. "It will be fine for a while, babies do not need much space for ages. We do not know the future. Luke might want to come back when more time has passed, but it will give everyone a space to breathe."

Rob and Alexis both spoke at the same time, both agreed that they would love to live in Luke's cottage. They loved the aspect of it, so close to the sea, not to mention the pull of the quirky shops, the cobbles, and the close-knit community. The icing on the cake was having Elizabeth off their backs, however this last thought was actually voiced by Rob alone. Alexis was uncomfortable about her feelings for Elizabeth...even her fake pregnancy had evoked feelings of sympathy and compassion. She hid her feelings, though, remarking instead, "Oh! But what about Mango? Are you going to take her to France?"

Luke made a face. "No, I couldn't put her through all that upheaval, rabies shots and that long journey, not to mention a passport! Do they have to have a photo taken? No, she loves living near the sea. That's if you'll have her? Are you a cat person, Rob?"

"I am now!" he said quickly, taking in Alexis's hopeful expression.

They all helped themselves to another ginger biscuit and raised their mugs to toast a new beginning. They stared at Luke as he suddenly announced, "The next thing on my to-do list is to find a solicitor and file for divorce against Elizabeth. I think she is guilty of unreasonable behaviour amongst other things. I'll ring her now and get the ball rolling. This procrastination has gone on long enough."

Luke settled himself on the bed in Céline's spare room. He clutched the phone, feeling nauseous at the thought of speaking to Elizabeth. He glanced towards the window, loving the view across the bare wintry fields edged by black copses of trees, hoping to steady and channel his thoughts with the ever-changing yet always reliable landscape.

Her voice made him jump, ridiculing his prayer that his call go unanswered. His throat seemed to close up, the words sounded cracked and dry to his ears. "Elizabeth. It's Luke here." He used the small silence to cough.

"Well, well. At last. I did wonder if you'd be in touch."

Another impossible pause, during which Luke realised there was nothing he wanted to say. He realised he was experiencing a wave of claustrophobia such as he had suffered from during the worst of his depression. It was a feeling that life was crushing down on him, pushing him headfirst into a narrow tunnel ending in a blind wall. Ironically, the antithesis of this seemed like a parallel; all he wanted was to be hidden away from sight, covered over, unable to see or be seen. The difference being that this would be a bolt hole of his own choice, with the freedom of escape when he needed it.

"I'm still here, Luke. Talk to me." Came the order.

"I'll save it for when I see you. Today okay? Expect me at two o'clock." He gave her three seconds in which to object before closing the connection. He dangled his hands between his knees, aware of the tiny droplets of sweat which had formed on his upper lip. That's more like it though, he thought, tell her as it is, don't give her chance to trip him up with her verbal traps.

Luke set off alone in the Volvo at midday. Rob and Alexis stayed with Céline to keep her company before having to drive home to Exmouth themselves by mid-afternoon, by which time Luke hoped to be on his way back.

Céline waved goodbye to Rob and Alexis, mournfully gazing after their retreating car with a rising panic reminiscent of being a child left alone in a strange place by one's parents. Unable to concentrate on even the simplest task, she sat at the lounge window, staring for so long that she was startled to realise that the sun had gone, leaving the hedges silhouetted against a clear, pale-greenish sky. She shivered at the sudden drop in temperature, cold enough for the possibility of a frost later. It was five thirty, time to turn up the heating and give thought to some sort of meal.

Luke arrived half an hour later, thankful for the warmth in the cottage, and to find Céline occupied in laying a couple of trays for a lazy supper. The smell of meat and onions weaved up from an ancient saucepan, brown with orange flowers, which had been in use ever since he could remember.

They ate comfortably with the trays on their laps, feet stretched towards the leap and crackle of an open fire that Luke had got going. Rob had kindly laid it before leaving, knowing the temperature was going to plummet overnight. Thomas had always insisted that the central heating was perfectly adequate, had balked at the prospect of dealing with coal dust and messy ash, not to mention rogue sparks blemishing the hearth rug.

"How was she?" Céline asked eventually, placing her tray on the floor.

Luke made a long-suffering face. "Perverse, as usual. I expected her to play the deserted wife, demanding that I return to her at once. But she said she just wants me to be happy again, and that she'd wait until I felt ready to go back to her! Said she was willing to do anything to help me through it…"

Céline looked surprised and encouraged. "Well that's good, isn't it? So has she agreed to be co-operative?"

Luke bit at his thumbnail for a moment before replying. "She wasn't sure about giving up her half of the cottage at first, but she soon realised it made sense to move back into her flat to be nearer to her school. It was a no-brainer when I explained that Rob and Alexis wanted to vacate the flat anyway, but I don't think she'd have been that keen if she knew that they'd be moving into my cottage."

"And what about the divorce?"

Luke shrugged uneasily. "She burst into tears actually," he said in a desperate tone of voice. "She said she couldn't even bear to think about it. She sounded gob-smacked… sorry, Mum, speechless with amazement. She had no idea that it was the next step in my mind…said she thought we were just going through this separation in order for me to get well…"

Céline bit her lip anxiously. "I hope you, what is it…put her right? She must face reality, non?"

"I told her, Mum. I said that I wanted a divorce, and would file for one on the grounds of unreasonable behaviour. She just said no. She refused to grant me one." He looked over to his mother with a perplexed expression. "I'd looked it up earlier on my laptop, just to be ready for this. So I told her that she could fight me in court. It would cost her loads, and she'd lose anyway. She ticks too many boxes on the list; refusing to let me share her bed when she was in a mood, not supporting me when I had my breakdown to name just two."

"I do not like to think of you and that harlot!" cried Céline heatedly.

"Steady, Mum…" Luke grinned. "That's not the right word, although it does have a nice ring to it."

"And don't forget how cruel she was to you when they told you that you may not be a father!"

Luke opened his mouth in astonishment. "Are there no secrets in my marriage?" he protested.

"Well, it's not a marriage any more so it doesn't count. Your father told me. I had to dig it from him though…he kept his cards closed to his heart, that one!"

Luke frowned in an effort not to correct her. He sat in silence, a mixture of sorrow and outrage washing over him as he remembered his fractured marriage.

Céline was on a roll and had one more example of unreasonable behaviour to throw onto the pile, not that Luke needed any convincing. "That trickster! To come to dinner with a pretend baby under her jumper! When did she think to tell you the truth? When she gave birth to a cushion? She's mad as a rabbit. Your father was right."

Luke deemed it sensible to get the conversation back on track. "Anyway, Mum. She's agreed not to fight me, just to ignore me. I warned her that living apart for more than two years will make it more obvious to a judge that our marriage has broken down irretrievably. She laughed at me and said two years from now I'd be on bended knees begging to come back. She said she could wait for as long as it takes."

Céline almost laughed in disbelief. "She is living in the world of cuckoos, isn't she? Quelle folie!" Then her face grew serious as she asked, "And what of her explanation of her last moments with my poor Thomas? What does she say to that?"

"She said that Thomas told her to get out of our lives, that he wanted her gone because she was poisoning our family. She said she was shouting at him because he was so nasty to her. He wouldn't listen…she told him he was mistaken, that it was him putting ideas into everyone's minds. She accused him of being the only one who hated her, when she loved us all very much, including him. She never meant to upset him, she said. All she ever wanted was to be accepted and loved. She asked if you could ever forgive her."

"Poor Thomas!" Céline whispered. "He was always like the firecracker just waiting to go off. Maybe it wasn't really her fault? She just got under his skin. She was in the wrong place at the wrong time, and so was he…"

Mother and son gazed at each other, unconvinced. The dying embers of the fire collapsed softly with a crumbling sound, like a last breath in a silent room.

Chapter Thirty-Nine

"A Clear Conscience Is a Soft Pillow"

Tuesday 8th March 2011

It was a blowy mild night. The sky was full of fast moving clouds, moonlight filtering through now and then only to be obscured again. Céline and Luke were aboard a Brittany ferry, set sail for St. Malo. They had embarked from Plymouth at ten o'clock that night, the same crossing that Luke had used to flee to France almost four months earlier. Mother and son had gone straight to their cabins which were adjacent to each other, agreeing to turn in, as there was a long drive to navigate in the morning. They were scheduled to land at eight o'clock French time.

They lay, waiting for sleep, a thin wall separating them, but the thoughts and worries pulling them away from the brink of slumber were depressingly similar. They could still hardly grasp that Thomas was no longer a part of their lives. They worried about each other, one so distressingly widowed, the other planning a divorce, and they drew comfort in the decision to face the next few weeks together.

Events of the last fortnight had moved smoothly and swiftly at least. Luke had helped Céline to close up the cottage, Dot next door was happy to keep an eye on things, and Céline had assured her she wouldn't be away for too long. Even Ron had offered to help, by driving in convoy to Newquay with Luke to drop off the hired car and drive him back.

Alexis and Rob had moved out of the flat over one weekend, putting a few things into storage; they didn't own a great deal as Elizabeth's flat was furnished. They had stayed a night in the Bridge Hotel in Exsham, keeping a low profile until Elizabeth had taken what was hers from the cottage. She had hired a small van to move her stuff to the flat. Luke had felt guilty that he hadn't offered to help her move, but he couldn't face seeing her again, and was convinced that she would have refused to leave at the last minute. The bank transaction to buy her share of the cottage was done, but not until he knew she was safely out of it and had posted her set of keys through the letter box.

If Mango was surprised to find that her owners appeared to have left home, only to have been replaced by these others who were a soft touch, allowing her to sleep on the kitchen table with her head in the fruit bowl and perform her morning ablutions on the draining board, she did not show it. Why bite the hand that feeds you? After all, one lap is very like another.

Elizabeth strode around her flat, searching for any signs of damage that she could hold Alexis and Rob responsible for. She was fuming, a continual state of fury which was eating away at her. She had been so convinced that the meeting with Luke would have ended in a tearful reunion, a mutual forgiveness and understanding, and a fresh start. But he had changed since his 'breakdown'. He had grown hard-hearted and sceptical. She should have put her foot down when he insisted on buying her out, but she was reluctant to give him another reason to stay away. However, she was relieved at the thought of moving back to her flat and not having to deal with prickly Rob any longer. Alexis was still a useful contact. She would deal with her later.

She began to calm down as she busied herself rearranging the flat and her belongings. At last it was beginning to feel like home again. She certainly didn't miss that poky cottage in Exsham! Smelly mud layering the harbour when the tide was out, scavenging seagulls sending her crazy with their continual screaming, and that wind coming straight off the sea, whistling through the gaps around the ill-fitting casements…she had never shared Luke's passion for quaint and quirky. And no more Mango, well, not until Luke had come to his senses and returned from his mad sojourn abroad. No more scraping evil smelling cat food into the bin, finding tangled balls of black fur on the carpet or coming across small headless corpses of birds and mice on the kitchen floor.

As for a divorce, she would do whatever it took to cling onto her marriage. Luke was her husband. He belonged to her. She wasn't going to let him go, not after all the hard work of catching him. She stopped in the middle of making up her bed with fresh sheets and sank down to sit in the edge of the bed. She picked up a pillow and hugged it, closing her eyes as she let the familiar daydream wash over her. It consisted of her and Luke, alone together in a sunny place, happy to be by themselves, away from his difficult judgmental family. They had all let her down badly, Thomas being the worst. She believed in her dream, she was patient, she could wait.

Overcome with adrenaline-induced exhaustion, Elizabeth lay down, still clutching the pillow to her breast, closed her eyes and fell into a deep sleep. Somebody once said, 'a clear conscience is a soft pillow.' As for Elizabeth, it seems that a complete absence of conscience appears to have the same result.

Wednesday 9th March 2011

Luke rolled the Volvo off the ferry and into the small port of St. Malo. It was a bright cold morning, the clouds having dispersed to reveal a pale-blue sky, a watery sun climbing slowly. Several seagulls stood dotted about on the tarmac, huddled into their own feathers, eyes closed.

"Warm enough, Mum?" asked Luke. Céline was wrapped up in a thick black coat and grey scarf thrown over her still dark hair. They had slept intermittently, aware of the ships engines rumbling beneath them.

She mumbled an unconvincing 'yes', and Luke promised to find a café as soon as possible. They both imagined a plate holding golden flaky croissants, mugs of creamy café au lait. As Luke drove through the old town, they admired the lines of ancient houses lining the harbour wall, the cobbled streets and colourful shop awnings. Luke found a large carpark, and soon found the perfect café down a narrow alley.

They sat down and breathed in the warm atmosphere, the sweet smell of baking bread, the mouth-watering sight of pastries filled with chocolate or apple puree and the crusty brioches, displaying dense milky dough when sliced open. Luke noticed his mother's cheeks losing their weary pallor, flushing pink as she raised the huge cup of steaming coffee to her lips.

He smiled at her, deciding not to mention the foam moustache on her upper lip. "Better? Do you fancy a short walk round after this? St. Malo is a beautiful city, but I didn't see it properly last time I was here. We could just stretch our legs a bit before the drive."

Céline dabbed at her mouth with a napkin. "Oh, yes please," she said with enthusiasm. She unfolded a twenty euro note from her purse and put it on the table, before excusing herself, trotting to the back of the café towards 'les toilettes'.

They made their way towards the beach, where the city curved out to the sea on a stunning natural harbour. They remarked on the long lines of bristling black stakes of wood driven into the sand, some lying on the sand and covered with grey shapes of mussels growing on them. Behind them, rising out of granite rock, was a maze of medieval streets. Luke pointed out the Cathedral of St. Malo dominating the early morning skyline, stained glass flashing. They walked along the ramparts of the ancient walled town, enjoying views of the city on one side and the harbour on the other.

Céline pointed to the islands and forts, scattered just out to sea. "Were these always cut off by the sea?" she wondered.

"Only at high tide!" Luke answered her, raising his voice into the sea breeze. "I think they let you walk out on foot to explore the islands when the tide is out."

Céline shuddered, imagining living there and getting cut off by the sea on her way home, arms full of shopping. Luke laughed at her overactive imagination. "Let's head back for the carpark," he suggested, taking her arm. They climbed gratefully into the car, already warmed from the rays of the climbing sun.

"A new start for us both, chéri!" Céline said softly, already feeling guilty of such a sentiment so soon after the funeral.

Luke glanced at her, thrown slightly by her choice of words. She was just accompanying her for a few weeks, wasn't she? He tuned the radio to a popular French music channel in an excuse to immerse himself in his own thoughts. The Volvo steadily ate up the miles as the sun rose in the sky, its warmth strengthening and brightening the further south they progressed.

Chapter Forty

"What Do You Want, Elizabeth?"

Friday 8th April 2011
Exmouth

The carpark was full as usual, the asphalt darkened by the frequent squalls of cold spitty rain, seemingly timed to drench the unsuspecting victim as they dashed from the rear exit of the hospital to their vehicle. Alexis wrenched open the door of her black smart car, its paint shiny bright with water. At seven months' pregnant, she clicked her seat belt closed with difficulty.

As she nosed the neat box of her car towards the exit, she became aware of a dripping person, enveloped from head to foot in a grey mac, pushing a bicycle in front of them. Once through the gate, Alexis paused despite there being no traffic. She looked back at the familiar figure behind her and turned left pulling up along the kerb. She leaned across to open the passenger window as Cheryl appeared alongside. "Cheryl!" she called. "Get in for a second! I haven't seen you for ages!"

Cheryl bent her head to peer into the interior, looking cautious until she saw who it was. She rested her bike against the wall and climbed in, her coat slithering soddenly as she moved. "What a dinky little car! I've never been inside one of these before! How are you, Alexis?" She turned to her friend with a beaming smile. She gasped as she saw the rising bump parting the opening of Alexis's now too-tight coat. "Oh my God! So this is what you get up to behind my back! Congratulations!"

Alexis laughed, holding on to Cheryl's hand. "I'm sorry it's been so long, Cheryl…it's crazy that we work in the same hospital and never bump into each other. I've seen you in the distance a couple of times…but always when I'm rushing somewhere. How are you?"

"Just the same!" Cheryl laughed. "Loads of night shifts because I need the money, same lodgings, it's not so bad. I just keep my head down. And I've made friends with a couple of new nurses. We go out clubbing once in a while!"

Cheryl blushed as Alexis teased her, "So! There's me knitting bootees and going to bed early while you're out downing Tequila Slammers! Good for you, you make me feel ancient, though." Her smile was slightly lopsided.

Cheryl looked into Alexis's eyes. "Something's happened, hasn't it? I know you too well…"

Alexis nodded, unable to speak. Eventually she managed to whisper, "Our dad died in February…heart attack."

Cheryl listened, full of sympathy as Alexis managed to bring herself to describe what happened. She was shockingly concerned by the news of Luke's breakdown and his subsequent leaving of Elizabeth, although this last bit of news brought an optimistic flush to her cheek. "What an awful time you've had!" she said, "I'm so glad you've got Rob. He seems like a great bloke…"

"He is!" agreed Alexis, realising at the same time with a guilty pang, that Cheryl's skin had a grey pallor, possibly just tiredness, but she thought she could detect an underlying joyless frame of mind which she guessed was a continual rather than a temporary state. "Do you fancy us meeting up for a catch up cup of coffee, starting next week? It's been my fault we've kind of lost touch. We should make it a weekly thing."

Cheryl's face broke into such a happy smile that Alexis's guilt at not looking out for her old friend sooner, nearly brought her to tears.

"Love to!" Cheryl replied. "How's Elizabeth bearing up by the way?

Alexis frowned before answering. "I don't honestly know. She was with Thomas when he died. Mum thinks they were arguing, but Elizabeth says she was trying to calm him down. We know he couldn't stand her and he didn't mince his words!" She grinned at the memory of him. "But apart from Luke, no one has seen her. Oh, yeah, she's moved back into her flat."

Cheryl looked alarmed at this news. "Don't look so worried. If she's got any sense, she'll just keep on avoiding us all."

"Where are you and Rob living then?"

"We've moved into Luke's cottage in Exsham! Only temporarily, until he makes up his mind about his future. Rob loves it, the smell of the sea, the wind flinging the seagulls around, and as for leaving Exmouth, it feels right! That's why I had to get a car…I passed my test ages ago, but I could never afford to buy a one! And Rob and I couldn't share his car, not with my different shifts at the hospital. This is the most economic one I could find, low tax and insurance, and I love it! It's like driving a matchbox!"

Cheryl nodded, admiring the quirky interior with its oversized dials like Mickey Mouse ears, and the funny little stick that just required pushing forwards to work the car through the gears. There was no clutch, and if she took her foot off the accelerator, the engine moved down the gears. It was like a child's toy car. She bit her lip, it was hard not to feel envious of Alexis. She turned to look out of the window. "Looks like the rain's easing off. I'd better get going. Right then, shall I text you when I know when I'm free next week?"

"Great, yes! Sorry I can't give you a lift now, but I don't think we'd fit your bike in here! Take care, honey! So glad I saw you today."

Alexis watched Cheryl climb onto her bike, wobbling slightly as she turned to wave. There was no side to her, she thought. She was just a kind sweet girl, and a true friend. She really was extremely happy to have bumped into her again.

Alexis buzzed along the Exeter road towards home. The rain was still throwing itself out of the sky in random icy bursts. She was looking forward to a big mug of tea and maybe a slice of hot buttered toast to take her through to supper time. As she passed the army barracks of Lympstone on her left, her mobile beeped twice from her bag in the foot well. She was just about halfway home, so she reckoned it would wait.

As she drove down Exsham high street, she laughed out loud at a small boy clutching his mother's hand and staring huge-eyed at her car. She waved at him and he waggled a chubby fist at her in delighted response. Her car was still quite a novelty, amusing particularly to the elderly and very young; middle-aged male drivers were a different kettle of fish…they cut her up on roundabouts, refused to give way to her in heavy traffic and often even made rude gestures at her for no reason at all.

Another irritated sound came from her mobile as she stopped a little further on at the delicatessen on the corner. She bought a carton of olives and a quarter of crumbed ham which fell in thick pink waves from the slicer onto waxed paper. Still ignoring her phone, she continued to the cottage.

She parked in her new spot, a small square recess where the low wall of their front garden gave way to the sloping stone landing slip of the harbour. Her car just fit there like a homing pigeon. She grabbed up her bag and dashed inside, thankfully shutting out the damp swirling weather. Her phone beeped again as she dumped her bag onto the kitchen table. She obstinately filled the kettle and slid two slices of nutty bread into the toaster before sitting down and delving into her bag.

The three messages were all from Elizabeth; 'Fancy a chat?' then, 'Just answer this, will you?' and lastly, 'Alexis, don't blank me! Please!'

Alexis gave a grunt of annoyance. Why did Elizabeth always push that little bit too much? That first text was sufficient. Did she think that people had nothing better to do than be at her beck and call? She realised that

Elizabeth was probably miserable and lonely, but since that disastrously embarrassing evening when Rob showed her up as a fraud, and the worrying circumstances of her father's death, Alexis was hesitant to encourage any contact.

She tossed a teabag into a mug and banged a plate onto the table, her movements jerky with vexation at having her precious homecoming spoiled. She had just lifted the kettle when her phone began to ring.

She jabbed the green button irritably. "Hello, Elizabeth," she said coolly, as if to a salesman.

Elizabeth waited a beat, seemingly expecting a warmer welcome and an inquiry about her well-being. When neither was forthcoming, she asked, "So, have you sent me to Coventry too, Alexis?"

The intended light-hearted note in her voice fell on unconvinced ears. Alexis formed her response carefully, fully aware that Elizabeth was never far away from either tears or anger. She decided to throw a question back, "What do you want, Elizabeth?"

"I thought you and I were friends," she replied sulkily.

Alexis felt an unfamiliar anger sweeping over her. This was like talking to a child who didn't understand that she had behaved badly. She knew that the temptation to lose her temper with Elizabeth was sinking to her level, and pointless. "We both have to move on now, you know that. Let Luke go, Elizabeth. You're an attractive woman…"

Elizabeth interrupted her, "Oh please don't patronise me! You can't just pat me on the head and dismiss me with a compliment, as if you're sending a dog away! We were friends, we still are. Don't be so harsh. It's not in your nature, Alexis! Let me at least come and see you, just once, please? What harm can it do? Are you at home now?"

"You're not serious! Why would you want to see me? I'm not going to act as a go-between for you and Luke if that's what you're hoping…"

"Since when did you become so cynical? I'm talking about us, how good we were as friends, that's all. I've no ulterior motive, honest. You are still my sister-in-law…"

Alexis was feeling ground down. She had always hated confrontation. Despising herself, she heard herself say, "Maybe…just so we don't part on bad terms. Your quarrel is with Luke after all…"

"Oh fantastic!" gasped Elizabeth. "When?"

"Um, soon…I'll text you…"

"What's wrong with now? I'm parked just round the corner. Get the kettle on, Alexis!" She laughed loudly, making Alexis shiver.

A cold finger of doubt seemed to tap her on the shoulder as she slowly muttered, "You don't know where I'm living now…how could you…?"

"Oh but I do! Luke told me he'd probably let the cottage out while he's away, and you know how nosy I am! So I drove over to see if I could see what sort of people were living in our cottage. I couldn't bear the thought of weirdos in it…so what a nice surprise I had! I'd parked up opposite, and who saunters over the road but Mango! I'd recognise that fluff ball anywhere! And she recognised me! Came running over for a cuddle. I couldn't imagine that Luke would abandon her to strangers, so I came to the obvious conclusion that you and Rob are our new tenants."

Alexis slowly put her phone down and waited for the knock at the door.

Chapter Forty-One

The Month of May Brought Balmy Winds across from the South

Tuesday 3rd May 2011
South-West France

Céline opened her eyes and lay quietly for a while. She could hear the cuckoo calling from a nearby wood, the twittering of starlings arguing across the road in a row of tall trees, and every now and then, if she listened carefully, she could hear a hoopoe calling to its mate in the distance.

She smiled at the thought of this small bird, no longer indigenous to England. It was more like a cartoon bird with its black and white striped wings, long down-curved bill, and an orange crest with black points which it raises when excited. Its flight was a series of jerky dips, its call a repeated hoo hoo hoo! The superstitious English deemed the bird unnatural, and had hunted it to extinction in the Middle Ages. The French were more romantic in their view, and the hoopoe was a common sight in Europe.

Life was enjoyed at a slow pace in this little hamlet of 'Les Petits Chemins'. It was the perfect place to lick her wounds as she gradually felt a new purpose returning. The sun was already throwing warm bars of light across the green and white chequered duvet. Céline loved this room with its French windows giving onto the small garden, the branches of the old pear tree knocking against the panes. She had heard the sounds of Luke's early departure for work some while ago.

Two months had passed since she and Luke had begun this mutual journey of grieving together and life had become a simple sharing of pleasures, painful memories easing and lessening. She knew that she had extended her visit far longer than intended, but she and Luke were easy in each other's company, and she was convinced that neither seemed inclined to end it. It had already been arranged that she would return to England for the month of June to be there for the birth of Alexis and Rob's baby.

She stretched deliciously, remembering the pleasant weekend just gone. The weather had warmed up considerably, and on an impulse, Luke had invited Gaston over for lunch on the Saturday. He arrived, pipe in hand,

Ella at his heels, an ancient jacket with a lamb's wool lining enveloping his spare frame. He brandished a bottle of red wine, the dusty surface garlanded with cobwebs, a good sign that it had lain maturing in his dark cellar for some time. Luke had lit the barbecue, the first of the year, and Céline had put a pretty cloth onto an old garden table and laid three places. Gaston had laughed as he sat down. "Only a mad Englishman would decide that a cold day in May is suitable for 'le dejeuner en plein air!'" he stated, knocking his pipe out on an ancient boulder.

Céline looked concerned. "Do you prefer to sit inside?" she wondered.

Gaston shrugged. "I have put on my warmest winter garment, and Ella will keep my feet warm," he assured her. He had been over to chat several times recently, and Céline enjoyed his dry observations and philosophical outlook on life. Over a meal of spareribs, sticky with sweet sauce, Luke and Gaston discussed work. There was a certain chap who lived in a nearby village who needed an artisan to help repair an old stone wall surrounding his property, which had collapsed in the winter storms so frequently experienced in this coastal area. Luke told Gaston he would be available in a couple of weeks.

The pork bones were thrown to an excited Ella who was not used to such treats. She ran round in circles, barking until Gaston ordered her to take herself and her booty elsewhere. She scooted off with her mouth full, showing the whites of her eyes in ecstasy. Gaston said she would bury the bones somewhere, probably in his vegetable patch, and dig them up again when they had reached an interesting stage of decomposition. Céline wrinkled her nose.

The vintage Bordeaux wine had loosened Gaston's tongue. He said he had not always been a bachelor, had indeed enjoyed several years of married life and had fathered several children. It had been his roving eye for a pretty woman which had been his undoing, in fact several pretty women, now he came to think about it. His long-suffering wife had kicked him out, and here he was thirty-five years later. This tiny hamlet by the sea was a far cry from Paris, but he was content in his old age. Céline informed him that she had also lived in Paris as a young girl, and indeed had met her husband-to-be in Paris, such a romantic city. She said she found it unbelievable that Thomas had been taken away from her already. Gaston had waved his relit pipe at her, announcing that the plans one made so conscientiously in the morning, so often became altered or abandoned by the evening. They contemplated this nugget of wisdom in silence for a few moments. Gaston rose to leave two hours and a second bottle of wine later. He made his farewells, and if Céline found herself losing count of the cheek kisses she received, she politely put it down to the fact that she was probably the first female to enter his lonely life for some time. When she shared this thought later with Luke over the washing up, he gently put her straight. Gaston was indeed known as the Casanova of 'Les Petits Chemins', he explained, having already formed a trail of broken hearts in the local vicinity. Céline reminded herself to study carefully those plump dark-clothed women, haggling at the Wednesday covered market with such rude vigour, for signs of unrequited love in those stern Gallic features.

The month of May brought balmy winds across from the South, the heated air suddenly shimmering with clouds of tiny flies, dispersing as huge black bees zig-zagged through them. Crickets began to sing in the long grass, silencing when Céline approached with her basket of washing, which would bleach clean and dry in the hot sun in only a couple of hours.

Luke found himself inundated with outside jobs that people had put off tackling until the warmer weather. He asked Gaston to join him to ease the load, giving the older man the lighter tasks while Luke strengthened his muscles even further with the shifting and digging work. They enjoyed working together, and Gaston was grateful for the extra tobacco money.

So it was that Céline began a therapeutic routine; a walk to the bread shop while the mists still lay across fields swelling with green shoots, the morning occupied with a few domestic jobs, weeding the small garden, adding touches to the cottage so that Luke would return to the rich aroma of some slow-cooked dish, a bunch of freshly picked sweet peas in a green and white jug, a pile of fragrant ironing on his bed. On Wednesdays, she drove across to the market town of Cozes, where under the huge wooden structure the sellers spread their produce as they had done for a hundred years. She brought home fresh prawns, ripe avocados, whole rabbits to be coated with Dijon mustard and simmered in red wine, and bunches of radishes, mâche and watercress.

In the afternoons, she drove over to Gaston's cottage. He would have returned for his midday meal and siesta, as befitting a man who would not see sixty-five again, while Luke ate his packed lunch on site, lovingly prepared by his mother. Ella would be waiting for Céline in the small courtyard outside Gaston's kitchen door. Céline would lift the latch of the old wooden gate and greet the dog with soft words. Not wanting to disturb her master, Ella would lick Céline's hands gratefully and follow her out to her car, only giving in to the urge to bark when they were flying towards the coast. She stuck her head out of the window, her fur on end, eyes closed against the salty wind. Once on the long sandy beach of Vergnes, Ella was allowed to run to her heart's content, back and forth to return the squeaky toy to Céline's hand, to have it thrown once again with dizzying excitement. This was one of Céline's favourite times of the day, when she could walk away the terrifying memories of Thomas's death, replacing them with the tender funny moments, which after all there were hundreds of, compared to that one black evening.

The weeks were melting away, and soon she would be back in England, welcoming another new life into the family. These days with Ella would end. Dogs were not allowed on the beaches during the summer.

Luke finally found himself able to begin the new wall-building project a week before Céline's flight back to the UK. He explained to her that it would be a lengthy job. The wall, which was made a little like the dry stonewalls of North Britain but with larger stones, had cracked and crumbled badly due to the unusual bouts of frost which had hit them the previous winter. He was secretly pleased that Céline would be happily distracted by the birth of Alexis's baby. He had loved having her near him for these difficult weeks since the funeral, but he was concerned that he would come to rely once more on her maternal devotion. It reminded him too painfully of his dark days of depression. He felt that once home in England, it would be sensible for her to stay there. She could not stay in France for ever.

Alexis had been on maternity leave since the beginning of May. She had been looking forward to a quiet few weeks, nesting and preparing for the birth as her body grew heavier. She never tired of sorting through the bottom drawer of her wardrobe, folding and refolding the tiny lemon and white Babygros and all in one vests. She would bury her nose in them, inhaling their just washed scent. At the bottom, Alexis added a rattle, a mobile, a fat yellow duck. Already the small cottage was struggling to accommodate the extras; the pram, the bassinet...but it would not be long before Luke would return. She and Rob would easily rent another flat with a second bedroom.

The trouble was, she could never feel totally relaxed. As the afternoons drew to an end, Alexis would find herself tensing up. Elizabeth had taken to dropping in without warning after her school day was over. The day and time was never the same, depending on what tasks she had to do before leaving the classroom. Alexis began to feel almost intimidated by not knowing whether Elizabeth would turn up or not. Sometimes, when the time reached four thirty or later, she would relax only to hear the dreaded sound of a car arriving. This panicked Alexis even more in case Rob came home early. She had not mentioned that first visit of Elizabeth's to him, knowing he would he would have been furious, and later, as the visits increased, it seemed too awkward to bring it up. In vain, Alexis had tried to hint that a warning text would be appreciated. Elizabeth had just laughed, saying that family had no need for such nonsense.

It occurred to Alexis that she was turning into a nervous wreck…just when she was supposed to be at her most calm and serene. She contemplated not being at home at that time of day, but realised how absurd that would be. She refused to be manipulated…but…there were days when she found herself close to tears. It wasn't just the unwanted visits. It was Elizabeth's insensitive manner. She would bring gifts, inappropriate toys, too large to store, or baby clothes which were not to Alexis's taste. And all these things had to be hidden from Rob. Elizabeth had even deemed it normal behaviour to wander round the cottage, poking her nose into cupboards and even rummaging through the baby's precious drawer of 'things'. Each time she eventually departed, she would hug Alexis for a beat too long, putting her uninvited hands onto Alexis's stomach, so that she recoiled in discomfort.

Alexis began to count the days down to the birth, to her mother's comforting presence, and then finally, to be able to move out of Elizabeth's suffocating reach.

Chapter Forty-Two

"I Didn't Realise How Thirsty I Was"

Wednesday 1st June 2011
Devon

Rob stood waiting in the arrivals lounge at Exeter airport. Céline's flight was on time, and the first few passengers were coming through, trundling wheeled baggage tiredly along, eyes brightening as they began to search for friends or relatives.

He spotted Céline straight away, her black hair clipped neatly away from her face, a smart dark-blue jacket and white jeans worn in the chic way that only a French woman could. She looked younger, refreshed. Rob waved, and then turned to beckon to Alexis, who had bagged a nearby bench, thankful to ease the baby weight off her feet.

Céline was grasped and hugged by both of them at once, Rob taking her suitcase, Alexis taking her arm. "You shouldn't have bothered to come, chérie!" scolded Céline, marvelling at how large her daughter had become.

Alexis laughed. "I need to keep the circulation going! And don't worry, Mum, the head isn't fully engaged yet."

Rob coughed in fake embarrassment. "Language, Alexis!" he admonished sternly.

Céline tutted. "We are not in the black ages now, Robert! We can talk of these topics without red cheeks, you know!"

Rob and Alexis exchanged childish smirks above Céline's head.

Céline was then peppered with questions by Alexis who wanted to know how was Luke? How was Madame Le Blanc? Did she still own four cats? How was the cottage? Did the electrics still blow if you switched the kettle on at same time as the washing machine? Céline did her best to answer, until exhausted, she claimed to now know how it must feel to be given the third degree.

Rob deftly manipulated his car through the busy suburbs of Exeter, and was soon on the way to Exsham on the Exmouth road. The rush hour traffic had mostly died down. It was getting on for seven o'clock, and the clear skies that had denoted a warm sunny day earlier, now heralded a noticeable drop in temperature.

Céline pulled gloves and a scarf out of her handbag, grumbling about the cold English climate.

Rob reminded her good naturedly that she had just flown over three hundred miles north. What did she expect?

Alexis had been concerned about the problem of domestic arrangements for when Céline arrived. Rob had offered to sleep on the settee, letting Céline share the double bed with Alexis. She was completely against this idea, reminding him that it might be for several days if the baby arrived late. He needed a proper bed while working long hours, and Céline needed her own space and privacy at her age.

The problem was solved unexpectedly when a neighbour who lived a few doors away heard about it from another neighbour over a garden gate, and was only too keen to offer Céline her spare room. Hilda Miller was a softly spoken lady in her mid-fifties, living alone. Céline took to her at once, and was happy not to have to put Alexis and Rob out.

Alexis began to relax at last. It had been a week since Elizabeth's last visit. Alexis had made it very clear to her that Céline was going to be arriving soon to help with the baby. At the mention of Céline's name, Elizabeth had turned pale, sitting down suddenly on the settee. "Céline? She's coming here?" she asked, sounding amazed.

"You didn't think that she wouldn't fly back to be with me, did you?" Alexis asked in surprise.

"No…of course…not…" stammered Elizabeth. "And she's staying here? Not much room…"

Alexis refused to give Elizabeth any details, she just glossed over the question, saying they could cope.

Elizabeth's eyes suddenly glinted with interest. "Flying back? From where exactly?" she queried nonchalantly.

Alexis stared at her, instantly deciding to reply in a vague sort of way. A half-truth would be safe enough. Lying did not come naturally to her as she could never remember what she'd said. She looked levelly at Elizabeth. "She's been staying with Luke for the last three months," she informed her quietly.

"But whereabouts?" Elizabeth quizzed through tight lips. She was dragging her fingers through her short hair, creating jagged points. Her eyes shone brightly, all signs of something simmering dangerously close to the surface.

Alexis refused to be tyrannized. "France," she said abruptly.

Elizabeth narrowed her eyes, a half smile lifting her mouth but not touching her eyes. "France is a big place…care to narrow it down?"

Alexis shook her head. "Stop it, Elizabeth!" she answered almost playfully. "You don't need to know, and I'm not going to tell you anyway. You'll have to go now, I've loads to do."

Elizabeth looked disconcerted, not used to Alexis's assertive behaviour. She stood up and hurried to the door. Alexis followed her, reaching round her to open the door wide, as if she would like to shove her sister-in-law out on her ear.

"I'll find him…somehow…somebody will let it slip…people always do…"

Talmont
France

Talmont was a small village, situated two miles south of Les Petits Chemins It sat on a rocky peak overlooking the Gironde estuary. Built in 1284, it still had its original layout as a 'bastide', the name for the walled towns found in south-west France. Towering above the village, the magnificent church of Saint Radegonde, symbol of the Poitou-Charentes region, sat like a guardian between the dwellings and the sea, still protected by ancient ramparts.

At some point, the village had been closed off to all but a few emergency vehicles. Early summer brought sightseers exploring the narrow, cobbled streets bordered by picturesque whitewashed houses, some allowing a tantalising glimpse of a flowery glade through an archway, or a view of a shadowy interior, blue shutters ajar, of a white cloth on a table laid for two, voices drifting from another room.

Almost every household had, over time, turned their front room into a shop, displaying fabrics, sundials, colourful scented soaps and candles, delicate white pottery decorated with blue and yellow flowers and butterflies, in short, the whole village was now an artist's paradise. No bread shops or supermarkets here…just simple paths weaving between tall hollyhocks, sounds of music, of waves crashing against the ramparts, the droning of insects. Restaurants were allowed, little covered tables spilling invitingly from enclosed secret gardens, rich aromas of crab and mussels wafting from a dark noisy kitchen, where sunshine, glowing through a lattice window, reflected ruby streamers from wine bottles lined up on its sill.

Sebastien Barbet had lived with his family in the small village of Barzan, situated on the coast, a couple of miles east of Talmont. On his twenty-first birthday, he had inherited a substantial amount of money which had been set aside for him from his grandmother's will. He was a steady intelligent boy, already working in a local bank with prospects, so his parents had advised him to use his inheritance wisely by purchasing a small house in Talmont. This was clearly becoming a very sought after village, a tourist trap, but still retaining its natural charm. The house had needed quite a lot of work doing to it, but was in one of the best locations, being set apart from other buildings on a grassy plot close to the foot of church. The end of Sebastien's garden was separated from the heady cliff drop to the tiny rocky beach below, only by a wide grassy path and a few stunted olive trees.

Sebastien painted watercolours in his spare time, winter seas beating on the ramparts, brightly coloured fishing boats returning on the tide in summer to navigate the narrow channels of water running inland from the sea, and always the stark black shapes of the carrelets, tiny fishing huts built high up on stilts, huge nets suspended like pelican's bills beneath them. They were the equivalent of the allotment, a husband's quiet retreat from domestic chaos. They lined the coast, silhouetted against the cold mauve hue of a winter sunset.

Sebastien had eventually amassed enough work to open up his small courtyard in the summer months. Here, at weekends and during the long summer evenings, he displayed his paintings, each with an unexpected edgy theme running through them, beauty startlingly brought down to earth. An empty white beach stretching long fingers of sand towards a turquoise sea, marred on closer inspection by the corpse of a gull, plastic garbage trapped bobbing among the seaweed, the lonely widower alone in his fishing hut, counting the days like beads on a rosary…counting down.

These themes had crept into his work gradually. At the age of twenty-seven, he had fallen in love with and married Yvonne, a local farmer's daughter, eldest sister to several siblings. She was two years younger than Sebastien, yet seemed to have been born with a maturity beyond her years. She seemed to Sebastien to have lived a life twice as full as his own, looking after her brothers and sisters, not to mention the chores, while her mother had worked on the farm, sinewy and muscled from wielding a hoe and lifting bales of hay. He loved her no-nonsense approach, the way she made his home make sudden sense.

In 1990, Yvonne died, aged only thirty-three, suddenly and swiftly struck down by cancer. Sebastien was heartbroken, his grief mirrored by the morbid turn of his art.

The only thing that remained worth living for in those dark days was Sandrine, aged seven. She was a solemn, beautiful child, with her mother's sensible old-fashioned outlook. She kept Sebastien on the straight and narrow somehow, with her quaint little observations and dry sense of humour.

Luke had been working on Sebastien's wall for nearly a week before he even knew that he had a daughter. This first day of June had been airless and close. A possible storm was brewing, distant rumbling out to sea, the sun suddenly obscured by solid purple blocks of cloud.

"Here…you must be parched. You haven't had a break since I got in from work a couple of hours ago!"

Luke looked up, sweat darkening his vision. He brought a handful of t-shirt up to mop his damp face. She stood on the grass next to the pile of white stones. The church loomed behind her, the light fading as the dusk and storm clouds joined forces in blotting out the setting sun.

She placed a small tray on the ground, on it was a tall frosted glass, bubbles bursting around chunks of softly clinking ice. Luke stepped towards her. At first he'd taken her for a young girl, in her denim dungarees cut off at the knees, tanned slim legs ending in white slip on shoes. Her face was not clearly visible in the sombre light.

"Thank you…I didn't realise how thirsty I was," he said. "I'm Luke by the way…"

"I'm Sandrine, Sebastien's daughter. Your French is very convincing," she observed, as if hinting that he might not be who he said he was.

"My mother is French." He smiled.

At that moment, a rosy ray of light from the setting sun broke through a gap in the clouds. It illuminated Sandrine's face. He was struck firstly by the straight fall of copper hair that reached below her shoulders. Close up, he saw that it was made up of several colours, ambers, oranges, dark browns, all merged together and shot through with sunlight. Her small nose was dusted across the bridge with faint freckles. She stared with interest at him, her black lashed eyes the dark grey of a stormy sea.

This was not the face of a young girl. It was a woman's face, but with the healthy glow and freshness of a young girl.

As he began to know her better, he would notice that her eyes changed colour dependant on the light. When waking her from a deep sleep, he would remark with wonder that her eyes were dark blue.

Chapter Forty-Three

Always Doomed to Be on the Outside Looking In

Saturday 11th June 2011
Exsham

"Are you sure you want to give it a try, Céline?" asked Rob, spreading chunky marmalade on his toast in a thick swathe.

"I must, Robert. The clock is ticking on. The baby is due in four days! If it decides to arrive in a rush, we cannot be waiting around for the ambulance to arrive like the slow boat from China. No, I will have a try this morning, after my croissant," Céline announced firmly, eyeing his toast with a critical frown.

"The roads will be pretty busy on a Saturday," warned Alexis with concern. Her mother had not driven much while Thomas had been around, but she assured them that she had driven every day while in France.

"As you, chérie, can no longer reach the pedals, then Rob will give me the lesson. We need a big empty space, n'est-ce pas?"

Alexis fearfully watched Rob manoeuvre her Smart car away from the cottage, Céline sitting next to him with a determined look on her face. The car only held two people, so Alexis had to stay at home, imagining the worst.

Woodbury Common lay only about two and a half miles from Exsham, on the Budleigh Salterton road. It was a beautiful area overlooking the Otter Valley. It consisted of rolling downs, woods and small beaten tracks running through the gorse and heather. This lovely heath was a vast empty area, even on a Saturday, with plenty of space for Céline to practise her driving.

The terrain was dry, and the track they chose was wide and flat, perfect conditions. Rob parked the car and got out to let Céline into the driving seat.

An hour and a half later, Alexis saw her beloved little car trundle up the road and nose its way into the neat slot beside the cottage. Rob climbed out of the driving seat and walked round to open the door for Céline. She looked less streamlined than usual as she walked unsteadily in through the front door.

Alexis pulled her into the lounge and manoeuvred her into a corner of the settee. "Well? How did you get on? It's a great little car, isn't it? So nippy!"

Rob disappeared into the kitchen in the quest of a strong cup of coffee.

Céline swivelled her dark eyes towards her daughter. "Nippy?" she echoed querulously. "There was nothing nippy about it! It was a very..." she searched for the right word, "muddled sort of experience."

"But you did drive it, didn't you? It's not that hard!" Alexis laughed encouragingly.

Céline gazed vaguely at Alexis. "I don't believe I did...it didn't seem like a car inside...it was more like a, what do you call it? A robber with only one hand. You know!"

Rob came in to the room at that moment bearing nerve-calming beverages and distributed them.

"What does she mean, Rob?" Alexis asked him, perplexed.

He sighed deeply. "Your mother found it difficult to grasp the concept of the gear stick. It reminded her of the lever on a 'one armed bandit', I think she means. So she kept pulling it towards her instead of away, we ended up going nowhere fast, not to mention with her braking at the same time. She wouldn't believe me that the car doesn't have a clutch pedal."

"Never mind, Mum!" said Alexis brightly. "At least you gave it a go! We'll manage!" Thank the Lord, she thought. One less thing to worry about.

Sunday 19th June 2011

One Thirty a.m.

Alexis lay rigid, on her back. Her head was turned so that she could see the green luminous numbers on the bedside clock. Rob's snores seemed to echo her breathing. She gripped the sheet tightly as another cramping pain moved from her back round to grip her vice like across her abdomen. She groaned loudly, no longer feeling the need not to wake Rob up. It was time...her contractions were lasting fifty seconds, and were occurring three to four minutes apart.

Alexis elbowed him unceremoniously in the ribs. "Rob! Rob!" she whispered urgently.

He was awake instantly, sitting up and leaning over to switch on his bedside light. "What is it, sweetheart?" he whispered back. "Are you okay? Is this it?"

"Yes! I think so! Oh Rob! I'm scared!"

"Why are we whispering?"

"I don't know…" Her giggle dissolved into a whimper of pain as another contraction weaved its excruciating grip around her.

"Stay there while I get your hospital bag, I'll ring your Mum too. Don't move, I'll help you dress in a sec."

Alexis bit her lip, overcome with so many emotions, but mainly grateful that Rob was so calm and reliable. She heard his voice coming from the kitchen. "Hello? Céline? Get dressed! It's time…Alexis is in labour! Are you there? We'll pick you up as quickly as possible…"

There was a short silence, and then at last he heard the mumbled sleepy voice of Céline. "Hello! Who is this? I was asleep!"

Sunday 19th June 2011
Nine Thirty-Eight a.m., French Time
'Les Petits Chemins'

Luke refilled the cafetière and brought it back to the table. He smiled at Sandrine, still not really believing that she was sitting there in his kitchen, that an hour ago they had been making gentle love in his bed. She sat at the table, wrapped in one of his spare dressing-gowns, nibbling a slice of golden brioche. She looked up at him through tousled hair and winked one blue eye at him, dimples appearing in her cheeks.

"Thank God your father is an open-minded man," Luke murmured, taking hold of her fingers.

Sandrine gave a husky laugh. "I am twenty-eight years old! He'll be relieved that I'm showing a healthy interest in the opposite sex at last. I've always been too busy looking after him, the house and practising recipes! What did you think? That he would chase you off his property with his hunting gun?"

"Silly!" He grinned. "No, I'm just grateful that he has accepted me so well. He's been very good to me, you know."

"Yes, I know! He is a very good man," she told him solemnly.

Luke poured fresh coffee into each of their cups. "Cheers then!" he said. "To us!"

Sandrine clinked her cup to his. "To us!" she repeated.

Just then the phone began to ring.

Luke reached behind him to pick up the receiver, raising his eyebrows at Sandrine. "Allo, oui…? Oh, Mum!" he said, a huge smile on his face. "What? Just now? Is she okay? Seven hours… is that normal? Okay… seven pounds, three ounces? Yes, yes, I'm writing it down! Give her my love, and what about a name? Okay, Mum, give them both a kiss! Bye!"

Sandrine gazed at him with wide-eyed anticipation. "Well? What is it?" she cried.

"A baby girl! They haven't decided on a name yet… Alexis is fine, just tired! Oh, I feel very emotional, I wish we were there. I can't wait for you to meet them all, Sandrine."

Sandrine nodded. "Me too, chéri. A whole family of people…" An expression of sadness darkened her eyes, and Luke knew she was thinking about her mother. She had shared her untimely loss with him, he had been very empathetic, knowing exactly what she had been through.

"I know, love. I keep thinking my dad should be here too, holding his first grandchild. He'd have been overjoyed."

Sunday 19th June 2011
Eleven a.m.

Elizabeth Johnson had been texting Alexis for hours. Weekends were hateful to her now; if she stayed in her flat, she drove herself mad, unable to concentrate on reading or television, even cleaning seemed pointless when she was the only person alive who knew whether it had been done or not.

She knew that Alexis's due date was the fifteenth of June, so she was desperate to know if there was any news yet. She also knew that she should not be texting Alexis. They had all made it plain that she no longer had any right to be involved in family affairs. She would never agree though. She would never give up, not as long as she was still married to Luke. The thought of no one letting her know when the baby arrived was driving her mad. On impulse and for something to do, she decided to go out for a drive.

She exited the flat looking slightly dazed. She had spent too many hours cooped up inside. She breathed in the heady scent of early summer, freshly cut grass and colourful freesias and sweet peas wafting their fragrant perfumes from neat front gardens. As Elizabeth climbed into her car, she realised with a jolt that without a doubt her intention was to drive to the hospital where she knew Alexis was booked in for the birth. She was soon on her way to Exeter, destination; The Royal Devon and Exeter Hospital.

Elizabeth parked and looked at the imposing red brick building in front of her. She took off her light jacket as she climbed steps and made her way through the entrance doors. The impetuous journey had brought a pink flush to her cheeks, her heart beat was raised and she gasped as a hit of pure adrenaline entered her bloodstream. It was the sight of the sign pointing the way to the maternity ward which had accelerated her pulse. Bittersweet sensations flooded through her as she followed the signs down the corridor.

Her trainers squeaked rhythmically on the linoleum as she walked, passing small family groups clutching flowers and cards.

Elizabeth entered the ward and approached the nurses' station. A plump woman looked up with a friendly smile, her blue uniform stretched across her generous bosom as she stood up. "Can I help you?" she asked, knocking a pile of papers together on the desk to even up the edges.

"Alexis Johnson?" she mumbled. "Is she here? Her baby was due five days ago. I've been away and I just wondered…?"

The nurse beamed at her. "Excellent! What good timing…she had the baby this morning! I'd not long started my shift actually… She's in the nursery at the moment, feeding the baby. Why don't you go and wave through the window, no visitors allowed inside, I'm afraid, but she'll be back on the ward shortly. Are you a friend?"

Elizabeth relaxed visibly at this friendly welcome. "I'm her sister-in-law, Elizabeth Johnson," she replied, wishing she had thought to bring a gift with her.

"Lovely! She'll be so pleased to see you!" gushed the nurse, directing Elizabeth to the nursery, with its long-glassed viewing window, a frieze of bunny rabbits and mice cavorting around the edges.

She stepped closer to the window. At first she could make out nothing but unrecognisable women dotted around the room, some seated, some standing at a counter making up bottled feeds, some just walking or swaying up and down the length of the room. They all wore dressing-gowns, pinks and lemons, all pastel shades. They looked like a docile breed of some secret sect, moving in a similar dreamy way, smiling, their lips mouthing some covert incantation.

She stared hard, concentrating, trying to make sense of these faceless forms…and then suddenly, there she was! How could she have not placed her straight away? What she had missed at first, suffering from some sort of tunnel vision, was that each woman was holding a tiny bundle, each wrapped in a soft cellular blanket.

Alexis was seated in a rocking chair, turned towards a large window, through which the sun's rays fell on her bright platinum hair, bent lovingly over the little shape wrapped in a pink blanket in her arms, curled close to her breast. Elizabeth gazed at length, tears forming as she stood there looking in… always doomed to be on the outside looking in.

Then she noticed the nurse standing behind Alexis's chair. Something about the stance, the way the arms were folded…she knew her but could not place her. The girl raised her head and locked eyes with Elizabeth. She leaned down to murmur something to Alexis, whose head snapped up like a deer alerted to danger.

Cheryl strode across to the door and flung it open. "Who said you could be here?" she demanded angrily. "Neither Alexis nor Rob want you here. He'll be back in a minute. I'd go if I were you!"

Elizabeth pushed herself forwards as if to enter the room. Her hand went up to the door jamb and grasped it hard. "I just want to see my niece and congratulate my sister-in-law!" she hissed. "Who are you to order me around? You're nothing!"

At that instant, Elizabeth felt the strong grip of fingers clasping her elbow. "Out!" said a low voice in her ear. "Now!" Before she could argue, Elizabeth was pushed discreetly towards the exit. As Rob ejected her unceremoniously into the corridor, he fixed her with such a cold stare that she flinched. The door shut in her face once more.

Chapter Forty-Four

The Scene Was Forever Shifting and Changing

Friday 24th June 2011
Exsham

"It'll be good for her, honestly! And it's lovely and warm." Alexis had been up since Sasha's six a.m. feed. "Come on, Mum! I'll fall asleep if I don't get out of the house."

Céline switched off the iron and raised the pile of pink and white baby clothes to her face, burying her nose in the delightful mix of fabric conditioner and subtle underlying smell of baby. "When you were born, it was suggested that we keep the baby inside for at least a week, away from people with their germs!"

"Yes, well. Things change." Alexis made a comical face at her mother. "You're not telling me that your mum didn't disapprove of your 'modern' ways when you had the boys?"

Céline thought back. It was difficult to remember those times without seeing again the puzzled hurt expressions on her parents' faces. Those special moments for herself and Thomas, the wedding, the births of the boys, had been tainted somewhat by Henri and Mathilde's disappointment. She didn't want to depress Alexis by such unhappy memories though, so she attempted a laugh, "Well, you are right…they didn't like the, what were they called? Displaced nappies? My mother was sure they would just fall apart!"

Alexis grinned. "Disposable nappies!" she corrected. This was when she missed Thomas with a flood of grief. The loving teasing of Céline when she tripped up over English words. She swallowed hard. "And how long did you have to stay in hospital?" she asked curiously.

"Two weeks with the boys! But they were born early, so it was different. Certainly this whisking in and out when the baby is three hours old? Well…c'est fou!"

Alexis had given Sasha her ten o'clock feed and left Céline to change her nappy and get her ready for the dangerous outside world while she brought the buggy round to the front door. Céline gently settled the well-wrapped, bonneted and mittened baby into the posh expensive pushchair, as she called it, that she herself had bought as a gift.

"Shall we walk down to the river?" Alexis suggested.

"If you promise to tell me if you get tired. You mustn't overdo things."

Alexis tucked her arm through Céline's, who had insisted on proudly pushing her granddaughter.

"Sasha is such a lovely name, so feminine," she commented.

The air was warm and sweet as they ambled away from the cottage and down the high street. They reached the end of it with only four interruptions, as women who hardly knew Alexis stopped them to look into the buggy with little cries of admiration and excitement. They turned right and began the slight descent towards the River Exe, where the Old Bridge Hotel, low down on the left, nestled close to the water's edge.

Thick reeds grew along the borders interspersed with clumps of tall bull rushes. They stopped on the old stone bridge, listening to the wild erratic cries of water birds, the rustle of the breeze as it blew through the long grass. Looking in the direction of the road as it zig-zagged away from the river, they could see flat marshland stretching each side of the road, for about a mile.

Céline studied the view with interest. "What are those houses in the distance?" she asked.

Alexis followed Céline's pointing finger. "That's the beginning of a tiny hamlet. That means a place smaller than a village," she explained. "That sprawling place you can see on the left is the George Hotel, and after that there's only a handful of cottages. There's no shop or anything…oh, I think there's a nursery, but that's all."

Céline glanced at Alexis. "A nursery? Bizarre, non?"

Alexis let out a loud chuckle. "No! Not for babies, Mum! It's a place where they grow plants and sell them! Oh, I'm going to miss you, you know…we haven't spent time like this together for ages. How long do you think you'll stay in France?"

Sasha began to whimper a little, so Céline resumed walking again to soothe her back to sleep. "I'm not sure, chérie. I am not frightened of living alone, but losing Thomas has made me think of the precious moments I must make with you and Luke. I will go back to Luke at the end of this month and then see how I feel. Luke is happy to have me there, I think, and after all, I am free now. I have rung Ron and Dorothy Mason; they don't mind keeping an eye on the house for longer. There's not too much to worry about. I said they could keep the pot plants, and they said that one of their friends' sons would be happy to take care of the garden while things are still growing so fast. The grass is like a jungle, they said! Isn't that kind? I offered to pay him of course…"

Alexis gazed fondly at her mother, content that she seemed to be coping so well. "Yes, you're right. Mum. There's no rush."

Céline put her hand on Alexis's arm. "You are such a good daughter! I am thinking…maybe I should think of selling the Cornwall cottage? Too many horrible memories. I should find something smaller and closer to you? But I don't want to be the millstone round your necks…" she said anxiously.

Alexis hugged her tightly. "That's something you could never be! But don't be too hasty, there are good memories belonging to the cottage too."

They stared sadly at each other, both thinking about Xavier, yet neither voiced their thoughts.

Friday 1st July 2011
'Les Petits Chemins'

It was four days since Céline had returned to the cottage. Luke had met her at La Rochelle and on the drive home she told him all about Sasha. She wanted to convey to him how adorable this child was, just describing her to him was making her voice quaver with emotion. He understood, the baby was giving them all hope after Thomas's untimely death. They discussed the possibility of Alexis, Rob and Sasha coming to stay sometime over the summer. Céline said she had suggested it to them recently, and they had been all for the idea. Rob was due two weeks' holiday and couldn't wait to show off his new daughter.

"It seems weird that so much has happened recently! I'm so relieved that Alexis has Rob now. He's a good bloke. Dad's death hit her hard. And how are you doing, Mum?"

"Good days and bad…you know. Loneliness is not nice, for anyone." She glanced across at him meaningfully. Luke kept his eyes on the road, feeling guilty that he had not yet told her about Sandrine. He could not put it off for long, and was sure Céline would be happy for him, but he could not shake off the underlying feeling that it seemed unfair for Alexis and now himself to have found a soulmate when hers had gone.

Céline was finding that she had too much time on her hands since her return. What with the hours of daylight lengthening, Luke was leaving for work earlier and returning later. He spent the bulk of the day working on Sebastien's wall, which was going to take a long time to finish, and he kept a couple of hours set aside in the afternoons for smaller local jobs. This kept him in the loop for any other work that could reach him by word of mouth from acquaintances.

Céline was finding that apart from small domestic tasks, there wasn't a great deal to do. She was not even needed to walk Ella, who more and more was allowed to run free by Gaston, in typical French style.

Friday had been the hottest day of the summer so far. There was not a breath of wind. Luke had not seen Sandrine properly since the previous weekend. They knew this would happen with the arrival of Céline, but it was hard. Sandrine had been practically living at Luke's cottage, so it made them feel like desperate teenagers having to steal lunchtime kisses when Sandrine nipped home to Talmont from her work in Cozes, where she worked in an optician's, to take Luke his baguette and bag of fruit. Now she sat near him, shared his lunch, and discussed the best way to introduce her to Céline.

"You're making me nervous! Is she very against me?" asked Sandrine glumly.

Luke smiled. "No, she'll love you…it's just that because Elizabeth refuses to grant me a divorce, I'm worried that she will say I should have waited before becoming involved with anyone else." He frowned worriedly. "She is a Catholic through and through. I don't want to put her in a difficult position." He stared thoughtfully out to sea as he picked at the peel of a satsuma.

"I would say that is closing the door after the horse has bolted, wouldn't you? We love each other…we are a grown man and woman. Elizabeth cannot stop you leaving her, so even if we have to wait, surely eventually you can divorce her because of the breakdown of the marriage? Unless you aren't sure about us?"

Luke sent her a look of pure shock. "Never say that, Sandrine! My life has dealt me some horrible challenges so far, as you know. At last it looks like happiness is in reach. I just don't want to risk anybody taking this away from me, from us…"

Sandrine sighed. "I understand, Luke. And I will always support you."

Luke reached out to run his fingers through Sandrine's hair. "I am so lucky to have found you. I'm not being fair to you, am I? I want her to meet you! Can I pick you up here after work? Seven o'clock?"

The beaming smile on Sandrine's face answered his question. "I can't wait to meet your maman." she announced firmly.

Luke knocked off work early that afternoon, apologising to the old couple whose decrepit old garden shed he'd been repairing. He made some excuse about having forgotten a vital tool. He refused a glass of wine and promised to return the next day to finish the job.

He entered his kitchen to find his mother taking a homemade quiche out of the oven. She stood there in surprise at his early return from work, the steam rising from the golden pastry full of the aromas of bacon, tomato, cheese, garlic and oregano.

"Mmm! That smells delicious. Any chance that it might stretch to a third person?"

"First, you are home early, then you tell me we have a mystery dinner guest! Is it my birthday?"

Luke dumped his work bag on the floor and grinned at Céline. "Put that down, mother, before you burn yourself," he ordered. She did as she was told and was startled further by Luke putting his arm around her and kissing her cheek soundly. "Come and sit down, I want to talk to you."

He led her to a small settee in the salon. This was part of the kitchen, an open-plan affair which meant that whoever was cooking would not feel cut off from other people. The settee was next to a large window which framed a view of fields of sunflowers and sweetcorn rolling away for a couple of miles to the coast, where the Gironde Estuary shimmered in the sun. Sometimes turquoise, bright blue or gun-metal grey depending on the weather, the waters were always dotted with seafaring vessels; from tiny fishing boats, to the huge cargo ships slowly navigating the estuary, or the cruise ships that lay anchored for several days. The scene was forever shifting and changing.

Luke waited until he was sure he had Céline's undivided attention. "Mum, I hope you won't think badly of me, and I wouldn't even be saying this unless I was absolutely sure, but I have met someone very special."

Céline's eyes grew round as she assimilated this information. She sat stunned for a few seconds. Luke waited for her to speak, trying hard to remain calm. "Well! I wasn't expecting that! I have only turned my back for a short while… That was quick work, wasn't it?"

Luke smiled awkwardly. "I know it seems badly timed, but it wasn't planned. It just happened. We've fallen in love, Mum. She knows I'm married, but with any luck, Elizabeth will want to divorce me on grounds of infidelity. Are you very shocked?"

"I am shocked! But because of surprise, not because I don't approve! Don't forget, I fell in love with your father on the day I met him. I am not in position to judge you badly, mon chéri! But I want to know all about her…what is she like?"

"You will find out in just under two hours actually." Luke laughed. "She is our mystery dinner guest."

Céline clasped her hands together in agitation. "Two hours to make an hors d'oeuvre, does she like radishes? Then a dessert, I can do something with the fromage blanc I bought yesterday… I think we have some good wine in the cellar, oh and yes, we have a ripe brie, too. You must take the duster and polish, then check the glasses have no marks…"

"Whoa! Slow down a minute… She is a receptionist for an optician, not the Queen of Sheba! And I would hardly call the two-foot hole under the floor boards in the hall a cellar!"

"She need not know this," Céline advised him solemnly. "We must be at our most first-class behaviour for…what is her name?"

"Sandrine," Luke said, covering his relieved grin with his hand.

Céline stood up briskly and trotted off to find the posh serviettes while Luke stared after her with mounting affection and respect. He heard her muttering, "Who is this Queen of Sheba? I have never heard of her…"

Chapter Forty-Five

Just an Ugly Little Maggot Sitting on a Leaf

Friday 1st July 2011
Talmont

Sebastien made his way home from the bank in Cozes, his car window wide open, but the hot wind blowing through it made no difference to the temperature inside the car. His shirt was sticking uncomfortably to him. He ran a finger inside his collar looking forward to a cool shower, a change into an old pair of shorts and t-shirt, and a cold beer in that order. He loved nothing better than being outside in the sunshine, so it was hard being cooped up in the dark bank all day. The hot weather was expected to continue for the weekend…good for tourists, so good for potential buyers of his work. His dream was to be able to give up his position at the bank and be able to rely on the sales of his paintings for his income.

He drove through the village of Seursac-Sur Gironde, over the roundabout and on towards Talmont. At five thirty, the light was changing, gilding the faces of the sunflowers as he passed their serried ranks standing shoulder. A field of stubble shone out at him, each stalk luminous with a bright green-gold lustre. He could smell the sea as he drove down the straight road, deep ditches on each side where the locals would catch large crayfish in season. He crossed another roundabout and then steered into the main road of Talmont, his tyres making a soft rumbling sound over the cobbles. He parked at the edge of the village, in a special carpark reserved for workers and residents.

On entering his small whitewashed house, he threw his briefcase on a chair in the tiled hallway, the tiles glowing butterscotch as the long rays of the sun slanted through the open door, highlighting them. He could hear the high sweet voice of Sandrine singing in the shower, and he smiled. He loved coming home to her, someone to share his day and a meal with, but he knew this was selfish of him. He couldn't expect her to take the place of her mother, no matter how many times she assured him that she was perfectly happy with the situation.

Sandrine had grown up more quickly than her friends, inevitably the death of her mother had meant that, even at the tender age of seven, she had become adept at small domestic tasks, helping her father wherever and whenever she could. She was quick to learn, and Sebastien found her determination to do things properly quite remarkable. He realised she must have been subconsciously watching her mother around the house, retaining an unusual attention to detail. Of course she was sad and tearful at times, but never self-pitying. She kept her compassion for her father, knowing immediately when he was feeling low, and being able to quietly shake him out of it with her bright chatter and her singing. She loved to sing, bringing a smile to anyone passing the house. They heard the childish voice wafting tunefully over the garden wall, not realising that the owner of the voice would just as likely be hanging out washing or weeding the flowerbed as skipping or playing with her dolls.

There had been a few dates, a couple of boyfriends who had morphed into just good friends, and certainly many suitors who had been skilfully yet gently averted. Sebastien was pretty sure that she had put a barrier around her heart since her mother had died, to make sure she would never feel such pain again. She was the image of her mother, a bittersweet reminder to Sebastien whenever he caught sight of her unawares, her bright head bent over some task. The realisation that she had fallen deeply in love with the good-looking young man building the wall at the bottom of the garden brought mixed feelings to Sebastien. He was relieved that at last she would have a new focus to her life, yet felt a fear that she might have her heart broken if this Luke was not worthy of her love, and what father really believes that any man is worthy of his daughter's love?

Sebastien headed upstairs, interrupting Sandrine's song to call out a hello to her. The bathroom door opened and she popped her head round it, her hair comically wrapped into a turban-shaped towel and her face covered in white cream.

"My God! Don't go near the window, you'll frighten the children!" he guffawed, dodging as a used cotton wool ball narrowly missed his eye.

"Papa! This is a very complicated beauty treatment! You mustn't make me laugh or my face will crack!"

"Sorry! We can't have that," he said in a serious tone of voice. "I take it this dangerous procedure is not for my benefit…?"

Sandrine flounced, her rabbit slippers and pink fluffy dressing gown somewhat spoiling the effect, down the hall to her bedroom. "If you're worried about missing out on your supper…there's a pan of onion soup on the stove and a wedge of Forme D'Ambert with some black grapes on the cheese board on the sideboard," she informed him over her shoulder.

Sebastien stared after her with a frown. "You sound very serious, chérie. Is everything okay? You were singing so cheerfully when I came home."

Sandrine turned round to face him. "That was my rallying the troops sort of singing," she told him. "I need to summon all my courage for tonight, Papa."

"What's going to happen tonight?" he asked with concern. "He's not taking you to see that latest arachnid film, is he?" he added, knowing how petrified she was of anything even vaguely spider shaped.

"Much worse," she answered. "I'm going to meet his mother," she announced grimly, as if she was preparing to meet her doom.

Sebastien struggled to keep a straight face. "Perhaps you should take a head of garlic in your handbag to ward off the 'evil eye' if you're that fearful," he advised solemnly.

Sandrine's face began to erupt like an earthquake, fissures branching off in all directions as the thick dry cream started to disintegrate round her uncontrollable grin.

Sandrine was still in a good mood when she ran downstairs to open the front door. She gazed at Luke appreciatively, taking in the black t-shirt, tight round his tanned upper arms, the biceps well developed after all his manual work. He wore crisp white jeans, freshly ironed by Céline, his dark cropped hair still damp from his shower. She leaned in to kiss him, breathing in the musky scent of his after shave.

"You're right…he does scrub up well! Is this the same man whom I saw this morning in his mud-stained overalls?" Came the disembodied voice from the hall.

"Good evening, Sebastien!" called Luke pleasantly. "I am stealing your daughter away again, as you can see."

Sebastien stepped into the doorway and folded his arms. "You are most welcome! I just hope she impresses your mother as much as yourself. Is she the ogre that Sandrine describes?" he asked with a grin.

"Papa! I never said that! Go away and heat your soup! Anyone would think I was a rude teenager! What will Luke think of me?"

"I think he will agree with me that you look beautiful tonight in your little yellow frock and ballet pumps, perfectly chosen for such a significant meeting."

Sandrine rolled her eyes and took Luke's arm. "Take me away from this terrible man! And it's a dress, not a frock!"

Luke parked his little black Ford Fiesta on the green triangle of grass which was just large enough to take three cars. The narrow road separated it from the cottage, which sat sideways on to the road. A green-painted picket fence ran down the side of the small front garden, a latch gate set into it halfway down. There was a shed and a small covered carport too, situated against a tall bay hedge which marked the end of the garden. Luke preferred to park Thomas's Volvo, under cover in deference to the memory of his father.

Luke opened the gate for Sandrine. Noticing her pale face, he took her hand in his, squeezed it tightly and led her along the long front of the cottage, past the front door, and guided her towards some French windows, thrown open to the warm evening air. They stepped straight into the kitchen, the rays from the setting sun behind them burnished Sandrine's hair into a cascade of copper fire.

Céline was momentarily blinded by the sun in her eyes and the blazing halo before her. Sandrine stepped forward at the same time as Céline, their outstretched hands met and their fingers warmly intertwined. The younger woman was pulled into the room, Luke hovering hesitantly behind.

"Mum…this is…" began Luke hesitantly.

"Sandrine!" said Céline softly, "Just as I imagined. I knew Luke was hiding something…and now here you are. At last."

All Sandrine's anxiety melted away as she stood there looking into the welcoming friendly face, the still beautiful dark eyes of her youth hardly altered.

Luke lounged at the long table, on which sat small jars holding squat guttering candles, listening with delight to the two women chattering to each other. It had gone better than he could have possibly hoped for. When Céline took a liking to someone, she had the wonderful knack of making them feel perfectly comfortable without overwhelming them. The genuine consideration for their feelings, shown by the attentive interested queries, the motherly offering of hearty home-cooked food, succeeded in helping Sandrine to relax totally.

She looked into Céline's face, just hesitating a fraction before speaking, "Céline? I have to ask you this before I lose my nerve…can you accept that Luke and I love each other?"

"And why do you ask that?" Céline murmured.

"Because we only met a month ago…and he is still married to Elizabeth." Sandrine's voice grew quieter and quieter, her eyes cast down to her lap.

Céline reached out and placed a finger under the young woman's chin, tilting her face up. "Look at me, chérie. I see that since meeting you, Luke is happier than I have ever seen him. I have seen him sink into the depths of depression in this unhappy marriage to Elizabeth. So yes, I accept that you love each other. I can see it in both your eyes!" There was a silence while both women stared at each other.

Luke cleared the table quietly and then coughed. "Um, have you two come back to earth yet? Do you fancy a walk? It's still amazingly warm out there."

The two women laughed self-consciously and jumped up. Céline leant Sandrine a cardigan and they made their way down the lane, commenting on the tiny bats darting and squeaking over their heads. The view across to the coast was a dark swathe of rustling grasses and crops, except for now and then the twin yellow beams of a vehicle highlighting the invisible road. The clamour of crickets sounded almost deafening in the otherwise complete silence, the noise dropping away as they passed and then resuming again.

As they turned right onto a slightly wider road connecting this village to the next, Sandrine linked arms with Céline and pointed towards the sea. "Look! There is my village…look how the lights twinkle and glitter in the distance."

In the full sunshine of the day, Talmont was clearly visible even at this distance, the huge church recognisable as it towered on the edge of the sea wall. But now, all they could see was the myriad of lights, pulsating as if a hundred fireflies were hovering there.

"I know Talmont well," Céline said. "When I came here as a child for the summer, I was always allowed to spend my pocket money on some little gift for a school friend."

"And what did you buy? Let me guess! Scented soap? Pink and white sugared almonds?"

Céline laughed. "Yes, I probably bought those things at ridiculous prices. But the only thing I ever really wanted was a little toy songbird in a cage. When you clapped your hands near it, it would sing like a nightingale. I was never allowed to buy one…my mother said I'd be bored with it after five minutes."

"They still have those! I'll have to buy you one!" teased Sandrine.

They turned back as the air grew cooler, wandering back up their road with its steep grassy banks on either side. Now and then they would see the bright glimmer of a glow worm amongst dark leaves.

"I used to take these home with me when I was young," remembered Luke nostalgically.

"Mon Dieu! Don't remind me! You were always disappointed in the morning when you looked in the jam jar, and instead of a glowing light there was just an ugly little maggot sitting on a leaf! Yet you never gave up!"

Luke laughed self-consciously. "I suppose I should have learnt my lesson from that!"

"Yes, that is a perfect description of Elizabeth, now you mention it," observed Céline naughtily.

Chapter Forty-Six

She Said How Nice It Had Been to See Them

Sunday 3rd July 2011

A Supermarket in Countess Weir Devon

Elizabeth breathed a sigh of relief. She had taken her car to 'Tom's tyre and exhaust' garage in Countess Weir, remembering the friendly assistance she'd received there when she'd had her flat tyre. Now they had serviced it and got it through its MOT. That was another irritating job done, another annoying reminder that these were the sort of jobs that Luke should be doing. She began to head back to Exmouth when she remembered that there was a supermarket not far along the main street. She pulled into the carpark, mentally compiling a list of the few items she needed.

Adding a pint of milk to the loaf, cheese and butter in her basket, she turned her head abruptly as she heard her name being called. "Hello there! It's Mrs Johnson, isn't it? How are you doing?"

Elizabeth took in the man walking towards her, slightly dishevelled, a crumpled shirt tucked into ancient baggy jeans. She knew his face, but couldn't place him.

"Not forgotten your old neighbour already?" he chuckled. "Bill Davis…from opposite…?"

She smiled faintly. "Of course. You were a Good Samaritan that day. How are you?"

"Fine thanks! Are you okay? I was sorry to hear about your marital problems…didn't even know you'd moved out 'til I spied that other nice young couple in there…and now a little 'un too."

Elizabeth felt exasperated that someone had been gossiping to this man about her marriage. "It's just a temporary arrangement," she snapped, before taking a deep breath and arranging her lips into a weak smile. "Alexis is my sister-in-law, she and Rob are just renting it for a while. I haven't seen them for ages actually…do you know how they're doing?"

Bill was about to reply when a lady joined them, clutching a basket containing a tin of custard powder and a packet of Bakewell Slices.

"Well…here's Hilda! She'll know all the gossip."

Hilda stood there smiling at Elizabeth. She wore mushroom-coloured slacks with a permanent crease, and an open-necked brown shirt showing a small string of pearls lying across the bony ridge of her collar bone.

Elizabeth raised her eyebrows. "Sorry, have we met?"

Hilda extended her hand, placing it firmly on Elizabeth's arm. "No, dear, but I feel I know all about you. Hilda Miller…your lovely mother-in-law stayed with me when Alexis was having little Sasha. Such a sweet little family."

Elizabeth felt pinned by the woman's invasion of her personal space. She could smell the sugary scent of her breath, see in unwanted close up the way her bright red lipstick had leaked into the lines at the edges of her mouth, reminding her of 'The Joker' in the Batman film. She moved slightly, dislodging Hilda's hand from her arm. "Is Alexis coping with the baby? I do worry about her. Exsham is such a quiet village."

"Oh, she's coping all right! Got a nice routine going there, so efficient. Of course she's a nurse, isn't she? She's started going to a 'mums and babies' group every Friday morning now too. Can I pass on a message from you?"

"Actually, I might turn up at the next meeting! I'd love to see them…don't tell her. It'll be a surprise. Where did you say it was?"

"It's in the village hall in the high street." Hilda supplied the information generously, always happy to be a helpful cog in the ever-whirling wheel of social events. "I think she said it starts at ten for a couple of hours 'til midday…"

Bill gave a discreet cough to remind the ladies of his presence. "Well, Hilda, if that's all you're buying, I suggest we shoot off. I always take Hilda shopping once a week. Breaks up the days, you know?"

Elizabeth said how nice it had been to see them…boring old ninnies. Still, it had been worth it.

Sunday 3rd July 2011
'Les Petits Chemins'

Luke had risen early, woken by the airless heat in the cottage, despite the circular fan next to his bed which whizzed and whirred as it sent a cool draught in a continuous arc, left and then right, like someone watching a tennis match. He opened his bedroom window which gave onto the length of lawn. The thick trunk of a palm tree cut his view in half. It was coated with a soft grey husk which shed continuously. The tree had grown tall, towering several feet beyond the cottage roof, its thick fibrous leaves always rustling in the breeze. Madame Le Blanc's husband had planted it the summer after Xavier had died, in memory of him, twenty-one years ago.

"Shower's free!" sang Céline. There was only one bathroom in the cottage, so a routine had to be adhered to. Luke shook off his thoughtful mood and began to consider how to spend this beautiful summer's day.

Over bowls of creamy café au lait and chunks of toasted buttered baguette, Luke and Céline sat outside on the grass at a rickety wooden table, discussing their plans for the day. The butter in its glass dish was dissolving almost before they could finish eating, despite the carefully positioned pink and green parasol.

"It has to be the beach. That's the only place to find any sort of breeze on a day like today."

"What's Sandrine doing? Are you seeing her?"

"I'll text her in a minute. She usually likes to get some housework done on a Sunday morning."

Luke's mobile beeped as he was just drying the last plate. Céline ran a cloth round the stone sink and then attacked the plastic bowl, squirting cream cleaner into it to remove the grease. She had Luke under a strict cleaning regime since she had arrived, but insisted that nobody could clean a sink as well as herself.

"What does she say?" she asked, hanging the rinsed cloth over the big old fashioned taps.

Luke grinned, reminding her of a small boy. "She says she'll join us on Vergnes Beach in a couple of hours. She's still got a few jobs to do."

The small carpark at the top of the sandy incline sloping to the beach was full, so Luke drove further down the road to where on the left there was a thicket of dense trees separating the road from the ocean. There was plenty of space to park along the sandy edge and enough shade to keep the car cool while its occupants went in search of the sun.

Luke led the way through the trees, the soft carpet of sand gritty with dust and debris from the road, full of pine needles from the trees, spiky barbs lethal to soft-soled feet clad only in flip-flops. He carried a beach bag and a parasol while Céline weaved along behind him, clutching her own bag and a striped rug, her eyes glued carefully to where she placed her feet.

The sun's rays flickered through the branches, the dappled light shifting, bright pools merging into black depthless shapes like swimming under water. Suddenly, they stepped into a wave of glorious golden heat as they left the trees, navigated a last steep path between clumps of marram grass and stumbled slipping through the sand onto the beach.

"It never changes," Céline said, sliding her sunglasses down to cover her eyes from where they had been perched on top of her hair. She gazed at the deep-blue water, the glasses slightly muting the silver flashes that sparked off the sea's surface. "Oh, how I love it here…"

"Come on, Mum," rallied Luke, "let's find a spot where we can see Sandrine coming."

Despite the full carpark, the beach seemed virtually empty. They chose a place halfway down, exactly between the trees and the water's edge. "Will this do?" asked Luke, dropping the parasol onto the sand.

Céline put her hands on her hips and looked at him. "Why does everybody ask that when they come to the beach? This square of sand is no different from anywhere else for miles and miles! And what if I said, 'no Luke, actually it won't do!' and what does that even mean? Will this do? Do what? If I knew what was waiting for me, I would never have married an English man!"

Luke busied himself screwing the pole of the parasol deep into the sand. "You don't mean that, Mum," he said affectionately. "You love our crazy language, and Dad loved you for questioning everything he said!"

Céline tsked, shrugging her shoulders. "He said I drove him mad."

"That was all pretence. It was a game you both played… You do know how much he loved you, don't you?"

Céline nodded as she peeled off her shorts and t-shirt, spread the rug, then her towel out on top of it and flopped down. "Yes, I do know," she agreed, lying back and closing her eyes.

"Don't go to sleep yet! You'll burn…did you bring your suntan cream?"

She sat up and reached for her bag. "This is a fine thing! I am not senile yet!"

Luke lay on his front, a novel propped up against the beach bag. Every few minutes he scanned the beach for signs of Sandrine. Céline was snoring softly beside him, her limbs already looking tanned. She looked younger than her forty-eight years, trim in a dark-green one-piece. He was lucky to have inherited her dark hair and skin that soaked up the sun effortlessly.

Half an hour later, a movement to Luke's right made him look up. He recognised Sandrine at once, with her cut-off jeans and orange strappy top, her way of moving, her shining hair. She approached with a happy smile, and now Luke noticed the figure behind her.

"I thought it would be more crowded than this! Look, I brought some fruit and crisps." She bent down to kiss him.

"Great…hey, I'm glad you came along! It's an absolute scorcher," said Luke, shielding his eyes as he looked up.

Céline began to wake from a deep sun-drugged sleep. She opened her eyes, pleased to hear Sandrine's voice. She raised herself on her elbows, turning her head.

"Hello," said Sandrine, "are you okay?"

"I'm fine, thanks," she replied, looking at the man the other side of Sandrine. He was crouched down, rummaging in a plastic bag.

"Meet my dad… I hope you don't mind me bringing him along?"

Céline sat up properly as the man stood up. He was standing with his back to the sun, and she could not make out his features. He bent down to shake her hand, and she twisted round awkwardly to face him.

She heard his sharp intake off breath, a pause, and then, "My God…Céline…how can it be?"

He leaned closer, turning his head slightly so that she could see his face. She put her hands up to her mouth, her eyes wide with disbelief. "Sebastien?" she whispered, her voice husky with shock.

Sandrine and Luke exchanged baffled glances as they stared at their respective parents, eyes locked onto each other, a frozen tableau.

Chapter Forty-Seven

"You Haven't Changed a Bit. Still the Young Girl with the Black Hair"

Friday 8th July 2011
Exsham 8.30 a.m.
Elizabeth dialled the secretary's number. "Hello, Margaret," she spoke in a subdued frail voice. "I'm sorry about this, but I've got some sort of bug…been throwing up since three o'clock this morning. I'd hoped to feel better…I know…I'd hate to pass it on to the children…okay then, I will. Thanks Margaret…yes, think I'll go back to bed for an hour. I'll take it easy over the weekend and hopefully be better by Monday."

She smiled at her reflection in the bedroom mirror. Plenty of time to get showered and dressed. What to have for breakfast…? She fancied scrambled eggs and bacon this morning. There was usually no time for anything more than toast on a school morning.

Elizabeth had sussed out the village hall in Exsham high street earlier in the week, and had found the perfect spot from which to watch for Alexis to pass with Sasha on her way to the 'Mother and Baby' group. Just off the high street, between a couple of small shops, there was a small rose garden surrounded by a low wall and accessible through an old stone archway. She had found a wooden bench, facing the garden with its crescent-shaped flower beds, and with its back to the wall just to the right of the archway. She could sit here, her back to the road but turned slightly to be able to watch people passing. With dark glasses on and a newspaper to hide behind, she was confident she would not be noticed.

Elizabeth settled herself on the bench at a quarter to ten. She had parked her conspicuous red MG well-hidden down a side street. There had been a young fellow sitting there when she arrived, but as she plonked herself down, shaking out her paper noisily and spreading her coat and bag along the seat, he had taken himself and his bad case of acne off and out of her way.

Twenty-five minutes later, she thought that Alexis was not going to show. Having no experience of babies, she had no idea that a baby will only take a feed when it's hungry, that it will probably fill its nappy after taking its feed, and then may vomit a small amount of milk back over its own clean Babygro or even more likely, over its mother's clean t-shirt just for good measure.

So it was that Alexis was seen, only slightly flustered, pushing a buggy quite speedily at a trot along the pavement at a quarter past ten. Elizabeth made certain that Alexis had actually reached and entered the village hall before she began to walk swiftly in the opposite direction towards the cottage.

Before posting the cottage keys back through the letterbox on that unpleasant day four months previously, Elizabeth was glad that she'd had the idea of having an extra set cut. She had no idea at the time as to why she did it, maybe it was just a symbolic gesture to reassure herself that she still had a hold on her past.

She walked slowly down the road, collar up and wearing a dark hat with the brim pulled down. She fought the urge to laugh. This was so ridiculous, but she just had to do it. She walked down to the harbour and then doubled back, made sure there was no one in the road, and slipped down the side of the cottage and quickly let herself into the kitchen. She closed the door quietly behind her, the bubble of adrenaline in her throat suddenly ruptured by the sound of a thud in the next room. She froze, holding her breath. The lounge door was slowly pushed open bit by bit…she considered hiding under the kitchen table…and then she saw the big black fluffy face looking at her with interest.

Scolded and hugged in equal measures, Mango followed Elizabeth up the stairs and into the bedroom. She stared around the room, a soft melting feeling running through her. This was all she wanted, to press the tiny clothes to her face, stroke the stuffed rabbit, set the bright colours of the cot mobile spinning. She would choose just one souvenir, take something home to cherish. She picked up a small frame from a chest of drawers, it showed Sasha at just a few hours old, but she did not dare take something too obvious that would be missed, much as she would have loved to place this by her own bed.

She felt the familiar waves of resentment and envy building up inside her. This should have been her baby…she had yearned and planned for it for so long. She took deep breaths in an attempt to calm herself down. She had to be patient…small baby steps. The thought made her smile. She fished out a soft, pale-lemon cot sheet from a neatly stacked pile in a drawer. This would have to do. If she took just one small thing every time, they would never notice. It wasn't much to ask.

Saturday 9th July 2011
France

"Has he said much to you, Sandrine?" asked Luke. It was their first chance for a proper chat alone since that weird Sunday. Céline and Sebastien had muttered something about being acquainted with each other a long time ago, but had brushed off any probing questions so that the rest of the afternoon had passed in uncomfortable silence.

Sandrine walked along the path next to Luke. It led up a slope and onto a grassy headland overlooking Talmont. The sea glittered on their right and a small vineyard spread out its neat rows on their left. "No, he's kept to himself. It's not like him. For a man, he's usually pretty easy to talk to. I daren't mention your mother, he just looks all broodingly at me. How is Céline?"

They came to a little copse of trees and Luke led Sandrine to a wooden seat tucked into a shady glade there. "She's the same. I asked her about knowing your dad and she looked like she was going to bite my head off, and then as if she was going to burst into tears! I think we just have to wait until they're ready to talk to us."

Sandrine took off her wide-brimmed straw boater and began playing with the brim. "I don't like it," she said sharply. "It seems like they are hiding a strong dislike of each other…we may never know why."

They looked at each other worriedly, knowing that this turn of events could have a strong impact on their own future together.

Céline sat next to Sebastien in his white Renault Clio. It had not been hard to find her cottage in 'Les Petits Chemins', there were no more than ten dwellings in all. He had made a quick phone call to Gaston under the pretext of needing to return some borrowed tool, who told him that Luke lived at number three. That was the trouble with mobile phones, their numbers weren't listed in the phone book. He knew that Luke and Sandrine were out walking somewhere and had acted impetuously before he could change his mind, parking on the green triangle of grass before banging on the front door of the cottage.

Céline had opened the door with a gasp of surprise. Sebastien placed a hand on her sleeve as if this had been arranged. She looked up at him questioningly. Apart from the dusting of silver glinting through the dark hair of his sideburns, and the deep lines at the corners of his eyes and mouth, he was the same. Tall and rangy, he looked ten years younger than his fifty-five years. Receiving no response from her enquiring looks, she let herself be led to his car.

They sat next to each other in silence while Sebastien drove aimlessly, pulling over eventually onto a dirt track running along a field full of sweetcorn. The tall spiky plants concealing their pale-yellow gossamer-covered cobs rustled in the light breeze. In the distance, they could see the silvery arc of the 'arrosage', the jets at the end of the huge coiled yellow hose sending huge amounts of water onto the parched fields, swinging from side to side, a rainbow coming and going through the sunlit deluge.

"You haven't changed a bit," he stated eventually. "Still the young girl with the black hair." He looked straight ahead with no expression. She wasn't sure how to read him. He seemed almost angry.

"I don't feel young. I am a widow and now a grandmother," she told him with a small smile.

"Yes, Sandrine told me about your recent loss. I am very sorry."

She nodded her thanks. "Sebastien, you must be so proud of her, Sandrine...she's a lovely girl. I'm glad that Luke has met her," she said carefully, wondering suddenly whether his stern demeanour was aimed at Luke. "Aren't you?" she asked recklessly.

He turned and looked at her then. His dark eyes seemed to swallow her up. "I love her dearly, yes, she has many good characteristics, yet with a fire and a bite to her words when she wants, just like her mother." He paused, with a pained expression, before adding, "And Luke is very good for her... yes. I'm glad they have met." He allowed a slight smile to touch his lips.

"Isn't it amazing? That they should meet each other, not knowing that we met all those years ago? You were so disdainful when you condescended to join all our crowd at those beach parties," she teased, feeling more confident suddenly.

"You were all so young, like puppies...wet behind the ears! What were you, seventeen?"

"Eighteen actually!" she pouted. "Our lives were just beginning...but you seemed to be so mature. You'd done it all..."

"I was twenty-six, as you well know. Too old to be spending time with your crowd, but certainly not mature. I had a lot to learn." His face was closed to her, like a shutter coming down. "Best not to look back at the past," he said harshly. "It can't be altered."

They drove back, Céline fearing to broach any subject that might touch a nerve. She felt a terrible sadness that he seemed so unapproachable, so when she went to open the car door to climb out, she was surprised to hear him say, "Would you like to go out for a meal sometime? For old time's sake?"

Chapter Forty-Eight
Happiness Tinged with Worry and Dread

Friday 15th July 2011
Exmouth

She shoved the staffroom door open with her shoulder and glanced at the handful of her colleagues around the room, engrossed in various conversations with each other. A couple of them glanced her way as she dumped her overstuffed handbag on the floor. She averted her eyes from the nods and smiles of greeting, turning away to flick through a pile of papers.

A woman approached her, everything about her shouted 'sensible' from her grey hair coiled neatly into a bun, to her polished brown lace-up shoes. "Good morning, Elizabeth, have you any plans for the holidays?"

Elizabeth looked sideways at her. "No, not really, apart from relishing six weeks away from thirty irritatingly moronic seven-year-olds with their half-witted babbling and infantile jokes."

Meg Taylor shot her a startled look, searching her face for signs of facetiousness, but could detect nothing but a deadpan stare.

The morning was unendurable. Elizabeth would not have turned up at work at all had it not been the last day of the term. The final assembly was painfully boring, what with that dehydrated Ms Carter droning on to the children, reminding them to be well behaved for their parents over the summer, not to let the school down and not to forget to keep up with their reading and writing.

Over at last, Elizabeth herded her class into a single file and back to the classroom, where the rest of the day was spent in the fruitless task of preventing the over-excited children from damaging school property or each other. It was the tradition on this day, to let them play games and have fun, but to hear the squabbling, the screams of outrage as a precious object brought from home were snatched at, the scuffling between small boys who needed to let off steam outside, anyone would think that some sort of punishment was being handed out.

It was just as the last little pest headed for the cloakroom and into the arms of its mother, who was probably dreading the next six weeks, Elizabeth imagined with a smug smirk, that she received a message to pop into Ms Carter's office before leaving.

If looks could kill, Ms Carter should by rights be lifelessly slumped over her desk once Elizabeth had entered her office. But she managed to sit straight and face with fortitude the obviously reluctant young woman standing in front of her.

"Sit down, Mrs Johnson, I won't keep you long," she said, waiting until Elizabeth had perched herself on the edge of the chair before continuing. "Is there anything troubling you at the moment?"

Elizabeth did not reply at once, then said stiffly, "My private life is just that…private."

Ms Carter seemed undeterred. "I don't expect you to divulge any personal problems, but when your behaviour at work is affected, then I need to know what's causing it."

"That's a bit vague. What are you trying to say?"

The headmistress looked Elizabeth in the eye, finding it increasingly difficult not to show her dislike for the woman. "Over recent weeks, I have been made aware of several complaints from other members of staff. These include unfriendly behaviour towards your colleagues, often arriving late so that staff have had to step in to look after your class, inappropriate comments made in front of the children concerning criticisms of other teachers, and even a harsh and unpleasant approach to the children."

Elizabeth put on a bored face and looked pointedly at her watch. "Oh dear, what a tirade. Who are these tiresome colleagues? Have they nothing better to do with their time than make up tales about me? I'm unfriendly? You make them out to be on the same level as the brats in the playground! Did I forget to say hello to them? Or perhaps I chose not to join in with their tiring gossip…"

Ms Carter's cheeks flushed a dull red. "Enough, Mrs Johnson! These are serious complaints, and you are speaking completely out of turn. How dare you turn this around? You are clearly not fit to continue working here. I have been putting it down to the stresses that you may have been enduring recently, but I now realise that this is no excuse for your disgraceful attitude. You have shown a complete disregard for your professional obligations, and I find myself in a position in which I have no option but ask for your resignation."

"Nothing would give me greater pleasure," was Elizabeth's parting shot as she left the room, crashing the door closed behind her.

Saturday 16th July 2011

'Les Petits Chemins'

Sandrine straddled the deep ditch between the surface of the narrow road and the rough chunks of ploughed earth at the edge of the field. "If the farmer sees what we're up to, he might get angry," she commented. "Besides, I can't get over. You'll have to give me a push."

Luke gave her a helpful shove, sending her stumbling in amongst the sunflowers. Their huge heads nodded at her in the breeze. "Just keep to the edge, where the tiny rogue ones are. We only need three or four to put in a vase. If anyone passes by, I'll yank you out."

Clutching the handful of baby sunflowers, Sandrine landed back onto the road. "I feel about five years old! You are a bad influence on me."

She walked next to Luke as they retraced their steps back to the cottage. They had walked as far as the next village, not even a mile away, passing a large, white stone windmill at the corner of the crossroads.

"It's a shame there aren't any sails on it, it could be made to look really pretty."

"I find the French are more practical than aesthetic…they'd only put sails on it if it was going to be made to work again," Luke mused. They walked on a way in silence. Luke then suddenly said, "I think we have to accept that my mother and your father are mad about each other."

Sandrine stopped walking and looked at him. She grimaced. "I know…it's quite disturbing, don't you think?"

"I suppose what bothers me, is how soon it is after my father's death. I want her to be happy, but is she being rational? And are they falling in love, or just in the thrall of some crush they may have had on each other thirty years ago?"

She smiled as they fell into step again. "Well…they're certainly old enough to know their own minds. As long as they're happy, and they're not hurting anyone, we should give them our blessing. I'm more concerned about us, Luke. What about our future?"

Luke turned to her, putting his arms around her. "Sandrine, I would like us to get married… It's nine months since I left Elizabeth. She must either grant me a divorce on the grounds of my infidelity or we wait for a two-year separation and hope she agrees to an automatic divorce then. I just want to get her out of my life as soon as possible."

Sandrine hesitated before insisting, "I know, so do I, but I'd rather she didn't know about us yet, Luke. From what you've told me, she sounds unbalanced! I'm quite scared of her to be honest…but I feel safe while you're here, far away from her. And if that was a proposal, then the answer is yes…"

They stood there in the road holding on to each other, happiness tinged with worry and dread. The crushed sunflowers lay ruined between them, a cascade of yellow littering the road.

Sunday 17th July 2011
Talmont

It was two weeks since that bizarre meeting on the beach. They had been drawn together almost without discussion, as if too much analysis into their intentions would not bear scrutiny. They avoided spending time with Sandrine and Luke, needing time alone to try out their feelings, like probing a sore tooth with your tongue.

"Are we being fair to our children?" Céline asked. She was sitting in Sebastien's small whitewashed courtyard, with a tall glass of iced water in front of her.

Sebastien looked up from stacking a pile of framed paintings against the wall. "I don't think that the children come into this, do they? They are not children anyway. They are making their own choices, as we are making ours." He grinned at her, "Why so serious? What could be nicer than this, if slightly unusual, combination? We have been given a second chance, as has Luke. And a new life for Sandrine…I think this is very fair all round, don't you?"

Céline nodded slowly at him. "I suppose so…" she answered doubtfully.

"It's Thomas, isn't it? It's all too soon…you feel it's not fair on him, don't you?"

"It's mad I know, but I suppose I feel guilty."

Sebastien walked across and sat close to her. He took her hand and his dark eyes bored into hers. "Listen to me…it wasn't your fault that he died, the doctor told you there were no warning signs. Our meeting again was pure chance, so why on earth are you feeling guilty? Has Luke accused you of anything?"

"No, of course not."

"There you are then…right, are you going to help me set up these frames? I think this is going to be a good day for a sale or two."

That evening, as the red circle of the sun disappeared into the sea beyond the church, several holiday makers were still trailing along the white dusty path past the house. The air was hot, clouds of tiny midges hovering. The variegated hues of the tall hollyhocks were still bright in the blushing rays; purple, white, palest pink and unexpected black.

There was to be a candlelight evening later; tea-lights placed along the paths would be lit, guiding wanderers through the village, as music wafted out from a copse of stunted olive trees. These stood in a hollow below the looming church wall, where a grassy glade formed a favourite spot for musicians.

Sebastien had sold four paintings that day and was feeling very satisfied as he finished tidying up. He placed a cold bottle of white wine on the small wrought-iron table, just as Céline came outside carrying glasses and a dish of battered crayfish garnished with crescents of lemon, and a bowl of homemade mayonnaise.

They sat down together, touching their glasses together just in recognition of a simple friendship rekindled. Sebastien brought a lighter out of his jeans pocket and leant forward to put a flame to a row of tea-lights set on the low wall, just as the last glow of the sun was swallowed by the waters of the estuary.

He sipped his wine again before setting it down. "Céline…if we had met for the first time two weeks ago, I would never dream of asking this…"

Céline interrupted him, eyes round with trepidation, "What are you going to say? Be careful…"

"I am being as careful as I can. But at our age, there's no point beating around the bush surely? I knew you as a young girl, full of dreams and impossible ideas. I now find a mature woman in front of me, but still harbouring those dreams…there are all those missing years in between. They are part of you, and they belong to you and Thomas, but they haven't changed you. You are still beautiful and I love that in my mind, and I think in yours, we are still young."

Céline nodded, a lump forming in her throat. Her voice broke slightly as she asked, "What were you going to say, Sebastien? Do you think our meeting again was fate? You're too down to earth for that!" She smiled at him.

"No, not fate…just coincidence. But too meaningful to ignore. I wouldn't be so crass as to ask you to marry me…"

Céline's crestfallen expression made his mouth twitch with amusement.

"…straight away," he continued. "But we can agree that this looks like a serious matter, wouldn't you agree? I can't think of anything nicer than to spend the rest of my life with you," he ended simply.

Céline's face was a picture of mixed emotions, joy, yearning, worry. Slowly she said, "I couldn't have put it better myself. But I think Sandrine and Luke have already guessed something of how we feel. How are we going to hide it?"

"We don't hide it. But we respect you and your children's memories of Thomas by not rushing into anything. What do you think about holding a gathering of close family, we don't need to give a specific reason, just call it a celebration of new beginnings, for Luke and Sandrine, Sasha, Alexis and Rob, and us, of course, but we just let them see us together. They will see how happy we are without any announcements needing to be made."

"Oh yes," whispered Céline, a look of huge pleasure on her face. "Where should we do this? And when?"

"Soon, I think. At the cottage in 'Les Petits Chemins? There's not much to plan really, just good food and wine for a small group. What about Saturday the thirteenth of August? That's a month away…we could send the invitations out tomorrow to give them time to think about it."

"Tomorrow? We don't have invitations! You are a crazy man!"

"Maybe, but I happen to have painted a series of little cards of scenes of the area. Perfect! We'll write them tonight!"

They both looked up as the kitchen door opened and Sandrine came through with Luke just behind her. They absorbed the sight of Céline and Sebastien relaxing in the half-light flickering from the tiny candles, the simple food on the table.

"Ah, just the people we wanted to see! Sit down, both of you," Sebastien welcomed, dragging two more chairs from a corner of the courtyard. He disappeared into the kitchen for another bottle of wine.

Céline smiled at both young people, making room on the table for extra glasses. "Bring some crisps!" she called. "And there's some pâté and bread left from lunch!"

"You see, it's come to this, when I'm being ordered about in my own house," remarked Sebastien, stepping smartly out of the doorway, an uncorked bottle in his hand, a crisply cold Sancerre no less, a white napkin over his arm. "Mademoiselle?" he inquired as he reached Sandrine's side.

"Hey! That's good stuff…what are we celebrating?"

"Good stuff indeed…I thought I'd brought you up better than that! We have something to discuss with you. I'll get the food in a minute, Céline…"

Luke looked round at the faces around the table, received a quick nod from Sandrine and said, "Before we sample this excellent choice of wine, there is something Sandrine and I would like to tell you too."

Chapter Forty-Nine

She Opened It Carefully, and There It Was

Thursday 21st July 2011
Exsham

At one month old, Sasha was proving to be an easy baby. She would take her last feed at ten o'clock in the evening and then sleep a good eight hours. This suited Alexis, who made the most of starting the day early. She loved following a routine, even one dictated by such a small creature, and it suited them both.

There had been a spate of deliciously warm sunshine over the last few days, so Alexis, knowing that Sasha would usually sleep for a good hour in the afternoons, decided on a walk. She settled Sasha into the buggy in a hooded jacket with just a light blanket over her.

By the time Alexis had been walking for an hour, she had a light sheen of sweat on her upper lip and had stuffed her jacket in the shopping tray underneath the buggy. Sasha had slept for most of the time, Alexis frequently checking that her head and hands were warm. She was approaching the cottage now, and the sun's heat seemed to have increased as the afternoon had worn on. It was close to five o'clock, one of Alexis's favourite times of the day.

Sasha opened her eyes as if sensing that she was close to home.

"Hello sweetie…!" Alexis gushed, using the special soft tone of the new mother to her child, unaware even that she was doing it. "Nearly home, and Daddy will be back soon."

On cue, as Alexis reached the front door and was delving into her pocket for her key, Rob's car rumbled to a stop at the gate. She watched him approach. His long-legged gait still had the ability to bring a smile to her lips. "You're home nice and early!" she called out.

Despite the heat, he looked relatively cool, his brown hair standing in tufts. He kissed Sasha first, a butterfly touch of his lips to her forehead which made her scrunch her eyes closed.

Alexis laughed and raised her own face for a less chaste kiss. "Who's been driving with the window open? Your face is freezing!"

"And yours is as red as a tomato…where have you been?"

"Thanks, you say such sweet things! Sasha and I have been walking for miles. I took her down to the footbridge at the Pathway Pub, you know, where the little ferry crosses. We walked over to the other side of the river and I pushed her a couple of miles along the footpath. I didn't dare go too far in case she got fractious, but she slept the whole way."

"She has a very accommodating nature, just like her father," Rob said smugly. He lifted Sasha out of the buggy and they entered the cottage together. "We ought to do that walk together at the weekend. I haven't done it in ages."

"Absolutely…" Alexis agreed. "It's so beautiful with the reeds, the water birds and the lapping of the river. We didn't see another soul, did we, honey?" she cooed, taking the baby from Rob.

"We could have lunch at The Turf Inn, it's right at the end as far as you can go. You can only get to it by foot, bike or boat."

"Trust you to plan something that involves a pint!"

Alexis grinned, laying Sasha on a change mat on the floor next to the coffee table while Rob went to put the kettle on.

"What's this? A letter from France? When did this arrive?"

Alexis deftly snapped the tapes of Sasha's fresh nappy closed over her tummy and blew a raspberry on to her soft skin. "This morning. I thought I'd wait for you to come home, as it's to both of us…open it, Rob."

He came into the room, slitting the thick white envelope open with a sharp knife. He looked at the contents and gave a grunt of surprise. "Well…it's an invitation from your mum and someone called Sebastien."

Alexis looked up with a frown. "What do you mean? What's it an invitation for? Does it say?"

"It just says you are invited to a small family gathering to celebrate, 'New Beginnings'. It's going to be held in the cottage, on Saturday the thirteenth of August at midday…"

Alexis sank onto the settee with the baby, preparing to breastfeed her. "This is mad! We can't just suddenly set off on such a long journey with a tiny baby! And who on earth is Sebastien? We'll have to say we can't go."

Later on that evening, Sasha quiet in her cot and their evening meal over, Alexis and Rob sat on the settee in companionable silence. Rob had lit the fire. Despite the earlier warmth of the day, the cottage felt cold once the sun had set. He leaned forward to poke a hole between the glowing lumps of coal. This sent up a wave of flames which caught hold of a scattering of small branches which had been laid on top.

As the amber sparks flew up the chimney, Alexis turned to Rob. "Are you sure? What are your holiday dates exactly?" she asked, sipping from her mug of coffee, and continuing the topic of the unexpected invitation.

"Monday the eighth of August to Sunday the twenty first. That would be perfect. I hadn't planned on going anywhere, but this would be a great chance for meeting up with the family and enjoying some sunshine. You want Luke to see Sasha, don't you?"

Alexis sighed distractedly. "Yes of course, but she's awfully young..."

"Oh you are an old worrier! She'll be over two months old by then. I'm thinking we could travel on Thursday eleventh of August, starting early, and could be there by the next evening, what do you think?"

She looked at him with round eyes. "You mean to drive? It's miles!"

Rob ruffled her hair affectionately, "Much easier than flying!" He laughed. And probably cheaper. Plus the fact we can carry all the paraphernalia we need for Sasha...we could even take her buggy. That'll make life so much easier. And we've got her a passport already, thanks to your clever mum telling you to get one early on in case we needed to travel at a moment's notice."

Alexis relaxed at last as she realised how much she would enjoy visiting her mum and Luke, the cottage of her childhood and the thought of the almost assured sunshine. She thought for a moment, and Rob was concerned that she was going to come up with yet another spanner in the works, but she said, "This is just an idea, and tell me if you don't agree, but I'd love to invite Cheryl to join us! We've seen a lot of each other recently, and she looks much happier...a holiday would do her good, and she is an old friend of the family. And," she added, flushing with enthusiasm, "she could sit in the back and keep Sasha amused while I help you navigate..."

Rod slapped his knees in delight. "Looks like you've talked me into it! I think that's a great idea. Cheryl deserves something to look forward to, that's for sure. We'll need to take the roof box in that case. I'll go on to the computer right now and see what I can book. We might have to travel during the night if all the day crossings are full, but I don't suppose Sasha will even notice."

Friday 22nd July 2011
Exsham 8.00 a.m.

A week into her supposed summer holidays, Elizabeth woke to another warm sunny day. She stretched and turned over, closing her eyes again. A dark depression had been settling over her since the school had closed its doors for the summer holidays. She didn't need the bloody school! She was free now, had enough money in the bank still to live comfortably for a long time. If it came to it, she could afford to buy a smaller flat and let this one again.

But the real source of her low mood lay in the realisation that her life and plans had spiralled out of control. She had at first reluctantly put it down to loneliness, but that had never been a problem. She had lived on her own for years, quite happily, with the ever-present knowledge that the next step was just over the next horizon. Meeting Luke, or someone like him, had been the initial part of the plan.

Then it had all gone wrong, events had taken her unawares, and she could not forgive….forgive whom? She had to blame someone, but not sure who, so she had blamed every one, set them all against her, and then blamed them again. It never occurred to her to question herself.

She sat up in her bed and gazed around, drinking in the sight before her eyes. Adrenaline came in a surge, lifting her mood and injecting her day with optimism. Next to her bed was the child's cot, padded and decorated in soft swathes of white material, a collection of stuffed baby animals sat in a row, and then, stacked on the floor were the plastic packs of nappies, a basket of bath products, piles of baby clothes, fluffy towels…it just went on and on, as if the entire contents of 'Mothercare' had been disgorged onto Elizabeth's bedroom floor.

She was dressed and ready in good time. She hardly bothered to sit on the bench in the rose garden this time, just stood in the archway, dark glasses obscuring her watchful eyes as she kept a look out on the moving people.

As before, she watched Alexis and Sasha passing by. Then she was entering the cottage once more, the actual deed of entering the cottage by stealth was enough to give her a buzz of excitement. She had no need to take another memento, just standing inside the house, breathing the same air as Sasha had was enough.

She stepped from the kitchen into the lounge, touching objects around her with sly, greedy fingers. There was a new photo of Rob holding Sasha on the mantel piece, the baby looking up at him with a gummy smile. Elizabeth picked it up to study it more closely.

As she replaced the small frame, she noticed the card sitting there. It looked like a birthday card. She picked it up and studied the front of it. It was a watercolour study of fishing huts perched along the edge of a craggy coastline. They were silhouetted blackly against the blood-coloured streaks of a winter sunset. She opened it carefully, and there it was. All the information she needed; the address, the date and time. It was an invitation to a small family gathering she noted bitterly, but one that did not include her, proof once again of her rejection as an outcast.

Chapter Fifty

Meanwhile Sasha Slept On, Oblivious of the Emotions Swirling Around Her

Friday 22nd July 2011
Exsham

Alexis laid Sasha down early for her afternoon nap. She seemed over tired, grizzling a little, her eyes wide open as she lay on her stomach. Alexis stayed near the cot until the papery pale eyelids closed, her breathing softly rhythmic. "Sleep Sasha..." whispered Alexis. The chaos of sound engendered by a room full of noisy babies and chattering mothers always seemed to tire Sasha out on their Friday visits.

Alexis went downstairs, made herself a cold drink and sat at the kitchen table with the telephone. At last, a moment's peace in which to call her mother.

She was glad to hear Céline's voice after the third ring. "It's me, Mum...I just wanted to say, we received your invitation yesterday..."

"Oh good! Will you come? I know it's a long journey, but Luke would love to see the baby, and I thought that we could all do with something nice to look forward to."

Alexis did not say that she had not been keen on the idea at first. "We'd love to come!" she said instead. "It must be really warm there at the moment? That's the beauty of the cottage, it stays cool even in a heatwave with its thick walls, doesn't it?"

"Yes, it does thank goodness. It is very hot here. Will Rob be able to take some holiday?"

"Yes, two weeks. So we'll travel overnight to France on the evening of Thursday the eleventh of August, and then probably be with you early afternoon the next day."

"Oh you're driving...so sensible with a tiny baby. Madame Le Blanc says she has a small cot if you need it... And you'll stay a few days, yes?" asked Céline hopefully.

"Of course, Mum, we're not driving all that way for two nights! By the way…who is Sebastien?"

The sudden question seemed to take Céline by surprise. There was a moment's hesitation before she replied, "Oh, he is just a chap that Luke is doing some work for. He has been very good to him, and of course he is a friend of Gaston, who cannot wait to see you again by the way! That's how Luke met him."

"Oh, okay…but…why is the invitation from you and Sebastien?"

Céline laughed. "That was a joke, really. I said I had no invitation cards, when Luke and I were talking about a little party, and so he kindly gave me some. He paints in his spare time, and so he joked that if I was going to use the little cards that he'd made, then it was only fair that his name should be on them too. And it will be nice way to thank him for putting so much work Luke's way."

Alexis was not convinced, but decided not to pursue it. She needed to ask something else, and this call was going to cost her enough as it was. "Okay, Mum…before I go, can I be cheeky and ask you whether we can bring Cheryl with us, if she's free? Obviously I haven't asked her yet."

Relieved at the change of subject, Céline was only too happy to say yes. "Of course, Chérie. I hope she can make it. She's a sweet girl. Shall I send her an invitation?"

"Please, she'd be made up to have one, even if she can't make it. Send it to me and I'll take it to her. By the way, are Oncle Jaçques and Tante Chantal coming?"

"Well, I rang him, but they will be on holiday in Spain with their girls and their families. It's such a shame we lost touch over the years…my only sibling…and of course, you've only met your cousins once…lovely girls…and now they have children of their own!"

Alexis could feel a trip down memory lane coming on, so she made a hasty excuse to end the call.

Céline put the phone down, a feeling of apprehension washing over her as she realised what a huge step she was taking. How would Alexis really feel about her mother with a new man? And so soon after her father's death? With Luke, it was somehow easier; he and Sandrine had confided their strong feelings for each other to her and Sebastien, so it had been possible to be more open about their own feelings. Céline had asked Luke not to mention it to Alexis. He had agreed, saying Alexis did not know about Sandrine either. Hopefully it would all go smoothly at the party when they would all meet each other for the first time.

Monday 25th July 2011

A Café in Exmouth

Cheryl came flying along the boardwalk pushing her bike. She parked it against the slatted wall of the café and bounded up the steps. Alexis was already waiting at one of the rustic wooden tables placed along the lengthy balcony, her face breaking into a welcome grin.

Cheryl peeped over at Sasha's sleeping form in the buggy, her face shaded by a white frilly parasol. Cheryl's expression softened as she gazed down. She got a hold of herself, sat down and took a parched gulp of iced Coke. "Thanks, Alexis! God, it's far too hot to be working!" she complained, looking ahead through the tubs of cacti, loving the sight of the beach stretching down to the hushed ebb and flow of the flat waves. A foamy coating was left fizzing on the wet sand each time the waves retreated.

Alexis brushed a damp tendril of blonde hair out of her eyes. "Well, in just over two weeks you'll be sunning yourself on a white beach overlooking the Atlantic! I'll show you all our favourite places. Rob's never been to that part of France either. Are you sure you don't mind taking ten days of your holidays? Not to mention keeping Sasha amused for hours in the car?"

Cheryl gave an amused grimace, "You are joking…what else would I do with my days off? The choice of sitting alone in my room, or swanning off to France with you lot doesn't take much mulling over! I adore Sasha, as you know, and I'm very grateful. Your mother's the best!"

Alexis sipped her drink, crunching on a chunk of ice. "She likes you," she said simply. "She felt so sorry for you when you moved into that awful house…any chance of getting something nicer?"

Cheryl shrugged. "To be honest, I haven't felt much inspiration to look, too many night shifts, just too tired, to be honest."

"When we get back from France, I'll help you look for a new place to stay. You are going to turn your life around, my girl!" she said cheerfully.

Cheryl sent Alexis a grateful smile. She was reluctant to wish the days away, knowing that the time in France would evaporate like mist. She would appreciate every second, the memories would have to carry her through the long days ahead. She could hardly bear to think of 'Life after The Holiday'.

Thursday 11th August 2011
Exsham

"Don't worry, there's bags of room!"

"Is the buggy in?"

Rob gave Alexis an old-fashioned look.

She put her hands on her jean-clad hips and made a face. "Just making sure! I must say, that roof box holds loads more than it looks..."

Cheryl looked relieved. "I didn't bring too much then?"

Rob laughed. "One little rucksack and a hand bag? I can always nip back for more if you've forgotten anything?"

It was early evening. Rob had collected Cheryl and her luggage from her digs after work. They had shared a simple meal that Alexis had made. "I hope you like Spanish omelettes? Thought I'd get us in the Continental mood."

Rob's Volkswagen Golf Estate had certainly swallowed up an alarming amount of baby accoutrements with still plenty of room for everything else. They stood in the road checking last minute items. Rob folded his arms. "As long as we've got passports, money, and tickets..."

"Don't forget reflective yellow safety vests, folding reflective warning triangles, survival foil blanket, spare tyre, tool bag..." came the disembodied voice of reason from behind them.

Rob turned around to see Bill Davis standing on his piece of pavement, surveying the group of travellers. "Well thanks, Bill, I think I've got all those items covered." Mango was sitting at Bill's feet, as if she had already transferred her loyalty to the next provider of sustenance. She gazed at Rob with her large green eyes full of disdain. Her look of contempt reminded him of someone...

Sasha was soon strapped into her seat, the last pieces of hand luggage placed on relevant laps and with the front door of the house firmly locked, Rob gave a wave to Bill and climbed into the driving seat. "Thanks for taking care of Mango!" he called, "Text us if there's any problems!"

Bill raised a hand as he watched them disappear down the road. "Looks like it's just you and me, mate, fancy sardines on toast for tea?" he said, bending down to stoke Mango, who was weaving round his legs, purring loudly.

Friday 12th August 2011
'Les Petits Chemins'
Mid-Afternoon

The long journey was almost over. Alexis had become more and more excited as she recognised the familiar landmarks as the countryside unfolded, the fields taken over by waves of golden sunflowers the further south they went. She had forgotten how different the buildings were too, with their whitewashed walls, the bright coppery tiles reaching as low as five feet from the ground on the side where the fierce winter storms would hit. Sasha had slept most of the way, Cheryl happily holding her hand and singing to her.

"Right, now we've got to see how efficient this Sat Nav is...unless you can take us to the cottage, Al?" asked Rob.

"I'll try, but it's been a long time...I wasn't even old enough to drive last time I was here!"

Between the two helpful voices of advice, Rob finally pulled up outside the cottage, having plumped for the Irish fellow's guidance rather than Alexis's hesitant comments: "I'm sure we used to go left here, oh, wait a minute...that house wasn't there last time was it...?"

Rob had already parked on the triangle of grass opposite the long low building and turned the engine off when Alexis gasped, "Oh yes! This is it!"

The white French windows in the side of the cottage parallel with the narrow road opened, and Céline stepped out on to the grass verge. She ran over to open Alexis's door, a huge smile on her face.

They all climbed gratefully out on the warm grass, hot, thirsty and cramped. Crickets sang out of the still hot air, the sky a deep blue as Cheryl looked around her. She felt spaced out, as if she was in a dream. The small garden in front of the cottage was a mass of pinks and oranges, set off by the hollyhocks and tall sunflowers which leant drunkenly against the white walls. The shutters at each window were painted a bright blue, and she drank in each detail as Céline showed them around, fussing about which they would prefer first, cold drinks or showers.

Cheryl sat upon a blue and white checked duvet covering the single bed. The room was unusual in her opinion in that there were no windows, but as the curtained glass-paned doors were opposite the front entrance, sunlight found its way into the room well enough. Her room was next to Alexis and Rob's. They had been given Céline's bedroom, so that with its external doors, they had easy access to the garden to walk around with Sasha if she was to cry at night. Céline had moved upstairs to a lovely room, a mezzanine above the lounge, with a slanting ceiling and a Velux window set into it, looking out over the estuary.

Céline knocked lightly on her door and put her head round it. "All right, chérie? Do you need anything?"

Cheryl gave a slow smile that seemed to stretch her cheeks. It was an unfamiliar feeling. "I'm fine thanks! I just can't really believe I'm here!"

Céline came forward to give Cheryl an impetuous hug. "I am so pleased you came…it is like having another daughter!" She laughed, and then as she saw the glint of tears in the girl's eyes, she said, "Well now, come outside, we'll have aperitifs, and then I have booked a meal at a restaurant down the road, my treat."

Rob and Alexis looked totally relaxed as they sat in the golden rays of the sun, which was growing larger as it sank towards the horizon. Alexis looked pretty in a white strappy dress decorated with tiny cherries, Rob in pale blue jeans and white shirt. Sasha was snoozing in her parents' cool bedroom.

Cheryl joined them. She also had made an effort in a pair of pink cut-off trousers and white gauzy top. Céline poured a drink for each of them and put out bowls of nuts and pretzels saying, "Luke should be back from work soon."

"Great…" said Alexis, sipping her white wine. "It seems longer than six months that we last saw each other…"

As she spoke, a car passed and drew to a stop next to Rob's. "It's him!" she cried, jumping to her feet like a child. Cheryl gave a start and stared in the direction of the road.

He was through the little gate and hugging Alexis like a flash. "Put me down!" He laughed. "Have you missed me?" One look at Alexis's quivering lips was answer enough.

His greeting with Cheryl was slightly more decorous, both murmuring greetings at the same time.

Rob was on his feet then, clasping Luke's hand and managing a half-hug at the same time. "How are you doing, mate?" he asked gruffly.

"I'm all right," Luke replied. "Good actually." Rob looked at him, thinking that, 'yes, he certainly looked good with his healthy tan and a relaxed demeanour that hadn't been apparent before.'

"And where's my niece? You haven't left her behind, have you?"

It was still light when they set off for the ten-minute walk to the restaurant, the sky a pale greenish-yellow, still warm, but with a bite to the faint breeze. Rob pushed the buggy proudly as he walked beside Luke. The road sloped down quite steeply, fields falling away to steep grassy banks at each side of it. Then they were in the village of Seursac-Sur Gironde, following the road down through the heart of the village; a hairdresser's, a bread shop, a church and then the restaurant tucked away to the left in amongst a row of dwellings. There were several tables set up on a patio that gave straight onto the road, the ambience softened with pot plants and candles set upon the low walls encompassing the eating area.

Céline generously ordered two bottles of champagne, saying that although the party the following day was the real celebration, she felt that tonight, with just close family around her was too special not to make a toast. Cheryl raised her glass with the others, a lump in her throat as she realised that she was truly being included.

Two glasses each later, and after the hors d'oeuvres had been set down, a wonderful assortment of coloured leaves, berries, and tiny glistening fish, Luke raised his glass once more. "To my mother, Céline....and to Sebastien!" he said warmly.

Alexis's eyes grew round, her eyebrows lifted, and Rob kept his face impassive. Cheryl looked on with warm interest, the two glasses of champagne on the empty stomach of someone who seldom drank alcohol more than once a fortnight these days making her feel decidedly rosy.

Céline glared at Luke whose only response was to grin. "What's up, Mum? It's fantastic news. What's the point in waiting? You were going to tell them tomorrow anyway?"

Céline had turned a very attractive shade of pink.

"Go on, Mum," said Alexis quietly, "what are you going to tell us?"

Céline swallowed and looked at her daughter carefully. "I have met an old friend. We knew each other a long time ago." She looked round at each face. "Sebastien is a very kind man, and I don't want to take anything away from how much I love Thomas, but I have realised that life is short. I could wait, and then possibly lose a very special second chance, so Sebastien and I have decided that we wanted to tell you all that we feel very strongly about each other. So that you will not be surprised at any later decision we might make." She risked a small smile.

There was a clamour of celebratory congratulations. Alexis continued to gaze at her mother, and then she burst into tears. Rob put his arm round her. Céline looked devastated, and Luke sat speechless. Cheryl was on her feet then. She stood behind Alexis with her hands on her shoulders and said, "I think Alexis has something to say."

Alexis blew her nose on her napkin and managed to splutter, "I do! I think that's the best news I've ever heard, Mum…" She dabbed her eyes as they threatened to spill over again. She reached across to hold her mother's hand tightly, putting the other over Cheryl's which was still resting on her shoulder.

Overcome with relief, Céline gave a shaky laugh, "I think it is my turn to get my own back. Luke has some news for you too…Luke?"

He was given a short reprieve while the plates were removed and the main meals arrived. He opened his mouth and closed it again, looking embarrassed. "Okay, well I wasn't going to say anything until tomorrow either…and I know that I am still legally married to Elizabeth, but I have met Sandrine, the most lovely, sweet caring girl in the world. In fact, you'll all meet her tomorrow, oh, and Sebastian, of course! I suggest we raise our glasses once more?"

The glasses chinked together, shining in the sudden inky dusk, a waitress busy lighting the candles on the walls and more on the tables. Cheryl hoped the dark would hide her shock. She swallowed the champagne which tasted warm and slightly sickly on her tongue, the bubbles had long since dispersed.

Meanwhile Sasha slept on, oblivious of the emotions swirling around her.

Chapter Fifty-One

New Beginnings

Saturday 13th August 2011
'Les Petits Chemins'

"When is Sebastien arriving, Mum?"

"He said about ten o'clock, chérie...pass me that pan, would you?" She turned from the sink to examine her daughter's face.

Alexis handed the omelette pan over. "What?" she asked, feeling awkward under the close scrutiny.

"You would tell me if you feel strange about Sebastien?"

"Ask me that question again after I've met him!" she teased. "It feels weird at the moment, of course it does, but I haven't had long to take it in. Do you feel 'strange' about him?" She laughed.

"But of course not!" Céline cried indignantly. "He is the most charming man!"

"Exactly! And that's what's important...we will accept him because you have. Don't look so worried!"

"What are you two whispering about?" asked Luke, coming through the French windows. He plonked a bunch of freshly picked chives onto the worktop.

"We're not whispering!" declared Alexis vehemently. "We were just chatting about Sebastien. I just told mum that I can't wait to meet him!"

Luke picked up a tea towel and began to dry the breakfast plates. "Well, I like him a lot." He smiled at Céline. "He's kind, funny and a good dad to Sandrine. By the way, Al...I didn't mention this last night, but just to warn you, Sandrine is Sebastien's daughter..."

Rob came through the hall door carrying Sasha. He heard Luke's revelation just as Alexis gave a shout of shocked surprise. "What! Why didn't you tell us before? This is crazy!" She took the baby from Rob and kissed her. "You poor child...what sort of mixed-up family have we brought you into?" She chuckled.

Luke looked at them both sheepishly. "I thought it might be a bit much to take in all at once..." He grinned. "It does seem unlikely that Mum and I should fall in love with a father and daughter combination!"

Cheryl, who had been sunbathing in the garden, appeared at the French windows. She stood there in her shorts and t-shirt, staring nonplussed at the sight of the four of them convulsed in helpless laughter.

Alexis was rummaging around in the boot of the car for a new pack of nappies. She looked up as a smart white Renault Clio appeared from the end of the road. There was usually very little traffic coming through this little hamlet, apart from the odd tractor, it being on the way to nowhere in particular. The car slid comfortably to a stop on the grassy parking area, next to Rob's. Luke had moved his dad's Volvo and his own car to a space outside Gaston's house, just a short way down the road, to make room for the extra vehicles.

Alexis waited for the man to step out of the car, a ready smile on her lips. He stood there, a pale-yellow shirt tucked into black trousers, a lock of dark hair falling across his forehead. He seemed younger than she had imagined. She stepped towards him, her hand outstretched, "Hello, you must be Sebastien? I am Alexis, Céline's daughter," she said in her best careful French.

"Enchanté Mademoiselle!" he greeted her warmly. "So blonde! You perhaps take after your father? I was so sorry to hear of your sad loss."

She nodded, touched that he had been brave enough to mention Thomas. "Yes, I do! And I think my baby girl may take after him too, although she hasn't much hair yet! Do come in and meet everyone."

They joined the others who were sitting outside at a long table shaded by a huge dark green parasol. They were drinking coffee in small dark red cups. "Having a coffee break already? You lazy lot! Look who I found outside," said Alexis. She introduced him to Rob and Cheryl before proudly leading him over to admire Sasha, lying in her buggy under a fig tree, mesmerised by the moving leaves above her. Céline proudly watched her own lovely endearing daughter making sure that Sebastien was accepted and made welcome. He sat down next to her, found her hand under the table, and squeezed it reassuringly.

The atmosphere was good, a lot of banter going on, and a few hilarious moments as complications of language arose. Poor Cheryl and Rob had virtually no memory of their school French, but Sebastien had a fair smattering of English, Alexis and Luke spoke French very well, and of course Céline was the one to translate from one language to the other.

Cheryl, who always dreaded social gatherings, found herself enjoying the company a great deal. Relaxed, she asked Céline, "How many more guests are coming?"

Everyone laughed, making Cheryl shrink with the fear that she'd said something stupid, but Céline reassured her,

"Only two more I'm afraid! I wanted just a close group of us. Gaston, my neighbour, is invited, because I have known him all my life, and of course Sandrine. Will she be here at midday, Sebastien?"

Sebastien gave a comical shrug. "That depends on what her beauty routine consists of this morning…she sometimes does strange things with cucumber slices, and I found her ironing her hair once…we must wait and see."

"Well…I am going to see what needs doing towards lunch…no, don't move! Enjoy the sun."

But everyone mucked in and helped to prepare the last food preparations; salads created, dressings shaken, cheeses unwrapped and left to breathe, wine opened. There was a joint decision to eat in the dining room, as no body fancied leaping up and down to shoo flies off the food, or to rescue cheeses and butter from sliding over the sides of their dishes in the increasing heat.

Elizabeth drove the hired Twingo carefully up the hill from Seursac-Sur Gironde. Her faithful Sat Nav had led her here from the Airport with hardly a problem. She slowed down as she saw the small road leading off to the left, down which the Sat Nav was ordering her to go. The ancient wooden sign confirmed that this was indeed the right direction for 'Les Petits Chemins'.

She had no wish to be spotted, and not being sure of the layout of the village, she ignored the Sat Nav and drove on further. The road continued between open fields, the hamlet seemed tiny behind her. She pulled over onto the grass verge and killed the engine. Looking back, she noticed that the dwellings of 'Les Petits Chemins' were tight knit. She was able to make out that the few roads and houses were actually contained in a very small area.

Leaving her car here for the moment seemed safe enough. She would explore on foot and form an idea of where to find…she pulled the sheet of paper out of her jeans pocket and checked the details she had copied down from the invitation…yes, number three, Rue D'Ancien Moulin.

She walked slowly back. There was a high wall surrounding the grounds of the first house on the corner. This followed the road round to the right as it led her twisting between an assortment of whitewashed houses and old barns. She jumped at the sudden sound of barking as a dog ran towards her and then round in circles, yapping excitedly.

"Ella! Arrêtés!" ordered a stern voice.

Elizabeth, who did not feel particularly threatened by this fluffy, friendly-looking animal, bent down to fondle the dusty golden fur. "She is beautiful," she commented in French, glad she had persevered with her recent refresher course in the language. She looked up at the bearded man standing there.

"She is not a very good guard dog…you saw through her straight away! Are you looking for someone?" he queried, noting her flimsy footwear and light clothes. She was clearly not a walker.

"I am looking for number three, Rue D'Ancien Moulin, is it nearby?"

Gaston stepped closer and pointed down the road with his pipe. "Just down there on the right. The cottage has a green fence, can you see? Are you coming to the party?" he asked.

She noticed a strong whiff of whisky on his breath and recoiled slightly. "I am a friend of Céline's…she doesn't know I'm here. I'd like to surprise her!" she told him.

He looked at her with interest, but before he could ask her anything else, they both looked up at the sound of a car. They stood watching it approach from that same direction. It slowed down and parked in the third space outside the cottage. The driver's door opened and a tall girl stepped out. Even from this distance, Elizabeth could appreciate the slender tanned limbs, the pretty pale-orange strappy dress, and the shining cascade of hair shimmering in the sunlight. Some movement, probably Ella's frisking tail, drew her eye toward them, and she raised her hand in a friendly wave before making her way through the gate and into Luke's garden.

Elizabeth raised her eyebrows questioningly. "A guest?" she asked.

"Ahh! That's Sandrine!" Gaston leaned closer with a sentimental expression, "She is the love of Luke's life… We are all delighted. They both deserve some happiness." The three glasses of whisky he had enjoyed earlier in anticipation of the party ahead had filled him with bonhomie. "In fact," he continued, not noticing Elizabeth's sudden pallor and twitching jawline, "it was down to me that they met! He met her while doing some work for her father, my old friend Sebastien!" He grinned at her, but her silence spurred him into action.

"Well! You go ahead. Would you say I'm on my way? Just have to take Ella to my friend Madame Le Blanc. She advised me that not everybody likes dogs…she will look after her for me. By the way, there is an old lean to by my house. You can park there if you want." He called Ella and went on his way. Elizabeth, hardly able to breathe properly due to the tightness of her chest, managed to stumble back to her car, deciding to take up Gaston's offer.

Sandrine followed the sounds of laughter and music to the French windows. She stepped through into the kitchen, where despite Céline's urging everybody to find a seat, people were happily standing with their backs to the work surfaces.

"Sandrine! At last! Come in, chérie, Luke, give the girl a drink." Céline smiled at her.

Luke took Sandrine's hand and pulled her into the room. "Don't be shy, sweetheart, let me introduce you; meet Alexis, my sister, Rob, her fiancé, and this is Cheryl, a friend of the family." Alexis gave her a hug and a kiss, delighted that Sandrine was so fresh and pretty. Rob gave her a brotherly embrace and Cheryl just about summoned up a convincing smile. "Oh! And I mustn't forget Sasha! But she's asleep in the bedroom and will say hello later," added Luke, smiling.

Sebastien moved around with a bottle of champagne, making sure that everyone was topped up, before joining Céline.

"On your invitation cards, we wrote that this should be a celebration of 'New Beginnings'. This was to be my way of introducing Sebastien to you all. I hope you will wish us happiness..."

Glasses were raised, a toast made. Then Luke cleared his throat to speak.

No one had noticed the figure who had crept in through the front door, past the bedrooms, down the corridor and was now standing in the doorway of the kitchen. Heads turned as she entered the room.

A silence fell as Elizabeth gazed from face to face. "Well, it's so nice to see you all!" she said brightly. "I can't resist a family gathering, everyone under the same roof. How lovely!" She moved closer to Céline and stared arrogantly at Sebastien. "And you must be my father-in-law? How fantastic to meet you at last!"

Puzzled glances were exchanged, shock rendering people reluctant to speak. Except for Sebastien, who said angrily, "Who are you? And what are you talking about?"

"Let me explain," she said slowly, as if speaking to a child. "I am Elizabeth, your son's wife." She cast a withering look in Sandrine's direction. Luke was staring at her with complete incomprehension. Céline took a step towards Elizabeth, her face a mask of horror and fury.

"You look as if you'd like to hit me, darling Céline. I wouldn't if I were you. Here, Sebastien, do you want the proof?" She took the envelope out of her bag, extracted the letter and spread it out on the table. "Shall I read it? Well, I'll give you the gist of it. It was written in July nineteen eighty-one, by a certain Sebastien Barbet to a Miss Céline Martel in Paris. It is clearly a reply to her desperate revelation that she is expecting his baby. In his words then…" she looked closely at the black words crammed furiously on the cream paper, "'I am so sorry Céline, but you must understand that I must ask you to end your pregnancy. I am not capable of becoming a father to your child, and you are far too young to even consider it. I have enclosed a cheque.' So gallant! And in case there's any doubt as to what the nineteen-year-old Céline thought of this suggestion, here, on top of your concerned words of advice, are the pencilled hysterical scribbled words; 'I will never abort your baby, never! I will raise it alone, but I will always hate you!'"

Elizabeth stood back to contemplate the reaction so far. Céline's face was chalk white. She was staring at Sebastien with terror as the truth lay before them. "Poor Thomas," Elizabeth continued conversationally. "He had no idea, had he? He thought you really loved him…"

"I did love him," Céline croaked.

"You loved that he stepped into your life at just the right time. You seduced him the first day you met him. You've boasted about it to me often enough! He was the perfect answer to your dilemma. It was bad enough that he had to hear how Luke let Xavier bleed to death that day, but when I showed him this letter and he realised that he wasn't even the boys' father, that you had just used him, well, it was too much for his poor heart… He told me once that I was an aberration, and I had to show him that his perfect family was not quite as perfect as he thought."

Céline flew towards Elizabeth, her hands stretching towards her throat, but Sebastien grabbed her arms. "Céline! What have you done? Was there another? Xavier? Oh my God…I had two sons…"

Turning away from the debris of broken trust before her, Elizabeth faced Luke and Sandrine, who were standing rigid, not touching. "So, you thought you could just abandon me like a broken toy, did you, Luke?" she hissed with venom. The black poison inside her just kept on flowing, seeping into and contaminating the lives of everybody in the room.

Luke watched Elizabeth's face, the face of such gamin cuteness that he had fallen for, that was now distorted out of all recognition by its destructive intent. "Does this bring you happiness at last, Elizabeth? You have broken every one of us, but what have you gained by it?"

"Revenge!" she cried. "And I haven't finished yet! This is the icing on the cake. She turned to Sandrine and stroked her cheek in mock sympathy. Sandrine flinched as if she had been burnt. "You poor thing! You thought your life was suddenly turning into a fairy tale, and now look! Has the penny dropped yet, you don't look very bright? Your lover is your brother! And let's not forget," she said and looked at Céline with contempt, "that

Céline knew that Luke was Sandrine's brother, and yet she was quite happy to stand back and watch them commit incest! What sort of mother does that make her?"

Sandrine gave an anguished howl of pain. She turned away as if she wanted to escape the cruel words ringing in her ears. Everyone's eyes were registering shock as they looked in her direction. Sandrine stood frozen for a moment, framed by the French windows. With the sun casting its beam through the glass panes like a spot light, the girl's outline was defined through the thin material of her dress, the swell of her abdomen clearly visible.

Cheryl realised Elizabeth's intention in a split second. With a scream of pure loathing, Elizabeth darted forwards, grabbing up a sharp knife from a chopping board, and hurled herself, not at Sandrine, but at Luke. But Cheryl was right behind her, lunging for the knife, and grabbing hold of Elizabeth's arm. Elizabeth jabbed her elbow back, catching Cheryl in the stomach. There was hollow groan as the knife sliced into flesh before clattering on to the tiles.

Cheryl slumped to the floor as Elizabeth suddenly ran full tilt out of the French windows, through the garden and round the side of the cottage. Her steps faltered as she heard the quavering sleepy cry of a baby. She ran to the closed French windows there and looked through the glass. Without a moment of hesitation, she opened the door, grabbed Sasha from her cot and ran down the road towards her hired car. How clever she'd been to book a car with a baby seat! She had planned this day for so long, firstly the destruction of the people who had denied her happiness, and then the snatching of Sasha, and she had done both. Poor Luke, he'd been so devastated when he'd been told that he was unlikely to father a child. How would he feel if she told him that she'd lied about her visit to the doctor? When she'd learned that she was the infertile one, that she would never be able to conceive a child? That stupid Cheryl had nearly ruined it though, she thought as she strapped the baby into the seat. Her fury began to mount again as she faced the realisation that it was unlikely that Luke would ever return to her. She slid behind the wheel and accelerated wildly down the narrow road.

In the cottage, an eerie silence had descended for a few seconds, swiftly broken by Alexis urgently requesting a first aid kit and something clean to staunch the flow of blood. At first she had thought that the blood was coming from Cheryl's side, so it was with some relief that she found that the knife had pierced the fleshy part of her left arm, above the elbow. She cleaned the wound with antiseptic solution and wrapped a clean bandage around Cheryl's arm.

"Are you okay?" Alexis asked her in a concerned voice. The poor girl was shaking violently, and Alexis was worried that she might be suffering from shock.

Luke stumbled over, looking pretty rough too. "You shouldn't have done that, Cheryl." he said in an awed voice. "You could have been killed..."

Cheryl opened her eyes as she heard his words. "She already tried to kill me once," she whispered. "I didn't care...I didn't want her to hurt you too."

Luke looked horrified at her words, swiping a hand across his eyes. He went back to where Sandrine was now sitting crumpled onto a chair, sobbing.

Céline stood like a statue, her hands over her face while Sebastien stared at her in disbelief and disillusion. Neither of them seemed able to speak to the other, fearing that once begun, the tirade of recrimination would damage them irretrievably.

They all jumped as a bellow of dread reverberated through the cottage. Rob came bursting through the door. "Sasha's gone! She's taken her! For God's sake, someone ring the police!"

Then there came an urgent knocking on the front door, but before anybody could move, Gaston appeared. "Come quickly!" he said, "There's been an accident!"

Chapter Fifty-Two

She Looked as If She Had Aged Ten Years

Saturday 13th August 2011

'Les Petits Chemins'

Confusion and panic took hold as they tried to make sense of what was happening. Then they were on their feet, the men on the move first, testosterone kicking in. It was Luke who began to take stock of the situation.

"Sandrine, I want you to stay and look after Cheryl, will you do that? Mum, I want you to phone the police, you'll be able to explain things better than me."

They nodded wordlessly, too distraught to argue.

Rob and Sebastien were on the way out of the door, following Gaston. Alexis looked wildly at Luke and together they followed the others. The sun was beating down, crickets clamouring their rasping music in the heat. Alexis could not think in straight lines. She just felt that there was a black hole in her brain, preventing logical thought.

The others were halfway down the road, approaching Gaston's house. Luke and Alexis caught up with them, their breathing harsh from the sudden exertion and the fear of what they would find.

Gaston looked back shouted, "Come on! Hurry!"

They ran to the end of the road and turned to the left, following the high wall which had belied out with age, obscuring the view of the road ahead. They rounded the corner, and there in front of them was a car, the driver's side was smashed into the off side massive wheel of a tractor. The driver of the tractor was standing there looking helpless.

"She was on the wrong side of the road, coming at me really fast. There was nothing I could do." He spoke quickly, looking at each of them in turn, a simple farm hand whose uncomplicated day had suddenly turned into a nightmare. "I've phoned for an ambulance…" he told them.

Rob was at the side of the damaged Twingo, staring in at the window. Alexis ran to join him.

Sebastien and Luke had dashed to the front of the car.

Rob and Alexis stared mesmerised at the tiny motionless form strapped into the car seat. "Sasha…" whimpered Alexis. It came out on a desperate sigh of finality. Rob opened the door and reached in.

Luke was staring in at the crumpled figure in the driving seat. "It's Elizabeth. She's not moving," he said emotionlessly. He tried opening her door, but it was buckled completely out of shape.

Rob released the car seat and lifted it out carefully. There was a tiny cry, the jerky waving of miniature fingers. "She's alive!" came his joyful shout. Luke glanced back at him, confused, thinking he was referring to Elizabeth.

Together, Rob and Alexis examined their daughter. "She's fine! Oh thank God!" They clung together, their eyes locked above their child.

Meanwhile Sebastien had opened the passenger's door. He was leaning in, trying to get some response from Elizabeth who seemed to have passed out. There was a large bruise emerging on her forehead. "She's not wearing a seat belt." Sebastien observed. "Oh… She's breathing…!"

A police car pulled up behind the tractor and two gendarmes got out. Gaston began to explain what had happened.

He said that he had fallen sleep in his armchair, and had missed the party. The noise of the crash must have woken him up and he went out to investigate. He had not realised that the driver of the car was the young woman he had spoken to earlier, but had gone to his friends at the cottage for help.

Sebastien had a quiet word with the gendarmes about earlier events. He insisted that the woman in the car had committed some serious offences. He was assured that everybody involved would be interviewed as a matter of procedure.

Elizabeth came round as the paramedics were easing her out of the undamaged front side of the car. No broken bones, they announced, just possible concussion. She would be taken to hospital for observation, and then questioned by the police. As the ambulance doors closed, Luke could see her white face, the livid bruise blooming above her left eye. She looked as if she had aged ten years.

The dishevelled group returned to the cottage. Moods were mixed; delight at the rescue of the unharmed Sasha, relief at the imminent arrest of Elizabeth, and the coming to terms with the damage inflicted by Elizabeth's poisonous behaviour.

Sebastien seemed to take charge as they all grouped once more in the kitchen. He suggested that they sit at the table. Cheryl had more colour to her cheeks now. Alexis had reassured her that the wound had been a clean cut and should heal without stitches, but said that it would make sense to have both Cheryl and Sasha checked out at the hospital. Céline had made a big pot of coffee and Luke and Sandrine were sitting side by side, not touching. Céline could feel Alexis's tormented gaze on her as she tried to understand how her mother could have lived a lie all these years. Her poor father had not deserved to be given the truth in that brutal way. Céline bent her head in shame.

Sebastien began to speak. "We are all in a state of shock. I can hardly begin to understand the reason why this woman has set out to hurt us all, but I do know that if we let her drive a wedge between us, then she will have done what she set out to do…she will have won."

Sandrine blew her nose, her eyes red from crying, "She has won! My life is broken. I have lost Luke. We have both lost everything!"

Sebastien smiled at her and then at Luke. They gazed at him as if he'd gone mad.

"Actually, this is one secret that this woman knew nothing about. Sandrine, I intended that you should never know this, but in the circumstances, it will be the best news I could ever give you. You are not my daughter." He looked at the surprised faces and continued. "Your mother was a young girl working on my parents' farm. She was only two years younger than me. There was a young man helping over the summer, he was a rough type, full of himself. One day, he forced himself on to your mother. She told me that he'd been harassing her for some time. I'm sorry, Sandrine, your mum made me promise never to tell you. He disappeared afterwards, and later Yvonne found out that she was pregnant, with you. Yvonne was such a sweet girl. It wasn't just compassion. We fell in love and married in June of nineteen eighty-two, and you were born seven months later. It seemed easier to let you believe that I was your father, and when she died when you were seven, I let the secret die with her. In my heart, you will always be my daughter."

Luke could hardly dare take in what this man was saying. It felt like someone had just handed him a winning lottery ticket. He turned to look at Sandrine, but she was so devastated at what her poor mother had been through that she could hardly take the rest in. Then she was crying and laughing at the same time.

Luke stood up and grasped Sebastien's hands. "I'm so proud to have you as my father," he said.

Sebastien opened his arms and Luke stepped into them and let himself be hugged fiercely.

Céline watched them all, broken-hearted at how much damage she had caused all these people by her selfish lies. She closed her eyes and was about to turn away, when she felt a hand in hers, another on her arm, pulling her back to them. She looked into her daughter's face, whether she deserved it or not, she was being offered a second chance. She wondered what Thomas would have advised her to do.

THE END